THE CASE OF
TWO IN THE TRUNK

A NOVEL

Anthony Celano

This book is dedicated to my family, Anna, Briana and Anthony
and the courageous members of the NYPD
who are the first to put themselves second in the face of danger.

REMEDIAL
INTERVENTION
–1998

JOE HORSE WAS IN A JAM. Being on parole greatly compounded the mess he found himself enveloped in. His dilemma was unnerving. If found with two dead bodies on his hands, he would no doubt be going back to jail. Sucking it up, he formulated a plan to address the two dead women sprawled out on his living room floor. He decided to use the downpour outside to his advantage. His strategy to get the departed duo out of his apartment while the rain was still coming down heavily—was sound. To accomplish this, he was going to need help. After taking in a deep breath, he took out his flip phone to summon the mover, his proven go-to man in all propositions involving risk. His soon-to-be accomplice, a reliable resource as long as the money was right, picked up on the second ring with a nonchalant "Hello?"

The voice calling on the phone was direct...and desperate. "It's me. I need you at my place with the truck."

Based on the tension in Joe's voice, the mover knew things were amiss. Something must have been seriously wrong to cause him to deviate from his usually relaxed state. "What's the problem, man?" he asked gravely.

"I got two large packages that need moving...like, right now," Joe said.

"Now? I was just chilling out man...getting ready to sit down." He sounded like a whiner. Joe Horse responded with an absoluteness that left no room for further discussion.

"Forget about that….I need you to come by my place right now….
Understand me? NOW, while it is still *RAINING* out…"

There were to be no details discussed over a phone. None were
necessary. The mover understood the significance of the call. Thinking
in terms of money, he calculated the desperation level of the demand
for service against what he felt he could squeeze out of the caller. Making
something serious go away was always an expensive proposition, but
since his history with Joe Horse was a long and profitable one, the mover
felt an obligation to cut his friend some slack.

"Okay man, sit tight. The cavalry is coming. It is gonna run you fifteen
centuries…okay?"

"Yeah…okay," answered Joe. "Just get over here."

Joe Horse had anticipated taking a haircut regarding the cost. He knew
his longtime friend, while loyal in times of crisis, was as greedy as they
come where a buck was concerned. But Joe overlooked that character flaw
because he understood. The two shared the same demanding financial
burden of heroin addiction, a monkey they had carried on their back for
years. Joe would have sprung for more than the fifteen hundred dollars—
under the circumstances, he was not about to quibble over expenses.

"Relief is on the way, man….I'm out the door," assured the mover. It
was the only answer Joe Horse wanted to hear.

The man with the truck rose from the kitchen table while watching the
old lady, her pronounced derriere protruding from the open refrigerator.
He observed his grandmother bent over with her head inside, snooping
around for something to prepare for her grandson.

"Don't bother making anything for me, Grammy….I gotta go out now."

The old Italian woman stood erect, turning to her grandson with what
could be construed as a stern look. "Where you go now?" she asked
crisply. The snap in her voice suggested she was put out by his leaving
before having a bite to eat.

"Work….I'll be home later," he answered as if irritated. "I'll grab
something outside if I get hungry."

"You go now? Stay….First-a you gotta eat!"

He picked up a banana off the table. "No time. I gotta go. This is
important…*big-a bus-in-ness*. I'll be back early."

After saying goodbye, he finished peeling the fruit, tossing the skin
in the kitchen pail before he departed his grandmother's house. Once he
was out the door, the old lady began muttering in her kitchen. "*Stronzo!*"
she said with frustration, not really meaning her grandson was a turd.

The vehicle was a light-duty box truck that he usually kept parked in
front of the house. Freshly painted yellow, the vehicle was impossible not
to see when it was parked on the residential block. Joe's friend had taken
an umbrella to protect against the drenching rain as he made his way to

the rear of the truck. He quickly looked into the back, checking that there were enough commercial quilts and ropes inside. He saw that there was still one flat-screen television remaining that he needed to sell. Jumping into the cab, he turned over the engine and carefully motored over to Joe Horse's house.

When he arrived, he saw Joe standing in the doorway of the three-story building, looking nervous. Stepping into the rain, Joe directed the truck to back into the wide driveway along the side of the house. After parking, the mover exited the vehicle to see Joe. They stood together in the doorway of the building to avoid getting wet while they talked.

"So, what have we got going on here?" The man with the truck presented a cool exterior as he asked the question.

Joe responded in a low voice. "I've got two bodies inside the house. Let's move them outta here while it is still coming down heavy and the street is empty."

"This is some fucked-up shit. What happened, man? You clipped them in your apartment? Why? What did they do?"

"Look, man...it's a long story, so let's just get their asses someplace else...okay?"

"Aren't we better off doing this shit at two or three in the morning?" suggested the mover.

"No....I want them gone from here. I can't stand the sight of these two anymore. It's flipping me out, man."

"Okay, Joe...I hear you. You got the scratch for me, right?"

"Yeah, I got the whole fifteen hundred...upstairs. How do ya want it... cash or product?"

"Cash."

Joe nodded. "Okay...so how are we gonna do this?"

The truck owner paused to look up at a sky that was still bleeding water in buckets. "Come on...let's go inside. Let me take a look at them first," he finally answered. "Just give me another minute, though."

The man with the truck entered the rear of his vehicle. He stretched out three ropes across the width of the truck's bed about a foot apart. Then on top of the three ropes he laid out one of the commercial quilts, making sure that it reached the edge of the truck opening. The mover wanted to have everything arranged so that there would be no wasting time jockeying things around once he got the bodies inside the truck.

Leaving the back door to the truck slightly open, he entered the rented duplex apartment with Joe. There on the living room floor were the lifeless bodies of two young women. A small white poodle was sniffing at the face of one of the corpses.

"You got my money?" The mover posed the question without caring enough to ask about the carcasses on the floor.

Without saying a word, Joe walked upstairs to his bedroom, returning a moment later with fifteen hundred dollars in cash, mostly in ten- and twenty-dollar bills. Joe handed the currency over to his friend, who in turn stuffed the bills into the pockets of his jeans without bothering to count it. He had too long a history with Joe not to trust him.

"What is the story with the people upstairs?"

"Not an issue...they are away," replied Joe. "So how do you want to do this?"

"The setup here is easy enough. Let's just walk them out one at a time like they are drunk."

They lifted the larger woman, an attractive blond in a long-sleeved black evening dress cut low at the front, off the floor first. With one arm wrapped around her waist, Joe slung one of her slender arms over his shoulder. His friend did the same on the other side, and the two men then walked the body out to the waiting truck. The limp head of the deceased remained pointed downward with each step taken. They hoisted her into the bed of the truck and gently placed her onto the center of the quilt. Luck was with them. As Joe had anticipated, the inclement weather kept the street deserted.

Once confident they had not been noticed, the duo returned to the apartment for the other body. With the rain making their footing slippery, they moved as quickly as they could without being careless. They followed the same routine with the second woman. She was smaller, so they found it easier to waltz out the plainly dressed brunette. They put her body on the quilt alongside the blond. Joe stepped down off the truck and pulled the door halfway down while his friend remained inside the vehicle's interior with the corpses. The mover proceeded to tightly entwine the legs and arms of the two bodies as Joe stood lookout.

"Get down that door further, willya, Joe?...This ain't no floor show! Just leave it open about a foot for me," the mover ordered.

Joe complied without answering; he did not like being ordered around. He took shelter in the doorway of his apartment as he awaited further instructions from his friend. Joe's friend flapped the quilt over the corpses, lacing it tightly within the embrace of the three ropes. Once the bodies were packaged, Joe's friend lifted up the back door of the truck, jumped off, and pulled down the door behind him. The mover then pointed, signaling Joe to join him in the cab of the truck. The special move thus far had been executed without incident.

"Okay, man, that's done....Now let's go unload this cargo," said the driver of the truck as he lit up a Marlboro. "Want a smoke?" he asked.

Joe reached for the cigarette with relief. "Yeah...gimme one. I left mine inside." He suddenly snapped his fingers. "Shit! Hold up a minute....I forgot something."

8

"What did ya forget?"

"That fucking mutt....It's not mine; it belonged to one of them."

"Best go get him then, man."

Joe hurried back to his duplex to take charge of the dog. After a minute or two, he emerged from the apartment with the small white poodle in his arms. He got into the cab of the truck with the canine.

"Where do you want to dump the girls?" Joe asked. "How about we take them to the foot of Columbia Street?" He thought the desolate waterfront area of Red Hook in South Brooklyn would be the most suitable destination.

The mover slowly shook his head. "We don't need to go that far on a shitty day like this," he answered confidently. "With all this fucking rain, I can find us a closer spot easy. But first you gotta get rid of that fucking dog before he starts pissing in the truck."

Joe Horse opened the door and abruptly tossed the dog out onto the Mill Road sidewalk without even a parting pat on the head. After abandoning the dog in the rain, they needed to travel along Mill Road only a short distance before the owner of the truck knew exactly how they were going to dispose of the bodies.

2

PORTRAIT
OF A
FANTASYMAN

"WELL, WHAT DO YOU KNOW?...Look who it is!" Thumbing through the photos, Fishnet had come across an unexpected mug shot.

Detective Bruce Milligan, known to coworkers as Fishnet, held up the photo to the light for a clearer view of the woman he had known many years ago. Letting out a snort, he slowly shook his head with disapproval. "Holy Jesus...did this bimbo sure hit the skids!" This assessment held not a trace of empathy.

Fishnet enjoyed passing time in the precinct squad room looking through old arrest photos. The mug shots were shown to crime victims for identifying those who had violated them. The detective found it worthwhile to revisit the old photos during periods of quiet. Aside from the entertainment factor, he felt it a beneficial exercise that kept him attuned to the criminals in his command. The ability to recognize a known criminal on the street is an advantage for those tasked with enforcing the law.

He pulled out all the old mug shots of the woman and laid them out across his desk in chronological order. The array clearly depicted her physical decline—from intoxicated young girl to a forty-something-year-old dissipated woman. His curiosity now tickled, he researched the record of his old acquaintance to discover that she had been last apprehended for propositioning men for sex. The nature of the arrest caused the detective to remember an incident that had occurred before her deterioration, when they sat quietly in his car in a secluded area of Prospect Park favored by lovers. Fishnet had had her polish off a couple of quarts of beer that night in order to loosen her up for what he had in mind. She was fairly attractive back then.

Beginning to feel depressed over the decline of one of his almost-conquests, he convinced himself that the photos were just a poor depiction of her. After all, no one looked very good in their police mug shot. The detective ended up regretting that he had ever made the discovery. The enlightenment caused him to cease looking at any more pictures. Fishnet's concentration shifted to doing something more productive with his time...like real police work.

But first he needed to placate one of his chronic mental impulses. On this occasion, his journey returned him to the beer-drinking episode in the car where he would relive the experience...only this time without any performance issues dampening the end result.

Bruce Milligan appreciated his nickname, feeling that Fishnet was a cool handle to have. He viewed it as a vibrant name that complemented his supreme rule inside a dimension that could accurately be described as the world of Fishnet. He was a Walter Mitty–like dreamer who excelled within the realm of his imagination. A consistent theme in his customized fantasies centered on his solving a spectacular case, one of epic proportions. These mental voyages aboard the ship of wishful thinking had but one objective...to wrap up the big caper in a fashion sure to generate public acclaim for himself. His imaginary escapades were always orchestrated for the front page, a necessity in attaining the legendary status he wanted for himself. His creations were bold headlines that were vividly clear to his mind's eye:

"FISHNET NABS SERIAL-MURDERING SEX FIEND"
"ANOTHER THUG FOILED BY FISTICUFFING FISHNET"
"WOUNDED FISHNET SUBDUES COP KILLER IN ROOFTOP STRUGGLE"

These invented excursions afforded the detective an opportunity to at least fictionally bask in the limelight, satiating his urge to experience the iconic status he so yearned for.

The more Fishnet contemplated fame, the more he detested his given name of Bruce. In the colorful orbit of law enforcement, he considered the moniker of Bruce an embarrassment. He thought the designation to be way too anemic, an effeminate title—totally devoid of machismo. He arrived at this deduction after overhearing someone state the name with a pronounced falsetto lisp. Taking it personally, Fishnet resented the insinuation of foppishness that had tainted his mother's favorite name.

Perhaps the most important drawback to the name of Bruce was Fishnet's fear that the press wouldn't be able to do much with it. Bruce was hardly anything like the attention-grabbing "Wild Bill" for sure. In the event he ever did make the six o'clock news, "Bruce" left the newspapers very little to work with.

Fishnet was no run-of-the-mill oddball. He was a functional psychopath, completely guided by a multitude of spontaneous off-the-wall inner thoughts. But he did have the ability to act in an apparently normal fashion even while being mentally removed from the present. When adrift, his psychosis transported him to a fantasy destination of his design in a matter of seconds. The invented world was a universe where the mundane morphed into matters of great intrigue, and people could be retooled to behave however Fishnet desired.

The detective drew many of his fantasies from perusals of ordinary cases such as the ones sitting atop his desk. Incorporating his own spin, he transformed average situations into sensational cases, rectifiable only by the personal cunning and extreme bravery of Fishnet. At times the villain was designed to be a cop killer who broke out of jail, an axe murderer, or some escaped lunatic wanted across the country. Each of these easily fit into his criteria. The script might at times vary slightly but always ended with the same finality...Fishnet eradicating the wicked after a fierce life-and-death struggle. He always relied upon administering a little "gold dot therapy," which was the common vernacular among cops when referring to police ammunition. Naturally Fishnet himself needed to sustain a wound or two from the gun or knife of the undesirable during the encounter. He envisioned such endings as an appropriate closure that would gain not just public accolades but also peer recognition and a dash of sympathy. The detective saw these encounters as a vehicle to inch him closer to the shamus hall of fame. The personal side of his life was also accommodated, where many of his social interactions were adjusted to meet the more preferable outcomes he conjured. The gratification he acquired from his imaginary happy endings was so pleasing that they surpassed those actual sexual happy endings that he worked so hard for (and that came along all too infrequently). His delusional spells came complete with their own moral code of professional ethics. It would be an understatement to say that Fishnet operated outside the parameters of normalcy.

Fishnet was a third-grade detective assigned to a precinct detective squad that covered Downtown Brooklyn, Vinegar Hill, and Brooklyn Heights. The hours he worked were dictated by a work chart that consisted of two evening shifts followed by two day shifts. His regular days off, referred to as RDOs, rotated. It was Saturday evening, and the detective was already halfway into his tour of duty. It had been raining heavily throughout the day, so it was anticipated that the squad would remain relatively quiet, assuming that most of the public would opt to remain indoors, where they could stay dry.

The squad room itself was desolate because Fishnet's team, which normally comprised four detectives, was down by three people. One detective had just retired, and a second was on extended sick leave, recovering from a hernia operation. Sidney Schiff, the fourth team member and Fishnet's partner, was away in Florida for a few days visiting elderly parents.

Sidney, a second-grader with twenty years on the job, was a patient man. Fishnet, with thirteen years of service under his belt, was another story. The latter's unpredictability was well known among his team, although the extent of his instability had never fully come to light. Fortunately, the two detectives complemented each other: Fishnet benefitted from Sidney's solid judgment, while Fishnet's aggressiveness proved fruitful at times. Sidney's nonconfrontational style helped keep Fishnet's John Wayne syndrome in check. So potent was the suppressive influence of Sidney that Fishnet referred to his partner as the anchor that held him at the dock. Had it not been for being weighed down, Fishnet's record might not have been as unblemished as it was.

Fishnet's Wild West style of working needed to be toned down at times in order to prevent his getting himself into trouble. It was doubtful that Fishnet ever realized how fortunate he was to have someone like Sidney Schiff around him.

After returning from his thoughts of having beers in his car years ago, Fishnet secured a cup of coffee and began reviewing his newly assigned active cases. He remained undaunted in his belief that one of these days an investigation would cross his desk that would propel him to that ceremony at 1 Police Plaza where he would be formally recognized. In addition to notoriety, the detective was aspiring for a promotion to second-grade status, an elevation that came with the salary of a sergeant. At forty-two years old, he had been in the detective bureau for five years without any spectacular results.

But despite this, Fishnet was a man not without a healthy ego. The magnitude of his vanity demanded that he maintain the best physical condition possible. Six feet tall and solidly built, Fishnet had tattooed arms—a panther climbed down his left inner forearm while a naked hula dancer shimmied on the inside of his right upper arm every time he flexed his muscle. The detective wore his straight black hair slicked back with a high part on the left side of his head. His black mustache was trimmed to perfection in an effort to emulate Clark Gable, the old movie heartthrob whom he actually bore a strong resemblance to. Fishnet worked hard at maintaining a professional appearance. Preferring conservative suits of blue, black, and gray, he was considered one of Brooklyn's finer-dressed detectives. He shunned the sport jackets favored by many detectives, thinking them not to be up to his standard.

He had earned the name Fishnet because he was so eager to put people in cuffs, much like a net that would drag the ocean floor and pick up anything in its path. When Fishnet was catching cases, the general consensus was that the person responsible was almost guaranteed to face arrest. On the surface, the reputation he had carefully crafted was one of a no-nonsense detective, not apt to be sympathetic regardless of any possible extenuating circumstances.

This bogus image concealed the fact that Fishnet was an opportunist, an unsavory sort who was readily willing to succumb to any temptation in his self-interest. Compromise was always a consideration as long as his concession tax was met, a charge that was scaled according to the law of Fishnet. This unethical component of Fishnet's makeup was something Sidney either did not notice or chose not to acknowledge. Either way, the nefarious attributes of Fishnet were not shared by his partner.

Fishnet considered not expecting some form of tribute for his largesse to be an exercise in foolishness. To some, Fishnet was considered a streetwise, savvy detective. To others, he was a shady operator with a gun and badge. He was both...and much more. The wayward detective honestly thought that he was performing the work of God...a labor that he believed was specifically designed to come with delightful perks that he made sure to capitalize on.

Where compensation was nonexistent, Fishnet fostered a reputation of heartlessness that had begun in his days as a police officer in uniform. His law-and-order image was jump-started with his writing a moving ticket to a seventy-eight-year-old senior citizen for running a red light.

When his radio car partner at the time asked him why he was penalizing the septuagenarian, especially after she had displayed identification indicating that she was the wife of a sitting criminal court judge, the explanation came without flinching. "She blew the light, didn't she? This is no charity. If anyone could stand the fine, this old bitch could. Besides, her old man is the same fucking guy who would give you ten years for pissing in the street." The elderly motorist would have fared much better had she included a double sawbuck along with her driver's license when Fishnet asked her to produce it. Twenty bucks always had a positive influence with the detective.

For better or worse, Fishnet was all about the performance of his duty. He was quick to address every investigation coming his way. Each case that could be adjudicated through clever massaging was up for negotiation. Fishnet turned felonies into misdemeanors and misdemeanors into incidents that were referred to civil court. In his mind, cleansing matters of an unwholesome nature was without question a viable option in many instances. As long as it wasn't a cop-related affair, Fishnet was more than content being the Houdini who made problems go away—for a price.

It was the rigidity of the department that contributed to keeping Fishnet from totally unraveling. Working in a paramilitary organization offered the structure needed to contain him. He was drawn to police work for the authority the position came with. He thrived on the added public respect he had gained by wearing a suit once he'd become a detective. For Fishnet, the gold tin gave him the necessary edge during interactions with those of a higher socioeconomic status. Detectives conducted investigations. They made cases against people that could result in financial and reputational damage. Those fortunate enough to be occupying a higher station in life felt compelled to listen more attentively to the words of Fishnet because he was now in a stronger position to hurt them. Those stationed at the lowest rungs, meanwhile, were already biddable. They had little choice other than to do anything but listen. In Fishnet's view, the common denominator among these opposite spectrums was fear. Fishnet was rather astute in his own perverse way.

In the detective's mind, the public was either at his throat or his feet. He always opted for the latter. He savored his role as the ultimate authority in determining who was to receive a pass for a crime, indiscretion, or error in judgment. His very job positioned him to eliminate problems or create them. It was a power that, when properly implemented, gave his voice the authority to humble others while exploiting them at the same time.

Raised as an only child, Fishnet was born out of wedlock to a working mother who cleaned houses during the day to meet expenses. Adept at pinching pennies, Fishnet's mother managed to run the fatherless household and have a little money left over to send her son to one of the parochial high schools in Woodside, Queens. Since getting out of line in the Catholic school meant, if caught, being cuffed around by the teaching brothers, Fishnet made it his business to avoid detection by those charged with maintaining discipline. Survival for a rule-breaker in what Fishnet considered to be an academic prison required proficiency in sneakiness, plotting, and taking calculated risks. The teenage Fishnet wasn't above having a smoke in the bathroom, looking up the dress of a female teacher from the bottom of a staircase, cheating on a test, or even bullying some bookworm....He was just above getting caught. Fishnet's educational journey netted him average academic grades and top honors in scheming. A stint in the army only provided the opportunity to hone his ability to connive. Upon return to civilian life, he began taking civil services exams, ultimately getting appointed to the NYPD.

Although a handsome man who was gifted when it came to attracting the opposite sex, Fishnet remained a confirmed bachelor. The detective lived alone in a one-bedroom apartment on Staten Island, where he gladly paid a paltry five hundred dollars a month rent. His good fortune had been self-orchestrated. It came about after he had caught a case involving a residential real estate brokerage firm. The owner of the business had been the victim of a substantial internal theft at the building where he rented commercial space. The business owner made it clear that if it could be shown that the actions of his landlord, or someone working for the landlord, had contributed to the theft either directly or indirectly, the insurance company would financially cover his entire loss. Fishnet reciprocated his complainant's bluntness by letting it be known that he was in the market for an apartment at a reasonable rate.

The two men spoke the same language. At the end of Fishnet's investigation, the insurance company paid the victim the full—and fully inflated—amount, and Fishnet moved into a nice, underpriced garden apartment. It was a classic win-win conclusion. For Fishnet, it could not have worked out any better. The last time he had received a deal from a landlord, he'd had to feed a poison hamburger to the barking dog of the landlord's neighbor. The detective was complex, a man with lots of demons. It would have taken a battery of doctors to get to the bottom of what was going on inside the head of the fantasyman.

3

BUSINESS OVER PLEASURE

"ERNESTO ROMERO, MY FUCKING ASS....It's the Mask!" Fishnet scornfully stated to himself as he read the complaint report. The detective was poring through a stack of his active cases when finally, nearly at the bottom of the pile, he struck upon a larceny case that tickled his interest. *This* investigation was one he wanted to pursue.

The crime had been reported by a married woman who accused a man, identified in the report as Ernesto Romero, of absconding from her home with her diamond necklace. What really put the sparkle in the eyes of the detective was the description of the suspect detailed in the complaint report.

Based on the information provided, Fishnet knew the true identity of the culprit, as would most cops assigned to the precinct. The story behind the incident had been repeated many times, with only the identity of the victim changing. It was a romantic tryst gone afoul, with the Lothario lifting the necklace as soon as the unfaithful wife busied herself elsewhere. There was only one possible viper fitting the description of the seducer...Tami Kwariani, a seedy scam artist who made his living feeding off vulnerable females. The scheming Kwariani was known to use a number of aliases. His memorable appearance led the men in blue on patrol in the precinct to dub him "the Mask," so named because of his large tomahawk nose, dark black glasses, thick black eyebrows, and black mustache. Even though he dressed well, there was no getting around his being a human facsimile of a plastic mask designed for the amusement of children.

The Mask was always good for an automatic guffaw when spotted on the street by the cops. They found his criminal antics almost as amusing as his appearance. Locking him up again would delight Fishnet to no end because he held a profuse dislike of the human parasite. The detective found it astounding how anyone as ugly as Kwariani could have such success at conning his way into the boudoir of his victims. Tami's bedroom conquests were anathema to the jealous sleuth.

The envious detective intended to take Kwariani down pronto, make money in overtime, and add another collar to his portfolio of busts. There was also a more nefarious end result motivating Fishnet. Never one to overlook a possible opportunity, he saw potential gain stemming from an interview with the affection-starved victim...providing she measured up to his liking. Fishnet reckoned that if the complainant had turned to someone as revolting as the Mask to satisfy her carnal impulses, then she might enjoy a session of hide the salami with a detective as well. With this thought occupying his mind, Fishnet mentally gravitated into the other dimension where he could be seen, martini in hand, sashaying his way into the exploited crime victim's bedroom. Luckily there was no one present in the squad room to hear the detective gleefully blurt out his standard victory cry of "Pass the sherbet, Herbert....The big boy is coming out to play!"

Once his pipe dream ran its course, Fishnet reached for his last nonfiltered Camel cigarette as if he had actually engaged in a workout. He always made sure to keep a spare pack of the suicide sticks inside a small pigeon coop locker that was located up against a wall in the squad room. Oblivious to changing times, he never took seriously the speculation that smoke-free workplaces would one day be a reality in New York City. In rebellion to the very notion, he used the center drawer of his metal desk as an ashtray, having no qualms as he flicked ashes and rubbed out his butts into the section that was supposed to be for pens and pencils. The block of attached green lockers was set aside specifically for detectives to house their smaller personal items. Fishnet was always certain to equip his coop with a tongue shaver, toothpaste and brush, mouthwash, razor, soap, and a bottle of Old Spice. One never knew when such things might come in handy.

Thumbing through his workload, Fishnet divided his cases into two piles: winners and others. Winners were cases that presented an obvious, easy arrest or a clear opportunity for personal benefit. Those winners requiring some imagination were his favorites. The rest were others, losing propositions that would require effort *without* the prospect of personal gain. Aside from the Mask affair, the active cases currently before him were underwhelming others.

It was about 8:15 p.m. when Fishnet reached for the phone with the intention of calling up the potential inamorata, who had fallen victim to the charms of the Mask. He was beaten to the dial by an incoming call. He picked up the receiver.

"Squad...Detective Milligan. How may I help you?" he chirped officially into the phone. "What was that...bodies? Where? A *double*? Okay, sit tight....I'm on the way!"

The detective was hot to trot as a result of the call. A double body count likely meant homicide and the potential for gory leading to glory, making this case a clear winner in his opinion.

Rising to his feet, Fishnet quickly shoved his open cases into a yellow folder. He then placed the yellow folder inside a weathered brown manila envelope, which he rushed to put into a locked file cabinet to ensure the privacy of those concerned. This could be the perfect storm for Fishnet.

Not only was he working without a partner, but he was also working without any in-house supervision. He put his charcoal gray suit jacket on over his blue shirt and quickly adjusted his blue tie, pulling the small Windsor knot snugly up to his throat. Removing a small mirror from his desk, he gave himself a quick look-see. He combed his hair, then checked out his black loafers to see if they were sufficiently shined. They were. Convinced that he looked good, Fishnet peered out the window of the squad room onto the street below. The downpour had finally stopped. He was hoping that the rain would not make an encore; he disliked working outdoors in bad weather. Rain ruined the crease in his pants, which meant a pressing fee.

Fishnet was old school when it came to appearances. To him, looking his best mattered. He had been taught early on that "a boy with a nice book cover greatly increases the chances of selling his book." It was advice he took seriously. Always appearing presentable, the detective was appalled at how many people never understood that there was no such thing as a good second impression. It was ironic that Fishnet neglected to take into consideration, in light of his own poor social skills, that first impressions also pertained to him.

Fishnet hurried to retrieve a set of car keys that were hanging off a small hook kept inside the squad commander's private office. He then, as required, made an entry into a movement log, signifying exactly where he was going and in exactly what vehicle he was using to get there. Lastly, the detective signed out a portable radio. By the time he hustled out the door of the squad room, he could not help thinking of how much the department operated like a parochial school. His religious teachers also had rules for everything, with the punishment for offenders coming swiftly and with certainty.

Fishnet drove to a location that was about a half mile from the precinct. Upon arrival he pulled up behind a radio car where Officers Kilmer and Milo stood waiting. The sector car team had been babysitting a large white Oldsmobile parked on Mill Road. Fishnet exited his unmarked car and nodded to the officers. "What's up?" he asked evenly.

Officer Kilmer, a veteran of fourteen years on the job, wore a sardonic expression as he leaned against the driver's side of the patrol car. Of average height and weight, the one sure thing that would draw attention to him was the wealth of thick red hair on top of his head. Holding a lit cigarette between his fingers, he raised his left hand slowly to acknowledge Fishnet's presence. This gesture caused the smoke from his cigarette to thin and widen on its path upward into space. The officer then lifted his chin, indicating the direction of the Oldsmobile. Kilmer's lack of enthusiasm was due to his being an unhappy camper. The officer felt that he had been unjustly flopped back into uniform from the mounted unit. His problems had begun when he had reached down from his horse and grabbed the wrong protestor by the collar. He had no way of knowing that the person he galloped into a parking meter, as he had been thoroughly trained to do, was related to someone in the mayor's office.

Officer Milo, olive skinned and soft spoken, came without baggage. The three-year veteran of the force, whom Kilmer referred to as a *buff*, approached Fishnet to fill him in.

"Hey, Fish," greeted Milo. "The Olds isn't hot....We already ran the plate. The patrol sergeant just left here. He went to see if the registered owner is home."

"Which sergeant...Maloney?"

"Nah, Skunk Fumes is on patrol." The officer did not try to hide his smile.

Fishnet returned a knowing look. Skunk Fumes, a white-haired old-timer, had been a sergeant assigned to the precinct forever. A stickler for the book, he loved nothing more than to point out the rules of procedure to his subordinates. His tutorials were classics among the rank and file. These sessions grew to represent a time of frolic for those cops not on the receiving end of the instruction. The name Skunk Fumes was coined by one of the sergeant's subordinates long retired. When Skunk Fumes went off on one of his long-winded spiels, he frequently stepped in close to his audience during the oration. His breath was so putrid that it made anyone in close proximity susceptible to upchucking. The intrusive aroma was so known for its potency that those not subjected to it struggled to contain their chuckles when they observed some poor unfortunate pulling his neck back to minimize exposure to the polluting breeze. For his part, Fishnet planned to sidestep the problem by speaking to the sergeant from the other side of the hood of the radio car.

Stepping over street puddles left over from the rain, Fishnet walked to the Oldsmobile. Once he saw the gaping hole, it was clear to him that the trunk lock had been punched out. Placing his pen through the hole where the lock once had been, he lifted the trunk door to take a peek inside. The detective saw feet in high heels coming out of the bottom of a rolled-up quilt. After a few seconds, he slowly eased the top of the trunk down.

Placing his pen back in his jacket, Fishnet looked over the immediate surrounding area. He could see that the prospects for developing leads appeared sparse. On one side of the Oldsmobile, there was nothing but a view of water. It would seem unlikely that any pedestrian would have been traveling on the pathway along the river on a day of heavy rain. On the other side was a closed school that was tucked in among residential houses. There was very little traffic flow moving along the street, likely because Mill Road led to no destination of any importance. At best one might see an occasional car passing through the area when a driver would be out looking for a parking space. There were very few houses in the neighborhood with driveways, making spots hard to come by for residents on days when alternate-side parking rules were in effect. It being a Saturday, the school itself was a ghost town. Fishnet was highly pessimistic about the odds of finding a viable witness to anything as far as the crime scene location was concerned.

When Skunk Fumes pulled up to the scene, he had the owner of the Oldsmobile in the back seat of his car. Fishnet pitied the poor passenger as well as the officer who had been cooped up with Skunk Fumes in such a confined setting. After a brief conferral with the sergeant, the detective requested that the Oldsmobile be removed to the station-house parking lot where it could be further examined in an enclosed location, out of public view.

Skunk Fumes assigned Officer Milo the task of moving the car into the lot. Milo relieved the Oldsmobile owner of his car keys without offering an explanation. The car owner instinctively knew that he had little choice but to go along with the program. Skunk Fumes and his driver transported the owner to the station house, where he was placed at a desk in the vacant squad room.

Fishnet notified the crime scene unit and the homicide squad, asking both specialty units to respond to the parking lot at the precinct. Despite the lack of obvious leads, this was Fishnet's type of case—it could very well be the big one he'd been waiting for. The Mask, while not forgotten, was going to be relegated to the back burner for a while.

4

THE DAILY DOUBLE—DEATH AND DEATH

DEATH IN THE AIR always seemed to have a silencing effect, thought Detective Sergeant Al Markie of the homicide squad. Here he was in a precinct parking lot filled with curious cops...each one highly trained to fire a weapon capable of snuffing out the life of one person in order to preserve the life of another. Depending on the person dispatched, a death can be either welcomed or regretted. Everyone, including himself, stood in silence as a token of respect for two dead strangers who were to be soon freed from their temporary coffin. Things remained somber in the lot until it was time for the curtain to go up.

Markie, who had the evening coverage for Brooklyn, was responsible for overseeing the investigation. He would spearhead the case from the office of the precinct squad commander, Sergeant Lance Parlatto, who was not present at this time. Part of Markie's job was to see that the case was explored as thoroughly as possible. He had assigned his most seasoned investigator, Detective Oliver Von Hess, to work with Fishnet. The sergeant was cautiously optimistic that the collaboration would be an amicable one. Markie had heard through the department grapevine that Fishnet Milligan was a loose cannon, someone who could be a handful to work with.

Sometimes the word *psycho* was tossed around in reference to the precinct detective. Markie would not allow himself to be influenced by such negativity without his own substantiation. He would form his own opinion, with the input of the fifty-nine-year-old Von Hess, concerning Fishnet.

The homicide squad's presence at the precinct preceded the arrival of the forensic investigators, giving Markie and Von Hess time to discuss working with the precinct detective assigned to the case. Von Hess was ambivalent about working with Fishnet but remained confident in his ability to ensure that the investigation would be professionally handled regardless of his counterpart's idiosyncratic tendencies.

Ollie Von Hess had thirty-six years on the job, thirteen as a second-grade detective. In all he had twenty-six years in the detective bureau. Closing in on sixty, the crafty detective had seen just about everything there was to see when it came to the final curtain. His exposure spanned the run-of-the-mill gunshot to the far-out send-off known as autoerotic asphyxiation. At an even six feet, Von Hess still maintained his full stature; the toll of age had not diminished him as of yet. Other than a gut, he appeared to be in good shape, still maintaining broad shoulders with evenly proportioned legs and arms. He wore brown-tinted glasses and had somehow managed to hold onto most of his sandy-colored hair. The only thing that might have dated him was a grandfatherly buttoned gray sweater vest that he liked to wear under his undertaker suits. A married man with a family, the Long Island resident represented the pillar of stability.

Von Hess was a man trained to win battles. Born and bred on the Upper East Side of Manhattan when the neighborhood comprised blue-collar working-class families, he enlisted in the United States Marines after graduation from Power Memorial High School. After his military obligation was satisfied, it was easy for Von Hess to segue into the culture of the police department once appointed to the force. His all-business demeanor served him well from the onset of his police career. His father-in-law, a retired captain, greased the wheels by getting him on a career path that ultimately led to his first promotion. After just a few years on the job, he was a detective catching cases in a precinct. He eventually was assigned to the homicide squad. It was here that he'd first met Markie.

Markie appreciated Von Hess because the veteran detective was a straight shooter, a loyal friend with no agenda, and someone who put the job first. When Markie looked at Von Hess, he saw Gary Cooper in the movie *High Noon*...a real man.

"No problem, Sarge. I can handle him," said Von Hess, whose self-assuredness helped ease any reservations the supervisor might have had.

Markie nodded. "I know you can, Ollie. But if this Fishnet gives you any shit...and I mean about anything...just let me know and I'll clip his wings good for him."

"No problem, boss...I got it covered. Thanks."

When the crime scene unit arrived to take charge of the scene for the purpose of evidence gathering, Markie noted that the responding forensic team was led by a young female sergeant in her early thirties. The appearance of a female sergeant caused Markie to blink. Seeing a woman in such a position should not have come as a surprise to him: the boys' club that was the detective bureau had been infiltrated by females long ago. The existence of the opposite sex in a specialized unit had been the norm for what seemed like forever. Still, it wasn't easy for Markie to erase twenty-two years of working in an environment that traditionally expected to see men at the helm in every corner of the department. The chauvinistic influence was akin to indoctrination, one that stubbornly lingered on internally, even though he was sufficiently advanced to embrace the changing times.

"Lay the bodies out on the floor so we can search them," the female sergeant announced. She then glanced over at Markie, giving him a courtesy nod. Markie returned the nod, appreciating the acknowledgment.

She next addressed the crowd of onlookers authoritatively. "Everyone step back....We are going to need some room."

The observing officers slowly began to step back from the Oldsmobile in compliance with the order given by the crime scene supervisor. They formed a wide half circle of police as they positioned themselves around the vehicle, all anxious to see the contents inside the trunk.

Everyone had been waiting patiently while the team of detectives from crime scene worked. They photographed, made sketches, and took measurements. Later they would powder the interior and exterior of the vehicle in an effort to lift fingerprints. It was a slow, methodical process. But at last the moment they were all waiting for arrived...the removal of what had been crudely stashed away in the trunk. The subsequent findings were guaranteed to be gruesome, so the wait at ringside was sure not to disappoint.

The crime scene investigators took hold of the large commercial quilt that contained the bodies. Fishnet pitched in, along with Detective Von Hess, to assist in carefully lifting the quilt out of the trunk. Sergeant Markie looked on from the sidelines with the same keen interest as everyone else. Finding bodies in twos came along fairly infrequently...the probability being somewhere roughly along the lines of birthing triplets.

Markie remained focused on the performance of his detectives as they helped lay the quilt softly onto the blacktop. Everyone gradually gravitated toward the vehicle to get a closer look. The sergeant from crime scene stepped in to again address the crowd.

"Come on, people...back it up," she ordered. "Give them the room they need to work, or else I'm going to rope off the yard."

Her warning was taken seriously, and the audience took a step back. One of the crime scene investigators stepped in to untie the three ropes that held the quilt together. As the crowd watched with interest, the detective began to pull back all ends of the quilt, extending it to the fullest length, revealing the dead bodies of two women. One crime scene detective was specifically assigned to snap numerous photographs at each step of this process. The forensic investigators were methodical in their work, ever alert to the smallest detail, cautious to never overlook anything or damage evidence in haste.

Fishnet looked on in fascination as he witnessed how the torsos had been joined together inside the quilt. The bodies were face to face, flush against each other, with their arms and legs interlaced. A senior crime scene member theorized that the corpses had been snuggled together in order to fit into the quilt. Fishnet was hoping that there was a lesbian connection to the deaths in order to make things more interesting. To his dismay, he had no choice but to accept a secondary role in the current activity going on in the lot. The detective felt as if he were a student being schooled; he'd never before paid this much attention to the details of the crime scene procedure. But this was different. This case interested him. Fishnet stood by, eyeing the separation of the two women as they were removed from the makeshift pod that had briefly served as their casket. It did not appear that the women had been deceased for an extended period of time as rigor mortis had not fully set in.

Once the two women were splayed out on the ground independent of each other, Fishnet managed to move in closer, gaining a superior vantage point. He took notes concerning what he was witnessing. He saw that both bodies were fully clothed. Aside from some dirt picked up from where the torsos had been placed, their garments appeared to be relatively clean. Fishnet was unable to detect any torn apparel or soiling.

As far as anyone could see, there were no indications of sexual violation having transpired. Fishnet could not resist the temptation to step in even closer. Being it was Fishnet's case, he was allowed to take the liberty of moving in for a better view. He looked over the shoulder of one of the crime scene people, who were bending over the bodies examining hands, looking for signs that a struggle had ensued prior to death. Fishnet nodded in agreement with the forensic investigator's assessment that there was no overt evidence of violence having occurred.

Fishnet glanced over at Markie to see if he was looking at him. The detective was leery of Markie because he did not know him. He had seen the sergeant from the homicide squad on other jobs but had never had an opportunity to interact with him. Fishnet had no way of knowing who exactly from homicide would be showing up at the precinct to

28

assist him. He knew Detective Von Hess from around the job as Ollie, an experienced old-timer with a solid reputation among his peers. Fishnet was glad when he learned that Von Hess was assigned to work the case with him. With Von Hess alongside him, Fishnet knew he had caught a break by gaining a low-key, under-the-radar workhorse who was not about seeking the limelight. This suited Fishnet fine because he was not one to willingly share the spotlight. Fishnet was less enthusiastic about Markie's presence, not because of who he was but rather because of what he was...a boss, just another layer of supervision that he would have to listen to.

The two deceased women had been cut down in the prime of life. What interested the detectives was the contrast in the way they were dressed, one being attired for an evening out on the town and the other garbed to wash the bathroom floor. The disparity made the detectives doubt that the two had been together for an extended period of time prior to their demise. The investigators thought it likely that the duo had met up someplace just prior to their deaths. There was also the more remote theory that they had died at different locations and were packaged together later for easier disposal.

Fishnet became fixated on the attractive blond in the long-sleeved black evening dress. He perceived her as a great beauty, overlooking the dark circles under her eyes, which projected a prominent contrast to her fair-skinned face. He eyed the dead woman's nicely shaped figure salaciously, and by the time he got around to ogling her ample cleavage, the detective had forgotten all about Markie, Von Hess, the crime scene, and his very surroundings. The madman entered into one of his mental pilgrimages, a journey to his special place where the deceased blond was a most welcome guest.

The detective invented personalities for those he invited into his world. He recreated the dead blond to be vivaciously bubbly during her interactions with him, someone enthusiastically receptive to his every advance. He designed her to look beautiful without the support of lipstick, rouge, eyeliner, or any other artificial enhancement. Her arms, although covered by long sleeves, could only be slender as were her legs. As a couple, the two were having intimate drinks at the Grand Havana Room, a private cigar club in Midtown, when he...

"Fishnet," whispered Von Hess to his new partner, who was staring at the blond woman as if in a trance. Receiving no acknowledgment, Von Hess tried again, this time in a louder voice. "Hey, Fishnet." Still failing to get Fishnet's attention, Von Hess aborted his effort—assuming the detective was either absorbed in his work or hard of hearing.

Von Hess was hoping for a private word with Fishnet; he'd been the aide-de-camp to Detective Sergeant Alfred Markie for years, so he knew his boss well. He intended to advise Fishnet on how to handle the sergeant. Markie was regarded as one of the more competent bosses in the detective bureau. He was the sort of boss who got involved in investigations not to outshine subordinates but to support their efforts. His sole objective was to solve cases, not score points with bosses. When it came to accolades, he was cut from the same cloth as Von Hess. Both were more than willing to take a back seat to others who felt a need for the limelight.

Markie, while reasonable, was unwavering in just one respect....He demanded that detectives understand that it was he who called the shots. Those questioning his authority came to regret it soon enough. This was what Von Hess intended to enlighten Fishnet about...the risk of crossing Markie.

It was the loud shouting of an officer from an upper precinct window, looking to get the attention of another officer in the yard below, that returned Fishnet's mind to the parking lot. The   detective stood confused for a couple of minutes until he got his bearings again. Once his composure was settled, he concentrated on the business at hand. Fishnet was disappointed that there were no visible marks on the body of the blond. The detective saw no blood; no ligature or finger marks on the throat; no bullet holes; no stab wounds; no bruises, lacerations, scratches, broken fingernails, defense wounds, or any of the other signs indicating foul play. Fishnet overheard one of the forensic people state to the crime scene sergeant that it was possible that there were marks on parts of the body that were unsuitable for examination in the yard. Fishnet was sorry to hear that they were not going to probe further. He held great curiosity in what lay underneath the clothing of the deceased. He had to placate himself with the knowledge that a thorough autopsy would at least provide answers as to the cause of the deaths.

A theory that the deaths had resulted from a robbery gone afoul was quickly eliminated: the gold earrings, gold neck chain, and black onyx ring on the body of the blond attested to that. The   same went for the second woman, a brunette with curly brown hair whose jewelry also had gone untouched. Her body was equally unmarked, clean with a plain silver ring and inexpensive watch still adorning her finger and wrist.

Fishnet noted that the second woman was substantially smaller in stature in comparison to the blond. Fishnet summarized her as being about average in every way. Her remains suggested that she was within range of normal weight. While sort of cute, she did not measure up to Fishnet's standard. Not making the cut excluded her from having a role in his secret world. Perhaps it was her modest attire that influenced Fishnet's decision to oust her. Her clothing did little to stimulate the detective: faded blue jeans, well-worn jogging sneakers, and a long-sleeved brown Mickey Mouse sweatshirt. Fishnet saw a crime scene detective remove a red dog leash from the rear pocket of her jeans. Fishnet concurred with the general consensus held by the other detectives that these two women had not been out on the town together enjoying a double date. Also recovered from the brunette were keys and a small wallet that contained photo identification, a credit card, and forty dollars in cash. Based on the photo ID, the brunette was tentatively identified as Barbara Allen, a thirty-two-year-old who resided several miles from where the Oldsmobile had been parked. Fishnet regretted that he was going to have to turn in the cash—the other detectives had already seen it in her wallet before Fishnet could get it into his own.

Another of the crime scene detectives handed Fishnet a small black dress purse that was recovered from the trunk of the Oldsmobile. The purse contained Three Hundred Forty Three Dollars, some makeup, an invoice, a small hairbrush, keys, and an empty rust-colored pill vial without a label. Based upon the information on the invoice, Fishnet was able to tentatively identity the deceased blond as Shirley Harris, whose address on the document matched the address of Ms. Allen. It seemed that the two women had lived together. The detective saw this connection as supporting his suspicion that the two women may have been gay. This possibility did not erase the pain he felt for having to turn in more than three hundred dollars. By his calculations, Fishnet's tour of duty had cost him three hundred and eighty three bucks at this point....It was enough money to upset his stomach. It took Fishnet some time to get over his disappointment at not being able to glom the money left behind by the dead women. The detective was spoiled. He had been used to easy pickings...scoring cash off a corpse found in the street or after rifling a residence when a person had expired at home alone.

It was going to take some time before the precinct parking lot was again functioning normally. The crime scene segment of the investigation was far from over. The medical examiner still had to come by to take a look, a response that could take some time because with the bodies now out of public view, the rush to get there was not as imperative. Once these tasks were attended to, the meat wagon would still have to arrive and transport the bodies to where the autopsies would be conducted. The Oldsmobile would also need to be held for evidence until a release could be obtained from the district attorney's office. Lastly, all of the personal property belonging to the deceased women would have to be safeguarded.

"Fishnet...I need a word with you," called Markie.

Walking over, the detective wondered what was on his mind. "Yeah? What's up?"

Fishnet's curt response revealed to Markie that the detective's commanding officer was letting the detective operate without restrictions. He evaluated Fishnet as being spoiled, undisciplined, and in need of straightening out. Markie was up to the job.

Markie pulled the detective aside for a private conversation. "Who was it that authorized you to remove the car from the street to the parking lot?"

Hand on hip, Fishnet frowned at what he was being asked. That was a mistake, but it was a gut reaction that the detective was unable or perhaps unwilling to control. Fishnet was well aware that moving the vehicle was an unusual decision for a detective to make. He felt that in this case it was prudent to do so in order to spare the public the discomfort of having to look at something so distasteful. Fishnet's intentions were honorable ones, but he had sidestepped the chain of command, a miscue in a paramilitary organization such as the police department. The detective compounded his mistake by his body language...which Markie viewed as disrespectful. This was something the sergeant had a problem letting slide.

"What are we looking to do here, sarge? Shock the shit out of old ladies and kids by leaving dead bodies all over the street?"

Fishnet's comment smacked of defiance, and Markie did not overlook what he now saw as a challenge to his authority. The situation presented sufficient cause for the supervisor to respond harshly.

"Look...you made the call on your own to move the Olds, and while I am not saying your decision was not a prudent one—"

"So where do you see a problem?" Fishnet demanded, interrupting Markie. "What, are you worried about ruining the chance for prints on the steering wheel?"

"Never mind what I'm worried about," snapped Markie. "There is a protocol to follow. I'm telling you right now that in the future, it would be in your interest to follow it."

"What protocol exactly are you talking about, sarge?"

It seemed to Markie that Fishnet was asking for it. He responded in a tone designed to cut Fishnet's legs out from under him. "The protocol that says you call me before you make a move on your own! Understand?"

Fishnet was listening attentively as Markie expanded on his answer.

"The protocol that says you don't do a fucking thing without my first approving it!" The sergeant was now on a roll, and the detective remained mute as the sergeant continued on. "I call my lieutenant to keep him posted...*and* you call me to keep me posted. It's called respecting the chain of command....Do you get it or not?" asked the sergeant firmly. He was prepared to go all the way with his subordinate if necessary.

The sergeant waited for a response, but none came, so he resumed.

"Let me spell it out for you, *my friend*....You don't go from point A to point B without my letting you. Now, if you have a problem understanding that, I'll stick a complaint up your ass where the sun don't shine....Maybe that will clear the cobwebs from your head. Am I clear enough for you to comprehend the protocol I'm referring to now?"

Fishnet was taken aback. He wasn't used to this type of heavy-handed reprimand. But the detective knew that with the way he conducted his affairs, the last thing he needed was the scrutiny of a boss like this. Fishnet was smart enough to retreat. Now playing the game, Fishnet answered Markie in the most respectful voice he could muster.

"My mistake....Sorry, boss. Now I know how you work. I got it."

"Good. Now, let's both get back to work." For Markie, the book was closed once Fishnet knew where the power rested.

Realizing that Fishnet was working his tour of duty in the squad without the benefit of a partner, Markie telephoned his office for additional support. The newly assigned detective, Olive Moore, picked up the phone. Markie instructed her to collect Detective Wyatt White, also newly assigned to homicide, ordering the both of them to respond to the original crime scene where the Olds had been parked. Once they were at Mill Road, their job would be to conduct a thorough canvass of the area to find a witness who might have seen something or could provide viable leads. For Markie, this was Homicide 101, a mandatory step to take. It was an easy assignment for the new members of his squad, one that came without anticipated complications. Markie then stepped back to allow his two teams do their jobs.

After his initial exposure to Fishnet, Markie was happier than ever that he had chosen Von Hess to work with him. His gut impression of Fishnet told him that the detective, even though having been around for a bit, still had a lot to learn. His hope was that by teaming him up with the old-timer, he would be creating the perfect teacher–student relationship. Little did Markie know that the student was a bedbug.

During lonely periods, Markie contemplated his future. With over twenty-two years in the department, he had covered a lot of ground as a detective and then a squad commander. His résumé was solid with his having worked in the most elite squads. These assignments came without shortcuts, beginning with his paying dues in uniform followed by years as a plainclothes cop jumping out of an undercover taxicab to arrest people in the act of committing robberies and assaults and carrying guns. With no promotional exams in sight, what to do next became the question. Markie had a decent education, which included advanced degrees that he rarely spoke of. He was well versed in how to play poker when interacting with the public, bosses, lawyers, and politicians. The problem was he was beginning to tire of dealing with all of them.

Something was different. The sergeant was smart enough to realize that all of these people hadn't changed....He had. They had always been a pain in the butt. He was at a place now where he found himself losing patience, especially with those younger ones who were in positions over him that he had to answer to. The sergeant had grown into manhood in the police department, a dangerous yet entertaining environment in which one can see and learn plenty from the best seat at the circus. Now at forty-three years of age, he was at a crossroad.

The divorce a few years back had sapped some of his strength. He had been married to a woman who took no prisoners. When she informed him that she was going to leave him and take along their three kids, she did her talking through a legal shark. It was no bluff when her attorney candidly communicated that they intended to take the sergeant to the cleaners. The financial haircut he took left him on the cusp of poverty. Remarkably, the sergeant didn't seem to really mind too much. He was the sort of man who looked at life practically. He knew he would have only gambled, drunk up, or pissed the money away, so living in a studio apartment in a rundown section of Brooklyn was good enough for him. Fortunately, Markie had the discipline to isolate his negativity at will. This ability to insulate from distractions permitted him to perform his job without impediment. Another thing working in his favor was an all-consuming work ethic. It helped camouflage the scars...probably saving him from self-destruction.

⊞ ⊞ ⊞

IN THE SQUAD ROOM, Fishnet and Von Hess got ready to interview the owner of the Oldsmobile. They decided to conduct their questioning in the lineup room, a square box that came equipped with a one-way glass for viewing. From inside the room, the glass just looked like a mirror. From an outside passageway, the room could be monitored without detection.

The cinder-block walls in the room were painted celery green. A pipe running along one of the walls was used by detectives to handcuff their prisoners to when necessary. Other than an unadorned square metal table and two metal chairs, the room was completely barren. The lack of visual distractions made the location an effective setting for interrogations. At the onset, it was agreed that Von Hess was to play the good guy role with all those to be questioned, while Fishnet's job was to act as the heavy. The first interview for the pair in the case was of Enrico Paparella, the owner of the white Oldsmobile.

"Have a seat, Mr. Paparella," said Von Hess to the short, bald man.

"Thank you," answered the little man as he looked about the room curiously.

"Would you like a cup of coffee?"

"No, thank you."

"Water?"

"Nothing, thank you."

"The Oldsmobile is in your name, correct, sir?" asked Von Hess politely.

"Yes....When am I getting it back? I need it for work tomorrow."

"We'll talk about that later," interjected Fishnet tartly. "For now, just answer the questions."

Fishnet stuck to his role as the bad guy even though Paparella seemed to be a very compliant person. Fishnet took his jacket off, lit up a Camel, and stood with his back to the entrance door of the room, facing Paparella's profile. His jacket came off to make sure that the gun hanging from his hip was clearly visible.

Paparella tried not to appear nervous. When he was asked to produce his registration to the Oldsmobile, he complied without question. Fumbling, he rushed to produce an up-to-date registration for his vehicle. The document reflected him as the registered owner of the car. He was then asked to produce a driver's license. Again he complied without hesitation and included a union identification card from the International Longshoremen's Association. These documents identified him as a fifty-eight-year-old dockworker named Enrico Paparel Paparella.

"Enrico...they named you after the great Caruso?" Von Hess asked.

"No...after the great Nobel Prize physicist...Enrico Fermi!" corrected Paparella proudly.

"Another good man," countered Von Hess after being corrected.

"If you like spaghetti benders, he was okay," added Fishnet dryly.

The comment was not immediately absorbed by Paparella. Von Hess moved on as if the remark had never been stated.

Questioning revealed that Paparella was a married man with three adult children, all of whom were married and with their own families. Paparella said that he was the only person with access to drive his Oldsmobile. An old-school type, he never loaned his car to anyone, including his wife. He resided in an apartment house just a few blocks away from where he had last parked the car on Thursday evening. Von Hess was conducting the questioning uninterrupted at this point while Fishnet stood by, silently sizing up Paparella. The car owner originally was a product of Calabria. He spoke English fluently and was easily understandable. Fishnet took a hard look at Paparella's hands. They looked powerful. The dockworker's face had a slight sag to it, but he still looked rugged enough to be holding up his end on the piers.

The Oldsmobile owner spoke with a certainty at times, giving Von Hess the impression that he could be quite stubborn and set in his ways. Other than that, the car owner was forthcoming in his answers throughout. When asked about the broken trunk lock, he readily answered without stammering.

"What happened to the trunk lock of your car?" Von Hess queried.

"Looks like somebody broke it," came the response of Paparella.

"You didn't have a punched lock when you parked?" Fishnet asked.

"Definitely not!" There was now a testy edge in the longshoreman's voice. He was pissed off. It had finally registered with the man from Calabria....He realized that he had been insulted by Fishnet with the earlier crack made about spaghetti benders.

The car owner was convincing in his claim that when he had parked the Olds for the night, the lock was in perfect working order. Paparella passed the smell test of both detectives. It didn't take much conversation before both were satisfied that he was not in some way involved in the deaths of the women. Frankly, Fishnet was a little disappointed. He'd secretly hoped Paparella was going to be a serial-killing maniac. That now seeming unlikely, Fishnet quickly became bored.

It was Von Hess who finally got around to apprising Paparella of some of the facts surrounding the case as it pertained to his car. Although he was far from thrilled that his vehicle was going to be held as evidence, he was as understanding as could be expected. While Fishnet and Von Hess could not totally rule out the possibility of Paparella having in some way had a contributing hand in the matter under investigation, they both thought it highly unlikely. The two detectives concurred in their opinion that the longshoreman was clean, just a working stiff whose vehicle had been conveniently used by those responsible for housing the girls in the trunk of his car.

"We unfortunately have to process your car," said Von Hess.

"Process my car for what?"

"Fingerprints...blood...you know, stuff like that," Von Hess explained. "With a little luck, the district attorney will authorize us to release the car back to you in a couple of days. Don't worry; someone will get in touch with you."

Paparella slowly began to rise to his feet. "Okay...can I go now?"

"Certainly," answered Von Hess. "Do you need a ride home?"

"No...that's okay. I'll walk. I might as well start getting used to it, I guess."

5

ALDO AND THE PRINCESS

THE MOST VALUABLE ITEM recovered from the scene was the photo identification of Barbara Allen. The document provided, in addition to her photo, a date of birth and an address. This left little doubt as to the identity of the modestly attired woman with the brunette hair. A fingerprint comparison would later provide positive confirmation as to the identity of both women.

There had been enough information gathered among the personal effects of the two women for Von Hess to run a criminal history check. Both had rap sheets in New York: Barbara Allen had been arrested three times for heroin possession in lower Manhattan and once in Nassau County on a charge of petty larceny stemming from an unsuccessful "five-finger discount" at a pharmacy. She had walked away from each of these arrests without jail time, but one of the drug busts was accompanied by an additional charge for felony forgery. That arrest resulted in a court-ordered vacation at a rehab center for drug addiction.

The arrest record of Shirley Harris was even more colorful. The blond had chalked up three arrests in New York. First it was disorderly conduct and criminal mischief resulting from a dispute with the manager of a movie theater on the Upper West Side. Another pinch, this time in the Greenpoint section of Brooklyn, saw her facing a judge on charges of sexual misconduct and prostitution with a minor in McCarren Park. Her last arrest came in an East Village shooting gallery where the law had caught her with a set of works, speedballing heroin and cocaine. This particular bust had found her also in possession of an unloaded .38 caliber Smith & Wesson snub-nose revolver that she claimed to be holding for a friend, who had also been arrested at the scene. She caught a break in court because the gun had been unloaded. The judge in the case took pity, forcing her into mandatory rehab.

After reviewing the criminal histories of the two women, Fishnet summarized them in just a few typically charming words: "Just a couple of fucking junkies."

Von Hess simply nodded. He had to concur; little argument could be made with his new partner's analysis.

"But you gotta admit, junkie or not, the blond bitch was primo... built like a brick shithouse," added Fishnet, looking for some form of concurrence from Von Hess.

Von Hess refused to dignify the comment. His failure to validate his remark puzzled Fishnet, so he pressed the issue, pushing for his partner's agreement. "What...are you telling me you didn't think she was hot?"

Von Hess turned to look Fishnet in the eye. "Cut the shit....What do I look like to you, some kind of necrophilia-loving pervert?"

Fishnet took no offense. "Fair enough," he answered with a chuckle. He actually was tickled by the senior man's tart response.

Fishnet was not looking for an argument with Markie's right-hand man. The detective had come across lots of long-in-the-tooth old-timers like Von Hess...puritanical souls who got uptight about any reference to things sexual.

The next step was to visit the women's residence. The recovered keys from the two deceased women would likely fit the lock to their apartment. Detective Von Hess recommended they go to the address after they first touched base with Markie. Fishnet went along without question. The detective apparently had learned his lesson as far as how to conduct himself while under the direct supervision of the sergeant from homicide.

As expected, Markie extended his blessing. The sergeant had already made notifications to the detective duty captain and to his lieutenant boss over at homicide, who was home when he received the heads-up. Markie advised Von Hess to remind Fishnet to give a courtesy call to his precinct squad commander, Lance Parlatto, who was also home. Parlatto, upon learning what was going on at his office, wanted to be involved. The squad commander reached out directly to the duty captain for authorization to go in to work. His desire was thwarted as a result of their conversation. Since it was also the captain's job to control overtime, he opted to side with frugality. Authorizing Parlatto to come in on overtime was out of the question as long as Markie was already on site to spearhead things.

Parlatto was irked by the decision. Aside from having a reputation for being a notorious glutton when it came to overtime, he desperately wanted to appear in the eyes of the higher-ups over in headquarters to be running an exceptional squad. He was prospecting for special assignment money...which meant a promotion that came with lieutenant's pay.

Not having Parlatto around suited Fishnet just fine. He already had Markie to contend with; he was not anxious to have yet another layer of supervision around, sticking a nose into his business. The detective disliked working under what he perceived to be a microscope.

"I'll put together the case folder," said Von Hess.

"Okay. I'll take care of the property," indicated Fishnet.

Fishnet locked up the personal property belonging to the women inside his pigeon coop for safekeeping and later vouchering. The action was a first for Fishnet. To his dismay, it would mark the only time he had ever put money in his coop with the intention of actually vouchering it. Once these tasks were completed, the time had come for the detectives to hit the street.

"Let's take my wheels....I'll drive."

"No problem, Ollie," agreed Fishnet. "I'll grab a radio."

At an even rate of speed, Detective Von Hess drove the unmarked police car to where the two women were believed to have lived. There was no conversation during the drive. Von Hess was mentally occupied, trying to figure out what could have caused a couple of young women to wind up in the trunk of a car as they did. Alongside him, Fishnet focused on writing into a notebook little reminders of the things he needed to do on the case. He drew a tiny dollar sign in the top right corner of the page as a reminder of how much money he was already out for having to later voucher the recovered money.

Arriving at the address, the detectives found a well-maintained, six-story, multifamily red brick apartment house in the middle of a residential street. After securing a parking spot on the block, they proceeded to the location. Two locked outer glass doors blocked their entry into the building. Through the door glass, the detectives could see mailboxes and bells affixed to a wall inside the vestibule. As he shook the exterior door violently in a last-ditch attempt to open it, Fishnet turned to Von Hess with a disturbed look.

"Don't you have the keys?" Von Hess asked.

Fishnet was embarrassed. He had forgotten the keys back at the squad. The thought crossed his mind to kick in the door to gain access. The detective was fit to be tied.

"How in hell do they expect people to get in this lousy dump?" asked

Fishnet with exasperation.

"Did you forget the keys?" Von Hess repeated.

"Yeah...I forgot the fucking keys!" Fishnet added in an angry tone.

Von Hess looked at Fishnet as if seeing him for the first time. He was surprised by such an over-the-top reaction.

"Relax, Fish....We are in no rush....Let's wait awhile. We don't have to go back to the squad right away. Someone will come by or leave soon enough. Let's give it a few minutes," came Von Hess's calm response.

Fishnet huffed and puffed at the thought of waiting. "How the fuck do they expect the mailman to deliver mail?" he asked aloud.

"It's a security precaution, I suppose....They probably had some break-ins. The mailman may even have the key," speculated Von Hess. "Who knows why things are set up the way they are?"

Fishnet collected himself well enough to accept the reality that he had to wait it out. The detectives sat back, making themselves as comfortable as possible in their car. Von Hess was shrewd. He turned on the radio so that they could listen to some mellow music in the hope that it would settle Fishnet down. His channel-surfing ended when he came upon the soothing voice of Mel Tormé. Fishnet began humming to the tune after a couple of moments of listening. Von Hess snickered as the man they called the velvet fog worked his magic in taming Fishnet. The musical therapy was interrupted after two songs, when suddenly Fishnet spotted a young woman exiting the building. The detective reacted with a speed that startled Von Hess, who himself had become complacent thanks to the music.

Racing across the street, Fishnet managed to catch the front exterior door before it closed. He eyeballed the woman's back as she kept moving forward, focused only on wherever she was going. She was lost in her own thoughts when she departed her building, never even noticing the sudden appearance of Fishnet coming out of nowhere.

Normally Fishnet would have looked to pick her brain in an effort to come up with possible information, but instead he chose to let her go because his quick action had left him slightly winded. When Von Hess finally made his way over to the building, the two detectives read the mailboxes together. Glued to the mailbox for Apartment 3R was a blue plastic strip with white printed lettering that spelled out the name *Allen.* Above the blue plastic strip was a small rectangular piece of white gauze tape that reflected the hand-printed name, in blue ink, of Shirley Harris. Fishnet produced a flashlight pen, which he pressed against the little dotted openings found on the face of the mailbox for Apartment 3R. Once the light was shed, he might have been able to read the labels on the envelopes inside—had there been any, but the mailbox was empty. He resorted to examining the miscellaneous mail left on the floor beneath the mailboxes, but none was addressed to either of the deceased women. A locked interior door still prevented their access to the apartments.

Von Hess saw a posting that indicated the building had a super in Apartment 1L. A look at the box for 1L identified Aldo Pagan as the super. Von Hess rang the bell to the Pagan apartment. The ring was answered by a female whose accented voice came through the intercom along with a loud and annoying static-filled blast. The responding voice was an energetic-sounding one.

"Who is it?" The words shot out of the intercom in rapid fashion.

"Police!" Fishnet barked.

The buzz granting entry came without delay, almost as if the detectives were expected. Once on the other side of the door, they proceeded directly to Apartment 1L. A short, sturdy-looking woman with a wealth of black hair answered the door, holding a small baby boy in her arms. A second little tyke stood next to her with his arm wrapped around the woman's knee. The boy's left hand was occupied with tugging at the bottom of his mama's gray clinging dress. Fishnet stood fixated on the singular wide streak of gray hair that ran from the center of her head down to her shoulder. He could see through the outline of her dress an attractive figure, even after having a couple of kids. Her legs appeared toned for someone not wearing shoes that would have helped tighten them. Fishnet liked the wildly thick hair that reminded him of a lion's mane....He found her to be sizzling hot.

The woman's dark, piercing eyes widened as she looked up at the detectives standing before her.

Having picked up on Fishnet's interest, the woman who came to the door had a defiant look about her when facing the two men. Their combined bulk was substantial enough to block her view of the hallway behind them. Fishnet mentally coined a name for her in seconds. Since she reminded him of the comic book heroine Sheena, Queen of the Jungle, the super's wife became his—Jungle Princess.

After he identified himself, Von Hess had to struggle a bit to get her to comprehend that her husband, Aldo, was not in any trouble. Once she was convinced of that, she softened. Her smile revealed ivory-white teeth couching a singular gold front tooth that stood out from the others in her mouth. She announced politely that her name was Millie Pagan. The detectives were compelled to pay close attention, laboring to understand her due to her limited command of English.

"Aldo is soo-pa.....He my huz-ban," she said while juggling her smallest child from one arm to the other.

"Yeah, Aldo...the sooooo-pa, where is he?" Fishnet was mimicking her.

"Out."

"Can you please call him for us on the phone?" asked Von Hess respectfully.

"Beautiful kids you have there," commented Fishnet as he watched the standing little boy at his mother's knee, tinkering with her dress. Each of the little guy's yanks flashed flesh, giving Fishnet a peek at his mother's thighs.

In answer to their discourse, Mrs. Pagan took a cell phone out of the open pocket of her dress to dial a number. After exchanging a few words in Spanish over the phone, she handed the device over to Von Hess so that he could speak directly to Aldo. Their conversation concluded with the super advising he would be home shortly. The detectives thanked Aldo's wife for her assistance and proceeded to their unmarked vehicle. Just as they were walking off, Fishnet turned slowly around to stare knowingly into the eyes of the super's spouse. Using his best Gable look, the detective's extended glance came across quite seductively. Refusing to flinch, she boldly returned the look, eliminating any suggestion of shyness. With a crooked smile of confidence, she lifted her chin slightly, which to Fishnet was an unmistakable signal that the light was green.

The unexpected attention Aldo's wife received broke the monotony of her routine. Fishnet turned away from her to look at Von Hess as he continued to walk off. Seeing his partner made him think of Markie. The thought was enough to make Fishnet forget about the super's wife in the real world. She would have to be resurfaced as Jungle Princess in his make-believe world at some point down the road.

Once the detectives were back in their vehicle, they again waited, this time for the arrival of Aldo. Fishnet glanced over at Von Hess behind the wheel. What he saw caused him to do a double take. The detective's stomach was brushing against the steering wheel. Fishnet never noticed that Von Hess had such an ample corporation. He was impressed at how the old-timer's gut seemed to diminish when he stood erect.

The super, who seemed to be taking forever, finally made his way home. Appearing to be in his late thirties, he seemed to be just a little taller than his wife. He was bone-thin, with chiseled features. Aldo walked with a slight limp, seeming to favor his left leg. He had an unclean look about him, with hands labor-blackened as if he had just finished working for hours underneath an automobile inside a garage. He wore his black hair plastered down to one side, and his thin black whiskers were spotted with small islands of bare spots. Aldo was dressed in a blue work shirt, matching blue work pants, and black combat boots.

Aldo approached the detectives with the ease of a family member greeting a pair of uncles. He knew exactly where he was going. The super jumped in the rear seat of the unmarked police car uninvited and without the slightest trace of uncertainty. Von Hess interpreted Aldo's ability to recognize an unmarked police car and get in it without being invited as a sign of an informant who was no stranger to interacting with the authorities. The possibility of Aldo being a snitch escaped Fishnet. The detective simply saw the super's ease with police as a refreshing surprise. Also, his English was excellent.

"You guys aren't from the precinct, right?"

Von Hess was the first to respond. "No, I'm from the homicide squad."

"Homicide? What do you need from me?"

"You *are* Aldo, aren't you?" Von Hess wanted to confirm whom he was talking to.

"Yeah, I'm Aldo....I'm the super for the building."

Thanks to Aldo, the detectives established that the two women had been living together in the same apartment for about three months. They learned that Barbara Allen had been employed as a cashier at Dixie's, a local twenty-four-hour diner. According to the super, Barbara had lived in the building alone at first, having rented her apartment about a year ago.

"She got the apartment through a real estate agent?" Von Hess questioned.

"Nah...her father got her the apartment and at a low rent."

The mention of low rent got Fishnet's attention. "Just how did he manage that?"

"Her old man knew the owner of the building."

"Do you know where he knows him from?"

"The girl's father is a doctor....He delivers babies, so I think that was the connection. I guess he might have delivered one of the owner's kids or something," conjectured Aldo.

Once Doctor Edward Allen was injected into the conversation, the detectives chose to pursue a line of questioning relating to him. Aldo explained that Papa Allen had paid the first four months of rent for his daughter. Aldo explained that he was aware of this because part of his duties included collecting rent for the landlord. Aldo's fluidness in providing information strengthened the view of Von Hess that the super might be a cheese eater. The guesswork left Von Hess cautious as to how he comported himself around Aldo. Experience taught him that a good rule of thumb was to never trust a snitch.

"Do you have a contact number for the doctor?" Von Hess asked.

Aldo faltered for the first time. The super's hesitation hinted that he was looking to protect the doctor.

Picking up on this, Fishnet nudged things along. "C'mon, Aldo...cut the shit. Give with the fucking number."

Relenting, the super reluctantly dug into his wallet for the contact information the father had given him when his daughter first moved in. At this point the detectives had a good read on Aldo. They eventually persuaded him to explain his arrangement with Barbara's father.

The story Aldo provided had the doctor slipping him a hundred dollars a month in return for the super keeping an eye on his daughter. Aldo stood firm in his claim that he was ignorant as to exactly why Barbara Allen needed to have an eye kept on her.

"How was that going?" Fishnet asked. "Was she behaving herself like a good little girl?"

"No problems," answered the super, taking notice that Fishnet was speaking in the past tense.

Aldo stood by his contention that there had never been any reason to report Barbara to her father, describing her as a good tenant who kept to herself. Von Hess had his doubts about this. He was tempted to ask Aldo to roll up his sleeves but then decided against it. Instead, he chose to inquire about Barbara's friends.

"Does Barbara have a lot of friends?"

"Her best friend is a small dog," said Aldo with a shrug.

"What kind of dog?"

"A small white poodle. She called the dog her little butterball....She takes the dog all over with her."

"Butterball was the dog's name?"

"No...just Butter," answered Aldo. "So what is all this about? Did she get in trouble...kill somebody?" The super was nervously joking as he posed the question.

Von Hess recognized that Fishnet was the impatient type. He figured that the time was fast approaching when his partner would look to cut to the chase. Von Hess was on the money with his insight; Fishnet threw it in first gear.

"So when was the last time you saw Barbara alive?"

That was all it took for Aldo's antenna to go up. His response came forth immediately. In an agitated, high-pitched tone, he launched into a series of questions of his own. "What do you mean, when did I last see her alive? She's dead? What happened to her?"

"We are trying to figure that out, Aldo. That is why we are here," advised Von Hess.

"How did she die?"

"We found her wrapped up in the trunk of a car," answered Fishnet bluntly.

Aldo stiffened. "The trunk of a car!" The super was astonished...and alarmed. "So what does all this have to do with me?"

"Relax, Aldo, we're only here hoping you may have seen or heard something," explained Von Hess.

"No, man, I got nothing to do with any of this. I am feeling uncomfortable here....Hey, do I need a lawyer or something?"

"What for?" snapped Fishnet, losing patience.

"Well, just so you know, I've been clean for years!"

"Really?...How nice to hear it," commented Fishnet sarcastically.

Aldo was looking to get out of the car. "I have to go. I got a lot of work to do...."

"Get comfortable, pal....We're not done with you," ordered Fishnet.

Von Hess had to take over in order to reel Aldo back into the fold. He managed to placate the super by taking the time necessary to explain the situation, reassuring him that he was not a suspect of any kind. Von Hess made it a point to emphasize to the super the particular importance of his cooperation. The liberal sprinkling of gratitude managed to bring Aldo around and back on the team. Von Hess gave him a Detectives' Endowment Association courtesy card to help him get out of traffic tickets in the event he ever got pulled over. That also went over well. The icing on the cake was the promise that the detectives would be through with Aldo shortly. This went a long way in stabilizing the climate.

Fishnet stared blankly into the passenger-side window as Von Hess resumed the questioning. The invisible smoke coming out Fishnet's ears was evident from the expression on his face. He did not like to be upstaged.

"Any boyfriends for Barbara?" Von Hess inquired.

"Nah, no guys ever come around here."

Fishnet's interest was now stirred. "Was she gay?"

"Nah, I don't think so. No women ever come around here much either." Aldo then corrected himself. "Well...there is this one girl who comes over once in a while."

"Who is that?"

"Some girl I think Barbara knew from work. I overheard them talking about customers in the diner one time...but I don't know her name or anything."

"When was it that you last saw her?"

"Who do you mean?"

"Barbara."

"This afternoon. She went out with the dog around one p.m."

"She was alone?"

"Just her and the dog I saw."

"What about the blond?" Von Hess asked.

Aldo inched up closer to the front seat when the conversation shifted to Shirley Harris. For the second time, Aldo was taken aback, this time after hearing the news that Shirley was also gone.

"Her too? Ohhh, man...this is some messed-up shit."

"Yeah, Aldo, it is. Now you know why this is so important....We have two dead girls on our hands," pointed out Von Hess.

The super described the blond as "nice" in the physical sense. Aldo suspected that Shirley worked in a nightclub or in some business requiring her to beautify herself. He told the detectives he had last seen Shirley on Friday when she left the apartment. He recollected her wearing a nice black dress and heels. Aldo conveyed that he was putting out the garbage when Shirley left the house. The super was unable to provide any information that linked either women to anyone specific. All Aldo knew for sure was that Shirley Harris often went out dressed up nice, returning at various times ranging from a few hours to a couple of days.

Aldo was put off by Fishnet's next question. The detective curtly asked Aldo if there was some sort of illegal activity going on inside the building with the girls. Aldo took the question personally. "No way," was his immediate response to the perceived accusation. "My building is a clean one!"

"We know that, Aldo," Von Hess assured.

Fishnet was again feeling some hostility toward Von Hess, who was turning out to be too good at his job for Fishnet's taste. He resented the older detective's style. To him, beating around the bush was babying people. These thoughts about Von Hess took him on one of his faraway journeys as he again stared out the car window. Fishnet pigeonholed his partner as prehistoric—a relic, an outdated device programmed with an old chip imbedded into a rusted metal skull that kept him on a singular track at an annoyingly slow rate of speed. The detective delighted himself as he envisioned the old warhorse headed to pasture...walking alone into a valley that led to someplace in Fishnet's world. Now that he had written the old man out of the picture, Fishnet was alone to nab desperados, to grab the brass ring that would bring him glory....

Von Hess's attention was pulled away from Aldo due to the cadence of recognizable clicking emanating from Fishnet. Turning to look at his partner, he saw Fishnet's hand in the side pocket of his suit jacket. The familiar clicking was Fishnet's repeated closing and opening of the handcuffs hidden in his jacket. Von Hess ignored what he thought to be a nervous habit.

The older detective was satisfied that he had gotten all he could from Aldo, so he let him out of the car. The sudden disruption of the car door being slammed shut returned Fishnet to where he actually was.

"So, what do you think?" Von Hess asked after Aldo was gone.

"Uhh...not sure. What about you?" Fishnet was stalling and in need to play catch-up.

"I don't think he knows much more," replied the older detective. "We'll be coming back later to the apartment with a boss to conduct a search. Maybe we can get more then."

"I'm with you," commented Fishnet.

46

6

BUTTERBALL

THE MIDDLE-AGED WOMAN could see that the white poodle belonged to someone. The red collar around the dog's neck seemed to be brand spanking new, so the dog was likely no stray. The animal appeared well groomed, clean, and very wet. The dog was behaving oddly, wandering aimlessly along Mill Road in an apparent search for something. The woman was not sure what exactly a bewildered animal should look like. But in her opinion, the canine seemed confused. After the dog looked up at her with saddened eyes that conveyed a need for help, she leaned down to reassure the frightened hound.

"What is the matter, baby?....You lost?" she asked, taking the dog's head in her hands.

The white poodle responded with a silent cowering quiver. Sopping up the sympathy, the dog lifted its paw and placed it on the woman's forearm.

"Aw...you poor thing...don't be afraid....No one is going to hurt you," she cooed.

The woman cradled the poodle to her bosom and rocked the animal for what would seem to a non-pet-lover as an excessive amount of time. She shortly came to the realization that she would be unable to abandon the dog.

⊞ ⊞ ⊞

DETECTIVE VON HESS took a stick of gum out of his pocket to chew on during the drive back to the station house. When the gum came out, it was a clear indication to those who knew him that the detective was mulling something over in his mind. His thoughts centered on figuring out the best way for him to handle his handicap. With Fishnet as the case officer, Von Hess was burdened with a short-fused partner with questionable social skills at best. This was a complicated dilemma that was not going to be as easy for the senior detective to navigate around as he'd originally thought. The pace of the investigation was moving slowly enough without adding the drama of a self-created problem. Unfortunately for Von Hess, he was in an awkward position.

Not being a boss, he lacked the authority, or willingness for that matter, to remove what he saw as a fly in the ointment...Fishnet. To expose Fishnet's less than professional behavior would require his stepping up to speak out against the detective. It was a move that Von Hess knew would not sit well among peers, not to mention the union. Without a palatable solution, the detective had no alternative but to accept the situation for what it was. He resigned himself to tough it out and play the hand dealt to him.

The one accomplishment achieved by the detectives was to establish time frames for the deaths of the two women. Given what Aldo had told them, the window of death for Barbara Allen was narrowed down to approximately seven hours, sometime between 1:00 p.m. to 8:00 p.m. on Saturday. As for Shirley, the margin was wider, a little over a day... sometime between 7:30 p.m. Friday and 8:00 p.m. on Saturday. The question was still not settled as to whether the two women had met their end at the same time and location or independently of each other. Von Hess was not ashamed to admit that they were going to need a break if the case was to go anywhere.

Fishnet offered theories that were all over the map. His mind had been working overtime in both of the planets he frequented. The detective liberally floated ideas that he bounced off Von Hess during the ride back to the squad. The senior detective considered some of his partner's offerings as reasonable possibilities, some as a bit of a stretch, and others bordering on the preposterous. Ever conscious of the importance of maintaining a healthy working relationship, Von Hess declined to dismiss any of Fishnet's proposals outright. With a noncommittal calmness, he listened politely to each of Fishnet's scenarios as he continued to chew hard on his gum. Von Hess injected an occasional "I see" into the conversation as proof that he was listening attentively. As his chewing

48

began to give his jaw the feeling of going through a workout, the veteran detective had a dark thought. He wondered if it was actually possible that Fishnet was playing with less than a fulldeck.

Arriving back at the precinct, the detectives saw there was still plenty of activity going on in the parking lot. They parked their unmarked vehicle on the street to avoid cluttering the lot further. After entering the parking area on foot, the detectives stayed on the sidelines, watching as the forensic investigators continued to do their thing.

Fishnet had little patience regarding the intricacies of forensic work. Aside from the perversion aspect of viewing the female bodies, he saw the entire process, while necessary, as too tedious for his liking. The detective's preference was to keep things simple, a leaning that came without time-consuming, technical mumbo jumbo. As far as he could determine, the crime scene people were still snooping around the car for latent prints, DNA, loose hairs, or whatever other stuff their unit scoured for. Personally, he was hoping they would come up with some kind of basic evidence that would simplify matters regarding the cause of death. A gun, a bullet hole, a bottle of poison—any of those would have been a nice discovery.

Gradually the crowd of onlookers, all wearers of blue, thinned out as the officers returned to their own specific duties. Fishnet was on the same page as his uniformed colleagues—once the bodies came out of the quilt, the real show was over. What remained to be done in the yard, however important, was still boring.

Having seen enough of the crime scene unit for one day, Fishnet retired to the second-floor offices of the detective squad, leaving the evidence specialists to their labors. Von Hess pointed his finger to the upper floors of the precinct, a gesture that made it clear to the crime scene sergeant where he and Fishnet would be if needed. Von Hess seemed to lag as he walked off. He kept looking behind him as he moved along, giving the impression that he still held some interest in the proceedings going on with the Oldsmobile. The truth was that Von Hess thought the work of a forensic investigator to be fascinating. Upon reflection, particularly after a beer or two, the one regret Von Hess had in life was not being able to pursue a higher education. Not even his wife knew that he would have loved to have been a doctor or lawyer.

Once inside the station house, the two detectives stopped by the clerical office. The civilian assigned to the office advised the detectives that a complaint report regarding the deaths had been submitted and a precinct complaint number assigned. Fishnet secured a copy of the complaint, which had been prepared by Officer Milo, who went on record as the first officer on the scene. After quickly looking the document over, Fishnet passed it to Von Hess for his review.

The details on the report reflected a pickup job, which is to say that the report was self-generated by the officer based on either his direct observation while on patrol or what was told to him by someone. Von Hess would have preferred the job to have been one originating from a citizen so there would have been at least someone to talk to, someone who might have been in a position to actually have seen something.

Without any witnesses, the investigators were left with just the area surrounding the location where the bodies were found. Mill Road itself provided zero in terms of opportunity for developing leads. No cameras existed that were positioned by the river, so there was no video to review. The hemorrhaging of rain from the sky deterred people from going outdoors, so the possibility of a passerby seeing something was remote. Mill Road was not a bus route, and there were no subway stations, cab stands, or car services operating in the immediate area. Von Hess contemplated all of these drawbacks in his analysis of the case. The facts thus far were not very encouraging.

Fishnet requested that the clerk send up a copy of the voucher for the Oldsmobile to the squad once it was prepared. He then walked to the staircase, located just off the clerical office, which led up to the detective squad. Before following his partner up the stairs, Von Hess took a moment to do a little digging. He wanted to see what the sixty sheet looked like, a document that provided an up-to-the-minute summary of all complaint reports prepared on incidents that had occurred within the confines of the precinct. The sheet of paper served mostly as a tool for bosses and investigators with an interest in the latest goings-on.

One entry in particular caught Von Hess's eye. It involved the recovery of an unidentified dog. Von Hess asked the clerk to see a copy of the full report, which he reviewed with great interest. His face remained expressionless even after reading that the rescued canine was a white poodle. Von Hess wrote the name, address, and telephone number of the person who had found the dog in his notebook. He decided to call the number of the animal-loving Estelle Stanley immediately after reading that she had found the poodle on Mill Road.

The ring of the telephone woke her up from a sound sleep. "Hello?"

"Is this Ms. Estelle Stanley?"

"Who is this?"

"This is Detective Von Hess of the homicide squad."

Receiving a call from a homicide detective alarmed her. With some concern evident in her voice, she answered, "Yes...this is Estelle Stanley.... Is everything alright?"

"Everything is fine, Ms. Stanley. Don't be alarmed." Von Hess began to put the woman at ease. "I'm sorry to bother you with this. I know it's late. I understand you took a dog into the precinct earlier, and I just need to

Anthony Celano

ask you a couple of questions about that."

"I rescued the poor thing....I found him wandering the street, lost. They said I could keep him if they can't find the owner," she responded in a defensive tone.

"No...please relax. There is no problem....We know that you helped the dog. I assure you...there is no trouble here," he said. "We are investigating a case about someone who passed away that may be the dog's owner. This is a routine call...just to see if you could help us with the identification, that's all."

"Oh...okay." The tension left her voice. "I was wondering what this was about. What do you want to know? I don't know who the owner of the dog is."

"Can we come by to talk to you?"

"Now?" she asked.

"Please...it would be just for a moment."

Realizing her studio apartment was a mess, she did not want to entertain visitors. "If you want, I can come in to see you. I can bring the dog with me if you like."

Von Hess was surprised at the cooperation he was receiving. "That would be great....I can send a police car over to pick you and the dog up, okay?"

"Okay."

It was 1:00 a.m. on Sunday when Von Hess caught his first glimpse of Estelle. He smiled confidently as he overheard the woman reminding the transporting officer as they entered the precinct that she was told she could keep the dog if no owner was located.

Von Hess judged her to be in her late forties. She was thin, of average height, and presented what he considered to be a youthful appearance in her black jeans and plain black pullover sweater. In looking at Ms. Stanley, the detective felt convinced he was viewing a good person. He based this on her willingness to be pulled out of her home at this time of morning over a dog. An abundance of hair, mostly gray, dominated her appearance. There was an army of curls of all sizes coming out of her head, sprouting in all directions and angles with little regard to uniformity. The hair on the back of her head seemed flattened out, an indication to Von Hess that she must have been lying down on her back when he called her. But none of this really meant anything to Von Hess. If she had come into the precinct in her birthday suit, he could not have cared less. There was only one thing that Von Hess was looking to ascertain.

The detective confirmed his suspicion when he saw that the small white poodle pressed snugly against the woman's chest was wearing a red collar. His audible expression of the word "Butter" was all it took to raise the ears of the poodle. The hound's perking up gave Von Hess everything he was looking for.

After introductions, Detective Von Hess took Ms. Stanley up to the squad room, where he sat her at a desk. Fishnet had been waiting for his partner patiently. After being filled in by Von Hess, he nearly busted a gut in his anxiousness to interview the woman with the canine. Once everyone was seated comfortably around the desk, Von Hess went over some of the facts while being careful not to alarm the woman unnecessarily. Her account of events was destined to be a concise one.

Ms. Stanley identified herself to the detectives as a painter who signed her work "ESSty," an abbreviation she used for her name...Estelle Sandra Stanley. Since she had never captured anything on canvas involving rain, the free spirit had decided to seize the moment and walk along the Brooklyn Heights promenade by the river. She took along her camera in the hope of finding something inspirational to photograph that she could later memorialize on canvas with her paints. By her recall, it was about 5:15 p.m. or so when she spotted the white poodle behaving in a befuddled way on the street. Von Hess took note that the location where she first saw the dog was about a quarter mile from where the Oldsmobile had been parked. Ms. Stanley indicated that she had made an effort to locate the owner of the dog by knocking on the doors of local residents. She conveyed that her initiatives were met with negative results. She said that she had taken charge of the poodle by removing the long strap on her camera case and slipping it under the dog's collar. With the help of the makeshift leash, she was able to walk the poodle to the precinct to report that she'd found it. That was the extent of her statement.

Fishnet's question about whether she had any knowledge of a blond in an evening gown gained no traction. Ms. Stanley was strictly a solid citizen, a compassionate pet lover who lived her life according to the rules. The dog lover managed to skirt by the entranceway to Fishnet's private world....She wasn't his type. Besides, the detective was not a big fan of animals.

After providing her statement, Von Hess arranged for Ms. Stanley to be driven home. She would be allowed to keep Butter forever unless someone more entitled stepped up to claim the orphan hound. It was going to be a good marriage. Von Hess was able to tell by the way Ms. Stanley affectionately rubbed her aquiline nose against the dog's snout as they left the squad room.

The detectives were glad to have gotten such a nibble, however small. They'd hoped to acquire more information, but at least they had walked away with something. With the dog lover now gone, Sergeant Markie, who had been standing by patiently, approached his detectives.

"What's the story?"

"We may have a little something, boss," answered Von Hess.

"We at least now know where the dog was found," piped up Fishnet, who had remained focused throughout the interview by keeping Ms. Stanley out of his other world.

Markie tried to be encouraging. "Hey, that's something....Let's take what we can get."

"It's a positive thing," agreed Von Hess. "My guess is that somewhere around where that dog was found, the two women must have met their doom."

No one challenged Von Hess after he made this observation.

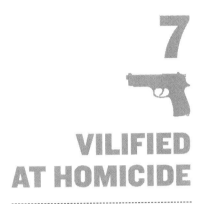

7

VILIFIED
AT HOMICIDE

THE TWO YOUNG DETECTIVES had been elated when their transfer into the squad finally came through. Their joy at entering into homicide was destined to be short lived, however. The first day in the office was to serve as their orientation. Instead of experiencing a smooth, welcoming transition, they were given a locker, a coop, and the cold shoulder. It was clear that they were being treated as a package deal: partners. It was on their second day that the newly formed team received their first assignment. The entry in the squad movement log indicated that they were heading to Mill Road to conduct a canvass on the order of Sergeant Markie. There was no discussion or goodbyes, just a frigidness emanating from distrustful coworkers who were doing their best to ignore their existence.

It would be untruthful to say that their being *persona non grata* was not hurtful. Since they were newly assigned detectives, being thrown out into the street on their own translated into a mild form of being baptized by fire. The task involved was nothing challenging to the detectives nor something they would be unable to handle. What was confounding was their being baptized by isolation. Even the homicide squad commander had few words to say to his newly inherited detectives. Experience had taught the lieutenant that sometimes things needed to be left alone so that they could work themselves out over time.

The two investigators stood at the entrance of the school, scrutinizing the front of the building as if they were examining it for imperfections. They viewed the property from all angles slowly, looking over every inch of the exterior of the building.

"Not a damn camera in sight," commented Wires to his partner.

"What do you want from these parochial schools? They have no money to spend on security cameras," she responded.

Wires shook his head. "Hard to believe they have no money....They must own the real estate. The Catholic Church owns more property than anyone in the country."

"So write the pope a letter," suggested Junior facetiously.

He shrugged his shoulders at her comment. "What do I care?...I'm no practicing Catholic anyway."

"Want to start the canvass of the houses?" Junior asked. "Might as well."

The newly formed team knocked on residential doors along Mill Road, hoping to develop leads that would further the investigation. After a while their efforts became monotonous as they found themselves providing more information to the curious residents than they were gathering. In a last-ditch effort, they began to flag down passing vehicles for questioning as they grasped for straws in their earnestness to achieve positive results. Their entire initiative on Mill Road proved to be a disappointing undertaking. Not even available employees who were assigned to work in the apartment buildings were of any value.

"This is a dead end out here," voiced the dejected Wires, knowing that the time had come to raise the white flag.

"I hear you....It makes no sense for us to be here any longer," agreed Junior. "Let's go to the precinct and see what they want us to do next."

"Why don't we just call in first?"

Junior shook her head indicating no. "If we do that, Markie may send us back to the homicide office. If I hear another word about Bill Clinton's cigar and Monica Lewinsky...I'll scream! That's all those guys talk about in that office."

Not replying verbally, Wires simply nodded, signifying that he understood. In his heart of hearts, he didn't see Junior's beef as a big deal.

⊞　⊞　⊞

OFFICERS KILMER AND MILO, the first officers at the scene, waited in the squad room to be interviewed. Now on overtime, they sat comfortably at desks, in no rush to talk to the detectives.

Kilmer was passing time leafing through wanted posters that were affixed to an old-fashioned two-hole wooden clipboard that he had removed off one of the walls in the squad room.

Milo sat in awe of his surroundings, evaluating the workplace of the investigators. The officer rather fancied the idea of being on the second floor with the squad. The thought of working in a relaxed atmosphere, no longer a slave to the division radio or the whim of any number of uniformed supervisors, appealed to him. After absorbing everything he could visually gather, he tried to figure out the fastest career path into the detective bureau. Without a hook—someone of influence to make a phone call on his behalf—he considered his chances of gaining entry into the gold-shield club to be pretty slim...unless, of course, he opted to be an internal affairs volunteer. If that were to be, he would have to come up with a credible story of how he had been "drafted" into the unit. But to Milo, it seemed too drastic a move. He expected he'd be in uniform until he could make the right connection.

Finally, when the time came, Fishnet interviewed Kilmer while Von Hess debriefed Milo. As expected, their stories were consistent, echoing each other without contradiction. The team had been performing routine patrol on the evening shift. It was near the end of the month, so they had been looking for summonses to write in order to meet performance expectations—a nice way of saying they had to meet a quota. Kilmer had been driving at the lowest possible speed alongside parked cars on Mill Road, giving Milo the chance to read vehicle inspection stickers without having to exit the prowl car. As he was doing this, he noticed that the trunk lock on a parked Oldsmobile had been punched out. His immediate impression was that the Oldsmobile was either stolen or had been broken into. Officer Milo alighted from the police vehicle to investigate.

Upon opening the trunk, he found a tied quilt. With a closer look, he learned the terrible reality of what was inside. Milo waved to Kilmer, summoning him to get out of the car to show him what he had discovered. After the second inspection, the trunk was closed. Milo radioed the division dispatcher, requesting the patrol sergeant to respond to the scene. By the time Skunk Fumes rolled up with his chauffeur, the officers had already run the Oldsmobile's plate to see if it had been reported stolen. After being advised by the dispatcher that it had not been reported stolen, they ascertained that the registered owner of the vehicle lived a few blocks away. The officers apprised the patrol sergeant accordingly, who then instructed the sector to notify the detectives while he fetched the owner of the Oldsmobile.

Once the officers finished giving their statements, their presence in the squad was no longer needed. All that remained for the officers to do was submit their overtime slips. Their tour of duty had concluded without their receiving any accolades. They received no pat on the back for a job well done. For the cops, it was all in a day's work. The officers had been conditioned to perform their duties without expectation of gratitude or sympathy. Their expressing anything to the contrary would have been considered limp-wristed by police standards. There was no tolerance among members of the service for whiners. On the contrary, people in blue were expected to exude a silent sturdiness on behalf of the people they served. Exhibitions of whimpering or sobbing would serve only to warp the crutch of security that the public relied on. When up against stormy weather, people can be relied upon to follow strength... never weakness. The few bucks in overtime that Kilmer and Milo were to receive for their efforts were sufficient thank-you as far as they were concerned. They slipped out of the squad room unnoticed, leaving the detectives to their work.

"So what do we do next?" Fishnet was looking to Von Hess for guidance.

"Let's get a boss and see what we can find out at the apartment. We also gotta work on notifying the next of kin."

"Yeah, let's see if I can get the doctor notification out of the way before we head out," agreed Fishnet. "We already know who the fuck he is."

"Want me to do it?"

"Yeah....Thanks, Ollie. I'll finish vouchering their belongings while you do that."

As Fishnet sat at his desk sorting out the property of the deceased, the phone rang. It was his partner, Sidney Schiff, checking in from Florida.

"Hey, Fish, what's doing?"

"You went away at the right time, Sid. I caught a nice one...a double, two girls in the trunk."

"No shit....Where?"

"Mill Road, by the school over there."

"You got any suspects?"

"Not yet. We're still working on it."

"Who are you working with?"

"Markie and Von Hess from homicide...and those two rat fucks they just picked up over there."

Schiff knew exactly who Fishnet was referring to. "I wish I was there with you, pal. I could have used the overtime."

"How are the folks?"

"They're doing good. My father plays cards every day with the old men, and my mother has her routine with the old ladies."

"With a little luck, we'll end up retired down south one day, Sid."

"I don't know about that, Fish. It is okay down here for a while, but then it gets kind of depressing...too much talk about aches, pains, and how sad the last send-off was. It's like everyone is waiting for the next ring from the man upstairs...and hoping that when they pick up the phone, the call isn't for them."

"At least the time there is well spent....The infection rate for STDs among Florida seniors is booming," pointed out Fishnet.

"I'll stick to perfume over liniment. See you when I get back, Fish."

After hanging up the phone, Fishnet spotted the newly assigned homicide detectives from his desk as they entered the squad room. He shot a quick glace over to Von Hess. With a sneer on his face, he tossed his head to indicate that Junior and Wires had returned from their canvass. It was no surprise to learn that the two had come up dry after combing the area where the Oldsmobile had been parked. Von Hess was pretty much indifferent when it came to the two newest members of his squad. He had been in the department long enough to have come across a lot worse. In terms of their performance, since he was not a supervisor, he did not hold much interest in their aptitude. The detective was not responsible for how effectively others carried out their duties. He knew that drawing fruit from a canvass in this set of circumstances was a long shot for anyone, so his expectations had remained low.

They called Detective Olive Moore "Junior" behind her back. The nickname was not administered with affection but rather as a reference used to malign. "Wires" was the negative epithet they bestowed on Detective Wyatt White. After completing their assignment, the two walked into the squad sheepishly amidst an aura of unease. The awkwardness stemmed from their knowledge that they were not wanted. No words had ever been used to communicate this fact—none were necessary. The silence that came whenever they entered a room occupied by their counterparts presented sufficient evidence of the hostility felt. Their self-consciousness was such that their very presence at any squad was an unpleasant experience for them.

Fishnet was one of the more alienating detectives. He was fast to perpetuate the animosity that strained cohesiveness. He had more seniority on the job than both Moore and White put together. He also had more time in the detective bureau and many more arrests behind him. This in his mind qualified him as their superior. Fishnet carried himself with smugness when around Wires and Junior. His brand of rudeness was not premeditated; it was behavior that came naturally to him. At the core of his disgraceful conduct was an innate cruelty. Fishnet was not a nice person by any stretch of the imagination. The isolation of Wires and Junior represented just another avenue by which he could express his vicious side.

"How can you work with those two weasels around?"

Von Hess was taken aback by Fishnet's complaint. "What's the problem?"

"The problem is you can't trust either one of those fuckers."

"What have we got to worry about? Aren't we playing it straight... following the rules right down the line?"

"Yeah, that's true....We are. We aren't doing anything wrong," answered Fishnet, knowing there was little else for him to say.

The poor reputation shared by the two newly transferred detectives was something that was self- generated. It stemmed from what was generally considered their unmerited transfer into a plum assignment over in homicide. They had squeezed their way into the unit by accessing a back door. The regular career path, the road taken by the other detectives in earning their way into the unit, required paying dues. Junior and Wires got their career wheels greased not by years of hard work, exceptional performance, or even heroism. They got to where they were by methods considered questionable by mainstream thinking, leaving them spoken of in the harshest of terms.

To her peers in homicide, Junior on the surface was a short, tubby, and spoiled woman. Wires, although impressive in appearance, was considered nothing more than an untrustworthy, opportunistic rat.

Junior's father was a long-retired veteran detective who, back in the day, had broken in a few of the current big bosses. As a result, he possessed the necessary juice to influence a transfer by calling in a favor. He had arranged the contract to homicide without any prior consultation with his daughter. The old man had been blind to the fact that fast-tracking Olive out of a community affairs unit would leave her with a high price to pay. The young detective saw no reason to abort the contract once she learned of it; she too had no idea of the ramifications that would come with the new assignment. Up to this point, everything had come easy to her as a very bright young woman. She saw the move into homicide not as an entitlement but rather as just another upward step on the ladder for someone with her talents. The presence of Junior in homicide created shock waves throughout the detective division. A resentment existed that was fueled by those prone to envy. It could be argued that it was a bum rap that Junior was receiving.

However, Wires was a different story. He had schemed his way into homicide on the strength of a distasteful arrest he had made when working as a precinct detective. Astute enough to capitalize on a departmental trend that rewarded acts of integrity, he set out to make it his business to make an arrest for bribery. The first sucker who suggested working something out was a local businessman, the owner of a bicycle shop.

Working in conjunction with the Internal Affairs Bureau, the detective set out to make a case against the shop owner. The businessman offered a free bike in return for Wires quashing a misdemeanor charge against a relative of his. Internal affairs demanded that the detective wear a recording device in order to properly memorialize the illegal arrangement.

The detective had not figured on his having to get wired up for sound for such a small bribe. He had no choice but to comply with the directive. For such high ethical achievement, the ambitious detective received his reward in relatively short order. His request for an assignment to homicide was rubber-stamped at the highest levels in the department, and he was transferred into the unit without even the formality of an interview. "Wires" was a moniker that stigmatized him as a wired-for-sound rodent whom fellow detectives hoped would be electrocuted the first time he stepped in a puddle. Wires soon came to realize that he might have been better off just declining the businessman's overture and be done with it.

Sergeant Markie received the two young detectives on his team without any signs of resistance. On principle, the sergeant had no use for anyone even remotely connected to the Internal Affairs Bureau. But being a fair man, he never let his personal prejudices interfere with business. He also had little respect for people who took shortcuts. The sergeant decided to pair the duo in order to, at first, minimize their interactions with other squad members until they at least got used to seeing each other. He felt that easing the unpopular two into his squad slowly was the best strategy.

Markie correctly recognized that his two teams working harmoniously together was sure to be challenging. He was certain that Von Hess would pose no problem. The seasoned veteran would never let a stubborn cloud looming over the reputation of any detective stand in the way of his doing his job. The sergeant's concern was Fishnet. He had his suspicions concerning the squad detective's dedication to inclusiveness.

But Markie knew it was his job to make things work: the sergeant needed to overcome a problem that could not be rectified merely by training babble or discipline or through some other authoritative method. Fixing this problem was going to require the young detectives to earn the respect of their coworkers—an objective that could not be attained overnight. Markie hoped that once enough time had elapsed, and as long as their performance met standards, people would warm up to the pair... enough for him to incorporate them into the mainstream of the squad. The sergeant stood rubbing his chin as he watched Junior and Wires quietly drinking coffee at a corner desk. They were about to prepare a report on the fruitless canvass they had conducted.

Markie did not mind reports containing negative results; when the time came to justify overtime, a fat case folder with lots of reports played far better than a thin one.

Part of the sergeant's strategy called for keeping Junior and Wires busy. He gave them simple jobs, ones that would keep them out of the crosshairs of their coworkers. The canvass he had selected for them had been a good start. Their next assignment came when Markie sent them out on a food run for the squad.

8

THE PEDIATRICIAN AND THE LITIGATOR

DOCTOR ALLEN WAS CLEARLY FRAZZLED. "Damn it! Let me think a minute, will you, Victoria...please?"

"So think, then," his wife snapped back. "Think of who calls you at home at this hour, Ed....It must be something serious!" She paused for a second and then continued, "You tell me. For what reason could it be other than something of major importance? Do you think that they want to tell you that you won the Publishers Clearing House sweepstakes?"

"Enough already," he said, sounding like a man worn down. Then, after having a thought, he added, "I don't know....It could still be nothing, but I suppose you're right. But why must you always have to assume the worst, though?"

This brought out the litigator in his wife. She was good at her job, and she had a counterargument to everything. "Oh, listen to you! Why on earth would you think the call is for something beneficial? Have you experienced something in the past that would lead you to this conclusion?"

"Will you please stop?" pleaded the medical man.

"First, I want you to go listen to the detective's message again....Does he sound like he's making a social call? Listen again, for heaven's sake!" It was frustrating to know she was right and yet to be unable to convince her husband.

Doctor Allen and his wife were bickering over a telephone message they'd received. As bright as he was, the physician still found it taxing to be doing two things at once when under pressure. He could not be distracted by chatter and concentrate at the same time. Both husband and wife possessed superior powers of logical reasoning when dealing with problems...as long as the complication pertained to others. The issue at hand was too close to home for either of them to be at their best.

He replayed the telephone message left by Detective Von Hess for the third time. Once more, they listened carefully to the recording: a simply stated request that they call Von Hess concerning a matter involving their daughter Barbara.

The doctor looked at his wife seriously. "So what more is there for us to discuss? I'll call...okay?"

"Certainly you should call. But don't provide any information about Barbara," she instructed. "Who knows? He may be looking to arrest her for something."

"Okay."

"And if he is looking to see Barbara, refer him right away to Hal Gordon. Believe me; they'll treat you better once they know a criminal lawyer is involved."

"Okay...okay...let me make the call."

"Do you want me to do it?" She did not have full confidence in her husband's ability to remember everything she had instructed.

Doctor Allen responded by just looking at his wife coldly. He dialed the telephone number for Von Hess. Once he got the detective on the line, he wasted little time in expressing his displeasure over receiving the call at such an unreasonable hour. He was intentionally venting his annoyance on the detective. He thought it best to put up a bit of a stink... at least in the presence of his wife.

"This is Edward Allen....What is the trouble, Detective Von Hess? What is the urgent situation concerning my daughter that has you disrupting my home at this hour?"

The doctor, being in the dark about his daughter's demise, caught Von Hess unexpectedly. He'd thought for certain that Aldo, since he was on the doctor's payroll, would have already provided his benefactor with a heads up. Von Hess explained to the pediatrician that there was pressing business concerning his daughter Barbara that he was unable to discuss over the telephone. The detective surprised the doctor by offering to come by his house to talk things over.

Barbara's father cupped the telephone to avoid being heard. He then began whispering to his wife. "The detective wants to come to the house."

Victoria Allen's mouth dropped. "Now?"

"Yes...I think so. Should I tell him to come over?"

"No! Are you crazy? What would that look like to these people around here with cops coming around at this time?"

"So what am I supposed to tell him?...We don't want to see him?" The doctor was stymied as to his next move.

"Ask him what this is all about," she directed. "Never mind, just give me the phone...."

Ignoring the request, the doctor proceeded to put forth his best argument to Von Hess as to why the detective should inform him over the telephone of what he needed to discuss. Von Hess explained that he appreciated the doctor's position as well as his reluctance to have him visit his home. Von Hess communicated that he had experienced such reactions in the past with other people, adding that he extended the offer to come by purely out of courtesy.

What Von Hess couldn't know was that sometime previously, Barbara had created a scene at the Long Island home of her parents. The stir came from Barbara's need of immediate medical attention one afternoon. The arrival of the police and ambulance had disrupted the serenity in a community where appearances were important. The very idea of the police again coming to the front door, along with one look at his wife... gave Doctor Allen cause to slip a couple of Tums into his mouth.

After some back and forth, the doctor offered to come into the precinct at a future time to meet with the detective. Von Hess convinced him otherwise. The detective was so adamant about the urgency attached to the matter that any notion of procrastination was off the table.

Again cupping the phone, the doctor turned to his wife. "This must be serious....We have to go to the precinct right now."

"What? No, we do *not*—"

"I'm going there now." Her husband cut her short, finally having his fill of being caught in the middle. "If you want to come, Victoria, get ready. If not, stay home." It was a rebellion that she had seen surface only a scant few times in all the years of their marriage.

Realizing that her husband had reached his limit, the attorney relented. "Okay, I'll get ready," she said quietly, trying her best to conceal her annoyance.

Doctor Allen, who was dressed and ready to go in five minutes, waited for his wife. Since she knew he was anxious to leave, it seemed to him that she was moving very slowly...purposely to get under his skin. The affection they once shared had ebbed with the passing of the years. As he waited, the doctor grew resentful, remembering the time she had pointed out to him that the ceiling in the bedroom needed painting seconds after they'd made love.

The couple exchanged just a handful of words during the depressing ride. The only noise inside their Mercedes came from the car radio reporting on the death of Frank Sinatra.

⊞ ⊞ ⊞

THE TIMING WORKED out perfectly for the detectives at the precinct. While they waited for the   Long Island couple, they polished off the wonton soup and pork fried rice that Wires and Junior had picked up from Wacky Liu's without having to rush. Wacky was Fishnet's contract. Wacky liked the cops because his operation was a twenty-four-seven affair that left him susceptible to episodes of overnight criminality. The many "eat it and beat it" types coming into his establishment overnight had been causing a financial sting. Not wanting to spring for the expense of private security guards, the situation left Wacky few options other than to take Fishnet's advice and embrace the local police. Once Fishnet put the word out that Wacky Liu's was good, it quickly became a favorite cop hangout. It didn't take long before people taking liberties with Wacky ceased to do so. If his math was correct, all Wacky had to worry about was taking care of a few hungry cops not looking to pay full freight for their food....The business owner looked at the situation as being cost effective.

The doctor and his wife arrived at the Brooklyn precinct a little over an hour after the conversation with Von Hess. They were directed to the squad room without being announced. Markie was not too happy about visitors just popping into the squad. Luckily the remnants of Chinese food had been cleaned off the desks, so the detectives were spared the embarrassment of being perceived as slacking off. The sergeant later made it a point to mention the oversight to the precinct desk lieutenant.

After the preliminary introductions, Von Hess and Fishnet found themselves facing off with two professional people. The detectives could see that Doctor Allen was at a level of stress that even the satisfaction of having a twenty-five-thousand-dollar Rolex on his wrist was unable to alleviate. His wife was a more complicated read. Fishnet's impression of Victoria Allen was that she was giving off vibes of being combat ready. Von Hess thought she weighed in somewhere between the lines of worry and resentment.

Both detectives had greeted the couple with the courtesy and respect that the occasion called for. "Please come into the office," said Von Hess warmly.

Doctor Allen nodded. He and his wife followed Von Hess into the privacy of the squad commander's office, where there was a comfortable couch for them to sit on and a private restroom at their disposal. Fishnet, a couple of steps to the rear of the trio, followed them into the office. As he began checking out the rear end of the doctor's wife, he wondered how old she was. Sergeant Markie was sitting at the desk in the office during the intrusion. He immediately rose from his chair, exiting the office in order to provide his detectives with use of the room. The sergeant's courteous behavior was not lost on Fishnet. He thought it admirable that Markie was thoughtful enough to step out.

"I'll get us something to drink," announced Fishnet. "Coffee alright with you, Edward? You, Mrs. Allen?"

"*Doctor Allen*," corrected Victoria, adding, "Coffee is fine for both of us, detective."

After a minute, the detective returned with two mugs containing the beverages. Fishnet regretted that he hadn't had time to spike Victoria's cup with a tiny squirt of urine. Seated next to each other on the couch, the parents of Barbara Allen were keen to address the matter that had taken them from their home.

"So what's this all this about, detective?" the pediatrician asked.

"I am afraid I have some very bad news for you," began Von Hess in a somber tone. He made the unpleasant notification as tactfully as possible. He had been careful to place his chair close to the couch so that he directly faced the couple. Fishnet assumed a more official position, settling into the cushioned chair behind the desk.

Von Hess leaned forward in a gesture of sincerity and chose his words carefully. He knew that his delivery would be an important factor in the success of a future conversation. To his credit, Fishnet recognized that sensitivity was required in such a delicate situation. Aware of his own limitations in this area, Fishnet opted to sit by silently, taking a back seat to Von Hess. This provided him with the opportunity to focus elsewhere as he commenced to mentally evaluate the couple.

Fishnet eyeballed Doctor Allen from top to bottom, assessing his worth as a man. In Doctor Allen he saw someone who appeared to be in his late sixties with enough gray hair remaining for him to put a wave in it. Of average height, Barbara's father weighed about 165 pounds. The fashionable glasses he wore contributed to his affluent look. It all worked well with his dark blue blazer, yellow shirt, and jeans. On his feet were dark brown bucks with orange heels that showed no signs of running down. The doctor's hands were exceptionally fine looking. His nails were clean, manicured, and highly polished. The total package reminded Fishnet of a guy he hated from his youth. The comparison so biased the detective's final evaluation that he factored Doctor Allen out of his thoughts entirely. There was no purpose for a clone of someone he detested having a place in Fishnet's world.

The emotional reaction of Barbara's mother was enough of an awakening to catapult Fishnet onto the road back home. The loudness of her outburst was surprising.

"Oh my God...*no!*" she cried out in a voice charged with emotion. She then began to silently weep. Absorbed in her own thoughts, she kept her pain contained as best she could.

"Good Lord...please, no!" The father's response was sad to witness. The doctor had tried to brace himself in preparation to absorb possible bad news about his daughter. He anticipated hearing about an arrest or perhaps even an accident resulting in hospitalization. What he neglected to expect was the news he received. The doctor took it hard. Try as he might, he found it impossible to control his overwhelming despair after learning of the death of his daughter. The devastating news reduced him to tears.

After a struggle, Doctor Allen eventually came to regain his composure. It was Victoria Allen who proved herself to be the rock in the family. Her recovery came shortly after her initial outburst. Once she wiped her tears, she engaged in no further display of emotion. She stiffened herself, flinching only at those additional details she found painful. The winces of discomfort on her face were something Fishnet found to be familiar. He recollected expressing the same grimaces after receiving an injection of penicillin into his buttock a few days after a brothel visit.

Once the distractions of the distraught parents waned, Fishnet was able to shuttle back onto the road to his daydream. Nestled comfortably in his personal zone, the detective began to concentrate on the lawyer. Victoria Allen was a tall woman, taller than her husband by a couple of inches. This was something Fishnet was not happy to see. It irked him to see a tall woman place her arm over the shoulder of a smaller man. He perceived such a sight as female dominance.

Victoria Allen was assertive, dignified, and professional. Such qualities worried the detective, who found it easy to interpret these attributes as pushy, snobbish, and arrogant. A trim woman whose body suggested a certain physical fitness, the attorney had blond highlights in the brown hair that seemed to fall stiffly along both sides of her face. Fishnet estimated her age to be somewhere in the neighborhood of her middle fifties. While attractive, she seemed hoity-toity to the detective, causing him to look upon her with suspicion. The black business suit and silk lavender scarf she wore suggested she was a successful somebody.

Fishnet disliked being out of his league...but she had now entered his world, a place where she was out of her league. His was a sphere where physical flaws meant everything. The telltale blue veins bulging from the back of her hands indicated that Victoria Allen had been around the earth longer than originally presumed. Her imperfection leveled the playing field as far as Fishnet was concerned. She was suddenly okay...now that he could refer to her as "the old lady."

68

"Are you ready?" asked Von Hess, addressing a partner who had entered a dimension beyond hearing.

As the parents were occupied dealing with their grief, Von Hess stood up and leaned over the desk close to Fishnet's face. "Fishnet!" he said in an abrupt whisper.

Snapping out of it, the detective acknowledged Von Hess. "Yeah."

"Let's go outside and leave these people alone for a while."

"Sure thing," answered Fishnet.

The detectives exited the office together, leaving behind the parents to console each other. Once outside, Von Hess tried to figure out what was going on with Fishnet.

"You feeling okay?"

"Yeah, sure...I'm feeling fine."

"You were out of it in there....I thought you were having some kind of spell. What's going on?"

"Nah, nothing is going on....I just got caught up for a minute thinking about the case and how we have to still find the family of the other girl."

Von Hess was not the sort of person who liked to unnecessarily stir the pot. Fishnet had not been drinking, and there were no signs of substance abuse, so he took the detective at his word. And he agreed about the problem of locating the other dead woman's family. "Yeah...that may be a job at that."

Von Hess thought the doctor was a decent guy. But a little conversation and the feel of his wife's masculine handshake was all it took for him to size up the attorney as a person accustomed to wearing the pants. Unlike Fishnet, Von Hess held an affinity for assertive women. After all, he'd married a woman who could have served the Army well in the artillery as the top gun...the chief of smoke who ran the show.

Sergeant Markie passed by the door of the squad commander's office several times. He was anxious to see how things were going inside Sergeant Parlatto's office. The last thing Markie needed was one of the parents having a heart attack as a result of learning shocking news without proper preparation. But as he hadn't heard any over-the-top eruptions, he assumed Von Hess had things under control inside the room. Age tended to provide a mellowing influence. Years of working on homicides had honed the skill of Von Hess when it came to face-to-face notifications of this nature.

When the detectives left the office, Markie was there to receive them. "How is it going in there?"

"No problem....We are just giving them a little time to regroup," advised Von Hess.

"How hard did they take the news?"

"You know how it goes, boss....Some people handle it better than others."

"I hear you," answered the sergeant, realizing the question he'd asked was a stupid one.

The detectives took advantage of their break. Von Hess visited the men's room to rinse his face with cold water in order to recharge. Upon his return he approached Fishnet, who was seated at a desk in the squad room, drinking water from a bottle. "Let's give them a little more time," he suggested.

"She took it better than he did," observed Fishnet. Being who he was, Fishnet found fault with the doctor. His twisted position was that as a pediatrician, the doctor should have held up better emotionally considering the fact that he had made a career in a business having to deal occasionally with death.

"Everybody handles this kind of shit differently," replied Von Hess pragmatically.

Fishnet had been looking for a different response from his partner. "Cold as the beaver of a witch, that one...," he said, giving Von Hess another opportunity to respond with an answer in line with what he was saying.

"Her husband must like her well enough. It'll probably hit her hard later, when she is alone and has time to think."

Fishnet decided to communicate his position bluntly. "Maybe...but her old man is as useless as boobs on a bull!"

Von Hess offered no response to his partner's observation. He could not think of anything appropriate to say.

It took about thirty minutes for Barbara's parents to adjust. Accepting coffee and water, the two were ready to fully engage with the detectives. Von Hess started out by clearly explaining the investigative steps taken thus far. He took the time to detail the purpose of the forensic team in terms of gathering evidence, as well as the role of the medical examiner in establishing the cause of death, which at this point still remained undetermined.

Most of the questions for the detectives were posed by Barbara Allen's mother. Her tone seemed to take on an added edge with each subsequent question. This suggested to Von Hess that she was impatient, which in her case meant normalizing.

Fishnet's attitude toward Mrs. Allen took a downhill slide once it came out that the woman was a civil litigator. Fishnet equated litigation with legal robbery. Considering her profession, the detective suspected that the lawyer was probably a man-hater. His instinct was to let Von Hess deal with her.

It irked Fishnet to see Doctor Allen sit alongside his wife quietly. As his imagination ran wild, he interpreted the interplay between the couple as

Anthony Celano

the doctor being emasculated, which in his warped mind translated into the diminishment of all things masculine.

Fishnet fumed in silence, watching what he considered a fellow man behaving like a small white mouse cowering in the corner of a cage, waiting to be devoured by a snake...when the reptile was good and ready to eat. What really tore the wound wide open for Fishnet was when the lawyer again corrected him concerning her husband's social status. She reminded the detective that it was *"Doctor Allen"* after he, this time, made the error of addressing her spouse as "Mr. Allen." Now out for all the blood he could draw, the detective took the gloves off. The attorney was summarily ousted from Fishnet's secret zip code. In real-world time, Fishnet's payback came in the form of his active participation in the questioning of Barbara's mother.

"Was Barbara having problems with anyone?"

"Not at all. Everyone loved Barbara. She was a wonderful girl," came the attorney's response.

"Did Barbara have any problems with her romantic interests? A boyfriend or maybe a...*girlfriend*?"

Fishnet's query came with a slight trace of sarcasm as he emphasized the word *girlfriend*. He was looking to push buttons. His efforts got a rise out of her.

Put off, she responded harshly, *"No* boyfriend and *NO* girlfriends!" Fishnet had scored his first point.

"Did Barbara owe anyone any money to the best of your knowledge?" Fishnet inquired.

"Barbara never had money issues," stated Mrs. Allen indignantly. "She held down a job, maintained her own apartment, and was preparing to go back to school."

"What about paying her own rent?" Fishnet blandly asked, casting a sly eye at the husband.

"Certainly she did. Absolutely! Why are you asking me these questions? So what does all this have to do with anything?" Another point scored for Fishnet.

Doctor Allen squirmed like a child caught with his finger in a cookie jar when Fishnet asked about the rent payment. He had been keeping his wife in the dark about the financial arrangements he had secretly worked out with his daughter, the super, and the landlord. The medical man was not sure if or how much Fishnet knew about the arrangements. Regardless, the doctor was relieved that Fishnet did not complicate matters by giving him up to his wife.

"I'm asking you these questions to try to come up with a motive or a lead," explained the detective, trying to legitimize his line of questioning. "Did Barbara gamble?"

More accustomed to doing the asking, the attorney was unaccustomed to the role of being on the receiving end of a question. "Barbara never gambled. She was too intelligent a girl to waste her money and way too smart for anything like that," the mother replied, clearly put off by the question.

Von Hess let Fishnet continue on without interrupting. Questions were being asked that needed to be asked, although a more decent manner would have been preferred.

"Did Barbara drink or use drugs?" Fishnet was looking directly into the attorney's eyes when he let her have it with this one.

"Please!" Victoria answered with exasperation. "Barbara *does not* use drugs!" Mrs. Allen turned to look at her husband for support that never came.

This last exchange caused Doctor Allen to squirm in his seat as he listened to his wife sanitize their daughter. Von Hess kept his eye on Doctor Allen, who was in turn watching Mrs. Allen.

Fishnet continued his torment of her. "Were you aware of Barbara's past drug arrests?" Fishnet's question came over icily.

"Why...yes...of course." Victoria Allen was taken aback by the question. Her reply came in a surprised tone. "But that was a long time ago...."

"You think she could have still been occasionally using drugs? Was she depressed?" Fishnet used a condescending softness in his voice as he posed these two questions.

Victoria was visibly irked. Her denial came out in a huff, through tightened lips that telegraphed her intense dislike of Fishnet. "Definitely not. My daughter successfully completed a prominent drug rehabilitation program in Florida and has been drug free for over a year!"

Fishnet paused, knowing he had her going. After several seconds of Fishnet looking at her, the doctor's wife finally came around. "Barbara went through the Rowland Return Program, one of the best rehabs in the country. The niece of a governor was there at the same time," she added as a form of proof regarding the worth of the program.

Von Hess finally stepped in. Hoping to put a halt to the tension in the proceedings he addressed the husband. "Doctor Allen, when did you last speak to or hear from Barbara?"

Fishnet was okay with Von Hess jumping in—he felt that he had gotten his pound of flesh for the slight he'd withstood.

"Friday night," said Doctor Allen anxiously. "She checks in with us religiously every Friday night."

"That is precisely correct," noted Mrs. Allen in a tone designed to set things straight. "She never misses a Friday. She has been very reliable, very dependable."

"Who was she close to? Did she have any close friends, perhaps?"

"She was close to her cousin Amy and also a girl she worked with... Wendy or a Wilma somebody," the mother answered. "No...it was Wyona. Yes, that was it....Her friend at work was named Wyona," said Mrs. Allen, who was clearly more comfortable dealing with Von Hess.

"What kind of work did Barbara do again?"

"She was working for a very successful restaurant owner."

"Dixie's on Third Avenue," chimed in Doctor Allen, looking to be helpful.

"Did you know anything about the other girl, Shirley Harris?"

"I believe she was a friend of Barbara's. I am not sure from exactly where, however," advised Mrs. Allen.

Doctor Allen promised to have Barbara's only sibling, an older sister named Michele, and his niece Amy contact the detectives because they had been close to Barbara. It was now 6:20 a.m. and time to break it off with the parents. Since cooperation was at a relatively civil level, Von Hess thought it appropriate to steer things away from questions and answers. He correctly calculated that since Doctor Allen contributed to paying the rent for his daughter's apartment, he would likely have a set of keys. Doctor Allen kept the key to Barbara's apartment on his key ring. Von Hess recommended that they go directly to the apartment without any further delay. The uniform patrol sergeant and his driver accompanied the detectives and the parents to the apartment. It would be their responsibility to secure the location.

Aldo had to be rousted to let them into the building because the doctor's key did not fit the outside door lock and Fishnet had again forgotten to bring the keys. Aldo and Doctor Allen exchanged nods.

"I had to give everyone new keys after I had the lock to the front door changed," Aldo explained. "I chased some kids away from hanging out in front of the house, and I think they came back and put Krazy Glue in the old lock."

Followed by her husband, the detectives, and the uniformed personnel, Victoria Allen led the way to the apartment without giving Aldo a second look. Her strides were long, quick ones, like those of a person with a certain intent to get to a specific destination. She had never been at Barbara's apartment before, but she charged toward it as if it were her own. Her husband rushed to keep up with his quicker wife. The rest of those present took up the rear. Doctor Allen placed the key in the lock and slowly turned it to open the door. Ever the gentleman, he stepped aside, allowing his wife to enter the apartment first.

After entering the apartment, they found themselves inside a one-bedroom domicile that was furnished completely but inexpensively. Of note was a dog bowl half-filled with dog food. There was just one dirty plate and glass in the kitchen sink, suggesting there had been no guests in the apartment. This was supported by an empty garbage pail.

The bedroom housed a made-up queen-size bed, an end table, a dresser, and a closet packed with clothes. A closed-up folding bed stood against one of the bedroom walls. Two large pink suitcases were standing alongside the portable bed, with clothes visible atop the suitcases. Several pairs of shoes were piled alongside the wall by the folding bed.

The subsequent search yielded a small black .25 caliber Beretta Jetfire. Fishnet recovered the gun from inside the pocket of a black woolen woman's overcoat that was hanging over the folding bed. Based upon the size of the coat, Fishnet knew the gun most likely belonged to Shirley Harris. After carefully scanning the room, he discreetly slipped the gun into his pants pocket. The detective was certain that no one had been looking at him.

The search yielded nothing other than some personal items that might have surprised only Barbara's parents. What Von Hess found of value was a small pocket-size datebook used to log telephone numbers and appointments. The book was discovered among the belongings of Shirley Harris. Von Hess made no secret of placing the book inside his jacket pocket. Von Hess, of course, had no knowledge of the small-caliber automatic Fishnet had stolen. That was to remain the disturbed detective's secret.

9

THE QUEEN
OF NOSTRILS

THE MATURE CASHIER had a pensive look about her as she rubbed the eraser end of the pencil against the area over her right ear. She had no itch to scratch; it was just something to do while she was thinking. Her lips were crunched tautly, causing little creases to appear around her mouth, as she strained her brain trying to best the puzzle in her crossword book. She was moving her lips as she thought without actually voicing anything.

"A three-letter word for *scoundrel*," her lips spoke silently. "*Rat*? No...that won't fit...too slangy....*Bum*? No, that doesn't work either.... Nobody uses that word much anymore...." Then suddenly it came.

"C-a-d...*CAD*! Got it....That works perfectly!" she declared triumphantly, allowing her words to be audible.

She had been doing puzzles while working the midnight-to-noon shift at the diner for a lot of years. While the word challenge strengthened her vocabulary, it did nothing to pull her up financially. Living paycheck to paycheck, she was not a woman in the habit of making excuses for herself. She took responsibility for paying the price for the fun she reveled in during the party days of her youth. Back then, the good times always took precedence, blinding her to any consideration of her future. With the accumulation of years, the fun came much more infrequently. Now her regular diet of pleasures was mostly limited to puzzles, lotto, and talk shows. The limitations placed on her frolic were the root causes of her negativity when she ventured beyond the world of what five-letter word fit into eight across. Absorbed in her puzzle, she never noticed the two detectives entering the diner.

By the time 7:00 a.m. rolled around, the stomachs of Fishnet and Von Hess were sending growling messages that were audible to anyone within range. Looking to appease the call for food, the detectives seized the opportunity to kill two birds with one stone by visiting the all-night eatery where Barbara Allen had been employed. They entered the diner right after Von Hess called into the squad to inform Markie of how things had gone at the apartment.

Once Markie was made aware that Shirley's datebook had been recovered, he wasted no time dispatching Junior and Wires to the diner to retrieve it. He saw the book not just as a source of new information but also as the perfect chore to keep the new members of his squad occupied without stirring up any ill will. The sergeant intended to have the second-string team go through the deceased woman's book with an eye toward identifying appointments she might have had scheduled prior to her demise. The book hopefully might also contain telephone numbers that could lead to the identification of relatives or people with knowledge that could shed light on the two deaths.

"I never realized that there was parking behind the building," Fishnet told his partner as they proceeded up the steps to the diner.

"I knew it," answered Von Hess. "I've been here before."

"Are they good?" Fishnet was curious as to whether the diner fed the police for free or at a discounted rate.

"It's been awhile...but I think they cut us a break that time once they knew we were on the job," advised Von Hess.

"They've got a lot of double-parked cars out front. Looks like a steady flow of people going in and out." Fishnet began conniving, figuring that the threat of a few tickets would ensure that the restaurant would be good.

The point was not lost on Von Hess. He was having none of it. "Whatever....If we have to pay full freight, then we pay full freight."

Fishnet decided to let it go. He wasn't going to mention the outside parking condition to the people in the diner.

A few seconds had elapsed before the woman behind the counter with the puzzle book realized that the two detectives were waiting for her to acknowledge their presence. The business was an establishment of decent size. The numerous tables and booths in the room were carefully spaced for maximum privacy and accessibility. There was a fully stocked bar as well as an impressive assortment of cakes for those with a sweet tooth. Dixie's was doing a decent business, with many of their seats occupied. Early-rising senior citizens, people coming off the graveyard shift, couples fresh from a workout at the local motel, and famished stragglers who were not yet ready to go home after bar-hopping could be seen occupying the tables.

The innovative breakfast special was a big draw at Dixie's. The selection was advertised as "Dixie's Full Boat," a composition of every kind of breakfast offering imaginable. The novelty dish came to customers delivered on platters that fed groups of two, four, and six people. There were few weight-conscious people opting for the specialty of the house.

Adjacent to the entrance sat the cashier. Her duties included greeting customers. As was the case with most people Fishnet encountered, the cashier came under his immediate scrutiny. He estimated her age to be somewhere in the vicinity of her sixties. She was attired in a white blouse, white sneakers, and a black skirt that ended at the knee. The black nylons she wore hid whatever embarrassments that might have existed on her legs. She was a woman of average proportions. Her once-golden hair had been invaded by lots of gray strands, giving her a faded, worn look. She wore her tresses combed back and up at the sides in a style that left her silver loop earrings exposed as they dangled from her ears. Fishnet had an affinity for hair worn in that style. He saw it as a sign of sophistication, making her appear queenly to him. It was this perception of regality that started the cashier on her way into Fishnet's make-believe world. The trip was short-circuited, however, once the detective got closer to the counter where the woman was stationed. The cashier's dark, mascara-sculpted eyebrows were a turnoff, as was the crossword puzzle she was working on. These were signs of a commoner. It was enough to bring him back mentally because it clashed with the mythical monarch his mind was conjuring up.

Then there was the other deal-breaker....The lower wall on the left side of the cashier's nose was half missing from an otherwise perfectly formed proboscis. This physical defect might have disqualified the cashier from entering his world, but it did not exclude her from receiving her own special name. The detective bestowed upon the cashier the sobriquet of "Nostrils," a name that would remain exclusively hers.

Von Hess approached the woman in a manner that made it immediately clear they were there on official business. Once he identified himself to the cashier, he got right to the point by inquiring about Barbara Allen. She did nothing to camouflage that she was the hard-boiled type. Von Hess could easily tell that the cashier had been around, likely coming up the hard way. Fishnet took it a step further. Now seeing his queen as a fading strumpet who had made the rounds of the castle more than once, he took an interest. Fishnet decided to take the bull by the horns concerning the questioning.

"So let me ask you a question....When did you last see Barbara Allen?"

"Friday night, I suppose....She worked the evening shift Friday. Why?"

Fishnet ignored her question. "What kind of a girl was she?"

"Okay....She did her job. Say...I asked you a question. What is all this about?"

"Would you say she was stable?" The detective did not budge.

"Depends on what you call stable. Look...she is a little out there, but we have no problems with her."

"Out there how?"

"I don't know...." She paused to think before continuing. "Like, when she started, she had the nerve to ask Chris if she could bring her dog to work. Wouldn't you say that was out there?"

"Chris?" Von Hess did not recognize the name.

"Chris Victore, the owner of this place."

"No problems with Barbara? Drink? Drugs? Money issues maybe?" pursued Fishnet.

"What do I know what she does?...I'm not her mother. She does her job...and I learned a long time ago to mind my own business," she declared. "So are you going to tell me what is going on here?"

Von Hess stepped up to answer her question. The cashier remained unfazed after learning the news of Barbara Allen's death.

"Do you know any of her friends?"

She looked at Von Hess with a tired expression. "No...should I?"

"How about a tall blond? Long hair, dolled up...low-cut black dress? She was a friend of Barbara."

"Look, I don't know....Tall and good-looking you say?" the cashier asked after a pause.

"Quite. You couldn't miss her coming in here," said Von Hess. The serious look the detective had on his face when he made the statement was one of a man tired of playing games. His look made it clear that he expected an answer.

"Okay...so there is this one blond who comes around. A real live one, you know the type...a party girl. She has the looks, but she also has the demons that come with it." The cashier seemed to be finally loosening up. She volunteered a little more. "She puts on way too much cheap perfume. You couldn't miss her. But Chris seems to like it, if you get my drift." She spoke with a trace of sarcasm in her voice.

"Her name again?" This time it was Fishnet who asked the question.

"Shirley...and I got no idea what her last name is. That is all I know," she added, anticipating the next question. Staring at Fishnet curiously, the cashier made a surprising comment. "Say...do you know who you remind me of?"

"No...who?" She got Fishnet's attention with the question.

She responded with surprising enthusiasm. "Who? Who do you

think?...Clark Gable! Anybody ever tell you that?"

This recognition pleased Fishnet to no end. The comment earned the woman he had dubbed Nostrils a reprieve. Reversing himself, Fishnet granted her a pass. The detective would find a place of prominence for her somewhere in his world....That was now a certainty.

"Yeah...I've been told that often," responded the detective happily.

"By the girls, I'll bet," flirted the cashier, making it clear that she was still willing to play the game.

The detective reacted to her flirting. "All the time," he answered in a sing-song voice. "So let me ask you something, sweetheart....You got a line on Shirley that could help us here?" He now spoke in a friendly, almost charming way.

"Look, sugar, all I know for sure is that she was real friendly with Barbara and Chris. Go ask Chris if you need details...and it was Chris who hired Barbara, not me."

"When is Chris around?" Von Hess asked brusquely. He was not a big fan of the sudden chumminess.

"He should be here within the hour. But then he goes to the track pretty soon after he stops in here. He goes every day to check on his horses."

This aroused Fishnet. "He's big into the ponies?"

"Thoroughbreds are his passion. This joint is just for giggles. You going to wait for him?"

Von Hess nodded. "Yeah, we'll grab a bite and wait."

The two detectives took seats at a booth by a window that faced the parking lot. From their vantage point, they were able to see the driveway and the parking space reserved for the owner. Committed to awaiting the arrival of Chris Victore, the detectives settled in. Holding up well, neither man showed signs of fatigue other than an occasional yawn.

A young, sleepy-looking waitress, about twenty-two years of age, came over to take their order. Von Hess contemplated asking Fishnet if he felt like partaking in the Full Boat. Once he saw the price on the menu, he abruptly changed his mind. Since receiving a discount was never a sure thing and something he would never demand, the senior detective ordered modestly. He asked for bacon and eggs on a roll and a cup of black coffee. Fishnet decided to have oatmeal with a cut-up banana in it, whole wheat toast, grapefruit juice, and green tea.

Von Hess was sensitive to the fact that the waitress was working many of the tables, so he intended to keep his inquiry with her brief. Their interaction was destined to be short lived once the detective learned that she had been employed at the diner for only a week. As a result, she was unable to provide anything of value other than the food that she later took to the table.

When Wires arrived at the diner, Von Hess saw him right away. He waved him over to the booth.

"Markie sent us for the datebook."

"Right," answered Fishnet coldly.

"Here you go." Von Hess handed over the black datebook to Wires while maintaining a neutral expression on his face.

Looking down into his coffee in order to reduce the chance of further conversation, Von Hess began to overstir the hot brew. Aware of Fishnet's feelings, he didn't want to get in the middle. When Wires walked off with the book, Fishnet muttered something inaudible under his breath. Von Hess did not bother to ask for clarification. He had a good idea it wasn't anything to promote the furtherance of harmony.

Since no one asked Wires he if was hungry, he just took the book as well as the hint and returned to his partner waiting in the car. Together they sped off to the precinct.

"Did you get the book from them?" Junior asked. "Yeah."

"Did they say anything?"

"Not a word. You know what? Screw them!" Wires was clearly irked.

By 8:15 a.m., Fishnet and Von Hess had long finished their breakfast. Nursing their fourth coffee at their booth, they both stared blankly out the large window facing the parking lot. A late-model black Mercedes sedan pulled into the lot, taking the spot set aside for the diner's owner. The driver energetically emerged from the Benz with the bounce of a young man. He went directly to the front door of the restaurant and entered. Fishnet looked over at Von Hess.

"Now, those are some wheels!" Fishnet commented enviously.

"Black is the only color for that car...just elegant," agreed Von Hess. Fishnet nodded in agreement. "Looks like our boy Victore is here."

"I'd say so."

The cashier was at her post, still absorbed working on her crossword puzzle, when the driver of the Benz came into the diner. He was a clean-shaven dandy about fifty years of age, who carried himself like a man with a healthy conceit. Regardless of whether his high opinion of himself was warranted, it was easy to see how he might be considered a charismatic charmer by some.

Solidly built, he stood just an inch or so under average height. He sported a deep tan. Nearly bald, he wore what little salt-and-pepper hair he had closely cropped to his bronzed head. On him, the meager topping did not detract from his overall appearance. Dressed in an open-collared red shirt, black slacks, red socks, and black tasseled loafers, he gave the appearance of a successful sporting man. A gold chain could be seen hanging from his neck with a gold horse head resting atop a bed of ample chest hair. It was definitely Victore.

He further identified himself by his actions. Going behind the small counter to get at the register, he brushed against the cashier as he reached into the till to pilfer cash. The raping of the register was his common practice, a task he carried out without gaining the attention of the cashier. It was obviously a part of the owner's routine that she had become accustomed to. She glanced up just to acknowledge the presence of the owner, then returned to her puzzle. When he turned his back to the register, Fishnet noticed the owner's right arm disappear somewhere down south between the register and the cashier. Based upon her reaction, the gesture had to have been something she had not been accustomed to so early in the morning. The sneak attack ignited the cashier enough to redden her face. The trigger pulled down below caused her to jump up out of her seat. Oddly, she seemed not to be offended in the slightest, making it apparent there was a relationship there.

The cashier's face quickly flashed a half grin of surprise that remained until she remembered her surroundings. Thanks to the presence of an ample amount of money that he readily spread around, Victore was in demand by many people looking to be taken care of...including his cashier. With alacrity, her eyes scanned the room to see if anyone had noticed what had occurred.

Feeling in the clear, her face took on a crooked, sardonic smile. The cashier turned back to the owner to face his silly lecherous grin. With the slight turn of her head, her eyes darted from Chris to where the detectives were seated. It was her way of signaling her boss without speaking.

Fishnet found it amusing that Nostrils appeared flattered by the sudden display of attention she received from Victore. The detective thought it not unusual that the cashier was alright with the early-morning groping she had received. The moment shared by the owner and his employee swiftly came to a conclusion once Victore got the message that the law was waiting to speak to him. Chris Victore was a very self-assured sort of man. He approached the booth where the detectives sat with the confidence of a crook who happened to be innocent this one time. He slid into the booth, taking a seat next to Von Hess. His smile revealed him to have rabbitlike buck teeth, causing Fishnet to consider asking him where he kept his carrots.

"I'm Chris Victore. What can I do for you gentlemen?"

Victore confirmed that Barbara Allen was in fact an employee of his. The restaurant owner expressed sincere shock upon hearing that his employee had been found dead in the trunk of a car. Barbara had worn two hats for Victore, working as a cashier and as a part-time bookkeeper. He described her as a flexible employee who would work various hours and days to accommodate the demands of the business.

Victore said that Barbara had secured her job at the diner based on a referral he'd received from a friend of his. It was at this time that the interview took an interesting turn.

"Who was the friend who referred her to you?" Fishnet asked.

"A girl I know asked me to do her a favor, so I gave the kid a job....That's all."

"What girl was that?" Fishnet had been expecting a more expanded response.

"Hey, what difference does that make? I prefer not to say—why involve her? My friend has her own issues."

"We need to know who the girl is...a name...so let's cut the song and dance." Fishnet was already losing patience.

The diner owner was put off by what he felt was aggressiveness on the part of the detective. "Whoa...relax, detective. I'm trying to be helpful here....No need for getting tough."

"You want me to relax? Then answer the question."

"What question?"

Fishnet abhorred this type of back and forth. He also disliked the restaurant owner's swarthy look; the rabbit teeth; his arrogant, egotistical demeanor; and above all his having the gall to try to sidestep his question. Fishnet pushed the envelope to the limit. "You want to get fucking cute with me, wise guy?"

"What do mean by *cute*?...What are you driving at?"

"Listen, Bugs Bunny," Fishnet said with a menacing edge, "if you want to go play with your ponies later, then you'd better start hopping along with the program. We are talking a dead girl over here, so let's cut the bullshit."

Von Hess was unhappy with his partner's escalation of the exchange. But he was not one to hide under the table once the rules of engagement soured. The older detective looked at Victore in a way that the restaurateur could be assured he was up against an uncompromising, united front... two against one, all rules and regulations from this point on.

"By the way, you got a liquor license for this dump posted anyplace?"

"Of course I do...hanging over the register," said Victore.

"And what's with all these customers blocking traffic outside?"

Getting the picture, Victore backed off. "Look, I'll play ball with you guys....What do you want to know?"

"I want to know who the hell the girl is," barked Fishnet.

"Okay, okay...easy...I hear you guys loud and clear. The girl who recommended her was Shirley, somebody I see once in a while."

"Harris?"

"Yeah, how did you know?" Fishnet's knowledge surprised Victore.

Von Hess communicated the facts of life to Victore concerning the unfortunate end of Barbara and Shirley. Victore was startled at hearing the news at first. But once the realty of the situation set in, he just shrugged his shoulders in a noncommittal way. All signs of his being saddened vanished as he moved to distance himself as best he could. Victore was somewhat skeptical that the detectives were unable to articulate the definite cause of the deaths, but he did not want to show that he cared enough to make an issue of it. Besides, a battle with the law was something he did not need.

Fishnet resumed his position on the mound, pitching questions. "So why is Shirley such a big secret?"

Putting on his best naughty boy look, Victore responded sheepishly, "Hey, look...I'm married. You see the picture...right? What are people going to say? What is he doing with Shirley...a professional girl? An escort! Forget about it!"

Fishnet perked up. "An escort....I see. You said she had problems—what exactly were Shirley's problems?"

"A doper...even spent time in rehab down south to fix herself up. She started to come around after she cleaned up." Victore spoke with coolness and without emotion.

"She was cleaned up as far as you know?" asked Von Hess.

"It was up and down with her. She would be okay for a while and then boom, another slide back into the pit. You know how it is once they get hooked."

"But she was functional, mostly?"

"Oh yeah...but hey, I don't ever ask anything, and she didn't volunteer much. I'm lucky to know what I know about her. When she wanted to get high, she did her thing, period....It made no difference to me."

"Who is her connection? Where did she get her drugs?"

"No idea, and that is square business. I hate drugs! I don't even give my nags Lasix!"

"What about Barbara? Drugs with her too?"

"Her I know even less about. One thing, though—Barbara knew that anyone using drugs would not be working for me very long. I couldn't take the chance and have someone like that working in my business. Shirley was extracurricular fun so you make allowances, but as far as Barbara goes...hey, business is business."

"Go on...."

"Look, the two girls were tight. They lived together...so it wouldn't surprise me if she got off now and then. But if Barbara was on drugs working in my place, she couldn't have been too bad because I don't miss much."

"Was Barbara an escort also?"

"Barbara? Nah...no way. Barbara was a nice girl, a smart girl...but a bit stuck up. I used to tease her by calling her the Countess." He reflected on his dead employee for a few seconds before continuing. "She was an okay kid, though. She came from money, so she had some class. She didn't need to go out escorting."

"I see," said Von Hess.

Changing the subject, Victore tried to be funny. "You know, Mona could have done alright as an escort back in the day."

"Mona?"

"My cashier...the one with the nose," laughed Victore. "Let me tell you guys something, and this is no bullshit; she is still good to go a couple of rounds."

Von Hess wanted to smack Victore. He did not see the humor in such a comment.

Fishnet thought about what Victore said. He found the woman he dubbed Nostrils in the role of an escort as something interesting to think about.

Von Hess continued with his questioning. "How did you first hook up with Shirley?"

"She used to come here all the time to eat, have a drink, sometimes just to freshen up. She would be dressed up nice, so I paid her a little attention. One thing led to another....Hey, what can I say? She ended up digging me."

"Okay," said Von Hess, "go on."

"Anyway, I started taking her to the track with me...showed her the stables, let her pet the horses, introduced her to the jockeys...things like that."

"She liked that sort of thing?"

"Loved it. We got together after that first trip to the oval. Like I said, she went for me." Humility was a virtue lost on Victore.

"Any family you know of regarding Shirley?" Von Hess asked.

"There is a mother in Florida who she used to live with. Tampa, I think it was."

"Do you know the mother's name?"

"I think Shirley said her name was Rose."

"Anything about the father?"

"She mentioned her father just once. I remember that she had to call him up. When I asked her if he was living in Florida too, she said he lived in Brooklyn someplace."

"Did she say where he lived in Brooklyn?"

"No...she kept a tight lip when it came to her father. I never even learned his name. That was fine with me. I didn't need to deal with any of that. I don't know anything more about her people."

"Do you know where Shirley was working?"

"Some place in the city, I think. She was a pickup for me. I got her direct number once I got close to her...so where she worked never came into

Anthony Celano

play."

Fishnet was skeptical. "If you were so close, how do you not know where she worked?"

"Tell you the truth, I didn't want to know about any of that—it sort of ruined things for me. I tried to keep our relationship like we were dating."

"You paid her to be with you, right? Paid her for sex?"

"Never money. I paid for the good times, yes...but no money." Victore's ego was attacked by Fishnet's question. "I don't need to do that," he emphasized. "Dinner, a weekend away, some jewelry once in a while... that kind of thing. But I never gave her any money to put out, and she never asked me for any. We were good like that."

"I see," injected Von Hess understandingly. "When did you last see Barbara and Shirley?"

"Barbara I saw Friday, here at the diner. Shirley I haven't seen since Wednesday. I wanted her to take a run with me to Atlantic City on Saturday, but she wasn't available."

"Why not? What was she doing?"

"Who knows? I never pushed anything with her. If she was unavailable, then she was unavailable. I never looked for explanations."

"When exactly was it that you last actually spoke to her?"

Looking at Von Hess, the diner owner answered, "I last spoke to Shirley on Saturday morning about eleven a.m."

"How did she sound?" inserted Von Hess.

"Hard to say. Tell you the truth, she could have been high. I know she was not alone because I heard voices in the background...but then again, it could have been the television."

"So she was indoors, you believe?"

"I'd say so."

Detective Von Hess had Victore reach out to Barbara's closest work friend at the diner, a girl named Wyona Symmons. Victore used his influence and saw to it that his employee was amenable to meeting with the detectives at the squad room. Von Hess called Sergeant Markie, requesting that he have someone pick her up at her house and drive her to the precinct.

Once the detectives finished their official business with Victore, the conversation strayed to lighter matters. The diner owner was given a DEA pocket diary by Von Hess as a thank-you for his cooperation. Fishnet took the opportunity to work in a few questions regarding horses. He was scheming, looking for a betting advantage. Victore was receptive to the conversation; he spoke about racing with the confidence of someone with a good deal of knowledge about the sport.

Fishnet asked Victore if he knew of anything good that might be running. Victore picked up a clean napkin and wrote down information pertaining to an upcoming race. He then passed the napkin to Fishnet.

"Tomorrow...Bitter End in the fifth at the Big A. Should go all the way as long as the track is fast and Roland is riding him."

"Roland is a winning jockey?"

"One of the best!"

"But remember one thing," Victore cautioned. "This horse runs without wraps. So if this baby is running with wraps on his front legs, bet him to place."

"Wraps?"

"Wraps can tell you if the nag is or isn't operating at full strength. Those wraps are put on for a reason. How is that for a tidbit?"

"This is a sure thing?" Fishnet was anxious for a yes answer.

Victore was amused. "Hey, Detective, this is horse racing....Anything can happen. The only sure thing is that you are going to eat in here for nothing this morning!"

Fishnet left Dixie's thinking that Victore was a pretty good guy after all. Von Hess still would have loved to have given the restaurant owner a smack.

10

THE
LEECH

MARKIE TOOK A SEAT BEHIND the desk in Sergeant Parlatto's office, trying his best to suppress a dire outlook. With so few pursuable leads, it was a chore not to be pessimistic concerning their odds of solving the case. The sergeant knew he had to appear optimistic that a break would come along at some point. Failure to lead without a positive attitude could destroy the interest of those reporting to him.

He picked up the cup of stale coffee on his desk. Since living on his own, he became accustomed to consuming things that were below par. After giving the cup a quick smell, he took a sip as he reached to turn on the small television that was kept in the office. After finding a station airing the local news, he waited until the coverage he was looking for came on.

"...two women found dead in the trunk of a car..."

...yada, yada, yada...

" ...police are saying nothing more than the investigation is ongoing at this time."

The sergeant was satisfied that there was nothing damaging to the department in the media coverage of the story. He took another swig of the lousy-tasting stimulant with an eased mind...and unsettled stomach. As he digested the drink, he digressed back to the more pleasant times of his marriage. He had to admit that he missed the home-cooked meals his wife, Flo, used to prepare for him and their kids. He could almost taste her deliciously smooth mashed potatoes, enhanced by pieces of mozzarella. His trip down memory lane was short lived when a few minutes later, the phone rang.

"Detectives...Sergeant Markie speaking." The sergeant spoke with the preciseness of an automated answering machine.

A confident, energetic male voice came over the wire. It was a reporter known to the detectives as the Leech.

"Sergeant Markie...this is Chick Aprile. How are you?"

"Good. You?"

"I'm terrific....The reason I'm calling is that I understand you are spearheading the double....Is that correct?"

Markie wondered where the reporter had gotten his information from. "Yeah," he answered cautiously, "I'm involved in the case."

The frown on the sergeant's face was derived from his knowing in advance what a nuisance the caller was going to be. Aprile was a newspaper reporter with a one-track mind when he got interested in a story. Within the law-enforcement community, especially among those who had something on the ball, he was known as a man to be kept at a safe distance. His tendency was to jump to conclusions. He was not above stepping over the line by taking statements out of context, overlooking certain facts, and massaging information in order to manipulate his narrative. And if he was really passionate about a story, he didn't hesitate to stretch the truth altogether...with no regard for the bodies sacrificed along the way. Working off assumptions in order to be among the first to get a story out was not unusual, and once on record...there was no turning back for him. He would remain unwavering as to what he reported. Insinuations of cover-up abounded when aspects of a police account were at odds with his own. To many in blue, the man was considered dangerous from a public relations standpoint. Some, using police parlance, would say the boy was a royal pain in the ass. Yet Aprile could always bank on his having a small fan club among those in blue. Friends would stand by him as long as their name made it favorably into the papers.

Markie answered Aprile's questions cautiously, without revealing much. He filtered his information, passing on only what he felt appropriate for public consumption. The Markie–Aprile interaction went swimmingly until the reporter became fixated on what he considered information being concealed. Thinking in terms of public interest, Aprile loved the idea of a story on two dead women found in a trunk. Their end fit the perfect ingredients for a tale that would not disappoint the most bloodthirsty of readers. Aprile sought out details that he could build upon and spin to further stimulate the interest of his audience.

"One girl was a prostitute," noted the reporter confidently, "so what about the other one? She was also a hooker, right?" The reporter already had this idea cemented in his mind.

Markie was surprised. "Where did that come from?" he asked. "We've got no confirmation of any of that."

"I have my sources, Sarge." The reporter's answer came with a trace of smugness.

"Well, you know more than me," said Markie. "We don't know anything like that."

"What do you mean?"

"I mean this....All we've got here is two dead girls. We're still working to figure this thing out."

Aprile did not challenge the sergeant's remarks. He moved on to other questions. "Did you hear from the medical examiner? Do you suspect it was a john who killed them?" Aprile was now posing questions in twos.

"There is no ME report as of yet. We have no persons of interest, and no cause of death has been established. We still need to confirm this mess as a couple of homicides."

"Well, what else could it be? Don't you at least have their names for me? Their ages?"

"We can't release anything at this point."

The reporter went on the offensive. "Why not? Why are you running interference? I have a story to put out, and you have an obligation—"

Markie cut him off abruptly. "Look, Chick, I'm sorry...but I gotta refer you to the department's public information people. They'll be posted as soon as we know more. Right now we have work to do, so adios. I'll be glad to talk to you later." Markie hung up abruptly, glad to get off the line after brushing him off.

Within twenty minutes, Sergeant Markie received a call from Captain North, the captain who had the duty. North was responsible for covering the city overnight and on weekends when the division captains were not working.

"Yes, captain?" Markie spoke into the phone with a hint of caution.

"Yeah...Markie...what did you say to Chick Aprile?"

"Nothing, boss—I just told him we are still working on the case. Why? He make a beef already?"

"Yeah, he called up public information," advised the captain, "and they called me. His squawk is that you are holding out on him, covering up the fact that the women were a couple of murdered junkie hookers. Do we know this shit for a fact?"

"Cap...the one girl worked for an escort service. As far as turning tricks when she bought it....we have no proof of that. Just so you know, though, one of the girls did take a pinch for prostitution."

"So the one girl was a hooker, then." The captain came to the same conclusion as Aprile. "Got anything else to tell me? Let me have your take."

"There's probably a drug connection here. Both girls have prior drug busts, and both were in rehab. I figure they took a fall from grace."

"I see. What kind of drugs?"

"Heroin. They were probably a couple of addicts."

"Were they ever busted together? In rehab together?"

"Nothing in BCI shows that they took a pinch together. I don't know about the rehab connection yet."

"So how do they end up in a trunk?"

"That's the mystery, cap."

"Did you tell Aprile any of this?"

"No, boss, I wanted to spare the families," explained the sergeant. "Bad enough they lost what they lost the way they did. They don't need to read any insipid crap spun by some thoughtless..." — Markie caught himself — "...*reporter* with a pencil."

The sergeant had worked himself up to getting his nose bent out of joint. And while he sympathized, the captain chose not to go down any negative roads with him unnecessarily. "I get it....We are on the same page with this, sarge. Have the families been notified?"

"Just one...the Allen girl. Her old man is a doctor, and the mother a lawyer. We are still working on finding out who the relatives are of the Harris girl."

"Any luck?"

"There may be a father in Brooklyn someplace and a mother in Florida. We are still digging."

"The blond is which one again? Is that the one in the fancy dress?"

"Yes, cap, Shirley Harris."

The captain seemed satisfied. "Alright, stay on top of this. If you need help, let me know, and don't worry about the overtime for now. Let's just get the job done."

"We're on it, cap."

"I know," said the captain confidently. "Remember...with Aprile involved, this could turn into a circus at a moment's notice, so watch your ass."

"Got it, boss."

"I'll neutralize the reporters," assured the captain. "Without the next of kin being notified, we are on firm ground being tight-lipped."

"Right, cap."

"Tomorrow is Monday morning, so anticipate hearing from people looking for updates. Keep me posted."

"Right, cap, you got it. Thanks a lot."

Captain North was an experienced hand who remained cool when under fire. Markie had a lot of respect for him. The sergeant knew that three things panicked bosses enough to tighten the screws: a timely case already being reported in the news, a cop-related incident, and an unhappy family with enough juice to create waves. All of these components had the potential to get the big shots to turn up the heat.

Markie looked at his watch. He was thinking of Fitzie's because he felt that he could use a drink. He resolved to visit his favorite haunt at the earliest opportunity. He looked out the second-floor window to check out the parking lot.

The forensic people were no longer working. The only sign they had even been there was the litter they had left behind. Prior to Aprile's call, there had been some media representation in the form of television crews who showed up briefly at the precinct to report on the deaths. Other reporters got their stories over the telephone from various sources. One radio station reached out to the squad, so Markie got to be heard over the air for a few seconds. All inquiries were answered with just enough information so that there was something to say but without really giving any substantial information. No details went out thanks to the law-enforcement escape hatch previously cited by the captain—a blanket declaration that there would be no further comment at this time because the facts were still being gathered and the families of the victims were yet to be notified. That was good enough to keep the wolves away from the door, at least for the time being.

Markie was an old hand when it came to the press. He had had his turn being scorched in the past, a result of his trying to be overly accommodating with members of the fourth estate.

Experience had taught him well how to step cautiously when navigating media land mines. But even armed with his experience, he knew it best to just stay away from Aprile. He was a reporter first and always. Never would the sergeant make the mistake that so many others in his position had been known to make in the past. Markie would never mistake the Leech for being something other than what he was.

⊞ ⊞ ⊞

WHEN FISHNET AND VON HESS returned to the squad, they found the office to be alive. By now there were day-tour detectives assigned to the precinct seated at their desks after reporting for duty. They were into their cases, hard at work. This was the last day tour for the team, so they were trying to tie up loose ends before they swung into their regular days off. They had no interest whatsoever regarding the women in the trunk—they were busy with their own work. One case centered on an elderly man bilked out of two thousand dollars; another was a missing person and another a landlord–tenant squabble. The sole female detective in the squad was seated at her desk, interviewing a victim of domestic violence.

Even though the trio of detectives were busy on their respective cases, it was a relief for Markie to know there were extra bodies available if needed. An added bonus was the availability of another female investigator. The sergeant thought having a couple of females around was an asset in investigations because women tended to lend a softer touch in matters involving other women and children. With the "two in the trunk" affair, Markie had no idea where the facts were going to take him, so having Junior and another female detective at his disposal was a good thing.

It being Sunday, working detectives sometimes had the opportunity to slip away for the purpose of attending church services. Although he did not personally engage in this diversion, Markie was okay with it if his people were so inclined. Attending Sunday Mass was a tradition that had been dying out in recent years. Since Von Hess, Fishnet, and Wires were not the religious type, they remained on the job throughout. It was only Junior who had taken the walk to the underattended church service to spend thirty minutes at Mass.

"How's it going working with Fishnet?...All okay?" Sergeant Markie was feeling out Von Hess.

Von Hess responded in a neutral tone. "That guy is a trip...but all is good, boss."

"No problems...right?" the sergeant asked warily.

"All good. He is just a little high-strung, I figure."

Markie was glad to hear this. It was one less thing to worry about. "Did you know that the press was here, Ollie?"

"How did that go?"

"They came and went," answered Markie. "No problem."

Fishnet was seated at his desk in the squad room. When he overheard the word "press," his interest heightened. He walked over to where Markie and Von Hess were engaged in conversation.

"Do you need me to reach out to anyone in the media and give them a briefing, boss?" Fishnet asked hopefully. "I got no problem talking to them."

Markie could not believe what he heard. He made short work of the offer. "No, we are all set....It's done. We have nothing to say to the press. I spoke to Captain North....He has the duty, so we are covered. Remember... no reporters!"

"Oh, okay." Fishnet was disappointed. He got the message loud and clear....Markie was a killjoy.

Anthony Celano

The sergeant still had more to say to the senior team. "The other team is out picking up the girl from the diner....She lives someplace on the other side of Brooklyn, so it will take a while before they get back here with her. Go take a break. I'll call you both when they get here."

Fishnet willingly agreed to take some time to rest his eyes in the precinct lounge. Before he went there, though, he first made a quick stop at the locker where he kept his uniforms.

The detectives maintained their lockers in a squared-off section at the farthest corner of the squad room. In this makeshift locker area stood fourteen large silver lockers. The lockers were positioned side by side, forming an *L* against a corner of the room. There were no windows to contend with, so the area provided the privacy necessary for the male detectives to change. Due to their being few in number, the female detectives in the squad maintained their lockers in the female locker room, an area shared with the general population of women on the patrol force.

Fishnet's locker contained more than just his police uniforms and related equipment. It also was home to a fresh set of civilian clothing and whatever else he thought he might need. There was no chance of a camera being secreted in the area where the lockers were arranged. Due to existing privacy laws, installing cameras in such an area was taboo. Once he was sure he was alone in the locker area, he removed the small black Beretta from his pants pocket.

The Beretta was capable of housing one round in the chamber and eight in the magazine. The clip was loaded to capacity. The chamber of the gun, however, had been left empty. This meant the weapon required pulling the top back in order to insert a round, which would then make the weapon ready for firing, or breaking the cylinder down to load the chamber with a bullet manually in order to fire. The chamber was probably kept empty in order to avoid an accidental discharge. Shirley Harris—or whoever had given her the Beretta—must have been sophisticated around guns. It seemed unlikely that the automatic had ever been used to kill anyone due to its small caliber.

Fishnet had had his eye out a long time for such a gun to use as a throwaway. He wanted the option of planting a gun if he ever needed to save his own skin due to an action he took in the street. The climate in the city was moving in a direction where the benefit of the doubt in a cop-involved shooting incident had somehow shifted away from favoring the civil servant. As a product of the street himself, Fishnet learned early on the importance of self-protection at all costs. The carcass of anyone he felled was going to be found armed because Fishnet had no intention of swinging for anyone.

Fishnet reached for his heavy woolen winter police overcoat. Shoving the other hangers aside, he opened the front of the overcoat. He went to the very bottom of the interior lining, where he had previously had a tailor install a small, secret pocket that closed with Velcro. He removed the 007 knife that was secreted in the lining and replaced it with the .25 caliber Beretta. The gun fit into the newly added pocket perfectly. It would be discovered only if someone were to specifically be looking for a weapon in the bottom lining of the coat. Fishnet slipped the knife into his pants pocket.

He'd had the secret pocket installed in such an odd place to protect himself against any routine, unannounced inspection of his locker. Fishnet was confident that to spot the secreted gun, a person inspecting would have to remove the coat off the hanger and examine the lower interior of the garment closely. He figured the odds of that happening to be a long shot. Superiors inspecting generally just glanced to see that an authorized coat, which was mandatory, was present in the locker. Whether the secret pocket was cunning or not was debatable, but in Fishnet's mind, it made a lot of sense.

After securing his locker with a combination lock, Fishnet strolled over to the precinct lounge, where he could sit in a recliner and watch television.

Von Hess, now tired, exercised better judgment. Taking advantage of the opportunity to rest, knowing there was no guarantee that he would be receiving another break, he opted to take his time in the precinct dorm. When Von Hess could not be found in the lounge, Fishnet sought out the senior detective. Once he located him, he took the lead of Von Hess and settled into the dorm where he too could be more comfortable.

94

11

WEEPY

AFTER COMMANDEERING the office of Sergeant Parlatto, Markie began to survey his surroundings. While he knew the squad commander through professional interactions within the police department, he did not know Parlatto on a personal level, nor did he care to. Being alone in his office presented Markie with the opportunity to nose around.

Markie began his exploration by fumbling with the items on top of Parlatto's desk, which was strewn with newspapers, loose gum wrappers, erasers, paper clips, pennies, and miscellaneous yellow Post-it notes. Given the sloppiness, Markie's immediate impression was that it was unlikely Parlatto had spent time serving in the armed forces. Markie looked at the paper in Parlatto's in-basket with amazement. Overall, the condition of the desk reflected someone totally lacking in initiative. The tray was overflowing with reports submitted by detectives and in need of review and supervisory assessment. Clearly, Sergeant Lance Parlatto was not a man to overwork himself.

"What on earth does this guy do with himself all day?" Markie wondered as he perused the reports.

Switching his attention to the desk drawers, Markie came across a stack of old magazines. There was nothing among the reading material that interested him. He derived little pleasure in going through old issues of *Soldier of Fortune* and *People*. Not even the centerfolds in *Playboy* held his attention for more than a few seconds. What did catch his eye was the bottle of Christian Brothers brandy he discovered. The sergeant found it wrapped in an old NYU sweatshirt in the lower right drawer. It had been a very long time since Markie had taken a drink of Christian Brothers. The thought of the brandy made him again think of Fitzie's.

The sergeant's snooping was interrupted by the squad room door slamming shut. Looking out the open door of the office and into the main squad room area, Markie could see Wires, Junior, and a young woman.

"Please have a seat by the desk in the corner," Wires instructed the woman.

"Alright. Thank you," the visitor answered politely.

"We'll be able to talk privately over there without any distractions," added Junior.

"Thank you," she repeated. "That would be fine."

The sight of the two detectives with the woman reminded Markie that there was a job he was charged to do. He was there to see to it that the detectives solved a case, not to evaluate Parlatto.

The woman's presence in the squad represented another lifeline—an additional turn at bat for the detectives in their effort to establish what had happened to the two women in the trunk. As Wires settled in with the woman about to be interviewed, Junior entered the private office alone to talk to Markie.

"We got the girl from the diner outside, Sarge."

"Good. See if she wants coffee or something, and then put her on ice. Let's give Von Hess and Fishnet the honors of talking to her."

Junior took his decision as a slight. She was more than just a little uneasy with her newly received transfer into the homicide squad. Part of her anxiety came from her still being heavily under the overpowering influence of her father, a man who took pride in his accomplishments during a time when there were few opportunities in the department for people of color. With his consistently reminding her of all the advantages at her disposal in the new department, she felt an extraordinary compulsion to exceed expectations...in order to prove herself in his eyes. The old man's active interest in her career only ramped up the level of her stress, adding a self-imposed pressure not to be an embarrassment. Subsequently, Junior was a highly sensitive individual.

On top of worrying about what her father would think, Junior had never been exposed to such isolation. She had begun to wish she could return to her prior assignment in community affairs, where all she needed to do was keep smiling and make nice with the people. Spending her time appeasing the locals came with a little less prestige among those playing cops and robbers, perhaps, but it offered more peace of mind.

"Okay, boss," replied Junior with a trace of dejection. She could not help but wonder if Markie thought her incapable of conducting the interview.

"I want you and your partner to work on that datebook. Check for appointments, names, numbers...anything that can give us a line. There has to be something in that book that can help get this case moving."

"Okay, Sarge."

Based on her less-than-enthusiastic response, Markie picked up on the fact that there was something wrong. As she went on her way, the sergeant called after her. Stopping in her tracks, she turned around to face him.

"Hey...hang in there. You guys are doing a good job—just keep doing what you're doing, and things are gonna work out fine."

That was all it took to right things. Junior reacted to the statement with a beaming smile, one large enough to cause Markie to notice her as a woman...as opposed to a female detective. Her attractiveness, regardless of the extra pounds, was something that he had previously overlooked. The encouraging words that she received from the sergeant came at the right time. It went a long way in boosting the spirits of a detective who had begun to feel sorry for herself.

"Thanks, boss!" She voiced her gratitude energetically and with utmost sincerity.

Markie checked out Junior as she walked off. Her movements gave him ideas. He was reminded that living alone in a studio apartment in a private house owned by an elderly couple had its disadvantages. He feared that bringing in overnight guests would raise questions and possibly his rent. He wound up slipping into a routine that was hardly conducive to a swinging bachelor lifestyle. The sergeant's ritual included putting out the trash, taking in the empty garbage barrels, and shoveling the snow off the sidewalk for his landlord, an octogenarian couple. In return, he benefited by enjoying an affordable rent, a home-cooked meal once in a while, and when he was around, an invitation to join them downstairs. It depressed him to think how he actually looked forward to hearing the old woman's voice calling up to him in the evening: *"Allie, it's nine o'clock,"* a coded message that meant it was time to come downstairs for cocktails.

Markie made his way over to the lounge looking for Von Hess and Fishnet. When he found the television off and the room empty, he immediately headed to the precinct dorm to look for them.

Arriving at the dorm, Markie saw Von Hess reclining back on a lounge chair, making music with rhythmic, long-winded snores. Farther off in a corner of the room reposed Fishnet on a bed. He was complementing his partner's concert with slightly audible whistles as he exhaled. The sergeant cleared his throat upon entering the unlit room. His polite effort to stir Von Hess out of his slumber didn't work. After this unsuccessful attempt, he walked over to where Von Hess was stretched out. The sergeant gently shook Von Hess at the shoulder without a semblance of arousal. The detective was in a deep sleep. Markie resorted to using some muscle to help wake up his detective. A brisk shaking finally woke Von Hess from his hour-long siesta. Once he came to, he was puzzled as to his whereabouts. As the head-clearing process began to take hold, Von Hess started to violently shake his head to accelerate his escape from the fogginess. Once restored, the detective was embarrassed to see the image of his boss standing over him. It was an uncomfortable feeling for a man like Von Hess.

The detective jumped to his feet with an unexpected swiftness that took Markie by surprise. The sergeant was impressed by Von Hess's agility, and he recognized that it was pride that caused the old warhorse to try to erase the image of his being on his back, indisposed. Von Hess had responded like a boxer who quickly rose from the canvas at the count of two...with the false hope that by getting up quickly, no one would have noticed him on the floor. Von Hess, ever the proud Marine, would never permit himself to appear anything less than fit for duty in the eyes of his boss. Markie could see the years in the face of the man whom he considered ageless. It saddened him to see the visible creases that appeared in the face of his ace investigator...his go- to man.

"Ollie...Wyona from the diner is in the squad room waiting for you. Get Fishnet and see what you guys can do with her," said Markie calmly.

"I'm ready!" Von Hess answered up with the pep of an acne-faced teen having his turn called in a cathouse.

Markie stepped out of the room to enter the bathroom alongside the dorm. After a couple of minutes he exited, passing through the door as Von Hess was entering. The two men simply nodded to each other as they crossed paths. Markie reentered the dorm, where he saw Fishnet in the corner making up the bed he had previously been sleeping on. As soon as Fishnet finished tidying the nest, he left to join his partner, leaving the sergeant alone in the dorm. Markie showed no hesitation at slipping into the comfort of a still-warm bed, where his own vibrating palate would soon undergo a short half-hour workout.

Von Hess and Fishnet relocated Wyona Symmons to the room with the one-way glass. She was seated at the metal table, drinking coffee across from Von Hess while Fishnet stood posted at the door. Ms. Symmons, a tiny red-headed woman in her thirties, was modestly dressed in black pants, a green pullover sweater, and white tennis shoes. Her face was interesting: heavily freckled with many prominent clusters of tiny orange dots visible on her cheeks and nose, she had no noticeable wrinkles or crow's feet about her eyes. Her nose was tiny as were her ears, which were noticeably curled over at the top. The black-framed glasses she wore afforded her the look of intelligence. Fishnet likened her to something along the lines of what he imagined a bibliophile to look like.

When Wyona was told by Von Hess that her girlfriend Barbara was no longer among the living, her reaction was surprisingly over the top. The anguish she expressed caused Von Hess to worry that the woman was going to collapse. Wyona engaged in thunderous wailing, supported by excessive tears and animated hand-wringing. Looking upward, Wyona threw her neck from left to right and then back again, loudly lamenting the passing of her friend. The scene reminded Fishnet of a grieving Olive Oyl in a Popeye cartoon.

Wyona worked herself up so that her face soon became fully flushed. It was at this time that Fishnet established what he considered an apt name for Ms. Symmons. The detective came to the conclusion that "Weepy" would be a fitting label.

Von Hess stepped away from the desk to retrieve a box of tissues. Upon his return, he placed the whole box into the hands of Wyona so she could help herself as needed. She accepted his kindness with a sniveling "Thank you." After the tank in her nose locker was emptied from excessive blowing, she successfully found her way back to full composure.

Once she was stabilized, Von Hess began to see indications of the intelligent side of the woman. She impressed him with her insightfulness. She demonstrated to the detective that she was cognizant of her surroundings. The woman was quick to recognize the obvious—something others in her position generally failed to notice. She, who had never graced the inside of a police station, conveyed to the detectives that she knew where she was being interviewed...in a lineup room as opposed to a room where she could not be monitored. The mirror side of the one-way glass made it quite obvious to her. Even Fishnet had to give her credit.

Von Hess initiated the questioning as Fishnet sat quietly. "Please tell us about Barbara. What kind of a person was she?"

The response came in nervous, quick sentences. "Barbara was a wonderful person, a good person! She helped me out a lot."

"How did she help you?"

"I lost my mother a couple of months ago....Barbara was right there for me, so supportive...like family."

"Sorry for your loss," voiced Von Hess softly.

"Thank you. You know, she offered to let me stay with her if I needed time to cope. Can you imagine? I didn't even know her very long. It wasn't like she was a lifelong friend or anything. But I can tell you this—she was a just wonderful person, simply a treasure."

"Why do you think she did that?"

"Because that was the way she was. She sometimes even cooked hot meals for her dog! God, she loved that dog. Did I mention that before?

She and the dog went everywhere together."

Von Hess had not figured on her being such a chatterbox. He steered Wyona back to the discussion at hand. "Did you ever know her to use drugs?"

Her face took on a stiffened look before she answered. "No."

"She *never* used drugs? Are you quite sure of that?" Von Hess asked in a skeptical tone. Wyona's hesitant reaction to the question was telling. She was holding back.

"Look...okay, we used to talk candidly to each other. She confided in me she had gone through a bad time awhile back. She was in a rehab program at one time."

"For what kind of drugs?"

"Heroin...and I think maybe cocaine."

"I see."

She quickly added, "But that was all behind her. She had been clean for a long time. She kicked that habit."

"Did you happen to know her friend Shirley Harris?"

"I met Shirley, but I didn't know her all that well. That girl was a little wild. I know that Barbara took Shirley in to help her out. That was the kind of girl Barbara was...all heart.

"Do you know how the two women knew each other?"

"From rehab in Florida. Barbara kicked the habit, but she used to say that she was worried about poor Shirley," recalled Wyona. "Did you get to talk to Shirley yet?"

"I am afraid Shirley met with the same fate as Barbara," stated Von Hess softly. He instinctively pushed the tissues back across the table, anticipating her need.

"Ohh nooo! How terrible! Who could have done this?" Her response was enthusiastic but without the accompanying flood as previously displayed.

Relieved, Von Hess resumed the questioning after a minute. "As far as you know, did they have any enemies? Could they have had problems with someone, perhaps?"

"Not that I ever heard about. Barbara was really loved, just a great all-around person, very supportive to a fault, always there for you...and smart! Like I've been saying...she was a wonderful person!"

"Did the two women have boyfriends?"

"No, no boyfriend that I knew of. Barbara was pretty shy when it came to boys. I think that could maybe be why we got along so well. I am the same way in that regard." She started to drift. "We were both sort of introverts around men. I personally—"

Von Hess cut her short in order to redirect her focus. "What about Shirley?"

Wyona hesitated for a second before answering. "Well, I think Shirley was going around with Chris...but please don't tell anyone I told you that. I need my job. It would cost me my position if Mr. Victore knew I mentioned his name."

"No problem. He does not need to know anything," assured Von Hess. "Do you know where Shirley worked? What she did for a living?"

"No, not really. I was not Shirley's speed, so we really never got close enough to confide in each other. She was Barbara's friend....I never imposed on their relationship."

"I understand."

"Barbara was just so great," she said sadly. "I am going to miss her so much!"

"When did you last hear from or see either of them?"

"I saw Barbara on Friday...Shirley sometime before that, I think."

Von Hess nodded understandingly. "What condition were they in... straight?"

"Yes...of course."

"*Of course*," echoed Fishnet. The snide remark went ignored.

By this time, Fishnet had closed the door on Wyona, dismissing her totally. He dreaded the thought of again hearing the words "a wonderful person" in reference to Barbara Allen. He decided it was time to make up an excuse to exit the proceedings. Fishnet rose to his feet as he spoke. "I have to check on something. I want to see if the other team had any luck with the book. Nice talking to you, Weepy," he said.

"I'm Wyona," she corrected.

"That's right...my mistake. Take care of yourself, Wyona."

⊞ ⊞ ⊞

BY 1:00 P.M., WYONA was on her way home. She was riding in the back seat of the unmarked police car, wondering to herself if she had done the right thing by fibbing to the detectives regarding Barbara's drug use. She held back the fact that Barbara had introduced her to smoking weed. The two had gotten into the routine of getting high after work whenever they were working together on the same shift.

Junior guided Wyona to the back seat of the unmarked police car before taking her own position in the front passenger seat. As the car moved along, the woman in the back seat gazed at the reflection of Wires, who was driving, in the rear view mirror. As she studied him, it came upon her that he was rather attractive in a rugged sort of way. She decided to feel him out to see if he was the friendly type.

Wyona leaned slightly forward to speak, making it evident to Junior that she was interested in the driver.

"Did you see the movie *Titanic* yet?" she asked, making conversation. Since Wires did not respond, Junior did. "No. I heard it was great, though."

"I heard the same thing," replied Wyona. "So, Wires, how long have you been a detective? I bet you get to see an awful lot in your job."

The two detectives in the front seat looked at each other perplexed. Junior then shook her head, smiled, and turned away to look out the window.

"Are you talking to me?" he asked.

"Yes....I was just curious...."

"What name did you just call me?"

"Wires."

"Wires? Where did you get Wires from?"

"Isn't that your name?" Wyona asked innocently.

"No...my name isn't Wires....What gave you that idea?"

"Oh...I thought Wires was your name because that is what the other detective called you."

The only attention Wyona received from Wires after this exchange was the dirty look he gave her. She was appalled by his sudden change in disposition. In retrospect, she came to realize that he would never have been the right fit for her. His temperament was not a suitable match, and the detective probably would not even approve of her smoking weed.

⊞　⊞　⊞

BACK IN THE SQUAD ROOM, Fishnet and Von Hess were kicking the case around between each other.

"Hey, Ollie, next time we talk to Weepy, remind me to bring a bucket and a mop," declared Fishnet.

"What can you do?...She is sensitive. Some people have their bladder in their eyes."

"Yeah," agreed Fishnet.

"But she is no dope, I can tell you that," noted Von Hess.

"How do you figure?"

"She knew her surroundings, didn't she?"

"You got a point there, partner. I noticed that myself," acknowledged Fishnet. "Well, we know how the two DOAs met anyway. But still, how in the fuck do they end up together in the trunk of a car?"

"Got me," sighed Von Hess. "Could be anything at this point."

"We are going to need a lot of luck or some kind of a break if we are ever going to figure this one out."

The old Marine was no quitter. "We have to keep punching and see if we can make our own luck."

"I'd say so," scoffed Fishnet. "After all, this Barbara was a real treasure, you know!"

"She must have had her good points," replied Von Hess.

"Yeah...too bad that the treasure got buried." It was another off-color comment made by Fishnet that Von Hess refused to dignify with a response.

Their conversation was halted when Von Hess heard the ringing phone in the squad commander's office. When he saw that no one was in the room, he entered to pick up the phone. It was the Leech.

"Detectives...Detective Von Hess speaking. How may I help you?" "Hello, Detective, this is Chick Aprile. Is Sergeant Markie there?"

"Not here, Mr. Aprile." He waved as he looked through the door at Fishnet standing in the squad room looking in at him.

"When will he be back?"

"No idea...could be anytime. Want to leave a message?" Fishnet had entered the office to listen to the conversation.

"I'm calling about the case of the two women found in the trunk," explained the reporter.

"Okay," answered the detective.

"The sergeant told me to call him after he firmed up that the women were drug addicts and working girls."

"Okay."

"So...did he firm that up?" he asked testily.

"You are going to have to speak to the sergeant on that, Mr. Aprile, or... if you like, you can call public information. Do you want the number?"

Fishnet showed an interest when he heard his partner mention the reporter's name.

"I called over there already. They said to call you guys." The reporter's displeasure was coming through.

"Okay."

"Why do you keep saying 'okay'? Are you going to give me a straight answer here or not?" The reporter was plainly angry at this point.

"Sorry...all I can tell you is that you have to either wait for Sergeant Markie or deal with public information. Do you want to leave a number?"

"Well, can you at least tell me if the family has been notified yet?" he persisted.

"Do you want to leave a number?" Von Hess repeated in a monotone that conveyed inflexibility.

"No, I'll call back! Thanks for nothing!" The reporter suddenly clicked off.

After he abruptly hung up, the detective had no doubt that he had completely pissed the reporter off, which was more than okay with him.

"So what was that all about, Ollie?"

"That reporter Aprile was looking for information."

"You didn't want to talk to him?"

"You heard Markie...no reporters."

"Oh yeah...that's right, Ollie. I forgot about that for a minute." Fishnet remembered that it was prudent not to go against Markie.

12

SCRAMBLED EGGS

THE TWO COUSINS FROM Long Island shortened their steps the closer they got to the building with the green lanterns attached to the façade. They had never been in a police station in their lives, so this experience was foreign to them. It was an encounter they entered into with trepidation. Their hesitation was never more evident than when they came to a standstill upon reaching the massive entrance doors. As they faced off, each was expecting the other to lead the way into the station house.

"You go in first," the acting teacher finally said to the dentist.

"Why me? You go ahead....You work in the city, not me."

"So what does that matter? I'm an actress who teaches acting....What do I know about police stations?"

The stalemate was short lived, with the deadlock broken by the officer assigned to the station house security post. Stepping out of the building, the man in blue greeted the women.

"Can I help you?" the officer asked in a friendly tone.

The dentist spoke up. "We are here to see the detectives about a matter."

Once convinced that the women were there on legitimate business, the officer escorted them into the building.

The teacher cupped her hand over her mouth as she whispered to her cousin, "Everybody here has a gun on their hip! Kind of creepy."

"Well, we are in a police station, aren't we?" answered the dentist practically. "If you came to my office, would you be surprised to see me with a drill?" she asked.

The acting teacher failed to see the comparison. "It's not the same thing....I never heard of anyone getting shot with a drill."

"How can I help you ladies?" the lieutenant on the front desk asked.

Looking up at the man in the crisp white shirt, the dentist responded, "We are here to see the detectives."

"You are...?"

"I'm Doctor Allen...the sister of Barbara Allen."

"One moment, please....I'll call upstairs."

It was 2:30 p.m. when Fishnet received the call from the front desk. Fishnet indicated that he would be right down to fetch the two visitors. Fishnet was always more than willing to extend himself when it came to interacting with females. Had the two visitors been men, he would have more than likely asked the lieutenant to send them up to the squad unescorted.

The detective returned to the squad room with the sister and cousin of Barbara Allen in tow. Once inside the squad room, the dentist took the initiative.

"I'm Michele Allen." She then slightly turned to her companion to introduce her. "This is my cousin, Amy Greene. The detectives spoke to my father about wanting to talk to us...."

"Yeah, we did. And you're Barbara's sister, a pediatrician like your father, right?" Fishnet asked.

"No, I'm Doctor Allen the dentist," she corrected, "unlike my father."

Fishnet's resemblance to Clark Gable piqued the doctor's interest in the detective. A romantic, she could picture Fishnet standing at the foot of her stairs looking up at her with the same raw masculinity that Gable cast in *Gone With the Wind*.

"I'm Detective Milligan," Fishnet declared to the pair confidently.

The doctor's face dropped immediately....Her infatuation was short lived. "Oh...you...you are Detective Milligan," she said with disappointment. "I see."

Standing perfectly erect with her shoulders pushed back, she now spoke in a different tone...one suggesting she had prior knowledge of Fishnet. Her lips tightened, transforming her mouth into a taut, straight line.

The detective nodded. "Yeah...I'm Milligan." He could see the obvious change in her.

Gable lookalike or not standing before her, the dentist could no longer bring herself to be anything other than icy. She had received an extensive earful about Fishnet from her mother. She now engaged the detective with a predetermined notion....It was her familial duty to abhor him. After picking up on her attitude adjustment, there was little doubt in the detective's mind that the dentist's mother must have put the *maloik* on him. Evil eye or not, Fishnet refused to allow the collision he had experienced with the mother to deter his efforts to conquer the dentist. The dentist warranted the extra latitude because Fishnet found her physically appealing. The professional woman's screen test impressed Fishnet enough for him to cast her in one of his psychotic, make-believe productions.

The detective escorted the two visitors directly into the vacant squad commander's office and suggested they make themselves comfortable on the couch. Von Hess entered the room to introduce himself. After the introductions, he then went into his usual routine of expressing his sympathy on their loss. He then thanked both for taking the time out of their schedules to come into the precinct.

Fishnet was not averse to Von Hess taking the lead with the two women. Once his partner arrived at the comfort level, his intention was to gradually ease himself into the conversation. Fishnet was wary of risking a misstep with the dentist. But it was too late; he would never be able to reverse the damage caused by Victoria Allen stigmatizing him as a beast. As a result, the cousins were more amenable to interacting with Von Hess, who had been described to them as the nice older detective.

For the most part, the cousins comported themselves in a businesslike yet friendly fashion. Both women declined the offer of something to drink. After a few minutes of settling in, the doctor then changed her mind. Directing her attention to Von Hess, she expressed that she would appreciate some coffee. Von Hess was fast to accommodate the request, leaving the room and shortly returning with a mug of joe.

"Not the best coffee in town but not the worst," the detective said as he handed over the blue mug with the detective shield logo on it.

The senior detective then shared some of the facts concerning the investigation. Von Hess did not profess to have all the answers concerning the death of Barbara. After responding to their questions as best he could, the time came for the detective to convey the need to interview each woman privately. Their reaction was one of total receptiveness. They had been won over by the older detective, readily accepting whatever he decided to put on the agenda.

Fishnet escorted the cousin of Barbara Allen into the squad room area, where she assumed a seat beside an empty desk. Ms. Greene assured Fishnet that she would be just fine sitting alone. "This is fine. I am okay waiting my turn here to see...Detective *Von Hess.*" She smugly emphasized the name of Von Hess as an intentional poke at Fishnet, also making it clear she'd spoken to her aunt Victoria.

The remark really got under the detective's skin. The slight represented a declaration of war to the unstable detective. Without saying a word, Fishnet spun around on his heel to briskly face away from her. Her punishment was to be more severe than mere banishment from the land of Fishnet; that would be too good for her. Amy Greene's fate was to be kept around long enough to be a torture victim in the tale he intended to conjure up. His spin envisioned her as a sex slave held captive in the basement of a predator...an STD-infected one to boot.

He slowly turned around to again face Ms. Greene. His smile reflected an evilness that could be detected only by someone who really knew him.

"Do you like Starbucks? There is one around the corner, and it's much better than the coffee we have around here."

"No, thank you," came her cool reply.

"You sure?"

Seeing him as pathetic, she smiled crookedly in response without saying anything. Fishnet was hoping she would at some point reconsider. He had every intention of lacing her drink with a healthy dose of speed. He kept the off-white powder inside a white handkerchief in his pigeon coop for just such an occasion. The spiked beverage would pay off Barbara's cousin and also even the score with the Starbucks manager, a man who had had the audacity to charge him for coffee when he first opened the business three months ago.

Fishnet returned to the office and took a seat behind the desk. Von Hess sat in the chair opposite Doctor Allen. Von Hess was again up from his seat after a few seconds. Excusing himself, he departed the office for a moment to get a fresh legal pad. The temporary departure of Von Hess gave Doctor Allen the opportunity to peruse her surroundings. The look on her face indicated that she saw nothing special. She was not to be faulted for not being impressed. The office, while well above average by department standards, offered nothing to sway her opinion. Outside of the private bathroom, the squad commander's office remained modest at best in comparison to the professional office space she rented.

Von Hess returned to his seat before she was able to give the room any further contemplation. He made it a point to ask Allen how her parents were holding up. As she became more relaxed, she assumed a softer demeanor, giving off a slight vibe of vulnerability. Fishnet saw the tender side being unearthed by his partner. While the chitchat portion of the conversation was playing out, Fishnet forgot all about the acting teacher to concentrate deeply on the dentist. The dentist tended to occasionally look upward, a movement that Fishnet somehow equated to the suppressing of tears. He felt compassion, a truly unique happening. Unbeknownst to anyone in the room, Fishnet had slowly inched over to the other side with Doctor Allen, who had just entered his conceived world...as his prize heroine.

Fishnet's fantasy had the detective bestowing pity on a fragile woman, wounded by the tragic loss of her sister. Not only would Fishnet acquire public acclaim, but the girl was also his to win in this imaginary escapade. Fishnet molded the dentist into his ideal...a keeper, a polished professional woman whose earning capacity served to sweeten the pot. His dreaming neglected to recognize anything that could undermine his world of make-believe. He tuned out the channel that aired the dampening possibility that the woman before him might one day morph into a duplicate copy of her mother. Nothing could taint his view of the dentist. He even saw good in the dentist's long, thin fingers. They reminded him of the young doctor at the VA hospital who had given him a prostrate exam. Her fingers were long and thin as well. Fishnet twisted the memory of an uncomfortable penetration into something enjoyable.

Doctor Allen was dressed in a newly pressed, form-fitting pair of denim jeans. A white long- sleeved silk shirt could be seen underneath a black jacket with brown elbow patches. She wore a very large diamond on one of her fingers, an adornment substantial enough to tempt many a thief. Her dark hair was of average length, as were her polished nails which were painted a subdued beige. For a woman closing in on forty, she really didn't need to wear much makeup. At this time, however, it made sense, serving to help hide any remaining puffiness caused by grief.

The dentist's diction was exceptional. She enunciated each of her words with a quality worthy of the stage. She was poised to a point where the average man would doubt his confidence around her. She informed Von Hess that she was Long Island–based with her own practice. During the course of the interview, Doctor Allen comported herself without a scintilla of arrogance or speck of superiority. Fishnet, while commuting between realities, remained constant in seeing her as something special... his ideal. He was able to distance the doctor's biological connection to her mother through an accepted scientific theory that prevailed in his world....The father's DNA had swallowed up the mother's when the egg got scrambled.

"Can you tell us a little bit about Barbara?" Von Hess asked softly.

The dentist faced the question head-on, getting right to the point. "Barbara once had a drug problem. She entered an excellent rehabilitation facility in Florida, which assisted her in overcoming her addiction. She was doing very well ever since as far as anyone in the family knew."

"Do you think it possible that she might have started using drugs again?"

While not exactly catching her by surprise, the question did stall her response for a second or two. "Anything is possible," she conceded. "But no...I honestly don't think that was the case here. We all considered her to be over the hurdle...hopeful that she wouldn't sustain a reversal in her progress."

Von Hess was impressed with her response. She was articulate and objective, two qualities that weren't always present in everyone under such circumstances. "Really?"

"Yes. You know, Barbara was an extremely bright girl, much more advanced academically than I. She could have been anything she chose to be. She was a wonderful intellect."

"That's been my understanding," said Von Hess, trying to be supportive.

Doctor Allen shook her head regretfully. "She had just fallen in with bad company, I guess, and lost her way." She looked up at Von Hess for further understanding.

"You are probably right about that," he reassured her. "When did you last see Barbara?"

"A couple of weeks back at a surprise birthday party for our aunt."

"How was she then?"

"She was fine. Not even a drink. She was nursing ginger ale all evening. That is why all of this is so unbelievable to us!"

"I hear you. Was Barbara seeing anyone?"

"Not to my knowledge. Amy would know better than I would. They often went out together."

"Did you know her roommate, Shirley?"

"No, I never met her. I did not even know Barbara had a roommate until Amy told me."

"Did Barbara have any enemies?" Now back in the game, Fishnet had put forth his only question.

She responded to the question with both defiance and defensiveness. "Not a one! That is what we simply can't understand! Everyone loved Barbara. She was so giving, big-hearted to a fault. A great sister and a positively wonderful person!"

There it was again...the words "wonderful person" in reference to Barbara. It was the one thing that consistently irritated the hell out of Fishnet. But since he was smitten, it was not enough to banish the dentist from the other world.

The detectives were both disappointed that they hadn't uncovered any new leads from their interview of Barbara's sister. While discouraged, Von Hess retained the determination to forge ahead, hoping that the sit-down with cousin Amy would push the case in a more positive direction. Von Hess was dedicated to trying to get to the bottom of the mystery so he could chalk up another one for the good guys.

When Amy Greene took her turn on the couch, Fishnet was still preoccupied with thinking about Barbara's sister. The thought that she might have been married had just entered into his realm of consideration.

It short-circuited his fictional concentration, returning him to reality in time to see Von Hess lean forward in his chair as he addressed Ms. Greene.

"Can I get you anything, Ms. Greene?" offered Von Hess, maintaining his gentlemanly manner.

"No, thank you, sir, I'm fine," she answered softly.

"Are you also in the medical profession?" Von Hess knew she wasn't, but flattery was always palatable.

"No, I'm an actress. I am also an acting teacher."

"Really? Have you acted in movies?"

"I have, but mostly I've performed on television in soap operas. I am now predominantly doing teaching."

"That's impressive. You reside and work on Long Island?"

"I just reside there. I work in Manhattan."

"That must be fun," commented Von Hess.

The teacher nodded in agreement. "I find it quite rewarding teaching others how to express themselves through acting."

"I can imagine you would. Many talented people never get the opportunity to express themselves. You are to be commended." Von Hess was hard at work with the shovel.

"Thank you. Sharing my skills in the cause of developing future actors is a passion I have."

"That is just great. Again, my kudos."

"Thank you. Inside everyone there exists acting potential. People just need the opportunity to bring their inner expressions to the surface. "

Taking in the conversation, Fishnet rolled his eyes. It was a gesture that luckily went unnoticed.

Ms. Greene liked the interest Von Hess had displayed. She further liked to hear herself talk, so the two got along very well. Von Hess let her go on so that he could stay ahead of the curve with her. The detective knew that artistic people in general were a strange breed, prone to temperamental outbursts. As a teenage prankster in an art class, he had once inserted a pencil into the backside of a one-eyed cyclops captured in clay by a fellow student. His dastardly act was met with an extremely volatile outburst by the creator of the art. The experience taught Von Hess a valuable lesson...to avoid running afoul of artistic people.

Ms. Greene was a free spirit in her thirties, attractive in an earthy way. She wore blue jeans, brown boots, a dark blue button-down shirt, and a brown corduroy jacket. Since she wore no earrings, her earlobes became more noticeable. They seemed to be hammered flat, like tiny sagging pancakes, with two prominent hole marks visible. Von Hess thought he saw a gold stud affixed to her tongue, but he was not sure. He was curious about it, but he certainly was not about to ask her to stick her tongue out. As it later turned out, he didn't have to.

Once the preliminaries were exhausted, Von Hess began his questioning. By the end, not much had been gathered. Greene had last spoken to Barbara a couple of days earlier, with the two making plans to have dinner. Barbara was described by her cousin as a person without vices and solidly rehabilitated.

The next question, put forth by Fishnet, came out of left field. "Is that a stud in your mouth?"

Both Greene and Von Hess were stunned by the audacity of asking such an intrusive question. Although offended, the woman recovered quickly, countering with a deliberate coolness designed to show she was unfazed.

"Yes it is. Do you like it?" she replied, taking the conversation a step further while looking directly into the detective's face.

"Don't it rust when it gets wet?" Fishnet asked with directness.

While anticipating a strained exchange, the teacher was not ready for that remark. Glaring, she answered in a huff, "No...it *don't* rust!"

Even though her miffed reaction gave Fishnet a degree of satisfaction, he was still disappointed that the opportunity to spike her coffee had not arisen. Von Hess, quickly trying to guide the conversation away from further conflict, injected his own question. "Did you know Barbara's roommate, Shirley Harris?"

"Yes, I met her," she replied, looking at Von Hess.

"Was she straight?" Fishnet bluntly asked.

"Straight in what sense?" Greene was legitimately perplexed by the question. "What and who are you talking about?"

"Either one of them," Fishnet shot back.

"Look, they both had their problems at one time, but they were functioning just fine."

"Are you sure of that?"

"Barbara might have done a little weed now and then, but that was the extent of it. That much I know, at least as far as Barbara was concerned."

Von Hess again stepped in. "Is there anything else you can tell us about Shirley?"

"Shirley was from Florida. Barbara met her when they were both in rehab down there." She then turned her attention to Fishnet. "What exactly did you mean by asking if she was straight?" She was not letting it go.

"Not under the influence of drugs." Fishnet had modified what he meant.

"Oh...well...yes, they were straight. And at least as far as Barbara goes, for a long time. She had been righted thanks to rehab."

"Do you know anyone she might have had a problem with?" Von Hess resumed the questioning.

"No, Barbara had no enemies. She was the greatest. Not just because she was family but because in truth, a more giving person didn't walk the earth. She was loved by all who knew her."

"That's what everyone is saying," offered Von Hess.

Fishnet reacted before he had to hear the word *wonderful* again. "Yeah, a real nice person. But tell me how nice people end up in the trunk of a car nose to nose, tied in a knot?"

The detective had crossed way over the line. Von Hess cleared his throat loudly knowing that the question was going to get the teacher's feathers ruffled but good. He braced himself for the storm he knew was coming. The teacher stood up from her seat in anger to blast the detective.

"I'm not sure what you are trying to imply, sir, but I do not appreciate your methods! Barbara was a victim, and you need to respectfully find out who did this to her!"

She entered the territory of what Von Hess remembered to be an artistic blowup. Fishnet, after being successful in his efforts to push her over the edge, knew it was time to back off.

"Okay, okay...take it easy. I'm not saying she wasn't a victim. I'm just trying to figure out what happened to her."

Looking not to exacerbate matters, Von Hess ended the interview; they weren't getting anyplace with Ms. Greene anyhow.

Detective Von Hess reconnected the cousins. Speaking to the two women privately, he made excuses for his partner's behavior, thanking both of the women for their cooperation. He did such a good job of mending the fence that there was no talk of making any complaint.

Fishnet took out a Camel and tapped it against the back of his hand prior to lighting up. He watched the two women exit the door out of the squad. The detective realized that he had little chance with Doctor Allen. Besides, with Amy Greene now added to his list of detractors, it was a sure bet he was to be buried even deeper during the ride back to Long Island. His disappointment was destined to pass quickly. Happy times were inevitable because things were always recreated to be far more amenable in the other place. In the other zone, under his direction, the detective was assured that the dentist would be more welcoming.

13

THE
DEATHMAKER

"WHAT WAS THAT?" he asked, not understanding the meaning behind what he had just heard.

"Say that again." The man with the raspy voice, whose words scratched through the telephone connection, was no longer asking....He was demanding a reiteration.

Nervously clearing his throat, the caller repeated himself. "What I'm saying is that I just heard the cops pulled a couple of dead girls out of the trunk of a car."

"So what the fuck is that supposed to mean to me?"

The caller hesitated before responding. He finally replied with an awkward cautiousness, not looking to arouse Red's suspicion. "You called me yesterday looking for Shirley, didn't you, Red? Well, one of the girls they found was dolled up and had long blond hair...so...well, you know..."

"I know *what*? What the fuck am I supposed to know here, Anthony Boy?" Red's voice turned sinister. Anthony Boy recognized the tone....It indicated he had better watch his step.

"Look, Red...I know nothing for sure. I just think it may be worth checking out...that's all," he explained. "You never know....Look, I'm calling you as a friend."

Red was not convinced. "Where you getting this shit from?"

"I got it from my friend....His brother was delivering soda to the precinct."

"What friend?"

"Georgie Cheese...."

"Since when does that asshole know anything?"

"It's all over the street," explained Anthony Boy. "Georgie's brother saw them taking the bodies out of the trunk in the precinct parking lot.... His truck was parked right outside the lot, so he was able to see what was going on because he was making a delivery."

"Did he say *who* the girls were?"

"He doesn't know that, Red....He was just delivering soda. The precinct is part of his route."

"What fucking precinct was this?"

"I don't even know the name of the precinct....It's the one right near the entrance to the bridges, down by Brooklyn Heights. You know, the one with the firehouse next to it."

"I know it. My daughter was supposed to be with you Friday night, wasn't she?" Red asked in an accusatory tone.

"Red...I just met her on the street for a second to straighten out with her....That was it," he replied defensively.

"Yeah...and...?"

"And...she came up to the car, and I handed her the cash...and that was it. I never even looked at her twice because I was busy on my cell phone lining up a new client...some investment banker from Jersey."

"Was she dressed up for work?"

"I don't even know, Red....Honest, I just paid her what I owed her. I only looked at her face for a second. I was focused on this pigeon from Jersey."

"I'm going to see about this, Anthony," Red said. He finalized the conversation by abruptly hanging up.

"Yeah...you do that, asshole," Anthony Boy said bitterly after hearing the dial tone. He regretted having made the call.

⊞　⊞　⊞

RED HUNG UP THE PHONE, feeling suspicious of Anthony Boy's motives. He knew Anthony as a man who could be too slick for his own good at times. Red had been trying to reach his daughter without success for a couple of days. This was a major violation of the routine he'd established since she had returned to New York. His edict called for them to converse every day.

Shirley Harris was under strict orders to get back to her father immediately whenever he called regardless of where she was or what she was doing. The rules he laid down were ironclad parameters, designed to keep his daughter drug free. The bulletin he had received from Anthony Boy was enough to cause him anguish, a sensation he did not tolerate well. His business was to cause discomfort, not be the recipient of it.

Red knew he would be useless until he found out for sure, one way or the other. He was conditioned to take the worst thrown at him regardless of who was involved, so coping would not be an issue. It was the lack of knowing the truth that freaked him out.

Red was not a timid man, so there was no question as to whether he would go out seeking answers. The doorstep of the station house was not exempt from his pursuit of information. Once determined to find out for himself about what had happened to his daughter, there was no power strong enough to prevent him from fulfilling his mission.

⊞ ⊞ ⊞

BY LATE SUNDAY AFTERNOON, Sergeant Markie was ripe. Due to this unpleasant condition, he made the time to slip back to his office at the homicide squad for a quick shower and shave. As with most detectives assigned to the bureau, he maintained a locker that was equipped to meet overnight needs, including a full change of clothes. What he had available to him was sufficient for the sergeant to recharge himself. Since his divorce, he had become accustomed to living without the domestic amenities connected to matrimony...like ironed shirts, fresh sheets, a spotless bathroom, and a stocked refrigerator. Markie's only downside to not going home to his apartment had to do with his having to use a throwaway razor. He found that they lacked the precision required for him to even his sideburns and maneuver around the corner areas under his nose.

With his refurbishment completed, Markie returned to the precinct feeling like a new man. Anxious to resume work, he immediately called the four members of his investigative team into the squad commander's office for a meeting. The sergeant felt self-conscious looking so presentable while the appearance of his detectives remained haggard. It was evident that the investigators needed shaves, showers, and some different threads to wear. Like a true mother hen, Markie was committed to rectifying their situation at the earliest opportunity.

After a recap of the information gathered so far, the sergeant felt compelled to keep the meeting short. Struggling to come up with the appropriate motivational words to stimulate investigative momentum, he had to be satisfied with just urging his crew to keep the faith. The detectives returned to their duties with the enthusiasm of someone walking into a gas chamber.

Wires and Junior scoured the datebook of Shirley Harris in an effort to come up with leads. The date boxes were found to be blank concerning appointments. All they had to work with were the telephone numbers recorded in the back of the book. They divided their work into two areas... exchanges with New York area codes and those out of state.

Wires devoted his efforts to the out-of-town numbers. He began with New Jersey. Someone named Ricky had a disconnected number. Next he left a message for someone with the initials of SL, instructing the receiver of the call to contact him at the squad. This was the pattern with all the Garden State numbers as well as the few in Connecticut, Arizona, and California.

Then he dialed up the only clearly identifiable Florida number, Ms. Natalie Furman of the rehab facility. The detective was hoping to secure information pertaining to any next of kin for the Harris woman. But since it was Sunday, Wires was unable to get anywhere. A security guard named Alvin advised Wires that it was impossible to locate someone who could access the records office. It sounded like a lot of baloney to the detective. He found it hard to fathom that the guard knew of no one he could call in order to gain access to the records. Alvin claimed that he did not even know anyone named Natalie Furman. Under the circumstances, the detective had little recourse but to take the security officer's word for it. Since the office staff in charge of record-keeping would not be back at work until Monday morning, there was little he could do other than wait it out. Wires made a final plea to motivate Alvin to move mountains, but his effort fell on deaf ears. Alvin was not about to extend himself under any circumstances. After Wires hung up the phone, he swore to himself that he was going to stick it to the first Floridian he came across. It went without saying that his vengeance was going to be double for anyone from the state of Florida named Alvin.

Markie, after learning of the results with the rehab center, tried to mitigate Wires's frustration by explaining that the Florida facility would probably require a subpoena before releasing any information. He advised Wires to try again the following day, requesting that the rehab center serve as an intermediary. It was likely they would agree to reach out to the next of kin of Shirley Harris, and he should ask them to call the detective. Wires nodded in agreement. His concentration was now directed toward his next losing effort: six numbers in Las Vegas.

Meanwhile, Junior was faring no better than her partner with the Big Apple numbers. Many came with just singular identifying names. The detective dialed up Buzzie, who claimed not to know anyone named Shirley Harris. The same answer came from Spooky, Mr. Flappers, Stretched Long, Milky Way, and a variety of other contacts Shirley

Harris had. Several messages were left with answering machines. Other local numbers in the book turned out to be disconnected, discontinued, no longer in service, or changed with no new number provided. The rest of her calls went unanswered. Oddly, there was no number for the owner of Dixie's or any of the people identified thus far in the investigation. The detective brought this to the attention of her boss. The sergeant was hopeful as she approached his desk in the squad commander's office.

"Any luck?"

"Nothing, Sarge. But do you know what I find strange?"

"What?"

"There was no listing in the datebook for Victore, the owner of Dixie's, or anybody else....Even Barbara Allen was not listed."

Markie had no ready answer to her observation. "Could be an old book, perhaps? Or maybe there is a second book she has someplace?"

"That's possible," she acknowledged, not convinced that was the answer.

Markie had another thought. "You know, we recovered no cell phone for either of those girls....She might have kept active numbers in her phone."

"That could be it." Satisfied, Junior returned to the datebook.

While the investigative team was treading water, exerting themselves just to stay alive at this point, Sergeant Markie went out to pick up the Sunday papers. He wanted to see what had been printed pertaining to the case. The incident was reported the way he had expected, with no identification of the two deceased women—so things were good so far. Just to keep himself busy, Sergeant Markie doodled. When he tired of doodling, he began drawing mustaches on people in photographs in the newspaper. Finally, he prepared a list of some unchallenging things to do:

- ○ Update bosses.
- ○ Prepare to deal with Chick Aprile.
- ○ Send out Wires and Junior for food.

After looking over his list, a flash of anger came over him. In his frustration, he ripped the paper from the pad and tore it up in disgust. He began to take a few deep breaths to contain his irritation. Few in his professional life saw this side of Markie, who was perceived by most as someone with a relaxed, self-assured personality. Yet such outbursts were not all that uncommon for the sergeant, who disliked not being able to gain traction on a case. Getting uptight was one of the reasons his marriage to his ex-wife, Florence, had collapsed. From his perspective, she was a relentless nag who wanted what she wanted... immediately. The fact that he was the same way escaped him.

Since there had been no notification made to any next of kin of Shirley Harris, Markie had no problems with Captain North: there would be no pressure coming from him as long as the press was kept at bay. Markie's strategy concerning the media was to stick to revealing as little as possible for as long as possible. He had seen instances where after the passing of time, a case would just fade off gradually into oblivion. This was especially true when breaking news took center stage, diverting all eyes elsewhere. He was secretly hoping for a major water main break, steam pipe explosion, or some other similar distraction to occur in midtown.

The sergeant did not fail to adhere to his own media battle plan. The reporter Chick Aprile called twice asking questions. Markie never took his call. He had Junior tell the reporter he was busy in the field. Little moments such as this left the sergeant feeling that it was good to be the boss.

With things having slowed down, Markie permitted three of his detectives to take the opportunity to return to their offsite lockers so that they could clean themselves up. They wasted no time returning to their home base to take showers and change clothes. The two detectives from the B team were further instructed by Markie to return with food for everyone. Von Hess was given the responsibility to see if any new cases had come into the homicide squad and to check for incoming messages. Fishnet had no place to travel because everything he needed was on site in his locker at the precinct. He was also told to take this time to tidy himself up. Sergeant Markie would remain on hand to monitor the office.

Wires and Junior returned with an ample number of sandwiches and sodas. That accomplished, the detectives were instructed by Markie to get the most recent arrest photos of Barbara Allen and Shirley Harris, and then to prepare their DD-5s, the follow-up reports that would reflect the work performed thus far. The general consensus at this point was that the case was on track to go nowhere.

Finally, a telephone call into the squad room put an end to the stagnation. Fishnet was the first person to get to the phone. It was the precinct desk lieutenant, informing them that there was a man named Harris in front of his desk looking to speak to the squad. Fishnet perked up immediately, asking the lieutenant to send the unscheduled visitor up to the squad. Fishnet, Markie, Von Hess, Wires, and Junior waited quietly with the hunger of a lion in Africa stalking a baby buffalo. They were hoping that this was going to prove to be the beginning of the break they so desperately needed.

The desk lieutenant did not like the looks of the visitor. Sizing him up as being the unsavory sort, the lieutenant ordered a radio car team coming off their meal to see to it that Harris made it up to the squad room without taking any detours.

The door to the squad room opened slowly. The father of Shirley

Anthony Celano

Harris, looking like a giant, stood at the threshold of the entranceway. He took a little time before he committed himself to taking the next step, one that would place him inside the squad room. Even after being beckoned by Fishnet to enter, he hesitated before penetrating the domain of gold shields and guns. He took a few seconds to cast his eyes around the room before he ventured forward. At that point he was all in.

His entry into the squad room manifested a slow, deliberate wariness — and the detectives were just as wary once they got a good look at their visitor. He was a hulk of a man right out of central casting, complete with the attitude. He stood about six-foot-four, weighed about 270 pounds, and had broad, rounded shoulders with Herculean arms that appeared capable of uprooting trees. Nothing about this specimen of man seemed gentle. His steel-gray hair was straight, worn plastered back away from his forehead with a little over an inch of distance between the hairline and eyebrows. All of this, coupled with the thickest of necks, gave him the look of a giant white simian. He sported hair stubble on his face, not out of fashion but rather due to missing a day of shaving. The most fearsome characteristic of the big man was not the scar over his right forehead or the flattened nose. Not even the intimidating dark sunglasses he wore took top billing. All of these paled in comparison to his hands. It was these two massive tools of destruction that truly frightened everyone; the very thought of being in their grasp could send shivers up a spine. Each of his fingers was sausage sized. Every independent digit sported a blue tattooed letter of the alphabet, which collectively spelled out the word "DEATH" on his left hand and "MAKER" on his right. Obviously the visitor was not a person afraid to advertise. His manner of dress did little to soften his persona. He wore a black collared shirt, black dress pants, black tasseled loafers, and a lightweight, three-quarter-length black leather jacket. Anyone who thought he had a black heart underneath it all would have been correct. This brute of a man walked with a bit of a shuffle, something similar to an over-the-hill pugilist who had engaged in one too many fights.

Von Hess automatically shot a knowing glance at Markie. Markie shared his vision of hope in the form of the man who had just entered the office. Now they had a streetwise guy playing the game — the detectives welcomed the chance to talk straight up.

Fishnet had absolutely no intention of getting cute with the big man. There was going to be no venturing off on delusionary travels because the detective could see that he needed to remain alert in the presence of Shirley's father. Fishnet solemnly motioned to the surprise visitor by extending his left arm, pointing in the direction of the squad commander's office. Fishnet, followed by Von Hess, cautiously trailed their guest into the office.

The big man looked around the small room, deciding where to sit. The detectives suggested that he settle himself down onto the couch. Once the large man was in place, Von Hess took his usual seat facing the couch. Fishnet chose to remain standing with his back to the office door. The more he saw of Harris, the more convinced he was that it would be in his interest to pay full attention to the big man. Fishnet was not going to take any chances—he had no intention of placing himself at the slightest disadvantage. There would be no reaching for a Camel either; he wanted both his hands free. Fishnet was no coward, but he was no fool either when it came to his own neck. Proving the saying that it takes one to know one, the crazy detective recognized a fellow psycho when he saw one.

Von Hess thought of extending his right hand to introduce himself to his imposing visitor but then thought such a gesture at the onset might come across as weakness to someone so formidable. He immediately noticed the big man's fingers, recognizing the blue ink often used in jailhouse tattoos.

Von Hess opened up the dialogue without formalities. "Nice tattoos."

"I know that you know where I got them." The big man was looking squarely at the detective.

"Are you Mr. Harris?" Von Hess spoke in his most official voice.

"Yeah, I'm Harris." The words came out in a rasp, as if the man were speaking with his neck tied in a knot.

"Can I ask you for some identification, please, Mr. Harris?"

Taking his sweet time, Harris responded in true wise-guy fashion. He made a big production out of pulling the small black wallet out of his pants pocket. He removed a New York State driver's license and turned it over to Fishnet, who jotted down the name, date of birth, and address. The detective never noticed that that the license presented was expired—and it would not have made a difference to the detective anyway.

"I'm Detective Von Hess." Von Hess then pointed in Fishnet's direction. "This is Detective Milligan."

Harris nodded at the two detectives. He then spoke about as directly as could have been guessed.

"Listen, I'm not looking for a love affair here with you guys. I heard you found a couple of girls in a trunk. One is supposed to be a tall, good-looking young blond. Is that right?"

"Yes...that's right," answered Von Hess.

"I've been trying to reach my daughter without luck. So I'm here asking you...is the girl you got named Shirley Harris?"

Fishnet found himself, out of pure reflex, responding first. He looked straight at Harris, man to man, and gave him the news.

"Your daughter is the blond we found in the trunk." The frigidness in the way Fishnet delivered the news caused Von Hess to look down and away, shaking his head.

The older detective tried to mitigate the bluntness of Fishnet's announcement. "Sorry to have to tell you this, Mr. Harris."

Harris took the news without blinking. He simply sat back in the couch, taking a moment to digest the revelation. Whatever scintilla of vulnerability he had in him soon vanished, and his look hardened once the news sunk in. Harris was taking deep breaths through his nose. Von Hess could see that his teeth were clenched tight. Then, after just a minute, Harris normalized, reverting back to his natural everyday persona.

"I want to smoke....Is that okay with you?" he asked calmly.

"You bet. Do you need a cigarette?" Von Hess asked.

"I got them." He took out a nonfiltered Lucky Strike, which Von Hess lit for him.

Fishnet liked the red circle on the packaging of the Lucky Strike brand. He also remembered how he liked the fact that the cigarette was advertised as being "toasted." The detective decided that if the brand suited the man before him, his own Camels were out. His next pack would be of the toasted variety.

"How about we take a time-out?" suggested Von Hess. He then offered Harris some water, which was declined with a wave of the hand. "Let's take five." Harris just nodded in agreement.

Fishnet left the door to the supervisory office open behind him so that Harris could remain under observation from the squad room. Once outside the office, Von Hess was handed several arrest photos of the two women that had been gathered by Wires and Junior. The photos all showed both girls with droopy eyes, indicating they were probably high on something when they had gotten busted.

Sergeant Markie signaled for Fishnet to join him at a desk in the squad room. "Let me have his information," he said, referring to Harris.

"Okay, boss."

Fishnet wrote out the scary man's name, date of birth, and address on a piece of paper and handed the paper over to the sergeant. Once he received the information, Markie then summoned Wires and Junior to come over to where he was sitting. Handing the paper to Junior, he instructed the two detectives to check out Harris.

After the five-minute break had passed, Fishnet returned to his position at the door, and Von Hess again settled opposite the couch.

Harris came out for the second round, asking the first question. "Do you know who is responsible for this?"

"We've got nothing as of yet," Von Hess said honestly. "How did you find out about it?"

"It's all over the street," responded the big man. "I didn't talk to Shirley for a couple of days, so I put two and two together and came over here."

Neither detective cared to ask Harris to identify the exact source of his information. Von Hess opted for an easier question. "Can you tell us anything about your daughter that could give us some direction?"

"Like what?"

"Was she depressed? Did she have any enemies? Was she having problems?"

A small smirk crossed the father's face. "Was she having problems? Where do you want me to start?"

Fishnet was paying close attention. Harris was interesting to him. Here was a street guy who obviously had come up the hard way. There would be no alibis, no excuses, and no uneasy moments of embarrassment. Fishnet instinctively knew that the word *wonderful* in reference to his daughter would never pass the lips of Harris. This big fellow was definitely going to be helpful to the detectives. In this assumption, Fishnet and Von Hess were on key, singing to the same music.

"How did she die?" asked the father, curious.

"Undetermined. There were no visible marks, so violence appears out," stated Fishnet. "We are waiting for the medical examiner to weigh in."

Harris nodded as if he were no stranger to the business. "Let me put it on the line. I am no altar boy. I've done things...been away to college. Green Haven...Sandstone...you get the picture."

Harris paused, looking for a reaction, but none came. The detectives appeared to be all ears, so he continued on.

"I'm no good maybe, but I was never mixed up in drugs. I've seen too many guys take a fall because of drugs."

Von Hess showed no reaction to the statement. "Shirley was into drugs?"

"Ahhh, c'mon, you know she was. Let's stop bullshitting each other. You don't walk away from that shit."

"How long did she have problems?"

"She got hooked in Florida, where she lived with that asshole ex-wife of mine...who is the dumbest of all bitches created," answered Harris.

The detectives offered no response to the comment.

"I paid to put Shirley in some half-ass clinic down there. It was me who insisted she come back to New York when she got sprung so I could keep an eye on her," explained the father. "She ended up moving in with this girl Barbara not too long ago."

"Do you know Barbara?" queried Fishnet.

"I met her. She seemed alright. Respectful kid...family has money, I think. But she is just as fucked up....She was in the same boat as Shirley... two dopers. They got tight at that Florida clinic."

"So they stayed close," noted Von Hess.

"Yeah, that's right. They reconnected when Shirley came to live here.

Anthony Celano

The plan was that they were supposed to hold hands with each other during the rough spots." The big man shook his head. "Let's get real....It was the blind leading the fucking blind!"

Then it hit Harris. "Shirley was found with another girl....Was that Barbara?"

Von Hess answered in a controlled, emotionless voice. "Yes, it was Barbara."

Harris did not flinch; his retort was two words. "It figures." It seemed like it did not matter too much to him. "So I'm here now....What do you need from me? I got things to take care of."

Von Hess spoke up first. "We are in the process of trying to retrace the steps of the girls to determine who they were last with. When did you last see either of them?"

"Shirley I saw Tuesday; she was looking good. We talked every day....It was a way for me to keep her honest."

"Makes sense," said Von Hess.

"I tried her on Friday night without any luck. I automatically saw it as a bad sign, so I kept trying. Then Saturday comes around and I try again.... Ehhh, you know the rest."

"What about Barbara?"

"The other one, I don't remember when I saw her. I pay no attention to her." Harris made a downward wave with his huge hand. He then lifted both hands and slapped them down against his thighs in frustration as he let out a deep sigh.

Von Hess continued. "Do you know where your daughter worked?"

"You don't know?"

"All we know is that your daughter used to dress up nice to go someplace," replied Von Hess.

Harris hesitated to ponder the question before responding. "Yeah, sure...I know. Shirley worked as an escort."

Fishnet did a double take. "You knew where she worked?"

"I knew all about it...and I know what you think, but it was a legit job... believe me!" Harris waited to see if there would be a response from the detective.

"*Legit*?" Fishnet asked, sounding surprised.

"Legit! Look...she was no hooker or anything like that. She knew I'd brain her and torch the joint where she worked if it was anything otherwise," expressed Harris adamantly. The detectives were listening attentively as Red Harris spoke. "The job paid her good money just to go out and eat and drink with some jerk-offs."

"So how did she get the job?" Fishnet asked.

The big man's answer came out slowly. "I don't know....She must have answered an ad in the paper or something."

Fishnet and Von Hess glanced at each other very briefly. The answer lacked credibility. "Yeah...maybe," commented Fishnet. "Do you know where the escort business was located?"

"Lower East Side, someplace on East Third around Second Avenue in the city." After a few seconds, he added to his statement, "The place is called Delightful Chaperones."

"Do you know who she worked for over there?" asked Von Hess.

"Some guy...Anthony. I know she was to meet him Friday. Go find this Anthony; he might know something...like where she was going."

Taking the information down, Fishnet and Von Hess both believed they were onto something. "Do you know Anthony's last name?"

"No." Harris lied, remaining semiloyal to his criminal code of honor. "So whose trunk were they found in?"

"It was some local citizen...a working man. His car was apparently parked in a convenient spot for whoever did this, so they popped the lock to his trunk," answered Von Hess.

"Any idea how they happened to wind up together like they did?"

"That's what we are still trying to find out."

The interview with Shirley's father continued on for almost an hour. The detectives answered questions, explaining perhaps too much of the case to him, and left off with what they figured to be a valuable resource to call upon if need be at some point down the road. The only real sign of emotion exhibited by Harris came when Fishnet showed him the arrest photos of the two girls for confirmation of their identification. Affected by what he saw, the big man leaned back, staring off blankly for several seconds. Von Hess for the first time detected what he previously thought to be nonexistent...a weakness. He now knew that is was possible for Shirley's father to hurt.

The veteran detective witnessed a dark transformation unfold. Harris started to speak in a slow hiss, as if his words were meant as a warning. "Best you go see this fucking Anthony sooner rather than later."

"Why is that?"

The detective did not receive an answer to his last question. What the detectives had heard were the parting steps of Red Harris as he walked out the door of the office.

Von Hess and Fishnet immediately filled in Sergeant Markie. By this time, Markie had a line on Shirley's father, which included his photo and arrest history. He decided it was time for everyone on his team to play nice in the sandbox. The sergeant called for another team meeting in the squad commander's office.

Markie assumed the throne behind the desk while his four detectives took seats inside the office. Markie emphasized that teamwork was going to be the key to their success from this point on. He summarized

Anthony Celano

the investigation up until the point of the Harris interview. Von Hess provided the details to the Harris sit-down, and then Junior articulated what she and her partner had learned about Shirley's father. Sounding official, Junior read aloud from her neatly handwritten notes.

"Joseph Pasquale Harris, age fifty-seven, born on February 20, 1941," she began. "Past addresses include 110 Skillman Street, Brooklyn, New York; 118 Walworth Street, Brooklyn, New York; 68 Avenue A, New York, New York."

"His driver's license showed an address on Vanderbilt Avenue in Brooklyn," noted Markie.

"Looks like he was originally a Bedford-Stuyvesant guy," commented Von Hess.

"Bed-Stuy and Lower East Side," Wires added. Markie signaled Junior to continue.

"He is known on the street as Red Harris, the Death Maker, Red Death Joe, and Joey Red Death. His rap sheet shows fifteen arrests."

"What charges?" Markie asked.

"In the Ninth Precinct, he was busted for untaxed cigarettes, two felony assaults and extortion, and two homicides. He paid a fine for the cigarettes and walked away from the other arrests clean."

"Nice," said Von Hess.

"Wait...there is lots more," said Junior. "It took five counts of extortion in the Seven-Nine Precinct to put him away for five years. Then on the Lower East Side, he racked up arrests for hijacking, gambling, murder, and burglary...beating all charges."

"Incredible," declared Von Hess.

"Is that it?"

"No, boss....A felony assault and an attempted arson finally put him away for another vacation. He did his time. He is no longer on parole; there are no warrants out on him."

"What did you get out of the puzzle palace?" Markie was referring to police headquarters.

"We did okay over there with the intelligence division....I got some good information."

"Okay....talk to me," stated Markie.

"I ended up speaking to Detective Bradley, who works over at one of the organized crime units."

"And?"

"Red Harris is connected to the Milano crime family as an enforcer for Carmine 'Champ' D'Angelo."

"I guess that is where the name Pasquale fits in," remarked Markie. He looked at Von Hess for confirmation.

Junior answered. "I said the same thing. Bradley said Harris is half

Italian, half Irish."

"Champ D'Angelo...," said Von Hess. "Didn't I read that he just died?"

"Champ died a couple of months ago. Red is now with the younger brother, Augie, who took over everything on the Lower East Side. They call him Swing Blade. According to Bradley, he was bumped up to capo," said Junior.

"Swing Blade D'Angelo? Sharp name." Fishnet was trying to be funny. "I wonder why they call this guy Red," Markie wondered aloud.

"I don't know," answered Junior.

"Could be some kind of reference to blood," guessed Wires.

"Whatever," said Markie. "At least we now know who we are dealing with, and we have a direction to go in. Anybody have any questions?" There were none.

Markie had to give credit to Wires and Junior. Regardless of their history, they were starting to impress him with their thoroughness.

"Okay...Fishnet and Ollie, you guys hit the escort service in Manhattan and see what you can come up with over there," ordered the sergeant.

"Right, boss."

"You other two go to the Ninth Precinct and see what they have over there."

"Right, boss," responded Junior, echoing the response of Von Hess.

"Keep me posted, and keep each other posted as well." This was the sergeant's final instruction.

On the way out the door, Fishnet turned to Von Hess. "What did you think of that guy Harris? He could scare a lot of guys, wouldn't you say?"

"I'd have to agree with you there, partner," concurred Von Hess. "One scary dude. I wouldn't want to fall behind on a shylock payment with him doing the collecting."

"His daughter must have taken after the mother," concluded the crazy detective.

"Certainly not the old man," agreed Von Hess.

"How would you like to go up against him in the street?"

Von Hess thought about the question before answering. "He is the reason why we carry a gun."

As they were walking, Fishnet stumbled after tripping over a wastepaper basket in the squad room. After experiencing the pain to his shin, he reacted in a fit of anger. The detective kicked the basket across the room violently. After Von Hess witnessed the incident, he looked at his partner curiously; the veteran detective could not help but think that Red Harris was not the only scary dude walking around.

Von Hess had no conception as to just how over the top Fishnet could be in answer to the simplest of life's problems. Once, after cutting his trigger finger on the sharp metal edge of an air conditioner he was

Anthony Celano

removing from an upper-floor window, he satisfied his rage by sending the cooling system airborne. The detective derived great satisfaction from looking down three stories at the broken air conditioner as he sucked the blood from his index finger. Even superiors weren't immune to the wrath of Fishnet. Many a boss would have given plenty to identify the culprit who had placed the thumbtack on the seat of the chair behind their desk. What remained unknown was that each authority figure shared one common denominator....They had pissed off Fishnet.

14

ALLEY CAT
AND
SAMMY ME

WITH EVERYONE ON ASSIGNMENT, Markie was left in the office with nothing to do but wait— something he was not very good at. He needed to do something to fill the time or he would start thinking of the past, specifically things that depressed him. Sergeant Markie considered himself a hybrid: his father's name was DeMarco; his mother was Nolan. Being half Irish, the saloon known as Fitzie's fit Markie's needs just fine because the Nolan influence prevailed. Since Papa DeMarco had not stuck around long enough to see the ink on his son's baptism certificate dry, the sergeant later rebelliously changed his name, going from DeMarco to Markie. In Fitzie's, the sergeant found a place to go when he needed to escape such memories. Since he'd already nosed around the office, poking into the affairs of the squad commander, he was now at a loss concerning how to occupy himself. He finally decided the time was right to take that visit over to Fitzie's.

Stepping out of the squad commander's office, the sergeant called over to the precinct detectives, who were seated at their desks making calls and preparing reports on their respective cases.

"I'm going into the field for a little while," he announced. "Don't give out my cell number. Just give me a call if anyone is looking for me." The sergeant strolled out the door of the station house, glad to be going someplace.

Fitzie's was only a short distance from the precinct, close enough to return from fast if he was needed. Owned by an old-time fighter, the saloon was a narrow hole-in-the-wall dive, configured like a long rectangle. It was a throwback establishment with prehistoric ambience; drinks were served on a bar top that extended from the entrance to the far end of the room. Time-worn leather stools were positioned sporadically up against the bar. There was no place else to sit other than at a single small wooden table located against a wall in the back near the dartboard and pool table. Affixed at the top of the wainscoting running along the walls was a narrow shelf that was just wide enough to hold a drink. There was one tiny unisex bathroom located in the back.

The Wurlitzer, situated to the left of the front entrance, was stocked with the recordings of old-time Irish vocalists. While people around the country were tuning in to a new television show about a woman known as Judge Judy and listening to recordings of Cher and Whitney Houston, it was only in Fitzie's where Carmel Quinn, John McCormack, and the "Irish Nightingale," Morton Downey, remained popular. Their songs were favorites of those imbibers prone to shed a tear at hearing sentimental musical reminders of days past. Continuing the theme of green were framed photographs displayed behind the bar of yesterday's Irish ring heroes in fistic poses. John L. Sullivan with his handlebar moustache was there, as was Gentleman Jim Corbett sporting a pompadour, Gene Tunney, Jim Braddock, the Toy Bulldog Mickey Walker, and even Billy Conn, who had borrowed the heavyweight title from Joe Louis until a late-round knockout reminded him that it was just a loan.

Featured most prominently at the center of the bar, celebrated over the register, was a huge oil painting of Fitzie's childhood idol, Jack Dempsey. Lining the walls were additional photos of celebrated people of varying ethnicities, some with names that are still remembered, others with long-forgotten claims to fame. Namath, Ali, Marciano, DiMaggio, and the Babe were some of the more easily recognizable. It was the identity of the long-gone notables such as Governor Al Smith, Mayor Jimmy Walker, billiards champion Ralph Greenleaf, golf's Bobby Jones, and race car driver Barney Oldfield that challenged those fond of drink who were interested in trivia...men such as Markie.

Since every fourth drink was a buyback and the boiled eggs were free, the sergeant could both tie one on and eat within budget. He was in a safe haven at Fitzie's, with his odds of getting in an off-duty jam remote. Old Man Fitzie kept his place peaceful and simple, so non-complex that spirits were dispatched to customers straight up...neat in a shot glass. The beer that was dispensed came in just two varieties...Budweiser and Guinness. Those patrons who became unruly when they drank were promptly bounced out, usually without any counter argument.

When Markie strolled into Fitzie's, things were very quiet. There were only three people in the entire place, excluding the bookmaker, who was invisible to the sergeant. One patron was a regular—an elderly woman who was busy counting out the coins that she had spaced out on the wooden bar. Once she set aside the correct monetary allotment, she used her index finger to push each coin toward the barmaid in order to pay for her next drink. When leaving, she could often be seen stumbling forward before catching herself after several quick steps...causing the other regulars to nickname her "Twinkle Toes."

The second occupant was a regular named Jasper, a senior citizen known to enter the bar hunched over with a bad back and depart still bent but beaming. When in good form, Jasper was called upon to sweep up. When he overdid it, Fitzie would put him to bed in his room upstairs from the bar.

Lastly, there was Alley Cat, the bartender. Alley Cat was a hard-looking, short-haired bleached blond with an English accent. She was alluring to those who preferred their women slightly rough around the edges. While hardly svelte, whatever extra poundage she carried was in the right place...her chest. An honest woman in her middle forties, she had been transplanted from London some twenty-five years prior.

Alley Cat had a thing for Markie—enough of an attraction to discreetly tuck her phone number behind the red pocket square of his suit jacket one night. But Markie never seemed to find the time to dial the number. He blamed his then-lack of interest on his ex-wife, Flo....He attributed her with causing him to sour on women. His unavailability only strengthened Alley Cat's resolve to attain his affection. Somehow his elusiveness made him that much more appealing.

"Hiya, copper!" she declared in a hardy voice. It was her standard greeting for him...that came along with her beaming face.

Pointing to her ample frontage, he responded, "Hi, Alley. How are they hanging for you?"

"Not below the belt yet, sweetie," she cracked. "The usual?"

"Yeah...please....and do me a favor. Give Twinkle Toes whatever she's having. Set up Jasper too."

"You got it." She continued to project a broad smile, making it very evident that she enjoyed seeing him.

The sergeant's consideration of others less fortunate was one of the things that made Markie special to her. He was the sort who, when out socially, was good to everyone. Alley poured out a shot of Jack Daniel's in front of Markie, backing it up with a short glass of Budweiser. After his first taste of the day, he turned around to look at the dusty framed photos adorning the wall opposite the bar. He knew who most of the faces were by now. One of his favorites was an old black and white of Johnny Broderick, a once well-known Broadway detective who had supposedly thrown the legendary gangster Legs Diamond through a plate glass window back in the day. Markie did not know whether that story was true or not. It didn't matter to him because it was Fitzie who perpetuated the legend; regardless of accuracy, Markie wanted to believe. The sergeant had been looking at the photo for a long time, so long that he almost felt he knew the long-gone detective. The sergeant pointed to his shot glass, signaling Alley to do it again, another quick one for the road.

Alley was looking to talk as she poured. "Still thinking of packing it in?"

"I don't know. What am I gonna do...take a trip around the world?"

"Not a bad idea....I've taken that the trip myself and never even had to leave the bar," she quipped with a smirk.

Markie laughed, shook his head, and stared down at the blue vein protruding from the back of her otherwise smooth hand. She had placed her hand over his when he reached for his shot glass. Her smile made her intentions clear. Responding to a body that was now urging him to engage, he stared into her eyes, making it clear that they were on the same page.

To the surprise of Alley Cat, she realized that she was finally penetrating his armor. "You came at the right time. There is no one here now," she said.

"I have to go to the little boy's room," he said.

Markie then threw his drink down—emptying the tiny shot glass. He left money on the bar and walked to the restroom without another word spoken. When he was joined in the john by Alley Cat two minutes later, he was more than a little surprised that they didn't crash through the bathroom door.

On the walk back to the precinct, Markie regretted that he hadn't made it with Alley Cat sooner. It angered him to have let Flo do such a number on him. It continued to excite Markie as he recalled Alley Cat's rapturous delight as he ravaged her with her back against a hardwood door. He replayed her every purr and passionate gasp in his head over and over as he proceeded to the precinct. The experience was light years away from the yowls that would emanate from Flo, whose missionary preference saw her resting her butt on a soft mattress. All such thoughts left his mind the moment he entered the station house.

"Anyone looking for me?" Markie asked aloud upon reaching the squad room.

"All quiet, Sarge....No calls," advised one of the precinct detectives he did not recognize.

"Thanks."

Sergeant Markie reflected on the days when he had been a detective working cases. He missed the responsibility of catching squeals, a dated

Anthony Celano

term used to describe complaints reported by the public. He enjoyed helping people deal with their problems, so from a public relations standpoint, he was a credit to the department in that role. When the telephone rang, the sergeant picked up on the second ring.

"Hello...this is Chick Aprile....Sergeant Markie?"

"Yes...this is Markie." *Here we go again*, he thought.

"So what is happening? Did you notify the family of the two women you found yet?"

"Yes, a few minutes ago." He spoke to the reporter lethargically.

"Oh, good," came the peppy response. "So what's the story, then? Can I get their names, where they worked, family background, and whatever else you can give me?"

"No problem, but you will have to get all that from public information later. They don't even have what you are asking for yet. I still have not even spoken to the duty captain."

"Who might that be?"

"Hang on a second." Markie checked the coverage sheet posted on the wall next to the desk. "Looks like Captain Moran currently has the duty."

"No problem. I know Sam Moran. But really, does it make a fiddler's fuck difference? They said for me to call you!"

Aprile's persistent tone was getting to Markie, who'd been up enough hours to drain most of his patience. "I have to go. All I can tell you is the investigation in ongoing, with my people out in the field pursuing all avenues. Bye."

"What avenues? All I'm getting from you is a lot of nothing," complained the reporter. Markie had not heard him as he had already hung up.

Sergeant Markie immediately called up the new duty captain to give him a heads-up regarding Aprile. Markie had never met Moran, but he knew that he was a new captain in the bureau. Word was out that Moran was called "Sammy Me" by his subordinates in the patrol force. Why this title had become his identifier was unknown to Markie. As a general rule, new captains coming into the bureau were a crap shoot....Sometimes they proved to be a natural fit while other times they left a lot to be desired. As a rule, most of the detective captains were well versed, knowing enough to gather facts, assess them, and then command accordingly. Some with less experience could be nervous types who unintentionally hampered progress. But Markie had come to realize there was another type to worry about: the ambitious captain. Markie was prepared for the worst.

"Captain Moran," the captain answered.

"Hi, cap. This is Sergeant Markie from homicide in Brooklyn. I'm calling to post you on a case we have going....We got two in the trunk—" Markie was promptly interrupted by the captain.

"I already spoke to Captain North, Sarge. So I'm totally up to speed as far as all he knew. Have you anything else to add for me?"

"Yes...both families have been located and notified. We also have a line on where the girls worked."

"Excellent!" The captain's response was enthusiastic. Such a hyperenergetic reply was viewed by Markie as a red flag.

"The one girl worked at an escort service in Manhattan," advised Markie. "I got two teams out there seeing what we can turn up."

"Escort service, huh? Interesting....This is sexy stuff; could be lots of media play here. A couple of junkie hookers?"

"Well, we have not confirmed any of that yet, cap. But what I wanted to do was give you a heads-up about Chick Aprile, the reporter...."

This interested Sammy Me. "I know Chick. He's a friend and a good guy....He's no problem. You just don't know him."

"Yeah...well, he is of the opinion that the girls were a couple of junkie hookers as well," said the sergeant.

"Sounds like a no-brainer to me," said the captain.

"He has been on my back looking for confirmation of this so he can make a spectacle of the case and put all the lurid details in his paper."

"Did he ask if you wanted to be quoted?"

"We never got that far, cap. I was able to stall him, but now that we made notifications to the family, I can't continue along that path."

"I see....So he has no information. Good. So what is the problem talking to him?"

"The guy is not reliable to be accurate. He twists things so that the story comes out the way he likes it to. I told him to call public information just to be done with him."

"That was probably smart of you," noted the captain. "He's alright... once you get to know him. That man will quote you and play you up big if he likes you."

With that comment made, Markie knew Moran was a hopeless case. "I'm afraid he's liable to throw us under the bus, cap."

After a second of thought, Sammy Me continued. "Okay...look...leave it to me. I'll handle this. Best you stay out of it. I'll call public information as soon as I get off with you."

"Okay, cap."

"Just give me all the details you have...names, ages, who the parents are, and whatever else you've got. Also, don't worry about Chick....It will be like a matador toying with a bull."

"Okay, cap. Good luck!"

A matador toying with a fucking bull! It was now clear to Markie why the patrol force called the captain Sammy Me. He was all about feeding his own ego while at the same time inflating his importance in the public eye. Markie was willing to bet his pension that Sammy Me's thirst for the limelight was going to result in problems. Aprile was no bull, and the captain was no matador.

"You and the team stick with it and keep me in the loop at all times. As for right now, I want to know every new detail. I am here all night if you need me."

"You got it, cap...and thank you."

"Remember...I'll take care of the press. You just refer all of their inquiries directly over to me."

Markie provided Sammy Me with the information he asked for. He hung up with the captain's parting words ringing loudly in his ears.

The sergeant had that uneasy feeling in his stomach, the kind people get now and then when they anticipate a problem coming. It was having to bend to the authority of wild cards like Sammy Me that made Markie contemplate retirement. Compounding the problem was that there was no one of higher authority around to reel the captain in. No one of a higher rank assigned to the detective bureau worked on a Sunday night. Sammy Me was a loose cannon...a glory hunter.

Markie had no recollection of any captain ever wanting to get into the middle of a media story as it was still unfolding. They avoided such positions whenever possible. After the fact, as long as things went correctly, there would be more than enough time to take center stage. In Sammy Me, Markie saw hiccups on the horizon. All he could do was keep his head low and hope for the best.

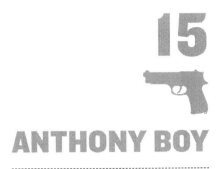

15

ANTHONY BOY

WHEN AUGIE D'ANGELO ENTERED his social club, he was greeted with the greatest of homages by everyone in attendance. Card players rose from their chairs to go over to him to say hello. Crew members, some of whom were made men in the family, kissed his cheek as a sign of respect.

Augie was the new boss, a capo in the Milano crime family. His promotion came at price, the passing of his older brother, Carmine.

The D'Angelo brothers were products of the Lower East Side, where they had established a reputation as bona fide tough guys with street smarts. The brothers supported themselves through a series of illicit activities that included running an after-hours club, hosting card games, shylocking, and narcotics trafficking. It was their carefully concealed drug operation that provided the funds for their fancy cars, clothes, and high-rolling lifestyle. Before long the brothers drew the attention of the Milano family hierarchy, who then began to show an interest in them. Once recruited as Milano family associates, their goal was to get their buttons... become soldiers in the family. The brothers correctly surmised that the quickest way to accomplish this objective was to fatten the envelopes going to the bosses. Their plan worked. When the time came for them to make their bones, a Milano prerequisite for induction, they carried out a couple of contract hits with one of the family's premier assassins,

Red Harris. Once rubber-stamped by Harris as willing and competent executioners, the D'Angelo brothers were proposed for membership in the family. The secret ceremony took place in the back room of a pastry shop on Second Avenue. Using their new status, money, and assorted front men, they opened a number of legitimate businesses that included a bar, a car dealership, a welding business, and a construction company. Their illegal enterprises were run out of an East Side social club. With Carmine gone, Augie had now inherited full control of their empire.

Augie was a daily visitor to his social club. Seated behind his desk, he waited patiently for Anthony Boy, an associate in his crew. Anthony Boy called for a meeting because of a beef he was expecting to have with Red Harris. Augie's connection to Red had blossomed since they had done their first work together. Harris, who was not a full-blooded Italian, wasn't a made man. He served as a mob associate, assigned to Augie's crew as the chief enforcer for his boss.

Anthony Boy Chiarello stood nervously in front of his silent partner, who was seated behind a desk that sat on an elevated platform in his private office. Augie liked the idea of sitting high... like a judge, staring down on a defendant who was awaiting sentencing. The office was isolated from the buzz of activity in the social club's main room, where members were playing cards and swapping stories. The junior partner, with the sweaty palms, was in the early stages of totally flipping out.

"Look, Swing...you know Red is fucking nuts," began Anthony. "I'm not ashamed to tell you that I'm more than a little concerned here."

"Anthony, c'mon...don't worry about it. I'll handle Red," assured Augie D'Angelo, whose street name was Swing Blade. "You got *nothing* to worry about, my friend."

But Anthony still had reservations. "Yeah...but if that maniac thinks we—"

"Hold it....Back up, Anthony....Where do you get the *we* from?" corrected D'Angelo, making it clear exactly where the liability lay.

"I mean *me*....If he gets it in his head that I was sending his junkie daughter out to lie down or *even* if he thought I knew about it...what happens to me? Forget it if he finds out about the drugs!" Anthony's last comment was reckless—he wasn't considering the serious penalty for admitting to drug involvement.

Augie's face stiffened. He now spoke with a stern look on his face. "You got no idea where you are going with this, my friend, so I think it would be wise for you to stop with the diarrhea of the mouth...unless you want to go on record."

Swing Blade's warning was paralyzing. Anthony Boy knew he had spoken too freely by mentioning drugs. Now he had a real problem because to go on the record regarding drugs meant that Augie would have to do something...such as impose a death sentence. He retracted what he'd said as quickly as he could. "Don't pay me any attention....I'm getting my words all jumbled up....I don't know what I'm saying over here anymore, Swing....I'm just all wound up."

This line of conversation sat better with Augie, who wanted to keep his financial relationship with Anthony Boy fluid. "Didn't I just say relax, Anthony? All you need to do is breathe," Swing Blade said confidently. "You just stay focused on our business and keep earning....I'll take care of the rest."

"That is exactly what I want to do...breathe! I'm scared, Swing....I don't wanna turn up like another Manny Bone...with my head found in a bucket of red paint someplace!"

"Anthony...get a grip on yourself! Leave Joey Red to me. You got no problems, my friend...so don't create any. Trust me."

"I trust you, Swing," Anthony answered half-heartedly.

Anthony tried his best to put up a brave front in order to hide his fear of Red Harris. The Death Maker's propensity for committing acts of violence had fractured the pimp's confidence in Augie D'Angelo's ability to neutralize the big man. As Anthony saw it, Red's proclivity for mayhem outweighed Swing Blade's competency at mediation.

D'Angelo did not appreciate the look of skepticism he read on Anthony's face. It bothered him that Red's reputation outweighed his own in the eyes of Anthony. He set out to clarify any misconception as to who possessed the greater authority. "Remember one thing, Anthony.... Joey Red fucking works for *me*." Augie jabbed his thumb toward his own chest for emphasis. "Red is my fucking man....He does what *I* fucking say!"

"I know that, Swing....I know." Anthony knew he had put himself in the middle of a no-win situation.

"You damn well better know that, Anthony! When I say there's no problem here, then there's no fucking problem. You understanding me?"

Anthony knew to back off. "Okay, Swing...I just got scared for a minute. I know with you having my back, I got nothing to worry about from nobody."

"Never doubt that, Anthony Boy...never!"

"I definitely won't, Swing. I just lost my head."

"Okay...forget it. Go say hello to my son-in-law in the bar. Tell Ernie I said to give you a double—no...a *triple* on the house."

"Thanks, Augie...I will."

"Cheer up, kid....We're having a real good year!"

⊞ ⊞ ⊞

FISHNET AND VON HESS rode over the Brooklyn Bridge into Manhattan. Upon arrival at Second Avenue and East Third, they saw nothing at the intersection that suggested the existence of an escort service. The detectives drove around the immediate surrounding area without results. They extended their search by traveling the full length of Third Street from east to west; again, there was no indication of an escort service. Next they proceeded north to south for a dozen blocks across Second Avenue, also without results.

Von Hess thought it time to throw up the white flag. He pulled the car over to discuss the situation with Fishnet. "You sure there was no listing anyplace for this escort service?"

"Sure I'm sure," answered Fishnet, surprised at the question.

"You got nothing with telephone information?"

"Not a fucking thing. Do you wanna get out and ask around?"

"Let's give information another shot before we do that. You may have gotten a stiff on the line. How about giving them another call?"

Taking out his cell phone, Fishnet placed the call. After listening to a recording that he hated, he was directed to hang on if he wanted to speak to an operator. Eventually a bored-sounding voice came on the line to offer assistance.

"I am looking for a business, Delightful Chaperones, on East Third Street, Manhattan. I need an address and number. Thanks."

After a second or two the voice spoke again. "I have no listing for a Delightful Chaperones on East Third Street....Sorry, sir."

Fishnet turned to his partner. "I told you...no listing."

"Ask them to just check on the name and forget the address," advised Von Hess.

"Check just the name, operator, or anything that comes close to it."

"One moment, please." After a few seconds, the voice returned. "I have nothing for Delightful Chaperones, but I do have a Delightful Chaperones, Inc. at 100 East Thirteenth Street. Do you want that number, sir?"

"Yeah, what is it?"

Fishnet, while jotting down the address and number, looked over at Von Hess and shook his head. After hanging up with the operator, he felt the need to let off steam. "Let me tell you....I hate dealing with these fucking people! First you get recordings, then mindless morons whose thinking you have to do for them!" vented Fishnet.

"Don't worry about it," responded Von Hess. "We got what we wanted."

"That ain't the point. I ask you, what's going on over here? Everything is a fucking recording now! Ever try calling a fucking government agency?...They put you on hold for two fucking days! Have things gotten nuts or what?"

"Welcome to the new world." It was all Von Hess gave him. But it was enough encouragement to keep Fishnet going.

"No matter what agency you call...it is always a recording! And if you do get a live voice...half the time you need an interpreter to understand what the fuck they're saying!"

"Yeah," agreed Von Hess, "things were a lot simpler once."

Fishnet was encouraged by his partner's concurrence. Von Hess did not need to say more because Fishnet took it from there. He was now on a roll, continuing on with his diatribe.

"People out of work all over the country and we keep fucking automating everything! Fewer and fewer postal workers, toll collectors, token sellers....Where are they taking us with this shit?"

Fishnet never elaborated on who exactly "they" happened to be, so all Von Hess could do was nod and look to change the subject. "So what's the address we're looking—?"

"These were decent-paying jobs with benefits and health insurance. Okay...maybe no one got rich, but it was enough to support a family on! Am I right or what?"

"You're right, Fish. A lot of people raised families on those salaries," agreed Von Hess.

"You know, they praise the gains being made by these computer geeks....I say we should be stringing their asses up from a streetlight!"

Von Hess began to look for an opportunity to reel Fishnet in. He remained without an opinion concerning Fishnet's call for public executions. Seizing a moment when Fishnet stopped to catch his breath, he broke in, attempting to get back to business. "So what is the right address? Where are we going?" he asked.

The first sign of cooling off finally arrived. After checking what he had just written in his notes, Fishnet replied, "100 East Thirteenth Street."

After having spoken his piece, the unbalanced detective then stared out the window into the building line as the car moved along to East Thirteenth Street.

Reaching their destination, the detectives viewed the location to be a four-story building. Parking in front of a fire hydrant, they walked to the front of the premises. The sturdy metal front door was unlocked. Entering, they faced a second door made of wood, which was locked. The names on the mailboxes for the floors reflected what the detectives were looking for:

1st Floor:	Ettore Enterprises
2nd Floor:	Adult Images Direct/Finest Adults, Inc.
3rd Floor:	Classic Massages, Inc.
4th Floor:	Delightful Chaperones, Inc./ACDC Fun,Inc.

Fishnet rang each of the bells to the commercial locations several times. No one answered. "Everything is quiet. There's no one around," observed Von Hess.

"Yeah," Fishnet agreed. "It figures."

Von Hess started his return to the unmarked car. As he was stepping out the front door, he heard a bashing sound to his rear. It was Fishnet giving one last try to access the building. The detective was engaged in violently trying to kick in the interior door. It had been solidly reinforced, so Fishnet's thunder kicks were to no avail. Once he got the fury out of his system, the detective caught up to his partner in the car. Both detectives settled back in the front seat, hoping their wait was not going to be a long one.

"Somebody has to come or go eventually," related Von Hess. The detective was seriously thinking about talking to Markie about Fishnet's behavior.

"This is all we can do right now. I just hope we aren't here all night," said Fishnet, accepting the reality of the situation. "You want to call Markie and let him know?"

"Yeah, I'll call him. You give the other team a ring. Might as well make sure they have the right address," said Von Hess in reference to Wires and Junior.

⊞ ⊞ ⊞

WIRES AND JUNIOR walked into the Ninth Precinct armed with the right address thanks to Fishnet's call. From the standpoint of the young detectives, this call from Fishnet was the first indication that they were being treated as truly part of a collective effort. For them, this small gesture of inclusion represented the hope that a thawing-out had begun—a process leading to acceptance. The detectives were being overly optimistic: Fishnet still couldn't stomach them. As for Von Hess, he never gave them a second thought one way or the other.

Flashing their gold shields, the two detectives strolled past the lieutenant at the front desk of the Ninth Precinct without challenge. They proceeded up the stairs of the Lower East Side station house to see the detectives. When they arrived at the squad, they discovered the open office vacant. Junior checked the movement log to find out where they'd gone.

"We just missed them; they signed out on a case fifteen minutes ago. They are heading to Queens."

"Ahh, shit," answered Wires. "It'll probably be awhile before they get back."

Junior nodded. "Let's go back and check with the lieutenant on the

Anthony Celano

desk downstairs."

The detectives asked the lieutenant if he would be kind enough to check the precinct business index for Delightful Chaperones. The lieutenant pulled out a small green metal box that was maintained behind the desk. The box contained index cards, in alphabetical order, for most of the businesses operating within the confines of the precinct. The detectives knew some of the cards would be up to date while others would fall short.

They kept their fingers crossed, hoping to catch a break. It was their day. The lieutenant produced an index card with the name and address of the contact person to notify in the event of an emergency at the business where Shirley worked. The two detectives knew that they had just hit the long ball. Considering the seedy nature of the business in question, they felt there would be no index card for it.

The lieutenant passed the card to Junior, who recorded the information into her notebook. Wires inquired if there had been any activity or incidents at the location in question. The lieutenant indicated that he knew of none. He then assigned the officer at the telephone switchboard to research the location. It was established that there had not been any calls for service at the address. There were also no apparent reports generated concerning the entity Delightful Chaperones, Inc.

Junior returned the commercial business card to the lieutenant. The detectives thanked their superior prior to leaving the precinct. Once back inside their car, the two detectives mulled over what to do next. Junior looked over her notepad and read to Wires what she had jotted down.

"Delightful Chaperones, Inc., contact is Anthony Valentino Chiarello, owner, 504 Eighth Avenue, Brooklyn, New York, 11215....There is no phone number on the card."

"Park Slope," informed Wires.

"Yeah...I think the address is right by Methodist Hospital," replied Junior.

"What did you say the guy's name was again?"

"Anthony Valentino Chiarello."

"That's Ant-nee," corrected Wires. "Ant-nee is one of your paisans, right?" joked Wires.

"Are you crazy?" Junior lifted the back of her hand, pretending she was going to swat her partner.

"What do you think?...Should we try to come up with a phone number for this guy and reach out to him?"

Junior nixed the suggestion. "No, Fishnet will have a shit fit if we do anything without him. Let's just call him up now so there are no surprises later."

Wires thought his partner had a point. "Let's call Markie instead so we don't have to deal with that asshole at all."

Offering no contrary opinion, Junior pulled out her cell phone and dialed up Sergeant Markie.

"Sarge, it's me. We were at the Ninth, and we got the name and address of the owner of the escort service. No phone number, though. The guy lives in Park Slope."

Markie liked what he heard. "Good work. Who is he?"

"Anthony Valentino Chiarello, 504 Eighth Avenue, Brooklyn."

Markie was pleased. "Fishnet and Von Hess called in a little while ago. They are sitting on the business....I'll hold them at that location for a while in case someone shows up."

"Do you want us to swing by Eighth Avenue on the way back? We can pass right by the place."

"Yeah...you two go to the house and see if you can dig up this Chiarello. Try to bring him home to Papa Bear...alright?"

"You got it, boss," she said. "Do you want us to try to get a number to call him?"

"No. We don't have any idea of what he has going....Our reaching out may rattle him. We don't want him to boogie on us. Let's just try to catch him by surprise and see if we can get his ass in here, okay?"

"No problem, boss." Junior turned in her seat to face Wires.

"He actually wants us to pick up the guy in Park Slope! What do you make of that?"

Wires shook his head. Shrugging his shoulders, he was not quite sure what to make of the sergeant's gesture of faith in them. "Go figure. I guess things really are looking up." For the first time, Wires and Junior were beginning to become cautiously optimistic in regard to their career in homicide. They started out for Brooklyn with a positive mindset.

The team pulled up to the Brooklyn address of Anthony Chiarello at a slow rate of speed. The detectives had plenty of time to overthink things during the ride. By the time they parked near the wide, four-story brownstone, their leeriness resurfaced; both were wondering what the catch was with Markie. They were curious as to the motive behind their being taken off the back burner. Their paranoia was getting the better of their common sense.

The Eighth Avenue brownstone had a large exterior stoop leading to three apartments on the upper floors. Access to the first-floor apartment was restricted by an old-fashioned iron gate. The name on the mailbox attached to the gate was McHenry. At the top of the brownstone stairs was an unlocked, oversized wooden double door that led into a vestibule, where bells and mailboxes were located. The name on the mailbox for the third floor said, "A. V. Chiarello."

Wires pressed the button, giving the bell two short rings. It took additional rings before the detectives were buzzed in. Once inside, they started up the steps to the third floor, where they were met at the top of the stairs by a corpulent man attired in nothing but a wifebeater t-shirt and powder-blue boxer shorts adorned with small images of Tweety Bird.

"Detectives!" Wires announced himself in a tone making it clear that the law was present.

"Who are you looking for?" the man in his underwear asked cautiously.

The detectives did not respond until they got up the steps. Once they rounded the banister onto the landing, the detectives were on equal footing with the man. As Junior spoke to him, she made it a point not to succumb to the temptation of looking down at the images of the little yellow birds.

"We are looking for Anthony," she said. "Are you Anthony?"

"What is this about?"

"Are you Anthony?" repeated Junior more authoritatively.

"Yeah, yeah...I'm Anthony. What do you want?"

"Chiarello?"

"Yeah, that's right. What is the problem? What did I do?"

"Does Shirley Harris work for you?"

Anthony's eyes opened wide as he now understood the meaning of the visit. "Oh yeah, I just heard about it. It was a terrible thing, her going like that."

"Who told you about it?"

"I heard it from a guy who works for me."

"What guy might that be?"

"Jimmy. He is my manager."

"Jimmy who?"

"Jimmy Regazzo."

"He works for you at the escort service and called you to tell you about Shirley Harris?" Junior was looking to be precise about the information she was receiving.

"Yeah...that's right." Anthony began to have the feeling that he might have said too much.

Wires and Junior exchanged confused looks. They were not exactly on the inside of things, but they nevertheless had gathered enough to give them the impression that no names had been released to anyone outside of law enforcement.

"Where did Regazzo hear about this?" asked Wires.

"Well...uhh...I don't exactly know where he got it from. Somebody probably just told him." By now he knew for certain that he had said too much.

"You own the escort service, right?" Junior wanted to know.

"Yeah."

Junior got to the point of the visit. "Anthony, you have to get dressed and come to the precinct with us. We know very little about Shirley, so we need your help...okay?"

There was some resistance to the female detective. *"Me?* I...have to go to the precinct? Why do I have to go to the precinct? Why can't we talk here?"

Wires stood with Junior by jumping into the conversation. "Anthony... if we could do it here, we wouldn't be dragging you along to the precinct. The boss wants you in. C'mon, let's go....Get dressed."

"But I don't know anything about Shirley! I can't tell you what I don't know!"

"Don't worry; this is no trouble that involves you," said Junior. "We just need your help to clarify a few things."

"Yeah, but—"

"Stop with the 'buts,' Anthony," Wires said firmly. "What are you looking to do here, start a beef? Get dressed; you will be in and out."

Feeling he had little choice, Anthony went along with the program. He accepted his unplanned date with the detectives. He took the law into his apartment, where the authorities waited patiently while he got himself dressed. Anthony's transition into street readiness turned out to be quite an interesting thing to behold. The detectives sat in the living room amused as Anthony selected his clothes. They studied Anthony as he paraded around his crib, meticulously preparing himself to go out into the world.

By the time Anthony was suited up, he presented quite a sight. At thirty-eight years old, he was under average height and shaped like an oversized pear. He had a fleshy face, complete with a few chins. His head pitched forward slightly, as if too heavy to be held up by his fleshy neck. The weight he carried in his midsection was not of the solid variety but rather a loose-hanging, soft flab.

The detectives were doubtful that Anthony ever did any escorting himself. He was not exactly a physical Atlas. Interacting with him, they soon realized Anthony's external deficiencies were countered by an extraordinary ability to think quickly on his feet. His phone conversations, which the detectives could overhear, revealed him as a decisive and persuasive speaker. He strung together his words convincingly and with skilled emphasis when looking to impose his will.

"A little exercise might do this boy some good," whispered Wires, covering his mouth.

"Yeah, the Navy could probably use him...as an anchor," quipped Junior. "But I have to say, this man can talk!"

"Yeah...you said it. This boy can go on with his throat slit!"

Anthony wore his sparse light-brown hair in a comb-over style. The most favorable thing about him was his blue eyes. His sense of fashion was bold, to say the least. He chose to wear a long-sleeved dress shirt that came in tight at the wrists and wide at the forearms. It was the type of shirt favored by swashbucklers, an expensive white silk with its first three brown buttons left unbuttoned from the neck down. From this garment, it was all downhill. His beltless harem trousers were something out of Ringling Brothers. Made of soft cotton, the waistband on the flowered aqua-blue pants found a home nestled under the shade of a kingly belly. Anthony's finishing touches included black socks with top-of-the-line black Nike sneakers. He was deciding which hat to wear when Wires gave him a nudge.

"Anthony...we aren't going to the senior prom. Are we almost ready?"

"Yeah...I'm ready," he answered. "Forget it....I won't wear a hat."

"You don't need one anyway. We got the car outside."

Once they had Anthony tucked in the rear of the unmarked car, Junior called Sergeant Markie. She was having a hard time getting through. After several attempts, she gave up. "What the heck?" she said, frustrated. "Why isn't he picking up the phone?"

"Maybe something is going on with the squad," opined Wires. "Give Fishnet a call."

With some reluctance, Junior called up Fishnet. Wires was listening attentively, anxious to hear how the conversation would go.

"Fishnet? I just want to let you know we got the owner of the escort service with us. We are on our way in with him."

"You do?" asked Fishnet. "How did you find him?"

"From the business cards at the precinct."

"So you snatched him up on your own," Fishnet replied in an accusatory tone. "What...all of a sudden now you guys are in business for yourself?"

"Huh? What are you talking about? We aren't in business for ourselves....Sergeant Markie sent us to pick him up."

"Why would he send you to do that?"

"You'll have to ask him yourself about that." Junior didn't appreciate having to answer Fishnet's questions.

"Forget it. Put him on ice until I get to the squad. But remember, this is my case, not yours, so I will conduct the interview."

"Don't worry; he's all yours." Junior clearly regretted making the call.

"What's up?" Wires was interested in what had been said on the other end of the conversation.

"The man is pissed off. Screw him! Who is he anyway? I've had it with this bullshit!" Junior had reached the end of her rope.

"Yeah...I hear you." It was all that Wires could say until his partner cooled off.

Wires remained in neutral for the entire drive to the precinct. It took that long for Junior to simmer down. Anthony was perceptive enough to see that something was upsetting the detective, but he had sense enough to remain quiet. Sinking into his seat, he gazed out the window to take in the scenery as it went by. There was silence in the car throughout the rest of the ride.

16

ANTHONY BOY SWEATS

WIRES MINDED HIS GUEST in the interview room as they awaited Von Hess and Fishnet. Anthony Boy was quick to look away every time he inadvertently made eye contact with the detective. It was an awkward situation for him; he'd committed so many crimes that projecting innocence presented quite an ordeal. His efforts to appear pure were complicated by the stress of not knowing if the detectives were restricting their investigation to the two girls in the trunk. His uncertainty prompted the need for him to do something. Hoping to gain some answers, he engaged Wires in conversation.

"So what happens now, detective?"

"You'll be asked a few questions, that's all," responded Wires.

"Questions about what? I don't know anything!"

"All you have to do is stick to the truth," Wires advised calmly, "and you'll be okay."

Things being no clearer, Anthony tried approaching it another way. "Who is going to be doing the asking? *You?*"

Wires looked at him, not sure if Anthony was being deliberately demeaning. He gave him the benefit of the doubt. "Not me. A couple of other detectives, the ones who are assigned to the case, will be talking to you."

"This is just about the two girls...right?"

"You'll see."

The vagueness of the exchange did nothing to ease Anthony Boy's doubts. Sticking to the truth was a ridiculous proposition, one that merited no consideration. Not knowing what to expect had Anthony Boy's mind working overtime. Trying to figure out how much the detectives knew about him was impossible. This was the first time he had ever been pulled in by the authorities solely for questioning. His past experiences with the law had been cut-and-dried affairs that saw his being taken into custody as the result of being arrested for specific crimes. These old busts were real-time incidents, his being charged for a crime he had been caught in the act of committing. He was unable to escape the feeling that his current predicament seemed to be more serious, something more involved. He was concerned that the detectives might be plotting to rope him into a major organized crime investigation. Anthony knew he didn't have a RICO case looming over his head because these guys weren't feds. But nevertheless, he was concerned. He took another stab at prying some information out of Wires.

"So this isn't your case then, detective?"

"No...I'm here to assist."

"You work in this precinct, though...right?"

"No. I'm with the homicide squad."

Anthony Boy gulped. *"Homicide!"* His words came out with emotion, as did the pained expression that came over him.

This was the first time Wires had identified himself publicly as a member of the elite squad. It felt good to him to announce that he was a big-leaguer, working in a unit whose day began only when the hourglass emptied for others.

Hearing from Wires that he came from homicide was an alarming revelation to Anthony. "Are you saying I'm involved in some kind of murder case here?" asked an astonished Anthony Boy.

"I didn't say that."

"But how do I fit in, then? I had nothing to do with nothing!"

"Sit tight, Anthony. The other detectives will be here shortly, so save the questions for them."

Again Anthony Boy was quieted without satisfaction, leaving his mind to work freely over whether or not to reach out to his lawyer. He concluded he could afford to wait a little longer before calling up his attorney. He disliked the notion of having to pay for a service he might not actually need....After all, it was not as if they had him in handcuffs.

The waiting gave Anthony time for his imagination to continue running wild. Now beginning to prey on his mind were the many stories he had heard over the years, endless tales of brutality exchanged among the old-timers he hung out with. His friends had lots of experience with the law, some dating back to the thirties. Their anecdotes about detective behavior, however embellished, were a continuous conditioning for him. He was convinced that once in the clutches of "the bulls," as those with gold shields were called back in the day, he was in for a bad time.

With this thought floating through his mind, Anthony Boy began to take a closer look at Wires. He attempted to measure the detective's ability to inflict pain in the event that was on the program. Completing his scrutiny, he decided to again engage the detective in conversation.

"How long am I going to be here? I got things to do...a business to run." "Not too much longer." Wires was being less than truthful.

Anthony Boy noticed how the detective had a nervous habit of flexing his upper arms, thus straining the sleeves of his jacket. Judging from the detective's barrel chest and wide shoulders, Anthony figured Wires to have an eighteen-inch neck.

"Jeez, they couldn't hang you, Detective! What have you got, a twenty-inch neck?"

Wires smiled at Anthony. "No, just eighteen and a half inches."

"You gotta be working out. What are you, some kind of athlete?"

"Just some weight-lifting, and I do a little boxing to keep in shape," advised Wires.

"Nice." A dour expression came over Anthony's face. Hearing that the detective was a civil-service Joe Palooka hardly put Anthony Boy at ease. Wires was real flesh and blood, someone who could hurt you, not some cartoon fighter in the Sunday comics.

Working himself up, the notion that he might take a shellacking became increasingly real to him the longer he thought about it. In short order he convinced himself that now, inside this house of pain, the roughhouse was inevitable. Anthony Boy hated violence. Spending his youth hanging with street thugs had exposed him to lots of unsavory conduct, but he always was able to get by on guile as opposed to muscle. Powerhouses like Swing and Red were the real tough guys....They were outright killers who pissed ice water. They took what they wanted and knew how to hold onto it. The two possessed what Anthony lacked and respected most...balls. The deep thinking about his two friends fortified Anthony with a newfound inner strength. He concluded that to appear weak in his current situation would not serve him well. He felt his best option was to try to bluff his way through by emulating Swing and Red. Anthony Boy was resolved to hang tough and not give the detectives anything.

Once 1:00 a.m. rolled around, Markie and his team had the squad room all to themselves. The evening-shift detectives in the squad had just gone off duty. The timing had worked out well. Markie, Von Hess, and Fishnet were in the squad commander's office getting the skinny about Anthony Boy from Junior. Fishnet was less than thrilled by having to sit quietly and listen to Junior. The few minutes he had to behave himself seemed a lot longer to him.

After Junior noted that Anthony Boy had known in advance about the demise of the two women, it was made clear to her that there was a suspicion that Harris was in some manner connected to the escort service. Markie thought that if correct in his speculation, Harris had played a role in getting his daughter the escort job.

"You guys go in and do the interview," Markie told Von Hess and Fishnet. "See what you can do with the fat boy."

Markie then looked at Junior. "You and your partner take a break; it has been a long run, and there will be lots more to do. I'll call you when I need you."

"We're okay," she said in response. "You sure you don't have anything else for us to do, boss?"

"For now, do as I say and take a blow. I'll call you."

The young detective maintained a poker face.

"Don't worry," Markie said encouragingly. "It looks like we are locked in for the duration here...so be grateful and take advantage of the few minutes you're getting."

"Got it. Thanks, boss." She was tired, so the order really had been what she wanted to hear.

Junior left the office feeling that Markie was not such a bad boss to work for. Later, when alone with Wires, she stated, "Markie is okay," summing up her feelings simply.

"Yeah," replied Wires. "Either way, this baby is turning into *mucho dinero* for us."

"That's true...but don't worry, we're earning it," responded Junior.

"Definitely. You know, I'd really love to solve this one." Junior nodded in agreement as the two headed for the precinct lounge.

⊞ ⊞ ⊞

INSIDE THE INTERVIEW ROOM, Fishnet and Von Hess were preparing to engage Anthony Boy. Fishnet went into his act by first removing his jacket. With his gun now displayed, the detective leaned against the entrance door to the room. Lighting up, he began taking long drags on his Camel, slowly blowing the smoke in Anthony's direction.

Seeing the way Fishnet carried himself reminded Anthony Boy of a guy trying *too* hard to show that he was a tough guy. Once the smoke started coming his way, he concluded that the detective was a real asshole. What *was* impressive, however, was the exposed roscoe. Fishnet's gun

Anthony Celano

fascinated Anthony Boy....It represented the equalizer. Having a piece at the ready eliminated any need to fear a Red, a Swing, or anyone breathing. Yet Anthony Boy was a realist....He knew he didn't have it in him to be a gun-toting desperado. He accepted his limitations—at best, he was still only a wannabe gangster.

Drawing from deep within, Anthony Boy went up against the questioning of Von Hess. He somehow mustered the resilience to hang tough. His back-and-forth joust with the detective was producing minimal information for the right side of the law. The only thing coming out of the exchange thus far that represented an indisputable fact was that Anthony Boy wasn't going to talk without the screws being put to him but good.

Markie could see this for himself as he stood alone in the hall, quietly spying from behind the one-way glass. Anthony Boy grew stronger with each passing minute as his confidence was restored. He proved to be quite adroit at answering questions once he regained his normal composure.

"So you're telling us that you don't know who it was that Shirley was slated to see?" Von Hess asked. "That you don't know your own customers...?"

"That's it....I have no idea."

Fishnet finally reached his limit, reacting harshly. "Don't hand us that bullshit, pal!" the detective shouted. "How the fuck could you possibly not know?"

"What can I tell you?" came the answer without any elaboration.

"You can tell us the fucking truth, you fat, blimpy fuck!"

Anthony was unmoved by Fishnet's insults. His reply came in the form of a casual shrug. By now, he felt he was in the power seat. He'd gambled correctly that hanging tough would see him through the storm. No longer was he concerned about a smacking around. He stood confident that if that were going to take place, it would have already happened.

Fishnet persisted. "C'mon, dickhead, tell us who the broad went to go see so we can move on."

"So sue me for having a poor memory, Detective. I got nothing to tell you," came Anthony's defiant response.

Markie had an unobstructed view of the escort service owner as he sparred with the detectives. The actions exhibited by Anthony when asked specific questions provided Markie with a good insight. Anthony Boy had a tendency to look down as he massaged his own left hand when asked key questions. For Markie, this was a telltale sign that the business owner was being less than truthful. The hand massage tipped him....Thanks to Mousey Flavin, the sergeant recognized the rub as the act of a bluffer. During a kid penny poker game played on a neighborhood stoop, Mousey Flavin had engaged in the very same nervous habit when he would boldly raise, knowing full well that he had failed to pull a card.

Markie could see that the detectives were traveling in circles. A new strategy was needed because they couldn't hold Anthony in a room forever. The best they had been able to pull out of Anthony Boy was that Shirley had been working for him on a part-time basis, going out on escorts for a few months without incident, and that she had been working out well. Markie was anxious to take a crack at Anthony Boy himself. He entered the interview room to advise that it was time to take a break in the action. He had Fishnet remove Anthony Boy to a new venue for interviewing...the squad commander's office.

Markie called Von Hess aside for a private word. "So what is the verdict?" Markie asked.

"You heard it, boss. He is not budging. He's definitely holding back... and he's smart enough to know we're on a fishing expedition here."

"How do you size him up?"

"Well, I don't see him behaving with the nervousness of a guilty guy who actually pulled a trigger if that is what you mean." Opinions provided by Von Hess were always respected by Markie.

"Do you think he is strong?"

"Right now he is. Things are going his way, and he knows it," he answered. "But unless I'm very mistaken, this guy would crack like an egg if we had a little something to pull on his short hairs with."

"What do you think we should do next?"

"Well, boss, we flopped with good guy–bad guy. He is not buying it... without some leverage, we're screwed."

"Can you think of anything?"

"We need something to squeeze with if we are ever going to get to the juice. What about we try it with a female on the team?...You know, a totally new and less imposing face to go at him,?" suggested Von Hess.

But Sergeant Markie had his own idea regarding what to do next. "I don't think so. Teams are not working with this guy. How about I go in solo?...You know, one on one."

Von Hess shrugged. "Yeah, why don't we give it a shot? If you don't mind going at him, we can use you as the bad guy leverage against him later."

"That's the ticket," agreed Markie. "You know, we still haven't run a criminal rap sheet on this tub of shit. Do me a favor; check him out."

"You got it, Sarge."

"And Ollie, don't forget to see if the organized crime units have anything on him. He can't be an altar boy....That is for certain."

"Righto, boss."

Anthony Celano

FISHNET SAT ANTHONY BOY on the couch in the squad commander's office. The detective sat across from Anthony as he waited for Markie to come into the room. The detective's mind went on one of its excursions. Fishnet had himself in the squad alone with Anthony Boy, taking his exercise as he used the pimp's head for a game of handball. Fishnet hated to lose—so Anthony needed to be put through Fishnet's imaginary wringer. The fact that he and Von Hess had not been able to succeed was unacceptable.

THE SERGEANT ASSUMED his rightful place behind the desk in the squad commander's office. Anthony Boy, slouched back on the couch, waited with what seemed to be a bored expression. His confidence evolved into smugness. This bothered Markie—he disliked it when the opposition got too comfortable. Without some degree of distress, the job of gaining information was made tougher. Markie engaged his prey psychologically, with a solid determination to break him.

"I'm Sergeant Markie from the homicide squad," he began officially.

Anthony wore an expression that demonstrated he was unimpressed. The escort service owner had turned from a Jekyll to a Hyde. In a remarkably short period of time, he had made the transformation from nervousness to arrogance. His strength was drawn from the belief that the detectives had nothing on him; if they had, that ship would have sailed by now. With that confident thought, Anthony Boy saw no reason not to go on the offensive.

"I'm talking to the man in charge over here, right?"

"That's right."

"Can I ask why I'm still here? I told you everything I know....Now, either pinch me or I'm going to leave."

Markie chose to ignore the ultimatum. "You own the escort business?"

"Look...you don't read me. I'm not doing this anymore....I'm outta here." Anthony rose from his seat.

"Where are you going?" asked Markie, raising his voice. "Will you sit down a minute?...I just want to talk to you for *Christ's* sake!"

Anthony Boy was taken aback. Surprised and not knowing how to take Markie, Anthony gave it a few more minutes. "What is this? You already know I own the business!"

"Sit down and relax a second," said the sergeant. "This is a serious matter. Think about it....How would you feel if Shirley was your sister or daughter? Let me tell you something, Red Harris didn't look to run out of here when we interviewed him....He looked to *help* us. Did you ever hear of Red Harris...Shirley's father? I think *he* would want you to help us."

Hearing the name of Red Harris caused Anthony to stiffen. He slowly sank back down into his chair, petrified at the very mention of the name. His body language revealed to Markie that the escort service owner did in fact know Red. Anthony Boy could see that the sergeant had a few unexpected cards up his sleeve. Unsure of exactly how much Markie knew, Anthony thought it best to settle down.

"Okay...so now what, sergeant?"

"All you have to do is relax, pal...that's what. There is no heavy lifting we want from you."

"Okay...but this is really bullshit now, and you know it. I think I may be calling my lawyer if I'm not out of here soon." There was now a noticeable quiver in Anthony's lips as he spoke.

The sergeant's face tightened, projecting a taut smile. In as calm a voice as he could muster, Markie responded to Anthony's mention of an attorney. "Certainly...you can have your lawyer anytime you say, but remember something....You are not under arrest here. Nobody is looking to put you in jail. I just want you to help us." Markie went into a pitch that he hoped would sufficiently rattle Anthony Boy enough to get him to say something of value. "Do you want the story in a nutshell...undiluted and straight up?"

Anthony Boy nodded cautiously. "Go on....I'm listening, sergeant."

"First off, let's look at the obvious from my perspective. You run a business....Is the business legitimate? Or are you operating an on-call whorehouse?"

The bluntness of the statement got Anthony's attention.

"The more I think about it, the more I wonder: how does the money come into this business? Cash? Credit cards? Where does the green finally wind up, and who gets what?" Markie was staring directly into Anthony's face. "These are just some of the easy questions to think about. Are there appropriate financial records maintained? Silent partners? No-shows on the payroll? Taxes on the up and up? I'm sure you have these answers...right, Anthony?"

Markie paused, looking for a reaction. There was nothing other than the sick look on Anthony's face. So he continued on. "Do we really need to sit here jerking on each other's chain while a couple of stiffs in the trunk of a car remain unexplained? You getting the landscape here, Anthony?"

In fact, Anthony Boy was struggling to comprehend where this was going. As a result, he offered no response.

"I don't know. Maybe I need some help on this....say, an IRS bean counter or some other fed, like in FBI. I know you would love to meet the feds...right, Anthony?"

Anthony Celano

The sergeant could see that Anthony was fading. He decided to step up the game and play a hunch: he was certain Anthony Boy was connected to organized crime. "How about your pals, Anthony? Your pals would thank you profusely for bringing around the heat of the federal government... wouldn't they, Anthony? And what about Red?...Do you really want to get on his bad side?"

Anthony was deflated. With his smugness long vanished, he reverted to the meek Dr. Jekyll. He looked at Sergeant Markie silently, with a dead seriousness, as he listened.

"*Capisce, mi amico?*" asked Markie softly, invoking the few words in Italian he knew, asking if his friend understood.

The words *fed* and *Red* hit their mark squarely. The ache in Anthony Boy's stomach dominated. These were people whom Anthony dreaded, and he responded as Markie had hoped. Anthony spoke in a low, controlled voice.

"Whoooo...Sergeant...let's try and be reasonable here." Anthony raised both his hands, palms up, for emphasis. "Where are we going with this now? There's no need to get crazy here," he said softly, looking to negotiate with the sergeant. "Let's talk about it....We can definitely work something out."

Markie responded from a position of strength. "Okay, let's talk. Keep in mind one thing, though. With me, it's all about talking....With Shirley's father, it isn't."

The truthfulness of the statement jarred Anthony Boy into sitting upright. "I know that."

Markie sensed that he had Anthony on the ropes. "I'm glad you understand we are talking about *your* future here...not mine."

Anthony Boy held his tongue as he hastily tried to figure things out. He was uncertain exactly how far behind the eight ball he actually was. He was sure of one thing....Aside from having to deal with Red Harris, he could not under any circumstances chance the exposure of the secret he had held for years.

"Here." Markie pushed the telephone on his desk toward Anthony Boy.

The two men were looking at each other intently.

"You see the phone....Do we start with the calls?" asked Markie coldly. "I'll even let you dial the numbers that will dismantle you."

When feigning ruthlessness, Markie could be very convincing. The possibility of ruin shook Anthony Boy up but good. There was no more hand-massaging to be seen now...just some sweat...especially at the thought of Red. Anthony Boy remained silent as he tried to hold in passing gas. He became a believer.

"Look, Sergeant, I don't need trouble with you guys. Try and understand...I got my reasons to consider. That's why I have to be careful."

"So let's get to the point and talk to each other, Anthony....What reasons?" Markie remained stern.

"You have to first promise to lay off regarding the feds."

"Okay...then talk to me....I have no love affair going with the feds myself." It was Markie's first step toward projecting himself as someone Anthony could play ball with.

Anthony Boy felt trapped between a rock and a hard place. He desperately wanted to do something but was not exactly sure what to do. He had unsuccessfully tried to figure Markie out. He had convinced himself to trust Markie because if he was being on the level, he represented a pathway. Out of sheer desperation, Anthony Boy took the plunge to commit before he even realized he was doing so.

"My first cousin is Ella Barone....Ever hear of her? She's the FBI agent who works on all the big mob cases."

This was more than Markie had bargained for. "Yeah, I know her. What's the family connection?"

"She's the daughter of my mother's sister...my aunt Marie's kid. So if you know her, then you also know how she gets off making cases and putting everybody away. Remember this, please....She can't surface. So do we at least understand each other in that regard, sergeant?"

"Okay...no problem," Markie assured him. "She'll be written out of the script."

At this point, even thinking about a lawyer was out of the question. The last thing Anthony needed was for a legal representative working for the family to find out about his secret.

"So what do I need to do here to straighten out with you?" Anthony Boy was approaching Markie from his crooked side. He was looking to see if he could first buy his way out by paying Markie off.

Progressing this far along with Anthony Boy gratified Markie. It made him feel good to have leverage enough to put an end to the cat-and-mouse game they had been playing. Anthony Boy had conceded a big advantage once he invoked the name of his FBI agent cousin. It was an edge that was going to be exploited.

"I know Ella Barone well. I worked joint cases with her when I was in the DA's office. We worked with her over in the Eastern and Southern District when our investigations overlapped." Markie let the words sink in before he went on. "We put lots of the boys who controlled the piers away."

In truth Markie had never met Barone, but he knew of her work on the waterfront by reading the papers. The sergeant began to press his advantage. "I take it Ella doesn't know what you do and who you run with?"

"Shit no....*That's* what I'm trying to tell you!" Anthony Boy was

Anthony Celano

starting to get agitated. "Please...she's got no idea what my business is. She thinks I run a fucking car service. Jesus...I even heard from my mother that she is in line to be bumped up....We got a regular J. Edgar Hoover in my family with that one!"

Markie laughed at that line. "I see the conflict."

"Why don't we just work this out? I can be very generous in ironing out this little wrinkle we got here. How about it, sarge?...Let's get together and we fix it...huh?"

Markie finally got the drift that he was being bribed. "Let's not go down a road that could make things worse for you, Anthony. You tell me the truth, and you walk away...no strings and no bullshit. You lie...well, it's your funeral."

Anthony Boy was annoyed at the sergeant's lack of pliability. After a deep breath, he responded. "Okay...okay, shoot." The words shot out of his mouth. He had grown tired of the futility of talking to a brick wall.

Once Anthony Boy threw in the towel, Markie got right to it. "So how does a guy like you get into the escort racket?...You need someone behind you...a friend, right? "

"True....A friend of mine holds up his end, and I run the business."

"He's a silent partner?"

"You could say that."

"You gotta have the right power behind you, a guy with the right juice... no?"

"Why you asking that? I thought this was about the dead girls," questioned Anthony warily.

"Would you prefer that your cousin ask the questions?"

"I hear you," came the defeated reply.

"Well, is that person your partner?" asked Markie.

"No....Well, yeah, sort of. My friend is like you said...a silent partner."

"Did you know the other girl...Barbara Allen?" Markie switched directions.

"No, I never even heard of her...on the level."

"I feel like a cup of coffee," Markie suddenly declared out of nowhere. "Want a cup?"

Anthony Boy answered up quickly. "I'm pretty hungry. You guys rousted me out of the house before I ate anything."

"I'll send out for bagels. How do you like your coffee?"

"Get me two...pumpernickel, cream cheese, and a large green tea with lemon, no milk."

"Okay, two it is. I need some time to think over this situation regarding this aunt of yours. I figure you have lots more to give." Markie left the office so Anthony could stew for a bit.

The sergeant was confident that the seed he had planted would eventually sprout large enough to break Anthony Boy and his harem pants wide open. He walked into the squad room. Fishnet immediately rose from his seat, as did Von Hess.

"I think we got him," Markie announced. "This bozo's first cousin is the FBI agent Ella Barone. He is scared shitless of this coming out, so we have an angle to work."

"Barone? She's the fed in the papers all the time," noted Fishnet.

"Tell you the truth, I don't even care about her. I just didn't want to make it look like I *didn't* know her," explained Markie. "Now she makes no difference. We have him hooked."

"Great!" Von Hess responded.

"You want me to go in there and step up the pressure, boss?" asked Fishnet.

"No, not necessary. You guys come in and talk to him nicely. Let him stew for a minute or two first. How did we do with the background on him?

On cue, Von Hess recited from his notes. "We got three arrests in Manhattan, one in the Fifth Precinct for selling fireworks, one in the Ninth for selling untaxed cigarettes out of the back room of a pizza parlor, and another one in the Ninth for running an after-hours club. He paid his fines and walked on all three."

"That's it?"

"No, actually there is one more...a pretty old one in Manhattan from when he was sixteen years old. They got him in a stolen car."

"You would have to be connected to run an after-hours club," observed Markie.

Fishnet then reported what he had gathered from intelligence. "Anthony Valentino Chiarello. They call him Anthony Boy. Our man is thirty-eight or forty years old, depending on which date of birth you believe. He is the godson of Fiore Jerome, now deceased—Fiore was an eastside Milano soldier. Anthony was at the wake of Carmine D'Angelo, and then he's at the Milano family Christmas party at the Log Room on Avenue C in Manhattan last year."

"So he is definitely connected....No wonder he turned white as a ghost when I mentioned Red Harris," injected Markie. "Go on."

"He was spotted at Belmont Park with Milano soldier Benny DiTulleo and capo Augie D'Angelo twice. Another time he is at the track with Augie alone. Then he shows up a bunch of times at the D'Angelo Brothers Social Club and the bar alongside it, The Adjustment Room."

"All good," commented Markie.

"All this is relatively recent shit too," Fishnet added. "It looks like the D'Angelo crew is where it's at. This fat prick we got here is mobbed up with them for sure."

Anthony Celano

"Good show," Markie stated with satisfaction. "Now we know how Shirley must have gotten her job. Red Harris is also part of the D'Angelo crew. The pieces all fit into place."

Fishnet added more to the conversation. "One more thing...the escort service...the building is owned by a woman named Angela D'Angelo. That's the name of Carmine D'Angelo's widow."

"Okay...here is the plan," began the sergeant. "I want you to lay it on thick about how tight I am with this Agent Barone, how we put away mob guys together on the waterfront, how I'm in solid with the FBI, and so on."

"Right, boss, got it," said Von Hess.

"I want you to tell him I'm prepared to call the agent to tell her who his playmates are. Be sure to mention the name D'Angelo. Dollars to donuts Augie D'Angelo is his partner in that escort business. It has to be!"

"One small question, sarge?"

"What's that, Ollie?"

"How could it be that Ella Barone *doesn't* know who her own cousin is?"

"Barone is no moron. My guess is that she probably does know about Anthony, covered herself by apprising her bosses, and everyone is just working around it. She is likely keeping things in the shade and away from her relatives without letting on that she is onto fat boy."

"Makes sense."

Markie had his detectives pumped, and he was genuinely struck by Fishnet going the extra yard concerning the identification of the owner of the building. (Fishnet, of course, never let on that it was Von Hess who had actually looked into it.)

After they grabbed the food, Von Hess and Fishnet went directly to the squad commander's office. Fishnet gave a separate bag containing the green tea and two pumpernickel bagels with cream cheese to their guest.

"Should we call the captain?" asked Fishnet.

"Not yet. No sense bothering the captain until we finish here. Once this piece is put to bed, then I'll make some calls," answered Markie.

The sergeant left the office so the detectives had time alone to talk to Anthony Boy. Fishnet and Von Hess wasted no time entering into the next phase. Anthony had wolfed down the two bagels in a New York minute. All he had left to work on was the tea.

"You know, this Markie is nobody to screw around with. He can be treacherous when he means business," cautioned Von Hess.

"I believe it!" acknowledged Anthony.

"The man is straight as an arrow...but don't let that fool you....He can be ruthless," Fishnet warned. "He'll cut your throat in a second if he doesn't get what he is after."

"For what? I'm already cooperating—"

Von Hess didn't let him finish his sentence. "Makes no difference to us how this goes, Anthony. We get paid either way." Then the detective became almost fatherly in his pitch. "You seem like a decent guy to me, so I'm just giving you a heads-up...but again, you do what you want. My advice, though, is to just give us whatever it is you know and be done with it."

"What is it he wants to know from me? I didn't do anything. Hey...do I need help here or what?"

"Yeah, you do...if you want the sergeant to call up your fed cousin and tell her that your partner is D'Angelo. C'mon, Anthony, smarten the fuck up ,will you?!" Fishnet's response came over as a counterpunch, fast and accurate. It did the trick....The final indications of Anthony's false façade of toughness toppled like a house of cards.

Anthony Boy's face changed instantly, turning a sickening color at the thought of the worst-case outcome. There was silence. His failure to deny the D'Angelo connection was as good as an admission to the investigators. That Anthony Boy was either partners with or fronting for Swing Blade D'Angelo was no longer conjecture.

"How did you guys find out Augie and me are partners?" Anthony asked once he gathered himself.

"Good police work," Fishnet quipped.

Anthony ignored the remark; he was not welcoming levity. With the desperation of a person who knew he was overmatched, he spoke up. "What do you want to know? Just guarantee me one thing...that my cousin and Augie don't find out about each other. If Augie gets wind of this...we are talking my doom here!"

"Relax and play ball, you will be covered," Fishnet guaranteed. "No one will know a thing."

"Leave Sergeant Markie to us. It will be okay as long as we have something to give him," promised Von Hess.

"So how did you come to hire Shirley?" queried Fishnet.

"It was Augie. He called me out of the blue regarding the girl. He says for me to hire Joey Red's daughter....I don't ask any questions on account I'm with Augie."

"Joey Red?" Von Hess asked.

"Red Harris....They also call him Joey Red."

"Where does the name Red come from?"

"Not sure....Something to do with red paint, I think."

"How does the money work?"

Anthony Boy explained the financial arrangements. "The girls pay us a turn-out fee of a hundred dollars for the privilege of working. We waived that cost for Shirley because of her solid bloodline."

"You decided that?" Fishnet asked.

"No, Augie made the call. I balked at the idea, actually, but Augie calls

Anthony Celano

the shots."

"We got it. Go on," encouraged Von Hess.

"The client pays us a flat rate of a thousand bucks a day for the escort regardless of what that involves. We split that money seventy–thirty with the girl, or guy, in favor of the house."

"Pretty steep, isn't it?" Fishnet was impressed at the profit margins.

"Not for my base....My clients all make big money."

"Same price for male escorts?"

"No. To deliver men, we charge women twelve-fifty a day. When the job calls for a GI, then we got a special on our hands and jack it up to fifteen hundred."

"What is a GI?" Fishnet asked.

"A GI is a gay interlude."

"This is some good business!" Fishnet held the enterprise with a newfound respect.

"Yeah, it really is, once you get the right clients....The sky is the limit when it comes to needing a little company."

"So you are putting them all out turning tricks?" Von Hess inquired.

"No...I send out escorts only. Any extra service my people provide, they do on their own and without any urging or knowledge of the office. Whatever they pluck the chicken for is theirs." This was a modified version of Anthony's pat answer whenever asked such a question.

"So you don't send them out just for sex?"

"It is not about sex from my end. We don't know all the moves, and we never ask. Some guys just want to be seen with somebody hot; others like to take trips to show off who they are. One guy just likes to make his ex jealous. There are a lot of crazy people out there."

"Did Shirley turn tricks?" Fishnet posed the question.

"She was supposed to be mostly used as an escort—unless, of course..." Anthony caught himself. He tried to salvage his comment, but it was too late. "Besides, pimping is something we never do. Augie made it clear that he wanted it that way."

"So now you are saying that she turned no tricks?"

"Look, as far as I know, she didn't. But who the fuck knows what she did once she was in with a client? Cash talks in this business."

"When was her last job?"

"Offhand, I don't really know."

"You guys keep a record of these calls for service, don't you?"

"Yeah, of course," answered Anthony to Fishnet's question.

"So when did Shirley last work for you?"

"I can't be sure. I got a lot of people going out."

Looking for an appointment confirmation, Von Hess stepped in. "But you do have a record of clients and when she was scheduled to see them, do you not?"

"Whatever I have is all in the computer."

"Let's go for a ride so we can take a look-see," said Von Hess, rising from his chair. The detective left the office, leaving Fishnet alone with Anthony.

Von Hess went directly to Markie. "Worked like a charm. We have him on board. They keep a record concerning the jobs they send the talent out on. We have to go check his computer to see what the trip sheet looks like."

"Call in with the results when you are done."

"Righto, boss....You got it," answered Von Hess.

17

GETTING
RED HOT

"OKAY," MARKIE TOLD THE desk lieutenant, "tell him I'm coming down now."

"Just do me a favor if you can; try to get this guy out of here quick."

"Why is that?"

"He gives me the creeps!" replied the lieutenant.

Sergeant Markie dragged his feet on his way to the stairs that would take him down to the first floor of the station house, where Red Harris was waiting. When he got to the top of the stairs, he stretched his arms and took a deep inhale, expanding his chest. He threw his shoulders back and sucked his stomach in, hoping to display as much physical impressiveness as possible. He wanted to appear as masculine as possible when meeting Red Harris. It was a guy thing. When the sergeant reached ground level, he became uneasy as he looked upon what appeared to be an angry Harris. Red's hands were balled into fists, his arms extended stiffly at his sides.

After noticing the sergeant, the big man turned his body toward him, giving the appearance of a man preparing to rumble. Red's advance was perceived as menacing enough to alarm Markie, whose experience had taught him how to react in such situations.

Standing his ground, Markie prepared to draw. He not-so-subtly folded his arms, placing his right hand inside his suit jacket. Reaching for the revolver hanging from his shoulder holster, he took hold of the weapon. With a firm grip on his gun, he lifted his left arm while opening the palm of his hand, signaling to Red that he should not advance any further. The Death Maker stopped in his tracks, believing that Markie was prepared to shoot him.

Markie had every reason to be cautious. Aside from his reputation as a stone killer, Red was a giant compared to the five-foot-ten sergeant. Even on his best day, Markie could never measure up to Red in a hand-to-hand confrontation. The sergeant's preparation for battle was a theatrical performance that turned out to be a successful ploy. Markie managed to distract Shirley's father, preventing him from doing anything stupid. Leaving nothing to chance, the sergeant felt that under the circumstances, this was the best way to react to a yet-unknown and possibly volatile problem. Red might have been halted, but he remained undaunted. He pointed a finger at Markie and hissed.

"You! I want to fucking talk to you."

With his machismo now on the line, Markie responded to the challenge without apparent fear or hesitation. "Alright. If we gotta talk, let's go outside and do it."

Taken by surprise for a second time at the temerity exhibited by Markie, Red looked at the sergeant curiously and slowly nodded his head.

Markie knew he needed to set some boundaries, to let the big man know that he could not just walk into a police station to treat a detective sergeant like one of his extortion victims. Once outside, Markie led Red around the building and into the parking lot. The spaciousness of the open lot afforded the sergeant the range he needed. He was either going to bullshit Harris until he could find a way to neutralize the big man's aggression or fence with him while waiting for help to arrive. Markie began with his standard strategy of finding common ground in order to reduce conflict. The tactic called for him to let it appear that he and his opposition were in agreement, both equally outraged over whatever it was that had crinkled the undershorts of his adversary.

But first he needed to find out exactly what that was.

"Listen," Markie began, "I can see that you got a beef...so talk to me." Markie was fishing...hoping to uncover what exactly the problem was.

Although Red was angry, his ire did not overcome how perplexed he was by Markie. The big man's intimidating manner of speaking didn't have the effect on the sergeant that he had become accustomed to. As Red wrestled with this thought, the sergeant sensed a reduction in his outrage. From Markie's perspective, this was a major breakthrough.... Red was willing to talk.

"I got a beef? My daughter is gone...turns up in a fucking trunk, and

Anthony Celano

you got the balls to tell me I got a beef? My daughter is called a *whore* in death, and you say that I got a beef?" Red raised his voice more and more with each accusation. "The world is told that I'm some fucking Al Capone who sired a junkie, and all you come up with is that *I got a fucking beef?*"

Markie offered no response. His strategy called for waiting Red out, knowing that eventually Harris would have to tire of talking.

"I go along with you guys and wind up with my shit being put in the street...and why?" Red then answered his own question. "So you hard-ons can get your name in the fucking paper! Talk to me about it, pal! Tell me about my beef....I'm listening!" The big man was roaring.

As Red was working his way toward mayhem—a destination he was not unfamiliar with— Markie remained quiet. Red looked at the sergeant as he waited for an answer. His expression turned to one of bewilderment as he began to wonder why the sergeant had not responded. Once five seconds of silence had elapsed, Markie chose to engage. Using a subdued voice, he hoped that his lowered tone would take their conversation to a better place.

"Listen to me for a minute....You've got the wrong guy here," began the sergeant. "You're singing to the choir. The one name you will not find in any newspaper is mine."

Red said nothing....He was listening. "You and me are on the same page here."

"Oh yeah? Tell me, what fucking page is that?" Red demanded to know.

Markie saw his opportunity to redirect Red's wrath elsewhere...to someone far away from where he was currently standing with Red.

"The name you saw was of some asshole captain. He's the guy who spoke to the papers, not me." Seeing that Red was paying attention, Markie continued. "Do you think I get up in the morning looking to talk to reporters? It's not the little guy....It's the brass who does that shit." Markie felt safe dragging the captain into the conversation because he wasn't anywhere in sight.

"What captain? Where does he work?"

"He works all over....The guy is a duty captain." Red wasn't familiar with the term. "What's that?"

"A detective duty captain covers the entire city when no other captains are working. Look...I've got no control over these guys, no more than you have control over whoever it is that you listen to."

"Yeah...well, let me tell you about captains....You can buy anyone of them hard-ons for five bucks and an ice cream," said Red angrily.

Markie kept his lip buttoned, allowing Red to rage on about all the unethical captains he'd come to hear about over the years. Once Harris exhausted his diatribe on captains, the sergeant again moved to shift the anger—this time away from the captain. He guided Red's venom to the media.

"You know, a captain can't control the press. It's the reporters who are the real shit-stirrers....A guy like Chick Aprile suckers the captains in by flattering them with attention. Once he gets a little information to work with, he'll paint a picture any color he likes. Aprile can take a stolen bike and turn it into the Lufthansa robbery."

"That's right! Aprile wrote that story. I know that fucking runt's old man....He's a midtown ticket agent and degenerate gambler."

Markie was glad to see he'd successfully shifted the hate to Aprile...a good place for wrath to be.

"That little piss is no fucking good!" shouted Red. "I know where he drinks, where he shits, and who he's screwing, and...forget about it.... You got no idea where that guy goes to dip his dick!"

Markie was out of the danger zone for sure now. There was one final person he needed to shift some blame to...Red himself. "We have to be honest with ourselves here, Red....The nature of our work, yours and mine, sells newspapers, and that's Aprile's job." The sergeant went full circle.

"People don't like me; I know that," said the big man in a mellower tone. "But why the fuck should they step on the dead to get to me?"

"Today it's you, tomorrow me, and the next day it's somebody else. Listen, Red, it's all about the story for these people. The victims, you, me, even the captain...we're all nothing more than pieces on a checkerboard. A big name like yours sells newspapers...so they make you a king in the game."

"I believe that!"

"Personally, I have more respect for you than that reporter," Markie lied. "This was all about exploiting a big reputation...yours."

"They want to sell fucking papers? They want fucking glory? I can give them good glory! Believe me—front-page shit that their kids will remember for a long time!" Red was living up to his Death Maker nickname.

"Forget it, Red...just as I have to. Screw them. You are who you are. Let's just try and figure out what happened so we can make it right and let your daughter rest in peace."

Red was still listening, which was a positive sign. The sergeant was making sense, the big man thought. "Sergeant...I gotta make it right."

"That captain and reporter are assholes....I know it, you know it, and so does everyone else who has half a brain." Markie felt he had turned the corner, so he kept going. "I got grief from the chief of detectives over that story. That captain threw me under the bus."

"Yeah, bullshit....You must have spoken to the captain!" Red had regrouped.

"What was I supposed to do? He is a captain; I can't deny him his due. Look, Red—"

The big man cut him short. "Wait a minute....How the fuck do you know to call me Red?"

"That's my job. How do you know things that pertain to your work? It's your job, isn't it?"

Markie was being careful not to undo his progress. Now he sought to wrap the conversation up. "Look...again...all I can do is try to make this right. Let me get to the bottom of it. Once this is over, I'll sit with you and give you the whole story, warts and all. My word on it. Other than that, I can do nothing more."

"I'm going to hold you to that, Sergeant Markie of the homicide squad... believe me." Red spoke with the extreme seriousness that convinced Markie he was going to have to keep his promise someday.

⊞ ⊞ ⊞

RED HARRIS HAD BEEN just one of the distractions for Markie. The first had reared itself earlier when Sergeant Lance Parlatto showed up at his office for work. As the commanding officer of the detective squad, Parlatto oversaw the precinct investigators. He was Fishnet's boss.

For a man in his mid-thirties, Parlatto still had lots of growing up to do. He was sort of a juvenile adult. In his spare time, he liked to amuse himself at home on video games. His current favorite was one that challenged his ability to safely navigate the Oregon Trail with his traveling companions. He had yet to make the trip all the way through without losing at least one member of the party he led. To make things interesting, Parlatto would assign each character in his party the name of someone in his squad. As the game stood, he had already lost Fishnet on the trail due to an infection.

The squad commander was not one of Markie's favorite people. Parlatto was another who put himself first. Whatever career achievements he had attained had been acquired thanks to his computer skills and knowing people. He came along at the right time to assist bosses who remained challenged by the intricacies of the automated electronic machine. Markie's experience in the Army and Von Hess's background in the Marines were believed to be archaic credentials compared to Parlatto's technological expertise. The veterans looked upon Parlatto as a whiz kid, all fluff and without much bottom to him. The man with the mouse had spent most of his police career holding down an inside job in headquarters that positioned him to rub shoulders with the highest levels in the department.

Parlatto's greatest deficiency rested in his limited exposure to the gutter, a basic ingredient in the makings of a good cop. Part of a respected reputation involved paying dues, which meant spending time getting dirty rolling around on city concrete. Parlatto's expertise, on the other hand, was focused on amassing statistical data, analyzing it, and then transferring the information onto easily understood charts. The finished products were considered Picasso-like masterpieces by some department executives who still typed with one index finger. There were no battlefield commissions awarded to computer geeks, just soft jobs and a few gold shields, with people like Parlatto at the head of the receiving line.

Parlatto, an averagely built short man, was clean shaven with a dark brown crew cut and glasses. He was a preppie who often came to work without the benefit of socks inside the burgundy penny loafers he wore. Tan slacks, blue shirt, and a blue blazer completed him. He kept a red and blue striped tie inside of his jacket pocket. The day-old *Sunday Times* he had carried into work was laid on top of his desk, open to the wedding announcement section. The squad commander took pleasure in reading about lovebirds—their accomplishments and those of their proud parents. Parlatto felt no embarrassment of this habit; he remained unfazed as to how such reading material might appear to those he worked with. To hardened detectives, having affection for hearts and flowers was considered to be the preference of wimps.

The squad commander had come to work with a bit of an attitude, carried over from the weekend. He was still smarting about not being allowed to come into work on overtime. A nine-year veteran of the force, Parlatto spent most of his career under the protection of his uncle, a man who was his hook on the job...a chief they called "Mean Mike." Once Parlatto had been promoted to sergeant, Mean Mike saw to it that he was shipped to the Internal Affairs Bureau for safekeeping. It was the very command where the chief had ruined enough careers to earn his nickname. The transfer of Parlatto was accomplished with a phone call and the stroke of a pen— acts that spared him from having to spend a minute getting muddied in the trenches of the patrol force. After two years of investigating his own, the sergeant returned to the well to ask another favor from his hook. Once again the chief came through, with Parlatto being awarded his own command in the detective bureau.

Parlatto's budding career was one built on smoke and mirrors. In Sergeant Parlatto, Markie saw a cunning slacker who used his guile to get over in a tough job. To those not in the know, Parlatto was an accomplished rising star. Fishnet was one of the few people who liked working for Parlatto, a boss he viewed as being unconscious. With Parlatto in charge, the detective knew he could do whatever he wanted. Fishnet still got a hoot out of every time he saw the sergeant wearing the beige corduroy suit he had gifted him. Parlatto had no clue that Fishnet had glommed a dozen of the suits off the back of a recovered hijacked truck one night.

"So how is my friend, Sergeant Markie of homicide?" asked Parlatto. "Thinking of retiring?...You should. Might as well enjoy yourself and your pension while you are still young."

Markie nodded, immediately standing up from the couch in Parlatto's office to greet him. Markie was aware of what was behind Parlatto's advice. His retirement would place Parlatto one step closer to a promotion that would give him lieutenant's money.

"I'm thinking about it. So what is going on, governor?"

"You tell me."

Markie promptly fulfilled his obligation of professional courtesy by giving Parlatto a full verbal briefing on the case. Markie's job was to support the efforts of Parlatto's squad, which meant that the investigation was Parlatto's ultimate responsibility.

"Can you believe that the duty captain wouldn't let me come in on my RDO?" Parlatto whined.

Markie ignored the statement, sending a hint that the squad commander should get over it. "Take a look at the case folder," said Markie. "It will spell out some of the things we did."

"Thanks. But let me ask you something....How could he do that? He knew that it's my squad, my case. How can he say that I can't come in to work it? How can that be?"

"What can you do? Forget it."

"Yeah...I guess you're right. Some people are just assholes." Parlatto's comment caused Markie to bristle.

Parlatto lifted the folder from his desk. He commenced scanning the reports with little enthusiasm. He knew he did not have to know too much....Markie had him covered.

"Just so you know, we have a full team of detectives out there working the day shift if we need them," said Parlatto.

The telephone rang, and Parlatto answered. It was the division captain. It was his first day back on the job after being off. Upon entering his office, he was met with a disturbing phone call from the police commissioner's office. It had to do with a newspaper article written by Chick Aprile. After receiving an earful, the captain called up Parlatto's squad for some answers.

Parlatto immediately went on the defensive. "No, boss, I have not read the papers yet." Parlatto was being less than truthful—he was aware of who the most recent newlyweds were.

"Well, go out and get them!" growled the division commander into the phone. "What the hell is going on over there with these girls in the trunk?"

"I just came in, boss....This is my first one back too, so I'm in the dark myself. I'm reading the case folder for the first time right now." Parlatto needed something to place between himself and the captain, so he sacrificed Markie. "Sergeant Markie has been handling the investigation.... He has been in charge of the whole thing from the beginning."

"Is he there now?"

"Yes, boss. He is right here next to me." To the squad commander's relief, Markie took the phone that Parlatto held out to him.

"Yes, boss?"

The division commander unloaded on Markie. "What exactly the hell is going on over there? The chief of detectives himself called me....He received a call on the double you got there. Look...we have a situation brewing," he warned.

"I understand," answered Markie.

"You'd better understand! Did you see the Aprile story this morning?"

"I heard about it," he lied, "but I didn't get to read it. We've been working straight through on this case. What is the problem with the paper?"

"The problem is that the Allen girl has juice. Her uncle is Senator Hadley V. Allen. Everyone is going batshit over there because it was reported that their prize package was a junkie with connections to a mob-run prostitution ring!"

"I didn't know....The family never let on."

"This is an election year for him to boot...so the real concern is that he could be hurt!"

"The family never mentioned any of this," repeated Markie.

"Why the hell would you dish out all that information?" The division commander was demanding an explanation.

Markie got defensive. "What? Boss...with all due respect, I never released anything. I referred the press to public information from the get-go. I know better than that."

"Well, somebody over there wised up Chick Aprile—he seems to have all the answers. I spoke to public information; they say they never spoke to Aprile. Now *you* tell *me*!"

"All I know for certain is that it didn't come from me." Markie was offended. "*That* you can take to the bank!"

"Do you know if Captain North might have spoken to him?"

"He could have, cap...but I doubt it. We were on the same page regarding the press. We were in agreement to give them zilch. Besides, we knew very little when Captain North had the duty. It was when Moran came on as the duty captain....It was he who got all the details."

The information seemed to have an effect.

"Moran is quoted in the Aprile story, but he swore he told Aprile nothing

Anthony Celano

he did not already know. He said you had already spoken to him. Captain Moran said that the leak to Aprile came from the squad side."

"How about that," remarked Markie dryly. "Did Moran tell you this before or after things got hot with the chief of detectives?" he asked, hoping to screw Sammy Me.

The division commander let out a disgusted noise under his breath. Sergeant Markie seized the opportunity to exonerate himself. "Do you want me to call Aprile, boss? I can do it now, to show you I never tipped him off. We can go over there to the paper even, if you want me to prove the point." Markie's tone was challenging, one that conveyed his willingness to go to the mat.

"Alright, take it easy. I had public information reach out to Aprile earlier to ask him who told him what."

"And?"

"Aprile told them to go read the papers...so here we are. Where are we going now?" It was clear the division commander wanted to move the conversation along in another direction.

Markie went on to enlighten him about Anthony Boy. Once he received the briefing, he felt a little better about things, and his attitude improved. "Listen...post me, will you? This is one I need you to get to the bottom of, or there will be no peace for any of us."

"Okay, boss, I'm on it. There was no leak here, though," emphasized Markie, not quite yet ready to let it go.

"Okay, okay...just do your best to figure this thing out."

"Will do."

"How many men have you got on this?"

"Two teams...four detectives, plus me and the squad commander."

"Alright...keep it going with the same teams working—they know the case, and I want consistency." The division commander concluded the call by hanging up the phone gently.

After finishing up the call, the division commander reflected back to when he had been a detective. He knew Markie would never have been so bold with him if he were on soft ground. To go so far as to extend the offer to face off with Chick Aprile at his office was evidence enough that Markie was in the right. But the division commander was no longer a detective. In the department, there had always been a fundamental conviction that bosses were supposed to stick together, circling the wagons when under attack. Sammy Me was a fellow captain, so he fell under this protective umbrella of solidarity.

After hanging up the telephone, Markie looked over at Parlatto but said nothing. When Parlatto asked what had happened, he received a crisp response. "I just added Sammy Me to my shit list. Let's let it go at that."

Parlatto immediately grasped that there would be no decent communication with Markie at this time, so he took Markie's advice and let it go. Parlatto looked down at the investigative folder in front of him and began reading the reports about the two women in the trunk.

Markie took out his cell phone to call over to the homicide squad to let his lieutenant know that he, Von Hess, Wires, and Junior were authorized to dig in for the duration. The captain's edict would override any overtime concerns that might be posed by his lieutenant. Markie took solace in knowing that there would be no bean-counting while the case was progressing. Later, perhaps, there would be questions—but for now all was good.

The next two developments came in as a one-two punch within five minutes of each other: Sergeant Parlatto fielded a call from the district attorney's office while Markie received a call from the precinct desk lieutenant informing him that Red Harris was in the building making an unannounced visit.

Parlatto made sure to have the case folder on his desk at the ready so that he had information at his fingertips. The call from the district attorney's office was transferred from the squad into his office line.

"Sergeant Parlatto. How may I help you?"

"Hello, Sergeant, this is ADA Hal Roberts calling for the district attorney."

"Hey," Parlatto responded casually, "how's it going? What can I do for you?"

"That's what the DA would like to know....How's it going?" Roberts sounded like more than just a typical prosecutor. His speech suggested he was a smoothie, something along the lines of a slick politician selling a bill of goods or spinning things to mitigate a problem. "The district attorney read about the two women in the trunk on his way into work this morning. I'm calling to let you know that the DA has expressed some particular interest in Barbara Allen." Roberts waited for a reaction.

Parlatto was prepared to respond. "I have my people on the case. We have been diligently conducting interviews, pursuing leads, and so on since Saturday. As we speak, I have my detectives interviewing the owner of the escort service where the Harris girl worked."

"The DA was interested specifically in the Allen girl. Do you have a cause of death yet?"

"There were no telltale signs on the body. We are still waiting on the medical examiner."

"There was a lot of information in the paper. Was it you who conferred with the press?"

"No, no, no! No sir, not me. Sergeant Markie handled that aspect of things. He was dealing with the press."

"Sergeant Markie from homicide?" "Yes."

"So we have no suspects or people of interest?"

Here Parlatto stammered. He was not sure who exactly might be a person of interest. "Well...not exactly. But I'm making headway."

"Okay. Let me know if anything breaks so I can pass it on to the DA. He is *very* interested. I'll see what can be done to move things along with the medical examiner."

"Thanks. If you want, you can call me anytime. My name, again, is Sergeant Parlatto. I'm the squad commander."

The sergeant hung up and let out a deep sigh. He thought he'd been through an ordeal. He had no idea about the heavy lifting Markie was doing with Red Harris in the parking lot.

18

DAMAGE
CONTROL

AFTER RED HARRIS LEFT, Markie returned upstairs to Sergeant Parlatto's office. He looked at Parlatto's relaxed face as he sat at his desk reading the wedding announcements. Markie felt a silent bitterness toward the scheming squad commander—a building resentment that was requiring some effort to suppress. Markie found it incomprehensible how upper management enabled people like Parlatto to thrive, overlooking ineptitude in key positions. Either that or superiors were just not paying attention to detail, missing the obvious red flags of incompetence. Markie felt a managerial upgrade of the detective bureau was needed, an ironic perspective considering how Markie himself had failed to notice a loony like Fishnet functioning right under his own very nose.

"We have to make some calls," Markie announced as he entered the office of the squad commander.

"Who else needs to be called? I already took care of the district attorney's office," apprised Parlatto.

"You did?" Markie was surprised. "So?"

"The district attorney expressed interest in the case," answered the squad commander.

"What did they say?"

"They said they're going to try to light a fire under the medical examiner's ass. I told them how you've been working on the case day and night since Saturday," Parlatto lied.

Markie nodded, but he doubted that Parlatto ever gave credit to anyone other than himself. "The squawk comes from a political connection," Markie told him. "A politician has the DA's ear."

Parlatto figured the connection had to be serious. "That makes this a big deal...right?"

"For now, yeah...but this too will pass. High interest never lasts forever. It's just something we need to stay on top of right now."

"What is the story with the girl's father?" asked Parlatto.

"Which girl?"

"The blond."

"That went okay. The story in the newspaper bent his nose out of joint. He's under control for now...I hope! We gotta call the parents of the Allen girl to let them know we didn't forget them."

Parlatto nodded. "I'll have Fishnet call them."

"No, better let me handle it. They're kind of high-strung; it'll play better coming from a boss."

"That makes sense," agreed Parlatto, without extending any offer to make the call himself. "Do you want to eat anything? I could send someone out."

"How about we hold off awhile? We still have some bagels out there if anyone needs to eat. Let's do a few pies and some sodas later. Maybe I could put the expense through on my end," offered Markie.

"Sounds like a plan." Parlatto then changed subjects. "What do you think of this merger with the transit and housing police?"

"We'll have to see. Hopefully it works out. They've been shooting for this for a long time. I guess merging the three departments isn't the worst idea I've ever heard."

Parlatto was not so sure. "I don't know how it'll play out with the troops, Al. I know Fishnet is dead set against it."

"Fishnet? What the hell doesn't he like about it?"

"He thinks the job is going to bend over backward to appease the housing and transit people in order to make it work."

"So?"

"So Fishnet figures the merger is going to reduce his chances to get promoted to second grade. He's afraid he might get passed over,," said Parlatto, "and frankly...I have the same concern. You think they'll spread some lieutenant's money their way?"

"I suppose they might," answered Markie. "But what are you gonna do? The mayor wants this to work."

"You know what Fishnet said I should do to make transit and housing feel welcome?"

"Enlighten me," said Markie with sarcasm. "What did the genius suggest you do?"

"Buy a Lionel train set and run some track straight from the squad to the shithouse to make both departments feel at home."

⊞ ⊞ ⊞

IT WAS 1:30 P.M. WHEN Markie got in touch with the father of Barbara Allen. He updated Doctor Allen concerning some of the progress made, revealing as much as he could. The sergeant was careful not to express assurances that he could not deliver on. Doctor Allen expressed surprise when he learned that the detectives had worked through the night. The courtesy call went a long way with influencing the doctor's opinion of the investigators....He now felt as if he were a part of the team.

Markie found the doctor to be an uncomplicated sort of man—easy to deal with. When the telephone was turned over to his wife, Victoria, things became more challenging. Her high opinion of herself made her a harder person to favorably influence. Markie caught on quickly that Victoria was a person of little tolerance...especially toward those she perceived to be of a lower social status. Her conversation with the sergeant came accompanied by an ample number of sarcastic remarks. But taking into consideration the circumstances, Markie never reacted to her liberally administered snide criticisms. The sergeant, thankful he didn't have to live with the woman, listened attentively as she chewed his ear off with complaint after complaint. Not all of the bile being drained from her system was without merit. The release of her daughter's belongings was in fact a process, and the medical examiner's report did seem to be taking forever.

Markie tried to explain that the time frame was normal, but she had a mental barrier preventing her from accepting the fact that toxicology reports often took days, weeks, or, in some cases, longer. When Victoria got around to Fishnet, things got interesting

"Detective Von Hess is someone I have all my faith in. But that other one...Milligan! Does that man have emotional problems?"

Markie had to laugh at that. He cupped the phone, pulling his mouth away from the receiver to mask his amusement. "What makes you say that?" he asked, sitting back in his chair in preparation for the long response he knew was coming.

"His behavior has been abominable...simply beyond belief," she began. "Aside from his being unprofessional, unsophisticated, and underwhelming, I find him...well, to be frank...disturbed mentally! Even his look is peculiar; he strikes me as being off."

"What exactly did he do?" Markie leaned back in his seat, knowing he was in for the long haul.

"Well...while I'm not professing to be a qualified psychiatrist, it is my opinion that the man needs some kind of psychological testing. My daughter said he looks like Clark Gable....Perhaps so, but his name should be *Crazy* Gable, not Clark!"

The sergeant listened until she wore herself out talking, which took some time. Once finished, the litigator felt much better for having expressed herself—as did Markie for not having to hear her anymore.

Markie concluded his conversation by promising to keep the couple apprised throughout the continuing investigation. To further keep Victoria happy, he promised to reprimand Fishnet and monitor him closely for indications of emotional disturbance. The sergeant made this promise just to humor her, not realizing how insightful she actually was. All was copacetic at this point, and Markie had been successful in making the couple feel included.

⊞ ⊞ ⊞

ADA HAL ROBERTS PROVED faithful to his word. He called the squad to inform Sergeant Parlatto that he had made headway after speaking to the medical examiner: enough pressure had been exerted to rush things along. Roberts asked no questions about the case at this time, indicating to Parlatto that things might have begun to settle down over at the DA's office. After Parlatto hung up, he stepped into the precinct hallway to dial up the division captain on his cell phone.

"Hello, cap, this is Sergeant Parlatto calling to give you an update on the case we've got over here."

"Good....How's it going? Anything?"

"Yeah, I managed to break the guy who owns the escort service. Looks like there is an organized crime connection here."

"What organized crime connection?" The captain pretended to sound surprised at hearing this, but he already knew as much because he'd read the morning papers.

"The blond woman's father is with the Milano family. That's how she got her job at the escort service," said Parlatto.

"How do you know that?"

"I got the owner of the escort service to fess up that he is partners with the D'Angelo brothers. Then I got him to tell me that an FBI agent is his cousin and..."

"Whooa...whooa...wait a minute....Hold up, sergeant." The captain had heard enough of Parlatto's self-promotion to sour him on any further conversation. "Is Markie still over there?"

"Yeah, cap, he's in the squad room."

"Get him," said the division captain curtly.

Parlatto walked into the squad room, holding up his cell phone to Markie. He signaled for the homicide sergeant to meet him inside his office to pick up the call. "It's the division captain....He wants to talk to you."

Markie took the phone from Parlatto. "Sergeant Markie."

"Markie...what the hell is going on now?" The captain was exasperated. "I just got things under control, and now Bill Gates over there is telling me about mobsters and FBI agents....Talk to me!"

"We have a lid on it, cap. We caught a break. The escort owner was giving us shit until we got lucky. Through questioning, he let it slip about his partner and cousin."

"What about them?"

"Swing D'Angelo is a capo with the Milano crime family. He's a silent partner in the business. The FBI agent Ella Barone is the first cousin of the up-front partner...Anthony Boy Chiarello."

"Barone? She is pretty well regarded over there with the feds. They're grooming that broad for bigger things....I think I remember reading that someplace recently."

"Exactly, cap. She's in line for a bump up. Anyway, here's the thing.... Anthony said that D'Angelo and the agent don't know about each other. Their link with Chiarello is the common denominator between the two. He's been dealing from two decks."

"Screwing around with Swing D'Angelo....What is he, a nut? This boy apparently likes to play with fire."

"For sure," Markie agreed. "Anyone who is blood to a fed is a liability to a guy like D'Angelo...and that puts Chiarello on the spot. If he gets found out, it's the ballgame for him. He *has* to go."

"How can you be so sure of that?" asked the captain.

"If Chiarello is ever *really* up against it, he has somebody friendly to go see and help negotiate a deal...you know, making it easy for him to roll over to the other side...to become a snitch," explained Markie. "We have Anthony Boy by the balls, cap, and he knows it."

"I see....So where are we going next with this?"

"My guys are taking Chiarello back to his business to check the trip sheet of the blond. If we can figure out where she last was, then we can work the case from there."

"Okay. Keep me posted, and tell everyone to spill none of this to the press. I'm going to call the chief of detectives."

"Right, cap. I'll call you later."

"Oh, one another thing, on a personal note." "Sure, cap."

"Do yourself a favor and keep an eye on this Parlatto. Do you understand what I mean?"

"I do....No problem, cap."

Hanging up the phone, Markie thought that if he were the chief of detectives, he would dump Sergeant Parlatto out of the bureau. He'd even bounce Sammy Me out while he was at it.

Markie sat on the couch in Parlatto's office. He leaned back, intending to rest his eyes for a minute. While he was doing that, Sergeant Parlatto returned to his desk and began looking over his newspaper. After digesting a couple of stories, he began to hear the small snores emanating from Markie's mouth. He thought he detected the slight scent of alcohol. He opened his bottom desk drawer and removed the bottle of Christian Brothers brandy. After examining the bottle, he couldn't be sure. To play it safe, he took out a magic marker and drew a small line on the bottle, marking off the point where the brandy ended.

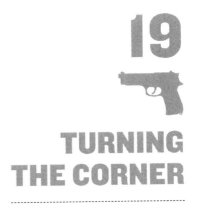

TURNING
THE CORNER

ANTHONY BOY SUNK DOWN as low as he could in the rear of the unmarked car. His greatest fear was someone seeing him being driven around by detectives. If that were to happen, he'd have to answer questions from the strictest authority he knew: Augie D'Angelo.

"Hey," he asked from the back seat, "where the hell are you guys going?"

"Your office...over the Brooklyn Bridge," answered a surprised Von Hess. He squinted at his passenger in the rearview mirror.

"No, no, no! Stay in Brooklyn; take me home....I got all the information you need at the house."

"The bridge is right here....We will be there in a couple minutes."

"Are you guys fucking nuts? I don't want to go into Manhattan.... Somebody with Swing Blade might spot me with you guys!" said Anthony emphatically, and then, more pleadingly, "Let's stay in Brooklyn...please!"

"Okay, I see. No problem, Anthony. We can turn around and go to your house," agreed Von Hess.

"Stay clear of Flatbush Avenue, Fifth Avenue...and Seventh Avenue... any of the big streets. Take Third Avenue."

"Hey, Anthony, we don't need you for a fucking road map....We'll get you there," chimed in Fishnet, resenting that their passenger was starting to give orders.

"I gotta be careful with this shit," protested Anthony Boy.

Fishnet did not like Anthony's speaking up one bit. "Why are you making such big fucking stink now?...All of a sudden you get shy? You had no fucking problem coming into the station house with the other detectives, did you?"

Anthony backed off; he knew he had to maintain his cool with the detectives. The newly minted cooperator bit on his tongue as he looked at Fishnet. After taking a deep breath, he replied in a subdued voice, "Your partners picked me up at my house....*That* I could explain. You guys are taking me home....My people will see *that* as a whole different story. To them it'll look like I'm in bed with you guys...and they won't be far wrong."

Both detectives knew that their passenger had a point. Over on the Manhattan side of the bridge, the risk did exist that Anthony might get spotted in the company of the law *without* wearing cuffs. Why take the chance? To Anthony's relief, Von Hess prudently switched course.

Anthony was glad that the detectives had taken him at his word when he told them that the information they sought could be retrieved from his home computer. He was taking a gamble. The truth was that his home computer housed only partial client records, just data he had personally entered. Anthony had never bothered to have an IT person come in and set up things right. As a result, the corporate business data remained divided, stored separately in two computers independent of each other. Really sensitive information never made it to a computer. The mob associate stored such tidbits in his head and on scraps of paper he kept in his wallet. Anthony was banking on having sufficient client information on the Brooklyn computer to bluff his way through with the detectives.

When Fishnet and Von Hess pulled up to the Brooklyn brownstone, there were no parking spots available. On the opposite site of the street was a bus stop that would have to do as a place to park. Anthony was able to move rapidly, despite his girth, when so inclined. He hopped out of the unmarked car, waddled swiftly across the street, and hustled himself into the house. The detectives followed his lead, although from a good distance behind.

When they reached the brownstone, Anthony Boy was waiting for them behind the entrance doors at the top of the brownstone steps. He marched the detectives directly up to his apartment. He led them to a small office adjacent to his bedroom that faced the yard.

Fishnet, who had been holding up the rear, was all eyes as he paraded through the apartment. His attention was drawn to the bedroom door, which was ajar, by the scent of lingering tobacco smoke that permeated the room. Poking in his head, he spotted a small scale atop one of the end tables next to the king-size bed. He noted the number of large

Anthony Celano

mirrors in the room, all seeming to cover the sleeping area. The sight of the mirrors caused his mind to wander off on one of his journeys. The detective pictured himself installing a hidden camera to memorialize his performances. He envisioned himself having Anthony Boy's job—an occupation that came with the wonderful trimmings he desired. He was pulled back to reality after noticing a couple of glassine envelopes on top of the bedroom dresser. Fishnet discreetly shut the bedroom door and joined Anthony and Von Hess, who were already in the small office.

"Hey, Anthony, mind if I use the bathroom?" Fishnet asked.

"Go ahead; it's off the kitchen," answered the mobster.

As Fishnet exited the office, he closed the door behind him about three quarters of the way. "I'll find it."

Fishnet hurried to the bathroom. Once inside, he rifled through the medicine chest for goodies. Disappointed, he entered the kitchen area where he began opening drawers and looking in cabinets. Fishnet hit pay dirt inside a cabinet above the sink where Anthony Boy kept his booze. Next to a scotch bottle was an old-fashioned Tiffany sterling-silver hip flask. Fishnet claimed the booty and placed it in the breast pocket of his suit. The find made the detective a happy camper. He figured his score to be worth at least a thousand dollars. Fishnet then tiptoed in the direction of the office. On the way, he stopped to peek into a closet. Inside the pocket of a leather jacket the detective came across something rare...a switchblade knife. The deadly weapon soon found a new home in Fishnet's other breast pocket. Spotting an open carton of Marlboro cigarettes atop the closet shelf, Fishnet helped himself to a couple of packs. Knowing his time was up, he then proceeded to the office where his partner and Anthony Boy were.

Anthony Boy's work area contained a desk, chair, computer, printer, and two-drawer black metal file cabinet hidden under the desk. The crowded desktop was home to business-related items, including an At-a-Glance datebook, pens, stapler, spare staples, and a calculator. There was also a wooden back scratcher, a dirty ashtray, a deck of cards, and the prior day's racing form. To one side of the desk was a paper shredder. In the corner of the room stood a wastebasket containing a couple of crumpled papers and an empty box of condoms. The basket stood beneath a six-foot stationary pedestal fan. The varnished wood floor had some scratch marks from the wheels of the chair. A large poster of Frank Sinatra was tacked to the wall directly over the desk; the singer's blue eyes seemed to peer at you regardless of where you were in the room.

Fishnet looked around the office and observed all of this, but he didn't see what he had been looking for. There was no sign of a weapon. His intuition told him that a firearm was likely secreted somewhere in the apartment along with some cash and drugs, probably in the bedroom...

an area that would be difficult for him to access under the circumstances.

Anthony Boy was seated at his desk, waiting for his computer screen to come up. Von Hess was standing at his side, looking over his shoulder. "Other people work out of here too?"

"No," Anthony answered. "This is just for me. My manager works out of the Manhattan office."

"These machines are pretty slow," commented Von Hess.

"Yeah, this is a piece of shit. I gotta get another one," answered Anthony. "It'll be up in another minute."

Anthony Boy rose from his chair to take out a pack of cigarettes from his pants pocket. After lighting up a Marlboro, he then dropped into his chair with his full weight, a plunge forceful enough that it shook the room. Anthony's crash-landing into his chair jolted Fishnet, enough to keep him away from any further daydreaming about what could be found in Anthony's bedroom.

"Jeez, I'd hate to be sleeping downstairs underneath you," the disturbed detective commented. "The ceiling could cave in!" Fishnet was the only one in the room seeing the humor of his remark.

Once the computer was up and running, Anthony Boy got down to business trying to pull up whatever Brooklyn clients he had entered into the system. He spun around in his chair to face the detectives and pointed happily to the computer screen. "Here it is....She definitely went out on a job in Brooklyn on Friday evening. This is the last time I had her scheduled to go out on a job."

"Where in Brooklyn?" asked Von Hess.

"All I've got here is Brooklyn...no address, though," he said, looking up to see the reaction of the detective. "Here...you could take a look for yourself."

Von Hess looked at the screen. "Who or what is JH?"

"The client's initials," answered Anthony. "But I'm not sure which client it was, though," he added quickly...hoping he could get by with his lie.

"If you don't know your own client...how does JH pay you?"

"He pays the escort cash, and she turns it over to me." Anthony was winging it.

Fishnet had reached his limit. "Who the fuck do you think you're bullshitting? Not even a name as to who she was escorting or a time?"

Anthony Boy just shrugged. "I don't know....Sometimes I rush to get things done and mess up making entries. As long as I get the money, who really cares?"

"So how do you keep things straight?" asked Von Hess.

"The accountant comes in—keeping things straight is his job."

"Didn't you see Shirley that Friday night?" asked Von Hess.

"Yeah...just to give her some money, that's all. Since she was Red's kid and we both live in Brooklyn, I'd meet her to square up. She would give me mine if she had money to turn in, or I would pay her off if I had collected up front. That was how we worked it. I did it as a courtesy, to save her a trip into the city."

"How much did you give her?"

"I think it was three hundred bucks or six hundred....I don't remember exactly."

"Check? Cash?"

"Everybody gets paid by me in cash. That works best."

"How do you get the money from the clients?" inquired Fishnet.

"Cash or credit card. But I got nothing on this last job obviously, so I'm out money," lamented Anthony Boy.

Fishnet got sore. He felt Anthony Boy was playing him for a chump. "You took a hit? Are you fucking kidding me? You know exactly where the fuck she went—now, let's have it, you fat fuck. Cut the crap or get ready for a little workout over here...a dose of TST."

Anthony gulped. He had no idea what TST meant, but he correctly figured it to mean something ugly.

Von Hess looked over at Fishnet, not sure if his partner was being serious. Playing it safe, he stepped in to prevent things from getting out of control. "Let's keep this simple. Let me see all your clients, Anthony. Print up whatever you have...names, numbers, and addresses...the works are what we need."

Anthony hesitated. He seemed nervous now. After a minute he realized he had little choice other than to present Von Hess with the information he requested. He gave the detective a list of the clients he had entered into his home computer, turning over information on thirty-three clients on thirty-three separate pieces of paper.

Von Hess was thumbing through the pages when the corners of his mouth took a slight upward turn. He neatly folded one printed sheet of paper and placed the document in the pocket of his black suit jacket. The other pages he rolled up into a cone and stuck into his back trouser pocket. Von Hess extended his right hand to Anthony Boy, who received it in his. Fishnet watched silently as the two men shook hands.

"Anthony, thanks for your help....It was good doing business with you. Don't worry about a thing."

Anthony was confused. "But what about my cousin and Aug—?"

Von Hess held up his hand, abruptly cutting him off. "Never heard of them. Have a nice life, Anthony....Nice knowing you."

"But stick around town just in case we have to come back to refresh your memory," added Fishnet. He regretted not having gotten a chance to take a closer look inside the bedroom. He would have loved to get a crack at some of the gravy that was bound to be there.

Once back in their unmarked car, Von Hess handed the rolled pages over to Fishnet for review. "What do you see?" he asked Fishnet.

"What? All I see here is just a bunch of names and addresses."

Then Von Hess removed the neatly folded sheet of paper from his jacket pocket and passed it to Fishnet. "What about this one?"

Taking the sheet of paper, Fishnet looked at Von Hess. "What about it?"

"This is the only name and address that should be of interest to you,partner."

After looking at the document, Fishnet suddenly came alive. "Hey! This fuck Spiros lives right in the neighborhood, not too far from where the Oldsmobile was parked...right on Mill Road!"

"Bingo! And it gets better. Unless I'm mistaken, that address is right near where the woman found the white poodle...good old Butter."

"Son of a bitch...we may actually get someplace with this stinking thing," exclaimed Fishnet, lighting up a Camel just for the hell of it. "Step on it, will you? I can't wait to get back to the squad with this."

"We'll get there soon enough. Call up Markie if you like," suggested Von Hess.

Reaching for his phone, Fishnet caught himself, realizing that he was acting too much like a buff. "Nah, I can wait....We'll be there in a few minutes anyway."

"Go ahead; call the sergeant. He'll be happy to know."

"You think so, Ollie?"

"Listen, I know the man. He'll definitely appreciate the heads-up. He lives for this stuff."

Fishnet called the squad and asked for Markie. By rights, he should have called his own boss, Sergeant Parlatto, but in his excitement he was not thinking of protocol. It didn't matter because Markie wasn't available; the sergeant was still heaving on the couch in the squad commander's office. Fishnet ended up talking to Parlatto anyway.

After posting Parlatto regarding what had occurred at the apartment, Fishnet sought direction. "Do you want to see if we could pick up this guy Spiros? We can go by the house now."

Parlatto knew that he was not strong operationally. He wanted no mistakes made. "Hang on a minute." He walked into his office from the squad room to arouse Markie.

"Hey, Al...wake up." Parlatto gave Markie's shoulder a gentle shake. Markie's eyes opened slowly.

"Jeez, I must have dozed off," Markie said, still groggy.

"I got Fishnet on the phone. They think they got the name and address of the last escort customer. What do you think...go pick the guy up?"

"Is he still on the phone?"

"Yeah."

"Let me talk to him." Markie stood up on his feet to pick up the phone. "Fishnet? This is Sergeant Markie. What's doing?"

Once Markie was filled in, he acted decisively, giving Fishnet explicit instructions. "Go with Ollie and see if you can pick up this Spiros at the house. If you strike out, come right back to the squad. No sense hanging out there when we don't even know what he looks like yet."

"Right, boss."

"Just give me the guy's information so we can check him out on this end."

Fishnet provided the requested information to Markie. After hanging up, he turned to Von Hess. "Markie wants us to go by the house and try to pick up Spiros."

"Okay," acknowledged Von Hess.

"But I see one fly in the ointment with all this."

"What?" asked Von Hess.

"Who the fuck is JH? Joe Spiros would be JS," Fishnet pointed out, "not JH...correct?"

"Correct...and I don't have the answer for that." While Von Hess had no explanation for the initials, he did have a question about something else. "Tell me something...what the hell does TST stand for?"

Fishnet looked at Von Hess wryly. "Tear-shedding time."

"Tear-shedding time? What the hell is that? I never even heard of the term."

"Nah...you wouldn't. I got that from my old man whenever he dropped in. That's what he used to say whenever he took out the switch to straighten me out."

Von Hess offered no response. He didn't want to go there. He dismissed the explanation as just more Fishnet nonsense.

⊞ ⊞ ⊞

AFTER HANGING UP WITH Fishnet, Sergeant Markie turned to Parlatto. "It looks like we may be finally cooking."

It was now time for Wires and Junior to be called upon. Parlatto looked forward to doing the honors. Meanwhile, Markie went into Parlatto's private bathroom to wash his face and compose himself. He hated using the squad commander's private bathroom—somehow it felt like he was imposing. Also, it irked Markie that Parlatto had such a decent office while far better people worked in offices where peeling paint was falling from the ceiling. It made him think there was no justice. When he finished in the bathroom, he called over to the homicide squad to fill in his lieutenant.

"It's me, Markie."

"Talk to me."

Once again Markie went through everything slowly, leaving nothing out. The lieutenant wanted to be sure of the information he was receiving so that he could accurately relay the details to his boss, the division captain.

In the squad, it was business as usual. At 4:00 p.m., the next new team of detectives was due in to commence their evening shift. They would be working together at the squad until 1:00 a.m. barring anything going down that would necessitate extending their tour or altering their assignment.

Wires and Junior resurfaced in the squad room with Sergeant Parlatto. The three met with Markie in Parlatto's office.

"We are okay to work through again, Lance," Markie announced. "They want us both to stick with it unless we hear different."

"Great," Parlatto said. "I already filled these two in on what we accomplished."

Markie addressed the two detectives. "I want you to do another thorough check, this time on a guy named Joe Spiros. I've got Von Hess and Fishnet out at his place, 8428 Mill Road, looking for him."

"Right, boss," replied both detectives at once.

"Keep the faith," Markie encouraged them. "The game is afoot!" It was a phrase out of Sherlock Holmes. He always got a kick out of using it.

20

JOE HORSE

"I'M HAVING THE BLT," announced Joe Horse as he chomped on pieces of hard candy. "What about you?" He asked his friend—the same friend who'd helped him with the most important move of his life just a couple of days earlier. "Order whatever you like....This is on me."

That was the music Joe's friend always liked to hear. "I think I'll go with grilled cheese and bacon. But let's have some coffee before we eat."

"You got it, man." The two men placed their order with the waitress at the diner. After she brought them their coffee, the pair went through ten sugar packages in order to sweeten the brew to their satisfaction.

The association between Joe and his friend the mover went back a long way. In their clean days, they bonded while playing in the same rock band. But the coolness of the music scene came sprinkled with the trappings of the drug culture. After the music died and the groupies were gone, the musicians were left with an unforgiving addiction. Once burdened with a horse habit to feed, they needed to supplement their income, which marked the birth of their careers in boosting cars and other petty crimes.

Unlike his friend, Joe Horse had a rich father with a guilt that needed pacifying. When the patriarch reached his tolerance limit over his son's drug-related shenanigans, he tossed Joe out of the house—but gave him a parting gift of ten grand to ease his own conscience. The donation was all Joe had to either make it or break it. After taking the money, the addict put it toward his business plan: an investment in heroin and coke. Remembering his father's business preaching about supply and demand, he began by pushing smack to the high school and college crowds. Some of these recreational dabblers remained customers of Joe's long after graduation.

Joe Horse developed a lucrative enterprise for himself. But along with his growing bankroll came a growing dependency on heroin. Joe was fortunate because he had access to enough of the dope to easily meet his needs. As the demand for his product grew, Joe took along his friend for the ride as a junior partner. The operation was successful enough for the friend to buy a truck and branch out on his own, freelancing on a smaller level as a drug-dealing mover and at whatever else it took to make lots of money. There were no hard feelings between the two men because the friend remained loyal, relying on Joe to be his connection to buy heroin and cocaine.

Joe kept his drug source as secretive as the formula to Coca-Cola. No one was clued in that his connection came out of Chinatown. Joe had an affinity for East Asia, with the Chinese being his preference when it came to doing business with suppliers. The way he saw things, the language barrier posed a tremendous obstacle for narcotics agents to overcome. With penetration into the supplier's operation complicated, all Joe had to do was not get sloppy on his end.

Joe was considered a novelty by the drug traffickers he did business with. Not overtly Asian in appearance, he amused them with his fluency in the language. The fact that he was half-Chinese served as an advantage that helped his entry into the underworld of the ethnic enclave.

Joe Horse held up the coffee to click cups with his friend. "Good luck, Franny....True friends are forever."

"Salute...to my dear friend Joe Spiros," came the response. "To our continued success!" The two men with the sunken eyes drank up, savoring the sweetness of their drink.

⊞ ⊞ ⊞

VON HESS PARKED THE unmarked car about a half block from the Mill Road address. One of the mailboxes was marked with the name *Spiros*.

"So far, so good," said Von Hess. He rang both bells to the house without a response.

Before knocking, Fishnet put his ear to the door. Hearing nothing, he rapped on the door with authority. Receiving no response to the knock, he gave it another try, rapping substantially harder.

"There is no one here, Ollie," declared Fishnet.

"If he's inside, he's got to be dead not to hear you banging."

Von Hess returned to their vehicle disappointed. Once inside the car, he called Sergeant Markie, who told him to return to the precinct. As Von Hess was doing this, he observed Fishnet shouldering the front door without success. He then began to try the windows to see if he could gain access. Watching from the car, the senior detective grew increasingly annoyed. "Jesus Christ Almighty, now what the hell is he doing?" said Von Hess with disgust. He then called out to his partner from the car.

"Hey, Fish...c'mon, willya? The boss wants us back at the house ASAP."

"I'm coming," answered Fishnet. The look on the detective's face indicated that he was growing weary of the restrictions being placed on him by working with Von Hess.

At 11:30 p.m., Markie, Parlatto, Fishnet, Von Hess, Wires, and Junior gathered in Parlatto's office. Fishnet looked somewhat tired, but he was still holding up well. Von Hess, going by the bags under his eyes, showed signs of weariness. His age, in addition to working with Fishnet, was taking a toll on him. Markie could see that his senior team was in need of a break—a condition he would soon look to rectify.

"This meeting is going to be brief," he began. "Fish and Ollie...you two are going to take a break after this, so hang in with me a little longer." Both detectives welcomed the upcoming recess without complaint.

"It's time to go all in. We are camping out for his guy Spiros all night if we have to," advised Markie. Turning to Junior, he asked, "What did you come up with regarding him?"

Junior had all the information written in her notebook. She was as efficient as a personal secretary to some corporate big shot. "Nothing came up on him over at headquarters regarding intelligence reports. The good news is that he *does* have a rap sheet and is on parole."

"What's the rap sheet look like?" asked Markie.

"Almost everything is ancient history, but... he is still on parole from a drug bust in Brooklyn. His full name is Joseph Anton Spiros, born December 13, 1958, 8428 Mill Road, Brooklyn.

Before that he lived on East Ninety-Fourth Street, Brooklyn. He has two street names, Joe Horse and Lofan Joe."

"Tell us about that drug arrest."

"He is currently on parole as a result of it....They got him with smack. He was caught with possession of a hypodermic needle and heroin in the Six-Nine Precinct...felony weight. He also had a suspended driver's license. They actually grabbed him in his car shooting up."

"Being on parole is good....And the other arrests?"

"Again in the Six-Nine Precinct for disorderly conduct, resisting arrest, and criminal possession of a controlled substance...heroin. He pled out and received time served. Then another possession heroin bust, this time in the Seven-Two Precinct, again time served, and a grand larceny auto collar in the Six-Two Precinct, where he received a conditional discharge."

"Another prize package," said Parlatto. "Wonder where the nicknames came from."

Markie rolled his eyes before he put forth the answer. "*Horse* is another name for smack....It's heroin."

"This case is infested with every junkie in town," commented Parlatto.

"It fits," observed Von Hess, looking at Markie.

"What?"

"JH stands for Joe Horse....JH was the customer Shirley was going to see."

"So what exactly is *Lofan* supposed to mean?" Fishnet directed the question to Junior.

"It's a Chinese word that means either *white devil* or just plain *white*," she answered. Junior was one step ahead of Fishnet. She'd checked with the Fifth Precinct, the command that covered Chinatown, and got the information from a Chinese-speaking detective.

Her diligence went unappreciated by Fishnet. "So what's the term for *black devil*?"

"I don't really know," Junior answered softly.

Fishnet gained some satisfaction after posing a question that she did not have an answer to— even if the question itself was irrelevant.

Addressing Wires and Junior, Markie gave his instructions. "Call the squads where he was pinched....See if you can get more of a line on him."

"Got it, boss," said Wires.

"Pull up his photo and then stake out the house on Mill Road. I want you to bring him in here to the squad...okay? He is on parole, so there should be no problem taking him in." Markie was looking to move in for the kill.

Junior belatedly spoke up. "I already spoke to the Six-Nine squad about him. They have information ready for us over there, sarge. They were the ones who told me he is known as Joe Horse and Lofan Joe."

"Go to it, then."

The unpopular duo had impressed Markie once again. He felt that these two just might have a future in the homicide squad after all. He then ordered Von Hess and Fishnet to take their turn at getting some rest.

⊞ ⊞ ⊞

WHEN WIRES AND JUNIOR arrived at the Six-Nine Precinct at 1:00 a.m., Detective Fermina Fernandez was waiting to receive them. She was a former narcotics undercover officer who had been recently assigned to the detective division. Being new to her squad, she wanted to do her best in her new assignment. Technically, at 1:00 a.m. she was scheduled to go off duty. She had every intention of waiting around longer, if necessary, on her own time to assist the visiting detectives.

Fernandez had two old color photos of Joe Horse that were not arrest related. "Here you go, guys," she said jovially as she handed over the photos. "I heard that it is nuts over there with that double."

"Yeah, you could say that, Fermina," acknowledged Junior.

Junior compared the nondepartment photos against the booking photos; it was definitely the same person. In one of the new images, Joe Horse was playing a guitar on stage, and in the other, he was standing alone in a room, attired in a white terrycloth bathrobe. He appeared to be in his mid-twenties in both pictures.

"Where is his file?" Junior asked.

Rather than respond, Fernandez made some idle conversation. She'd been working the tour alone all evening, and she welcomed the opportunity to talk to the visiting detectives. "Somebody said you have a father who is retired....How does he like it? Does he like being retired?"

"Yeah, I guess so...but he is driving my mother crazy by being home."

They all laughed at the statement. Detective Fernandez had a pleasant laugh that revealed her to be a very good-natured person. Her warmth made it difficult for many civilians to believe she was a detective. It was this same appealing characteristic that had made her a superior undercover in the narcotics division for several years. The drug dealers never saw her coming. They would do hand-to-hand transactions with her without hesitation, never figuring she was the law.

"So do you have a file for us?" asked Junior again.

"A file? Not really....What I told you is that I know a lot about him." "Ohh...I took that as meaning you had a file on him."

"No...I have no file, just some personal intelligence on him."

"I misunderstood....So what can you tell us about Joe Spiros?"

"Now they call him Joe Horse. They used to call him Lofan Joe."

"Lofan Joe...that means white devil, right?" asked Wires.

"*Lofan* in Chinese means white....I don't know about the devil part. Joey is half-Chinese and half-Greek. Did you know that?" asked Fernandez.

"Not really," responded Junior.

"Nice combination," said Wires.

"Officer Murphy locked him up for smack and a hypodermic needle in a car awhile back. Listen to this....Murphy interrupted him in a car with the needle still sticking out of his arm. Poor Joey never even got to pull the trigger." The detectives shook their heads in concert at the thought of Joe Horse having such bad luck. "They found some weight in the car...so he did some time."

Chuckling to himself, Wires looked at his partner, who just shook her head. "Jesus, now, that is a tough way for a junkie to take a bust," he said.

"You know he did time for that, right?" Both Junior and Wires nodded in the affirmative. Fernandez put forth more information in hopes of further being helpful. "He's a bad addict for sure. The sad thing is that he has a real good brain...or at least he had one. Can you believe that he was going to be an accountant?"

Wires did a double take. "An accountant?"

"Yeah, but I don't think he ever graduated. Anyway...from what I hear now, he has a boatload of money. I know the Spiros family is in some kind of business. Maybe he works for his father."

"You never know," said Wires.

"Did you know he used to play in a band when he was young?...Actually it was his own band. The band was named Spiros...after him. He rocked.... Joey was very handsome back then. You could see it in the pictures.... Even his skin was clear."

Wires and Junior looked at each other after listening to Detective Fernandez. Junior could not resist asking another question. "How is it you know so much about him?"

"Oh, well...years ago I used to follow his group....They were really good. Actually, to be honest, we went to school together....I guess I was sort of a Spiros groupie back then."

"So you can tell us where his birthmarks are?" Wires commented with a gloat.

Fernandez laughed off the remark, taking it good naturedly. "I *don't* think so," she answered. "How is Fishnet doing?" she asked. The conversation reminded her of the wayward detective.

Junior was surprised at the question. "You know Fishnet?"

"We worked night watch a couple of weeks ago, so I was with him all night. He's a trip....We were all over Brooklyn on jobs. It was a crazy night."

Wires and Junior had no time to dawdle. Aside from being aware that Fernandez was off duty, they were anxious to head out directly to the Mill Road residence of Joe Horse and make good on their assignment. They were determined to reverse the reputational damage they'd sustained. By their calculations, the only way to accomplish this was to prove themselves as dogged investigators with the best work ethic in the squad. They intended to rise above not only the mediocre and average squad members, but also above the best detectives in order to remove the stigma hounding them. They were shooting for the moon...to be exceptional.

The two detectives secured a parking spot on Mill Road. The unmarked car they were in was located close to the front door so they could easily see who was entering or exiting the house. Armed with the photos of Joe Horse, they sat outside for about an hour waiting.

Junior was the first to get antsy. "How do we know he is not back in the house already?"

Anthony Celano

"All the lights are off."

"So? He could be sleeping."

Wires tilted his head to one side, considering Junior's remark. "You're right. We really don't know, do we? How about we get a number and call the house....What do you think?"

"No, a call might spook him, tip him off that something is up. We should try to grab him cold – by surprise, totally unaware." Clearly Junior had been paying attention to Markie.

"Want to give a shot at knocking on the door?" asked Wires.

"Let's do that. If he's home, we can snatch him right off. If not...at least we know to look for him coming home."

The detectives duplicated the efforts made previously by Fishnet and Von Hess with the same negative results. They returned to their vehicle prepared to wait their man out.

It was after 2:00 a.m. when Wires first saw Joe sauntering alone along the dark street. He took steady strides and didn't appear like a man under the influence. There was no fading off or periods of standing still...slowly bending over in a nod out. The detectives knew for sure that they had their man because the subject was wearing the same black shirt with the single yellow stripe down the front that he had been wearing in one of his mug shots. Joe Horse was about five-foot-eight with a slim build. He had a full head of black hair that he wore in the style of the early Beatles – but at his age, thanks to the bags under his eyes, the look was more reminiscent of Moe from the Three Stooges. He was clean shaven, wore pink-tinted glasses, and had a couple of old acne scars that were visible on his face. The jeans he wore over his black boots were of the latest design.

The detectives wasted no time – they pounced on him like a couple of panthers about a second after they recognized him. The detectives never had to identify themselves. Joe Horse was a street guy. When in top form, he would have been capable of spotting cops from a mile away with blinders on. At this hour, while still functional, he was not at his best. Wires made the overture while Junior stood alongside him, letting her partner take the lead.

"Hold it up, pal," he said commandingly.

"What?" Joe Horse raised his hands in a defensive gesture.

"Where you coming from, Joe?" asked Wires, looking to confirm he had the right man.

"No place...special. I've been at Quigley's on Henry Street all night."

Wires was all business. "We need to take a ride to the precinct. You have anything on you that you shouldn't have?"

"No...I'm clean, man." He spoke in a nasal-sounding whine.

Wires noticed the outline of a thin, cylinderlike object in Joe's pocket. He figured it for a weapon...possibly a pen gun or a knife. It was a hypodermic needle, a criminal offense that constituted enough to arrest Joe. "Okay...c'mon, what other toys have you got? Empty your pockets on the hood of the car."

Joe Horse complied but very slowly—carefully placing his property on the hood of a parked car for the detectives to inspect. Not taking any chances, Wires patted Joe Horse down. He needed to be sure Joe didn't have a weapon on him. Joe's additional property consisted of house keys, a comb, a black wallet containing over seven hundred dollars, and a candy bar.

"Are you sure you don't have anything *else* someplace on you that you shouldn't have?" Experience had taught Junior that it was possible Joe might just have secreted a stash of drugs in private areas.

"No...nothing, man. I told you I'm clean."

"Okay...let's go, then. In the car," ordered Wires.

"Go where?

"The precinct."

"Go to the precinct for what? I've been straight. I got no open cases on me. I'm not chipping or anything, man."

"You're in possession of a spike, aren't you?" Wires asked.

"Don't tell me you guys are pinching me for a spike, man!"

"We have to talk to you. You are going into the bull pen for possession of the spike. So let's go....You're coming with us."

"C'mon, man, why can't we talk here and forget about the arrest? Take the money. It's not mine anyway. I just found it. I was going to turn it in...."

Wires ignored the bribe attempt. "Let's go....Put your hands behind your back....You are starting to piss me off." The last thing he wanted was another bribery arrest.

The detective made it clear that there were no options. After putting the cuffs on Joe, they placed him into the rear seat of the unmarked car. Once inside the vehicle, Joe inched up in his seat to speak to the detectives.

"So this is definitely an arrest, then?"

"You are in cuffs, aren't you?" asked Junior.

"For just having a spike?"

"Yeah, for just having a spike. Are you forgetting about parole, pal?" countered Wires. "Do you think your parole officer is around?"

Joe Horse quieted immediately. The comment made by Wires was a vivid message alerting Joe to go along with the program. Joe took the ride without so much as a murmur. After a few minutes in the car, Joe Horse dozed off, falling sound asleep with his head resting against the rear window of the vehicle transporting him. The silence during the trip back to the squad was interrupted just once, when Junior made a call to alert Markie that they were bringing home the bacon.

21

GIDDYAP JOE

MARKIE DECIDED THE time was right for him to tell Parlatto that he was going out to run an errand. It was a diversion he had been thinking about and was looking forward to. All of the detectives were accounted for, and there was no brass sniffing around. The setting was perfect for him to take a bit of relief and go see Alley Cat. Markie's boss over at homicide was long off duty.

Barring any new crisis requiring the duty captain, the sergeant from homicide was home free to pursue an interest that was beginning to overshadow his desire for drink.

"I have to go out and take care of something, Lance," he announced. "I'll be back in a little while."

"No problem....I got you covered," answered the squad commander without hesitation.

Parlatto was only too happy to see Markie occupy himself someplace off site. The homicide sergeant's absence meant Parlatto finally was going to have some time for himself. He was unaccustomed to having to share his office for extended periods of time.

"Do you want me to bring you back something from outside?" Markie asked on his way out.

"No, I'm good. Take all the time you need....I'm here." Parlatto was anxious for the solitude that was about to come his way. "Don't worry; I'll reach out to you if something comes up."

Markie headed over to Fitzie's without apprehension, confident that Parlatto could be relied upon to hold down the fort for the short time he intended to be gone.

"Finally!" expressed a relieved Parlatto once Markie was out the door.

Parlatto took the opportunity to make the most of his privacy. Locking the door to his office, he eyed the couch as he took off his tie. Stepping behind his desk, he reached down to remove a container of milk from the small refrigerator stowed underneath the furniture. He opened one of the desk drawers where he kept a clean glass and package of mint Oreo cookies. After filling the glass with milk, the sergeant turned on the television to channel surf, stopping at an old western. The squad commander then eased his way over to the couch, kicked off his shoes, and put his feet on the chair he used as a footrest. Dipping an Oreo into the milk, he became engrossed in the imminent danger facing the wagon train, which was circling the wagons in preparation for the Indian attack. Awaiting the invasion, Parlatto's vigilant eye was out for the chief of the tribe. He had sat though enough oaters to know that if they could take out the Indian in the colorful headdress, the raiding party would likely cease their onslaught. Strategizing against cinema Indians was a hell of a lot more fun to Parlatto than trying to figure out what had happened to a couple of junkies.

⊞ ⊞ ⊞

LOOKING TO WASTE NO time, Markie picked up his pace as he hustled over to Fitzie's. He was anxious to again bask in the one environment in his life that remained consistent. The distinct smell of the barroom, the unembellished surroundings, and the solitude to think uninterrupted were all appealing. And now with Alley Cat...the pot was sweetened.

There were never any changes taking place at Fitzie's. It was an old-school gin mill that had not undergone a single improvement that anyone still around could recall. Fitzie was the most precious relic in the place. At age eighty-four, he was a throwback. Fitzie managed to draw in his customers based on his reputation as a former boxer and great raconteur. He'd been a heavyweight contender whose claim to fame was being rated in *The Ring* magazine's top ten for the championship. As a storyteller, there was no one better. His impressive rendition of the lengthy poem "The Face Upon the Barroom Floor" was legendary. Holding the attention of every half-stewed customer in his audience, his oration was administered perfectly, stanza after stanza, never faltering. The conclusion of his recitation came with a unique and memorable touch....

He would fiercely slam his hand down on top of the bar as he emotionally put forth the closing line, "With a fearful shriek, he leaped and fell across the picture—dead!"

Daytime patrons of the emporium were an aging bunch whose numbers managed to replenish year after year, regardless of the death toll. Fitzie's geriatric crowd drank throughout most of the day as if on shifts, with cliques of men coming and going. He drew working men in by cashing their paychecks, allowing them to take a slice of the pie before they turned it over to their wives. The blue-collar crowd drank, watched a game, talked sports, and racked the felt table to play a little nine ball for quarters.

In the evening hours, the bar became a favorite haunt of some of the younger people in the neighborhood, particularly on weekends. The pool table and dartboard were tools used to identify the loser who was going to pay for the next round of drinks. Perhaps it was a goof for them just to hang out in an old-timer's place, or maybe it was the cheap prices that drew them. Whatever the case, the local youths were a welcome addition because they paid their tabs and caused no problems. Besides, having a few young girls coming around was always good for business.

"Koufax was the best pitcher ever," a middle-aged man told a young woman and her boyfriend as the two stood at middle of the bar sipping mugs of beer. "Nobody could touch Sandy in his prime."

"Yeah... in baseball he's all that," the woman allowed. "But Ali is my favorite overall athlete."

"That draft dodger! Are you kidding me?" blurted Pat, an old-timer seated nearby at the bar who had been listening in on their conversation.

"You sound like my grandfather, Pat," she groaned. "Why can't you people understand that the man had a religious conviction?"

"So did Fighting Father Duffy," the old barfly snapped back. "It didn't prevent him from serving his country up at the front!"

"Fighting Father *who*?" she asked, smiling at her boyfriend.

Markie squeezed by as they continued their debate, taking a seat on an empty stool at the very end of the bar. The barmaid had spotted him when he entered, and by the time he got settled in, Alley Cat was on her way over with a bottle of Jack Daniel's and a shot glass.

"What happened to you, cop?" she said as she poured the shot. "You look terrible!"

"Working....I haven't been home since I last saw you."

"Poor baby...a big case?" She filled a short beer glass with Budweiser. "We are still working on those two girls in the trunk from the other day."

"I read something about that!"

Markie glanced around at the crowd. "These young people sure wake this place up, don't they?"

"They're not so bad," Alley said. "Not exactly the big spenders...but they're okay."

Markie doubted that anyone could be considered a big spender at Fitzie's place. "Next time I come by, I'll give you my college pin...you know, 'Boola Boola.'"

She laughed. "I'll give you some 'Boola Boola!..but I can't talk to you now. The lad over there is signaling me for a refill. The place has been like a soph hop all night! I'll come by again in a minute."

"Okay, but pour another before you take off." He threw down the first shot in order to make room in the glass for the second.

Markie liked drinking. The more he drank, the less uptight he became... and the more he liked Alley Cat. His fondness for alcohol was a vice that rarely seemed to get the better of him. He was one of the lucky ones who could consume a good deal without getting sloppy. The sergeant looked over at the framed photo of Detective Broderick hanging on the wall. His hero was wearing a conservative dark suit, black tie, white shirt, and light-gray fedora with a thick black band. The hat was worn with a tilt, pulled down to one side, giving Broderick a real tough-guy look. Markie loved that picture. He smiled and raised a glass to the wall. "To you, old-timer!"

He finished his whiskey and the beer chaser, and he took out money from his thinning billfold, leaving enough on the bar to cover his drinks and a little something extra for Alley. He wanted her to think well of him. As he headed out, Alley Cat spotted him.

"Hey, you leaving already?"

"I have to get back on the job."

"Oh," she said with disappointment. "Okay. I guess I'll see you next time."

Markie looked at Alley Cat's red lips as she spoke. He reached over the bar to pull her toward him. He then gently kissed her cheek as he said goodbye. It seemed to her to be a long, drawn- out peck. It was at this point she knew he wanted to get back into her pants.

The sergeant walked out without any further fanfare. He returned to work to do his duty, wondering how long it would be before he could jump Alley Cat's bones.

⊞ ⊞ ⊞

JOE HORSE WAS BELIEVED to be the key to the door that would lead to solving the enigma of the two women in the trunk. It was the wee hours of the morning when he was sitting quietly in a chair in the interview room, cuffed to a pipe affixed to a cinder-block wall. He was looking uneasily at Fishnet as the two men waited quietly for Von Hess to arrive.

Fishnet kept his back up against the closed door, doing his best to project a hard stare as he sized up his man. It was Camel time for him. Taking his first deep drag, he entertained himself blowing circular smoke rings in Joe's direction. The detective was disappointed that the other team had been successful in picking up Joe. Fishnet's preference would have been for him to have grabbed Joe at his home...where he'd have had a shot at grabbing some cash and drugs.

The thought of missing out on the chance to get his hands on Joe's stash irritated him to no end. The more he processed the lost opportunity, the more ornery Fishnet grew. He began to look for ways he could persecute the prisoner. Noticing a tiny mark along the vein on the back of Joe's left hand, he ordered Joe Horse to roll up his sleeves and reveal his arms.

"What?"

"Come on...up with them. Let me see those fucking arms, asshole." Joe complied, slowly unbuttoning the cuff to the left sleeve of his shirt.

"Now the other....Come on, hurry it up," ordered Fishnet.

Joe Horse repeated the process with his other shirtsleeve. Right then, it was plain as day to the detective the depth of Joe's addiction. His fondness for the needle had riddled his arms with two trails of discolored flesh...the marks of an addict. Fishnet now knew one thing that he could take to the bank about Joe Horse....It would be just a matter of time before he would be needing another fix.

Self-conscious, Joe Horse was dismayed at having to reveal the condition of his arms. Viewing his discomfort was cause for Fishnet's personal euphoria. He derived tremendous gratification at seeing the misery of Joe Horse.

"Okay, now the shoes and socks, and up with the pants legs," ordered Fishnet.

Joe Horse slowly complied, revealing his additional telltale scars of drug addiction. Fishnet's sneer projected him to be a man who felt totally superior, a master of men who lorded over those he conquered.

As a result of his humiliation, Joe got a little testy with his captor. "What is this really all about, man?"

Before Fishnet could respond, Von Hess entered the room. Looking at Joe Horse with his sleeves rolled up, shoes and socks off, and pants legs rolled up, the senior detective turned to Fishnet seeking an explanation.

"What gives?"

"Just making sure *Joseph* has nothing on him that he shouldn't have."

Von Hess thought there might be more to it, but he accepted the answer. "Okay, Joe, get your shoes and socks on," he ordered.

After Joe Horse put his shoes and socks back on, he again asked for an explanation. The even- tempered Von Hess read Joe his rights, after which he responded to the question. "It's about two dead people. Did you hear about the two girls found in the trunk on Mill Road?"

"Yeah," replied Joe cautiously, "I saw something in the papers. So what?" A certain flippancy could be detected in his reply as he slowly lowered the sleeve on his cuffed arm.

Von Hess wore his serious-as-cancer look. He threw his reel into the water, hoping for a bite. "So somebody said they saw you with one of the girls...a good-looking blond. What about it?"

Joe Horse reacted with a sudden jump that saw him straighten up in his chair. "Me?" he asked, with his thumb pointed to his own chest. "Well, *somebody* made a mistake. You got the wrong guy, man."

"The person who told us is somebody you know very well, asshole," needled Fishnet.

"Who are you talking about? Saw *me*?" When no response came, Joe Horse continued. "Just so you know, I'm not some jerk-off....I went to school. I don't have to talk to you here....I know my rights, man."

Fishnet had his opening. He was in the bad-guy mode all the way—a part he enjoyed playing. "Yeah...you're no jerk-off; you're an intellect who got flaked with a mother lode of smack. When you did your stretch, did you pleasure yourself with a CPA prep book?"

"That was—"

Cutting Joe's explanation short, the detective came across even harsher. "Cut the shit, asshole. We know you were with her Friday night, so let's have it."

Joe Horse let out a protracted sigh. It was apparent the detectives had done their homework. Fishnet's behavior was not unexpected. It only confirmed Joe's suspicions that he was in for an unpleasant session with the detectives.

"What do you want from me?" Joe spoke in a low voice, looking down at the table. He looked depressed because he knew all too well what was coming next.

"To rethink things, pal...and don't forget that spike you had on you."

"You were really an accounting major in school?" Having enough of Fishnet, Von Hess had reentered the conversation from a different, softer place.

Letting out a slight sigh, Joe answered Von Hess. "Yeah, for almost two years."

"I'm impressed...and that's no bullshit. I always wanted to be an accountant. Let me ask you a question....Was it very hard?"

Joe thought the older detective was being authentic, so he answered accordingly. "Not for me. It came easy to me."

"How exactly does a guy like you, who obviously has a brain and who probably comes from a decent family, take the slide downhill you took?"

"What slide? I'm doing good," the addict stated defiantly. "I got plenty of money...more than you guys will ever realize in a lifetime, man!"

"You have no argument from me on that," Von Hess conceded. "But I'm not smart like you."

Joe nodded with pride. "I got the brains. *That* you can't take away from me."

Fishnet held his tongue at the remark. Leaving Von Hess to continue on with the questioning, he permitted himself to stray off on a journey. He was soon traveling in a world where he was the managing partner of a huge CPA firm...a famous accountant with celebrity clients. It was all cocktail parties in the Hamptons, ascots, pocket squares, and ambitious women jockeying for position just to be photographed standing next to Gable's twin.

"That is why I am so curious....I can see that you have the brains. So how is it that you got hooked?" Von Hess asked.

Joe Horse tossed his head to one side and snickered. "That is something I keep asking myself."

"You had a tough family life?"

"Nah...nothing like that. My father owns businesses, and my sister is a financial advisor in Manhattan....They both do real good." Then he added, "Funny thing is that I'm smarter than both of them put together."

"But here you are...sitting with us."

Joe took no offense. "Yeah...here I am sitting with you guys."

"What kind of business is your father in?" asked Von Hess, sticking with his friendly tone.

"Laundry....He owns about a dozen places."

"Lucrative?"

"Big time....Anytime you have a cash business, you can't lose. As long as those machines are operating, the coins keep adding up."

"You're father's a Greek, right? What happened?...He didn't like the restaurant business?"

"My father's brother is in that business....That's his thing."

"You aren't all Greek, are you?"

"Greek and Chinese....My mother is from Beijing."

"He's Greek-ese," injected Fishnet after coming back into the real world.

"We're trying to talk seriously," barked Von Hess at his partner, angered that Fishnet was disturbing his momentum in lowering Joe's resistance.

The expression on Von Hess's face didn't escape Joe's attention. It made it plain he was tiring of Fishnet. This went far in making an impression on Joe. He was now able to relate to a detective who he felt stood up for him. Maintaining his cool, Von Hess shifted the conversation to the pertinent business at hand.

"How exactly did you get hooked on drugs? I'm still baffled by this whole story."

"Music, music, music," came the answer in a drawn-out way. "I was a musician in high school and college, had my own band even. My father always hated the music scene. He wanted me in business with him."

"Oh...so a beef with your father made you turn to drugs?" Von Hess was intentionally coming across as dumb.

"I'm not saying that, man. It was party time for me...playing the guitar, doing lots of different girls, plenty of weed, then pills....You know the story. It was all about sex, drugs, and rock and roll."

Joe Horse for the moment forgot that he was talking to detectives. With his guard down, he began talking about himself. "The drug thing just sort of snuck up on me. I guess you could call it an occupational hazard. In time, everybody, the whole fucking band, got hooked on one drug or another."

"But you still had the smarts to get into accounting," Von Hess noted.

"Yeah, I was always good in school...especially in things pertaining to business. It was my own band too," he said with obvious regret. "I handled the financial end, controlled the money, negotiated gigs, hired musicians, the works."

"What school?"

"I went to Baruch College."

Seeing that Joe Horse was loosening up, Von Hess stayed the course. "Then?"

"Then...things went south. It was the drugs, man. I started skipping classes, the band started blowing jobs...you know, the usual shit. We were showing up high, nodding off between sets. It got pretty fucked up, man. When the work dried up, the band folded."

"You gave up on music and accounting?"

"Carrying the monkey, it became all about money. Next thing, I start getting caught doing shit, and...well, now here I am with you."

"So what about you and this fucking blond girl in the trunk?" In one leap Fishnet got to the heart of things.

"I told youuuuu....I don't know any fucking blond." His response was one of exasperation. "Didn't I already tell you that, man?"

Fishnet, fully focused in the present, made his move. He decided to push the addict into a corner. "Smarten up....Save the sob story for somebody who really fucking cares. We'll get the parole officer in here to hold your hand, and you can go down memory lane with him."

Joe Horse again straightened up in his seat fast. Von Hess detected the stress on the doper's face. It was his cue to be the good guy again. The first time Joe looked away, he signaled Fishnet to leave the room. On cue, Fishnet reacted.

"I can't listen to this guy's shit anymore. Let's get the parole officer down here," he said harshly just before bolting from the room.

Now alone with the prisoner, Von Hess tried reasoning with the suspect by coming over as fatherly. "Listen, Joe, before my partner starts picking up the phone, take a minute to think this out. You and I both know you are going to talk to us eventually. How about we make it easy on everyone, including yourself?"

"I have nothing to give you, man."

"Tell you what; let me talk to the boss while you mull it over. If you play ball, maybe we can do something with the parole officer. Sit tight."

Von Hess left the room and asked Fishnet, who was waiting outside, to remain in place and keep an eye on the prisoner. He then scooted over to the squad commander's office. When he got there, he found the door closed. Von Hess knocked on the door and waited. After a minute, Markie opened the door. Sergeant Parlatto was seated on the couch.

"So?"

"I think we'll get there in due time. Patience is all it is going to take with this guy," opined Von Hess. "We have him in the room, letting him stew."

Markie massaged his forehead with his fingers. He was on the verge of having a headache. "Wires and Junior just ran out to grab something to eat. They'll be back shortly. When they get here, they can step in for you guys. Let's try a change of faces and see what those two can do with Spiros."

Von Hess concurred; he thought it a good idea. Fishnet would hold a contrary opinion, but he had no say in the matter; it was Markie's call.

When Wires and Junior got back, Markie sent them to the interview room to pursue the effort in trying to roll over Joe Horse. No offers of nourishment were extended to the man with the addiction. The young detectives commenced their interview with more of the same, a monotonous verbal good guy–bad guy exchange that would remain unrelenting until a penetration into Joe's defense could be made. It took some time before Joe Horse finally began to show signs of weakening. It was Wires who scored the first point in denting the addict's armor.

"Look, friend...think about it. It was the escort service that gave you up! Can't you get that through your thick skull? How do you think we got to you...huh?" Joe Horse looked at Wires as he thought about what the detective said.

The detective pressed on. "You think a pigeon flew in the window with your name on a piece of paper stapled to his ass? C'mon, willya! You are supposed to be a smart guy!"

In an effort to better his circumstances, Joe chose to offer the detectives what he thought was a limited, nonincriminating bone. A small concession might do him some good in working the angle he had cooked up. Joe decided to approach the weakest link on the other side of the table...Von Hess.

"Okay...I did have a date with Belle. But I'm only talking about his to the old detective."

"*Belle?*" Junior turned to look at Wires. The detectives were unfamiliar with the name.

"I want to talk to the old guy," Joe was insisting.

Wires summoned Von Hess and Fishnet to return to the interview room. Once there, Von Hess assumed control of the interview.

"I spoke to the boss, Joe....There may be some wiggle room for you. Who's Belle?" Von Hess asked.

"The big blond," clarified Joe. "What kind of wiggle room you talking about?"

"Tell me about Belle first....I have to know what we can get *before* I know what we can give."

Joe understood his point. "I know the blond as Belle. The paper said her name was Shirley something,...I forget what."

"How did you contact her, and when was that?" Fishnet asked.

Joe looked at Fishnet warily and then over to Von Hess, as if asking for permission to answer. "Go ahead," encouraged the senior detective.

"I always go through the escort service. Whenever I call, they send the best hookers over to my house. It costs a bundle, but it works out for me. Lately I've been asking for Belle to come over specifically. I've had her over a few times....She was cool. We got along good."

"When was the last time?"

"It was on Friday."

"What time?"

"About 7:00 p.m. or 8:00 p.m., somewhere around that time."

"Where were you going with her?"

Joe Horse looked at Fishnet with surprise. "Going?"

"Yeah, going!" responded Fishnet, raising his voice. "She was supposed to fucking escort you someplace...wasn't she?"

"I never leave the house with them. Girls would just come over to service me....And let me tell you about Belle; this girl knew her business."

"Really?" replied Fishnet.

The face of Von Hess tightened at hearing this. Not interested in such details, he posed the next question to get back on track. "When did she leave you?"

"She always stayed awhile...until the next morning. She left about 6:00 a.m., I think. It could have been earlier or even maybe a little later. I don't exactly remember."

"She spent a lot of time with you," noted Fishnet. "That had to cost. Where do you get the money?"

"I *know* how to make money," he said defiantly. "I got plenty....Don't worry about that." The addict failed to indicate how he earned his money.

Fishnet wasn't worried...just enthusiastic about the possibility of worming himself into Joe's house. "You must have a pretty good bankroll tucked away somewhere."

Joe Horse could see the dollar signs registering in Fishnet's eyes. Knowing that he had Fishnet's attention, he forgot about Von Hess. He decided to propose the plan he had devised to Fishnet.

"Look...I got *lots* of green...all at home. It's enough to spread around nice. Maybe it's a good idea for us to go to my place....I can fix myself up and then maybe give everybody a little something for their trouble—"

"Not a chance," replied Von Hess in an unwavering voice.

Fishnet did a double take. As he turned to give Von Hess a look, his expression clearly indicated, *Why not?*

Joe appealed to Von Hess. "Listen, I can even give you plenty of information about a lot of shit out there. Once I'm okay...we can work together." Joe was grasping at straws. "We can come right back here and resume if you want...*after* I'm fixed up. I'll work with you, man."

Fishnet looked at his partner as if to say, *How about it?*

"Forget it," advised Von Hess coldly.

"Yeah...forget it," Fishnet echoed, pissed at having no other choice than to concur.

Joe needed time to think, so he put on an exaggerated faking act. He placed both hands against his stomach. Rocking forward, he began to complain. "My stomach is starting to bother me. I have to use the bathroom."

Von Hess asked Wires to take Joe Horse to the bathroom. The squad room was very quiet. Parlatto's precinct detectives had finished up their shift and were long gone by now.

During the break in the action, Markie and the rest of the team were briefed by Von Hess. "Joe admits to having sex with Shirley Harris at his place. He knew her as Belle. He said she was with him between 7:00 or 8:00 p.m. Friday night and Saturday morning sometime around 6:00 a.m. Joe said that he was unsure of the exact time she left because he was high."

"A hooker...right?" Sergeant Parlatto asked.

"Yeah, looks that way."

"How much?" Parlatto asked.

"According to Joe Horse, a lot. When we asked where he gets his money from, he just said he has lots of money."

"Where is he now...still in the room?" asked Markie.

"In the bathroom. He said his stomach is giving him problems."

Fishnet had to give it a try. "He's got to be dealing drugs in order to pay that kind of freight. Girls like that don't come cheap. And where he lives? He's dealing for sure. Maybe we should go to his house and see what's there."

"We would need a warrant," said Markie, dismissing the idea.

The sergeant made a decision to have Fishnet and Von Hess continue to work on Joe Horse. He then took a moment to talk privately with Wires and Junior.

"You two are doing good work."

The faces of the two detectives expressed surprise at receiving the accolade.

"I just want you to know that your work is not going unnoticed," said the sergeant. "I know it has not been easy."

"Thank you," was their joint response.

"Trust me...just hang there the way you have been, and things will work out fine."

After the detectives left him, Markie sought out Sergeant Parlatto. "Why don't you get something inside you? I'll hold down the fort now. Just bring me back a piece of lemon pound cake if you don't mind." Parlatto felt like a piece of lemon cake also, so he readily agreed.

⊞ ⊞ ⊞

VON HESS AND FISHNET resumed the grilling, and the time soon came when Joe Horse showed signs of actual decline. He no longer had an appetite. It was only a matter of time now that the addict was weakening.

They continued to chip away at Joe Horse, asking him to repeat answers over and over with variations of the same old questions. The barrage of questioning finally tripped up the junkie.

Joe Horse leaked to Von Hess that Barbara Allen had also been at his apartment. The revelation served as nourishment to the detectives, an energy pill that saw them double up on their effort.

"Okay...Belle stayed with me longer into the next day than I told you. She asked me if her friend could come over to my apartment and hang out. I said, 'Why not?'"

"What time was that?"

"The other girl got to my house about...I don't know...in the afternoon....I don't remember exactly."

"On Saturday?" Von Hess wanted to make it clear.

"Yes, Saturday."

"Did the two women leave together?"

"They both left after a while. The other girl came by with her dog. I hate dogs; I'm allergic to them....So for that reason I got rid of them both. I told them that I was having difficulty breathing."

Fishnet wanted more. "And?"

"And that is it." The reply from Joe Horse came fast and definite. He stayed entrenched at this place in his narrative, unprepared to offer up any more until he got some assurances.

Von Hess called up Sergeant Markie, asking him to respond to the interview room so that he could hear what they had learned directly from Joe Horse. Markie looked at Joe Horse carefully. He listened to him repeat what he had told the detectives. Taking Joe's clammy appearance into account, he decided to clear the room and go one on one with him.

Once everyone else was gone, Markie took a seat at the table opposite Joe. Markie's plan was to rely on his specialty...working the head of those seated across the table from him.

Von Hess and Fishnet had left the interview room to assume standing positions behind the one- way glass. Fishnet was put off by what he considered the sergeant's intrusion. He voiced his dissatisfaction to his partner. "This isn't fucking right," he hissed. "He has no business sticking his nose in now. We had this junkie on the ropes."

"Give the boss a chance," Von Hess advised. "Believe me, he is good at this."

"I don't give a fiddler's fuck if he's Charlie Chan and the junkie is his number one son....He has no fucking right to interfere like this! I'm going to talk to the union delegate about this shit."

"What the hell are you talking about?" Von Hess snapped. "Just chill out, will you?! And don't worry—you can be sure that you'll get *all* the credit if this goes anywhere."

This statement made Fishnet hold his tongue; he was now willing to live with Markie's involvement. Once the intrusion issue was resolved, Fishnet was able to concentrate on monitoring what was happening on the other side of the glass.

"Listen, my friend," Markie began, "this is nothing personal. You are who you are....How you got to where you are is not for me to judge. So I won't. Can you understand that?"

Joe Horse just shook his head slowly, trying to figure out where the sergeant was really coming from. The sergeant's style of approach was new to him, and a boss being up front and asking the questions was another first for him.

Markie continued. "You could have gone out and committed a triple homicide...and I still would figure you did what you did because you had your reasons."

"I committed no homicides!" Joe said loudly.

The statement bugged Joe Horse out, heightening his nervousness. This left Markie with the impression that he'd touched on something close to home. He now felt certain he had the right man in his midst. He was so close to the prime rib that he could almost taste it. All he needed to do was stay the course.

"I'm not saying you killed anybody....I'm leveling with you here, Joe. We have been going around in circles, with you giving it to us in bits and pieces. You know it is only a matter of time before you tell us....You know that," he stressed. "You are here on a pinch. You are on parole, and you are probably already getting sick...right?"

With his head down, the dejected addict absorbed the points made with silence. "You are already cold. I can see you are already starting to sweat...."

"I'm not sweating!" Joe Horse had a burst of defiant energy at the implication.

"Okay...so I'm stretching the point....You're not cold and sweaty," conceded Markie.

"Look...let me repeat myself. You've got a habit; let's face it. You are going to require fixing at some point...right? On top of that, you're on parole, and we got you with a spike on you. You have no options....Am I right or what, Joe? Yes or no?"

"Yeah."

"So why are we sticking to denials? If you murdered these two, I understand you sitting tight. If you didn't, then why are we procrastinating here? You got the time for that?"

Markie was now listening for a response. None came.

"You have to play it smart, Joe. Do you understand what I'm trying to tell you here? Whatever happened...happened. You just need to explain it now, unless you intentionally shot them in the head or some shit...which I know you didn't."

"Go on...," came the response from Spiros.

Markie continued, sensing he was getting someplace. "There is no sympathy or help for someone who brings nothing to the table. You have family?"

"Yeah...I got parents and a sister." Upon mention of his family, Joe Horse was starting to appear even glummer.

"Good people?"

"Yeah, they're real good. I was the big disappointment even though I'm making money."

"Forget that." Markie was coming off with the confidence that people gravitate to. "We can turn all that around if you just listen to me. If your folks are good people, all they really want is for you to meet them halfway."

Markie paused. He was looking at Joe Horse to see if he was still getting to him. He felt that he was.

"Look, a hospital visit is likely in the cards for you at some point down the road. Medication of some kind will keep you safe. We can wait, or you can take the trip to relief ahead of the curve. What is it going to be?"

Joe Horse answered in a tone that suggested he couldn't convince himself. "But I told you everything I know."

"Stop!" Markie scolded. "That kind of talk will land you into the arms of an unsympathetic parole officer, who will put you back in the can for a lengthy stretch if I have anything to say about it. But why go that route? You have to trust me on this. I can help you."

After Markie was relatively sure that what he said had sunk in, he kept going.

"This is one of those times when the truth is the only answer. The truth will give us something to work with, something to tell people. There was an accident, you made a mistake...or there were extenuating circumstances. Whatever the real story is, it will be alright. Spill it and we can run with it. Do you get the picture?"

Markie received no response for a couple of minutes. He was a patient man, prepared to wait.

"Listen, Joe...I can provide you with some light at the end of the tunnel....How about it?"

Finally, Joe Horse was preparing to deliver the answer to a riddle that had perplexed the detectives for days.

"Can we take a walk?" Joe seemed unexpectedly calm when he asked the question.

"You bet. Let's go." Together the two proceeded to walk around the precinct halls while engaging in conversation. Due to the late hour, there was little activity at the precinct, so the two enjoyed a degree of privacy as they walked.

"You win, Sarge."

"So talk to me," encouraged Markie.

"Any chance we can go to my house so I can straighten myself out first?" "Can't do it....You know that. Might as well just start talking now."

"You can't blame me for trying."

"No, I don't blame you for trying."

"Can money fix this for me?" "C'mon, Joe, get real. Let's hear it."

"Belle came over to the apartment not just to have sex with me. We would hang out, get it on, and cap things off by shooting up smack. That was our routine. She called up the other girl, Barbara, to join us, and the three of us got off."

"Barbara worked for the service? You had a triangle...three-way sex?"

"No...nothing like that. She was just a friend of Belle. No sex....Barbara was only about the heroin."

"You knew Barbara previously?"

"Yeah. The three of us did it before."

"No sex, though, with Barbara?"

"No...there was no sex with Barbara. Just H with Barbara."

"What time was it that Barbara got to your place?"

"Around 2:00 p.m. or somewhere around that time, I think. Don't hold me to the exact time, though."

"She came with her dog?"

"Yeah. That mutt was always with her."

"And then what?"

"So Barbara shoots up first."

"Heroin? She injected herself, or did someone help her?"

"Yeah, heroin....I'm Joe *Horse* right?" he said sardonically. "She shot herself up."

"Go on."

"So Barbara gets off first, then Belle. I'm about to get mine when first thing I know, Barbara falls out in my living room. Me and Belle are holding her up to keep her off the floor....Then all of a sudden, Belle's legs cave in....She collapses on me too. Now I got the two of them knocked out at my feet!"

"Jeez...what did you do?" Markie feigned understanding.

"I checked them for a pulse, a heartbeat, and get nothing...both are gone. So now I'm dead, I figure." Joe seemed relieved to get the story off his chest.

"Then what did you do?"

Joe Horse stopped walking so he could emphasize his point face-to-face with the sergeant.

"Hey, Sarge, look; I'm on parole for drugs....What can I do? How can I have them found like that in my crib? I had to get them the fuck out of there...right?"

"I see your point. So what did you do next?"

"Well...I'm not exactly thinking straight myself at first, but then I come to terms with the situation. All I know is that I can't have these two broads found in my place....This violates me for sure, and I don't want to go back in the can for nothing."

"Did everyone share the same needle?"

"No, I had my own set of works. The girls shared the needle Barbara brought over, though."

"You provided the heroin?"

"No, no! Definitely not! Barbara brought all the junk over and a set of works for her and Belle to use."

"Who paid for the smack?"

"I don't know where she got the shit. Nothing exchanged hands with me. Whatever the arrangement...it was worked out between the two women. I told the detectives before that I paid the service a lot of money to get Belle to come over and put out, so they had the money."

Joe Horse stared intently into Markie's face. Markie knew better than to believe Joe's tale in its entirety. The sergeant figured that Joe had to have sold the dope, bartered it, or made a present of it to the girls. He assumed that Joe knew the best way to articulate his story in order to minimize his exposure.

Markie tried approaching things another way. "Did you pay Belle off in drugs on any of her visits?"

"Never....I always paid cash, enough so she and the other girl always had enough to bring the drugs. That was the way we did it."

Markie felt sure this had to be a fabrication, but he had to work with what he was given, so he didn't press the point. "What did you do after you realized the girls were gone?"

"To tell you the truth, I had to make a visit to the little boy's room first thing. It gave me time to think things out while on the throne. I ended up calling a friend of mine to help me remove the bodies. I got off myself while waiting for him to come over, so I was okay."

"But you didn't fall out, did you?"

Joe Horse was at a loss for an answer to the question. Markie moved on. "What friend?"

For a second, Joe Horse hesitated. "A guy I know, he owns a small box truck. He is sort of a mover who does small moves."

"What is his name?"

"Do I have to give you that?" Joe Horse knew he did. "Franny."

"Franny who?"

"Franny Preto."

"How old is Preto? Is he a Brooklyn guy?"

"Yeah, a Brooklyn boy who lives on Fort Hamilton Parkway someplace... same age as me."

"Okay, then what happens?"

"Franny came over pretty quick with his truck to help me out."

"What time was it that he got to your place?"

"Between four and five, maybe even later....I am not really sure. All I know is it was still raining heavy when he came."

"And?"

"We took the girls out of the apartment one at a time and put them in the back of his truck."

"How was it no one saw you?" Markie asked. "Risky, wasn't it?"

"Not really. The truck was backed up onto the driveway, so we only had to go a few feet. Besides, it was raining like crazy."

"Not many driveways where you live. You were lucky. How did you take them out?"

"We had an arm over each of our shoulders and walked them out erect... one at a time. We made like they were drunk. We loaded them on the truck, and Franny tied them in the blanket. The whole thing only took about five minutes."

"Blanket or quilt?"

"I mean quilt."

"Why would Franny do all of this? He must be a good friend."

"We go back a long time, but trust me, it was not out of love. I had to give him fifteen yards up front to get him to help me."

"Fifteen hundred bucks...were you okay with that number?"

"What could I do under the circumstances?"

Markie said nothing in answer to this question. He hated to think what he would have done if he were being stuck up for fifteen hundred. The sergeant remained dubious about certain parts of Joe's tale, but he thought the addict was being truthful about this last portion. His story flowed too well to be anything less than the truth.

"What did you do with the spikes?"

"Right down the sewer, along with the packaging."

"Did the two girls have phones?"

"Yeah, they did....I tossed their phones in the sewer too. It was the only thing of theirs I went south with. Franny wanted to take their money and jewelry, but I said no. I'm no grave robber."

"You did the right thing there. Don't forget about you getting rid of the dog," Markie pointed out.

"Yeah...we dumped the dog too. But the mutt didn't go down the sewer, at least...right?"

"That is true. Where did you go with the bodies?"

"With the rain, it was kind of dark out...like night. Mill Road was desolate, so we didn't have to go far."

"I know that by where we found them," said Markie.

Joe Horse continued his account. "Franny punched the lock of the first car he saw with a big trunk."

"Again...weren't you afraid to be seen?"

"No. Franny double-parked the front of the truck alongside the rear of the car, preventing anyone from seeing him punch the trunk lock. Then we carried the bundle on the side of the river, where no one could see us, stuffed it in the trunk of the car, and took off."

"What kind of car was it?"

"A Lincoln or a Caddy, maybe even an Olds....I'm not too up on cars."

"How hard was it to punch the trunk?"

"Franny did it easy—he was a top car thief when he was a kid. Boosting cars was his specialty."

"His specialty now is...?"

"Anything for a buck," answered the addict.

"Then what did you do?"

"We went to my place. We both took a shower and ordered some pizza."

"What time was that?"

"I don't really remember the time....I'd be making it up."

"Okay, Joe. Let's walk back to the office. I want you to tell this story to the detectives. Once that's done, I'll see about straightening you up. I'll also see what I can do for you with the district attorney....You are no killer."

Joe Horse, the almost accountant, believed him.

22

THE LAW

ONCE JOE HORSE SPILLED the beans, he began a journey down a road of no return. He knew better. He was sophisticated enough to realize it would have been smarter to keep his mouth shut. The addict's cooperation, even while suspecting it was against his best interest, was primarily prompted by his declining stamina and inability to control the nervous tension that came with his addiction. He had reached the point where he was incapable of continuing to tread water—he had to make something happen. The need to keep things moving had caused him to embrace the illusion that he could somehow walk away from it all. There simply was no leeway in the law that would provide the elbow room for him to slip through the bars of a cell.

Fishnet and Von Hess settled down to business with Joe Horse. Since he'd already revealed his story to Markie, the detectives had no difficulty extracting the same narrative. The prisoner remained faithfully committed to his account of what had happened to Shirley Harris and Barbara Allen. The more he repeated his story, the easier it became for him to believe whatever portions he had fabricated.

Fishnet and Von Hess were in agreement that the story provided was credible—with a single exception. When it came to the origin of the heroin, Joe's version of events just didn't ring true. This was a pill that refused to go down easily for the detectives. Their quandary rested in their inability to prove that Joe Horse was the one who had furnished the heroin to the two women.

By 8:00 a.m., the squad would liven up when detectives arrived to commence a new tour of duty. Processing the prisoner was going to take time. Since it was Fishnet's case, he was naturally the arresting officer of Joe Horse. He booked his prisoner, prepared the arrest papers, and assembled all the related available paperwork in the case folder for presentation to the district attorney's office. Included were the reports prepared by the detectives who'd worked the case, detailing the investigative steps taken and numerous interviews conducted over the days worked.

During this period, Joe Horse surprised everyone—maintaining more physical endurance than he or the detectives had originally thought possible. Nevertheless, it was generally felt that the time might come when Joe Horse would have to be carted off to a hospital for treatment. Fishnet was hoping his luck with the addict's resilience would continue. The detective wanted to avoid the inconvenience of having to take his prisoner to a hospital. If Joe Horse were able to hang on long enough to enter the custody of the Department of Corrections, Fishnet would be relieved of the responsibility of the prisoner's medical care. Once Joe entered the correctional system, he automatically became their headache instead of Fishnet's.

For this reason, Fishnet did all he could to take good care of Joe Horse, including pampering him with plenty of sweets in hopes of keeping him still. Fishnet's backup plan was to slip Joe Horse a couple of the confiscated pills he kept secreted under the bullets in his box of .38 caliber ammo. Each pill was hidden under a separate cartridge that was housed in its own Styrofoam hole.

Sergeant Markie and Parlatto had been sitting quietly in the supervisor's office watching the clock when Parlatto's detectives signed in to start their tour. The supervisors had been waiting for 8:00 a.m. to arrive so they could make their required notifications to the bosses coming on duty. Von Hess, Wires, and Junior had completed their obligations. They were cut loose after having performed their jobs well. The precinct detectives on hand would be tasked with transporting Fishnet and his prisoner to central booking for further processing. Once there, Fishnet would have Joe Horse lodged until the prisoner was ultimately transported to court for arraignment and transfer to the Department of Corrections. What remained unanswered was the question of the appropriate charges to lodge against Joe Horse.

Sergeant Markie telephoned his lieutenant over at homicide to inform him that the case had been solved. The news made his boss happy, and he indicated that he would apprise the division captain after the consultation with the district attorney's office. Both were confident that those at the northern end of the managerial pyramid would be throwing confetti at hearing the news. Blue DD-5s—the form used for closing a case with positive results—were always well received.

Markie's next call was to the medical examiner's office. To his great surprise, he learned that the preliminary results of the autopsies were available even though the full results would take four to six weeks. What was not a surprise was the cause of death for both women: both Shirley Harris and Barbara Allen had died of an accidental heroin overdose. As Markie knew well, this meant that there were definitely no murder charges that could be filed. A charge of murder would have required proof of intent to kill, which was not the case here. The district attorney, if inclined to stretch things, which was unlikely seeing that the case could not be proven, could consider manslaughter as a possible top charge.

Sergeant Parlatto dialed up the district attorney's office to speak to Hal Roberts, but Roberts was away from his desk, so the sergeant left a message. Markie was slouched back on the couch with his hands folded behind his head. His eyes were staring blankly up at the ceiling, looking at nothing in particular. He was thankful that his work was finished on the case. He was feeling too tired to even stop at Fitzie's for the morning pick-me-up he had been considering. It was a weariness he very well knew he would get over once he hit the fresh air. From this point on, Fishnet and Parlatto were on their own. It was their responsibility to handle the DA—*and* tie up any loose ends.

Markie was rubbing the grit out of his eyes when he heard Parlatto addressing him. The sergeant turned toward Parlatto, amazed at how the squad commander continually managed to walk barefoot on hot coals without getting his feet burned. Markie was certain that Parlatto had learned nothing as a result of the case—a point that only furthered Markie's disdain. He knew Parlatto would never progress to where he knew how to run a case on his own or even begin to comprehend how to successfully navigate the turbulent waters created by media.

"The charge isn't going to be murder, is it?" asked Parlatto.

"No, Lance—without proof of intent, that's definitely out. Let's just wait and see," Markie said through a yawn.

"I figured as much," Parlatto said.

"How's that?"

"It's simple. Prosecutors hold their trials before they get inside a courtroom in order to protect their batting average. They want every case to be a winner...right?"

"Right...your point?"

"So," reasoned Parlatto, "why would they even consider taking a chance on a manslaughter charge? I figure they won't go for it."

Markie had failed to give the squad commander enough credit. He had underestimated Parlatto, surprised that he possessed sense enough to arrive at the conclusion he articulated.

"Whatever....The case is solved, and that's the bottom line," said Markie. He rose to his feet to stretch. "This Joe Horse is a pretty clever guy....I'll give him that."

"In what way?"

"He never once admitted to giving the girls the drugs."

"So?"

"So...if he does," explained Markie, "then we have him cold on manslaughter because by injecting them, or just by giving them the drugs, an argument could be made that he acted recklessly."

"So what exactly have we got?"

"All we have is his saying that the girls had their own heroin and administered it to themselves."

"Yeah, but that has got to be bullshit," Parlatto replied. "You know that."

"I do, but Joe Horse is off the hook because we have no way of proving otherwise."

Parlatto sighed. "So that's it."

"The DA is going to know that Joe Horse was the candy man, but what can he do? It makes no sense for that office to take up the challenge and try to prove something they most likely can't."

"I see."

Markie had one final thought. "The only thing that might move the district attorney in the direction of a manslaughter charge is a political push...which is unlikely at this point from what I can see. Things have apparently died down on that front."

"So what do we charge him with?"

"Let the DA enlighten us. But then again, you can also go ahead and charge what you like, and the DA can drop those charges down when he draws up the affidavit."

Parlatto was confused. "So...what are you saying to do?"

"Since this case did have some political interest, even though the concern seems to have subsided...you never know. I'd let the district attorney make the call from the get-go; then you can refer questions directly to their office. Let them handle it," said Markie.

"Makes sense," agreed Parlatto.

⊞ ⊞ ⊞

IT WAS AFTER 9:00 A.M. when Hal Roberts returned Parlatto's call. After hearing the facts, he told Parlatto that he would have to get back to him concerning the charges. As promised, thirty minutes later, Roberts called back, advising that the charge would be "improper disposal of a body," a non-penal law misdemeanor.

"A misdemeanor! That's it...improper disposal of a body?" asked Parlatto with amazement as he glanced over at Markie.

Roberts answered without any emotion. "That is it, sarge."

"Really?"

"Hey, what can I tell you?...We don't make the laws down here, sarge."

"Okay, got it. Thanks, Mr. R." Sergeant Parlatto hung up the phone.

For Markie, once he let his lieutenant know about the DA's verdict, his job was officially over. Now, all that remained was the responsibility of the squad commander. Parlatto had to worry about Joe Horse getting sick, the spike they had found on him, his parole officer, and the second piece... Franny, the mover who had helped dispose of the bodies. Whatever else surfaced from this point on was on Parlatto's shoulders.

But Markie did take a moment to telephone Barbara Allen's parents before he signed the log to go off duty. The medical examiner's findings finalized things. The couple took the news quietly, without any expression of emotion. There was not much for them to say. By now they were resolved to the fact that their daughter was gone due to an accidental overdose while among fellow junkies. All the parents could do was to accept what they found distasteful....Their daughter was an addict who had fallen off the wagon. The truth behind the why and how of their daughter's death meant little to them now because they would invent their own version— something a little more palatable— that would imply the police had dropped the ball concerning what they would forever refer to as the "murder" of their daughter. Since there was no winnable legal battle, the couple did their best to put the whole mess behind them. Barbara's parents did not obsess over what the outcome was going to be regarding Joe Horse. Victoria Allen no longer cared if Fishnet had all of his marbles or not. It had simply become time for her and her husband to move on.

Markie knew that he was obligated to make one last call. He was in no hurry to pick up the phone to engage in what he knew might turn into a taxing conversation. Instead, he stalled— accompanying Parlatto into the squad room to apprise Fishnet of the charges. The detective was disappointed at the news. The case was not the big one that he was hoping might propel his career and advance his quest for fame.

After receiving the news, Fishnet looked over to where Joe Horse was lodged. Joe was lying down on his back on the stone bench inside the cell with his forearm covering his eyes. As Fishnet stared at his prisoner, he was trying to come up with a creative reason that would get him into his prisoner's apartment. Knowing that a search warrant was not feasible under the circumstances, he was left only with his imagination. Gazing off, he made another mental escape...this time to the abode of Joe Horse, where drugs and cash were in abundance. A slight trace of glee could be seen on his face as he envisioned himself stuffing his pockets with drug money.

Eventually, the homicide sergeant rose to the occasion. He held the phone in his hand for a few seconds before he dialed. He was thinking about what he was going to say to Red Harris. He was in luck; there was no answer, allowing him to leave Harris a message to call him at the homicide squad. Markie was glad to avoid a conversation with Shirley's father. He wanted to be at full strength for that.

Markie went off duty to enjoy his time off. He was sure to duck out of the building quickly...just in case Red got his message and was nearby. When he returned to work, the sergeant would talk to Red about what he figured to be the most expensive misdemeanor case ever investigated and charges that took many years down the road to make it into the penal law.

23

ALLEY CAT PURRS

THE REJUVENATING EFFECTS of the outside air temporarily made a new man out of Markie. The breezes bestowed enough feel-good for him to hum his way over to Fitzie's for a quaff. Walking over to the bar, he passed people on the street, some of whom looked twice as he happily sang to himself. When he entered the gin mill, he saw Fitzie behind the stick serving customers. The business owner smiled broadly when he spotted Markie.

Markie always received a big wave of acknowledgment from the owner whenever he came in. The warm greeting made the homicide sergeant feel wanted. In general, Markie had an aversion to any special treatment; he never wanted to owe anyone anything. But the friendly welcome he always got at Fitzie's was something he welcomed. It was a gesture that made him feel good about himself.

"Hello, Sarge!" Fitzie called out. "How have you been?"

"Good, Fitzie. No complaints."

"Hope everything is going good for you....I haven't seen you around, sonny boy. What happened?" The bar owner asked this with some concern. "Were you sick or something?"

"I've been around; I guess we just keep missing each other. I've been busy working, so I've been in and out."

"You look a little tired."

"Nah...I feel fine," said Markie. "Well...maybe just a little tired."

Markie knew that he was kidding himself—his newfound pep would soon fade. He also knew that once he occupied a stool, he'd be in for the long haul. After a drink, he would be too tired to even want to get up on his feet. Since he was swinging out and would be off from work, there would be no rush to go anyplace.

"Take a seat, Sarge," the proprietor ordered. "I'll fix you up good.... How do you feel about a flat roof?"

Markie cast an unknowing look at Fitzie. "What's a flat roof?"

"On the house!" came the old man's reply as he poked a thumb into his own chest. "You never head of that term? Where have you been living... in a cave?"

Looking at the gray-haired, ruddy-faced proprietor, Markie laughed before responding. "Sure thing, Fitzie....Nothing fancy, though—just give me whatever you've got open."

Markie slid onto the vacant stool, which he found to be a little uncomfortable. He didn't mind. With his fatigue, after the second one, he knew he would be numb. While he waited for Fitzie to come back, the sergeant, as usual, made it his business to be oblivious to the presence of the bookie seated at the front of the bar. He figured what went on at *that* end of the rail had nothing to do with him at his end. Markie looked the other way at what he figured to be the offering of a service wanted by people who came to drink in the bar.

Fitzie soon returned with a bottle of bourbon to pour Markie his drink. "Here you go—Old Grand-Dad, 101 proof...strictly for the pleasure of one of New York's finest. This should help curl the nails on your toes!" The owner smiled as he filled the oversized shot glass. "Here you go...three fingers. Bud chaser, right?"

"Perfecto...thanks, Fitzie."

Fitzie, still robust in appearance, liked to work his charm behind the bar, dispensing booze and shooting the breeze with his clientele. His tales of the ring were always a favorite. They were stories he told with a conviction that left little doubt in the mind of listeners. Fitzie went into one of his stories as he poured. "You know Jimmy McLarnin, the old welterweight champion? He is over ninety and still alive! Now, there is a little guy who whipped thirteen champions...."

A couple of hours later, Markie could be seen struggling to keep his head off the top of the bar. Even in his unstable condition, he knew that once his skull touched the mahogany, he would be a goner. Desperately in need of sleep and with little food in his stomach, the destructive liquid assault on his body had gotten the upper hand. Refusing to put his head down, the sergeant succumbed to sleep while sitting upright on his stool with his head bent to one side over his shoulder. Markie looked like a man hung...minus the rope.

Fitzie could see the sergeant would never be able to make his way home. The bar owner, who owned the building, kept an apartment for himself on the second floor for those days when he had his own trouble making the return trip. After recruiting a couple of regulars, he had them guide Markie upstairs and put him to bed. For a fleeting moment, Fitzie pondered whether it would be a good idea to take the sergeant's gun and hold onto it for safekeeping. But the gun went untouched, left undisturbed in the shoulder holster. Fitzie did not want to run the risk of offending his friend in law enforcement. After all, he reasoned, a bar owner never knows when he may need a favor from a cop.

Alley Cat was scheduled to start work at the bar at 7:00 p.m. She could always be relied upon to show up about ninety minutes early when she worked this shift. She would bring something to eat in order to fill up before she started work. Today was no exception.

"Alley...do me a favor: eat upstairs in the apartment so you can look in on old Markie for me."

"Sure, Fitzie....Is he okay?"

"He overextended by a few, but he'll be okay. I just want to be sure before I go home."

"No problem, Fitzie. I'll babysit."

When she entered the apartment, Markie was still sound asleep. Alley checked her watch. She had plenty of time before she needed to be behind the bar. She called downstairs, alerting Fitzie that she was putting on coffee for when Markie finally woke up. Looking at the prone sergeant, she gently shook him. Seeing a slight stir from him, she smiled as she began to stroke his hair with evident fondness. It turned her on to see him helpless...where she was in control. Markie soon came to realize that he was experiencing one of those pleasant wake-up dreams that men are always up for...only this time it was the real McCoy.

24

FED
BY RED

BY THE TIME MARKIE returned to work, he was feeling better than ever. Now that he was in solid with Alley Cat, he was ready to tackle the world. As a rule, he was always anxious to get back on the job. He was a man who for the most part loved his work, amassing huge amounts of time off on the books due to his not wanting to be away from the action. After scratching his name in the squad sign-in log, he scooted through the squad room toward his own office in an effort not to prolong the gauntlet of greetings that awaited him.

"Good work on that case in Brooklyn Heights, sarge," said one detective as the sergeant made his way past the coffee maker.

"Nice going!" said a fellow sergeant.

"I heard you killed it, boss," voiced another detective.

"Another one for the good guys....Nice job," was the accolade Markie received from his lieutenant after he peeked into his superior's office to let him know he was present.

Accolades aside, being back in the saddle felt good to the sergeant. He was content being at a place where he belonged. He later brushed off the praise by pointing to the three detectives in the office as the people most deserving of credit. This in and of itself came as no surprise because everyone knew of Markie's modesty. What did cause some unsettlement among squad members was when Markie referred to Wires and Junior as detectives with a great future in the squad. That pronouncement was a stunner. The public acknowledgment was met unenthusiastically, and people, not knowing what to make of the situation, silently resumed what they had been doing prior to Markie's arrival. This reaction did not faze Markie—he knew that the duo's transition into the squad was going to take time. His gesture merely planted the first seed of positivity.

On his desk, Markie found a small yellow sticker on the receiver of his phone. The message written on the sticker advised that a Mr. Harris had called and was expecting a return call. Hearing telephonically from "Mr. Harris" was a hell of a lot better than receiving notice that "the Death Maker" was waiting for him downstairs.

Markie didn't hesitate to contact Shirley's father. This time the call was answered promptly.

"Hello...this is Markie from homicide."

"Markie! Where the fuck have you been?" The identity of the person on the phone was unmistakable. The gravel in his voice was Red's calling card.

"I've been off....This is my first day back. I tried calling you the other day, but no one answered your phone."

The big man offered no explanation why he had not picked up his phone. "So what have you got for me?"

"Everything you want to know," answered Markie. "When are you available to get together?"

"You know Leon's...near the Cyclone on Surf Avenue?...How about 7:00 p.m.?"

"I know the place. See you there at 7:00 p.m.," confirmed the sergeant. "Come alone." Red was in the habit of dictating terms.

⊞　⊞　⊞

WHEN MARKIE ARRIVED AT Leon's Restaurant in Coney Island three hours later, Harris had already secured a booth in the most private section, at the rear of the eatery. Red was having an espresso when Markie sat down. The sergeant's attention was noticeably drawn to the bottle of Sambuca on the table. Markie had never been a big fan of espresso. On those rare occasions when he ordered it, he always opted for anisette.

"Drink?" offered Red. He picked up on how Markie had zeroed in on the bottle of 'Buca.

"No...thanks. I don't drink," said the sergeant with a poker face.

"I want you to talk to me straight."

"Really...I quit drinking....Square business." Markie misunderstood what Red was referring to.

"I don't give a shit if you swill down a fucking bottle a day," said the big man with a surprised frown. "Tell me about my daughter!"

Markie felt foolish having made such a blunder. He got right to the point. "Both girls died of accidental overdoses...and that comes straight from the medical examiner."

Based upon his reaction, this was no big news to Harris. "Go on. What else?"

"We made an arrest. The guy we grabbed was charged with improper disposal of a body—a misdemeanor."

"That's it...a fucking misdemeanor?"

"Afraid so....The charge isn't even in the penal law—it comes out of the health code, I think, or some other half-ass book of laws."

"So how exactly does she end up in a fucking trunk?"

"The guy was a steady...*client* of your daughter." Markie sought to choose his words carefully because he knew the ground he was treading could collapse at any moment.

"What *kind* of steady client?"

"They had...an arrangement of some kind," answered the sergeant.

Red looked at Markie, waiting to hear more. He knew Markie was trying to sugarcoat the facts. "Just give it to me fucking straight, willya?... Don't treat me like I'm some fucking pussy."

"Okay...whatever you say. Anyway, they shoot up in this guy's house, and the two girls overdose on heroin right on the spot as a result." Markie was attempting to pass over the rough patch as swiftly as possible.

"What's the arrangement they had, sergeant?" demanded Red, dragging the conversation back to the ground Markie had attempted to skirt.

As requested, Markie gave it to him straight. "Sexual...after which they would get off on smack."

"Are you telling me the snowbirds had a threesome?" Harris was expressionless.

"No, no...nothing like that. The second girl joined them in the apartment after the sex part was over. The other girl was there strictly for the heroin," clarified the sergeant. "My guess is that he supplied both women—he probably either sold it to them or they had some other arrangement worked out. Either way, we are unable prove anything."

"So the escort service was sending her out...turning tricks?"

"The position of the owner of the service was that Shirley was sent out strictly as an escort," Markie explained. "Whatever else she did was done on her own. They apparently didn't really care."

"That's bullshit!" thundered Red. "Don't buy it....That little fat bastard doesn't miss a fucking trick....He makes his money knowing which customers want what from the girls! He knew what the fuck was going on!"

Markie shrugged, neither agreeing nor disagreeing. He was taken aback by the remark about "that little fat bastard"—it was practically an admission that he knew Anthony Boy a lot better than he had originally let on.

"What about this mutt you pinched? Who is he? What's his story?"

"The guy is a junkie."

"So he sent her out to see a fucking junkie!" Red didn't hide his disgust. Then he exploded. "Don't tell me no more, and don't tell me the service didn't fucking know about what was going on here. That cocksucker goes along with whatever the customer wants as long as it brings in money. He'd take it up the ass himself if you wrapped a five-dollar bill around your cock!"

Markie didn't even try to respond. His silence was taken by the big man as agreement. Once Red cooled down a bit, the sergeant again spoke. "The guy is a functional junkie who seems to generate a lot of money," explained Markie. "We think that his cash comes through drug dealing."

"He's fat with money, you say?...That cinches it. They sent him over a playmate he can relate to...the bastards. The service knew what was going on!"

"Anyway," Markie resumed, "this guy was on parole for drugs. After the girls collapsed in his apartment, he called up a guy he knew with a truck. They transported the bodies and ended up dumping them in the trunk of a parked car. That's the long and the short of it."

"I've seen hopheads like that, junkies who can function once they get their stuff," said Red. "This guy is in the can now?"

"Yeah, he's in. Don't worry; he won't be coming out on the street for a while because his parole was violated. He'll be in the joint long enough to get himself healthy again."

"What was he on parole for again?"

"Heroin possession....I'm talking weight."

"Son of a bitch!" Red Harris caught himself before he went off again. "Does he have a name, this motherless fuck?"

Markie hesitated for a minute before he answered. Since it was public record anyway, Red was entitled to know. "His named is Joe Spiros. His street name is Joe Horse, a Brooklyn guy."

"Never heard of him. What is he, a Greek?"

"Half-Greek and half-Chinese."

The waitress came by to ask if they wanted to order anything. The sergeant indicated he did not. She placed a fresh espresso in front of Red Harris.

"Take that shit back. Give me a scotch....Make it J&B on the rocks with a splash of water. Then give us a couple of steaks, mashed potatoes, and some spinach," ordered Red. Then addressing Markie, he asked, "How

Anthony Celano

do you like your meat...medium?"

"Medium rare," answered the sergeant obligingly, realizing he was going to have to eat. "Also give me a Coke."

After taking the order, the waitress walked away from the table. The big man was obviously a known entity at the establishment. It appeared to Markie that he might be sitting at Red's regular table. Markie suspected Red was likely to have a piece of the place.

"So the escort service was sending my daughter out to turn tricks?"

"I didn't say that. The girls make that decision on their own; at least that's what I was told. The house collects a flat fee from the women for the privilege of their working for the service. There was a seventy–thirty split on the take, with the house getting the lion's share. Whatever else the girls did, it was done on their own with nothing going to the house... as far as I know."

"Did the service know about the drugs?"

"That never came out, so I can't say yes or no to that."

"Who was it from the service that you talked to? Was it that guy Anthony?"

"Yes."

"Who was it who helped move the bodies? How did they do it?"

"Joe Horse had a friend—a freelance mover he knew, stepped up to help him. They walked the girls out to the truck pretending they were drunk."

"Who is the mover? He's got to be the junkie's crime partner to do something like this."

"Franny Preto...another Brooklyn local."

"You busted him too?"

"No, that is for the squad detectives to do now. It is up to them to follow up."

"So Preto is still on the street, then?" asked Harris.

"As far as I know....Look, just leave it for the law to handle."

"Of course," answered Red innocently as he took his drink to his lips.

When the steaks arrived, the two men devoured them. Markie declined the offer of dessert.

When Red saw that the sergeant had finished his meal, he addressed Markie for what would be the last time. "You want anything else?"

"No...this is enough for me, thanks."

"Then that is it, sergeant....Our friendship can now be considered over." The Death Maker closed the conversation.

Markie took it as his cue to leave. His obligation met, he left the diner, glad to be out of there. The sergeant was not quite sure what steps Red Harris intended to take, if any. Whatever was on the Death Maker's bucket list, there was nothing Markie could do to alter it.

He looked at his watch, wondering if he had the time to make a swing by Fitzie's for a quick one. He got in his unmarked car and headed there, but before he arrived, he received a call from Von Hess.

"Markie speaking."

"Sarge, it's me, Ollie."

"Yeah, Ollie...what's up?"

"We got a new one that just came in...a woman in an apartment stabbed to death. The lieutenant wants us on it."

"Where is it?"

"The Seven-Two in Sunset Park. Top floor of an apartment house at Fifth Avenue and Fifty- Fourth Street."

"You at the office?"

"Yeah, boss."

"OK, wait outside for me. I'm in the car. I'm on the way to pick you up. See you in a few minutes."

There would be no visit to Fitzie's for the time being. On the drive over to pick up Von Hess, the sergeant wondered if there was anything he could do to put Red Harris in check...but he drew a blank.

⊞ ⊞ ⊞

FISHNET AND HIS PARTNER, Sidney Schiff, now back from Florida, knocked on the front door of the townhouse. A woman in her early forties answered the door. Upon seeing the two men at her door, she quickly began to adjust her reddish-brown hair.

Fishnet immediately began to evaluate the woman. She was thin and tall, wore glasses, and had a recently trimmed pageboy haircut. She was attired in a cleavage-revealing button-down red shirt and tight jeans. What solidified Fishnet's approval was the ruby pendant hanging from her neck. He figured the piece of jewelry to cost big bucks.

"Mrs. Gertrude Albright?"

"Yes, I'm Trudy Albright. Are you the detectives from the precinct?"

Fishnet produced his gold shield. "Yeah, I'm Detective Milligan. This is my partner, Detective Schiff."

Trudy picked up on Fishnet's lingering stare. She found herself flattered that the Gable lookalike was checking her out from head to toe without the slightest trace of hesitation. "Please come in and take a seat. Can I get you anything to drink?"

"No, thank you," replied Schiff.

"I can't begin to tell you how embarrassed I am over this. I never even told my husband...not that I talk to him very much anyway."

"What does your husband do?" Fishnet asked.

"He's an investment banker."

"You own or rent this place?"

"We own it." After hearing this, Fishnet was sold on her.

Seated on the couch next to the crime victim, Fishnet opened the manila folder he was carrying. He took out a photo array containing six pictures of white men, all with mustaches and glasses, to show Trudy. After producing the array, he asked, "Do you recognize anyone in this array?"

Trudy's response came instantaneously and was to the point. "THAT'S ERNESTO!" Clearly impressed, she asked Fishnet how he was able to identify the man who had stolen her diamond necklace so quickly.

"That's our job. This fellow has a history of committing these type of crimes," said Schiff.

Trudy hardly heard what Detective Schiff said. Her interest was in Fishnet. "I'll bet Ernesto isn't really his name....Am I correct?" She was locking eyes with Fishnet as she asked the question.

"Nah...his name is not Ernesto....We call him the Mask," answered Fishnet, continuing the intense eye contact.

"The Mask? You have to tell me all about him...." Trudy's broad smile revealed her delight in the conversation she was having with Fishnet.

Detective Schiff could see that Trudy's interest in recovering her missing diamond necklace was a secondary concern for her. Not wanting to be a third wheel, the detective excused himself from the room. By the time Schiff made it back to the car, Trudy was in the middle of mixing a Harvey Wallbanger for Fishnet.

25

SWING BLADE'S RULING

RED STOOD ON THE CORNER as if he owned the block. His jaw was lifted, shoulders back, and his feet were firmly planted on the sidewalk. He was wearing his lucky black porkpie hat—something he did only when was packing heat. He stared across the street at Augie D'Angelo's Skylight Social Club on Avenue B and East Tenth Street. The storefront was located alongside another D'Angelo stronghold, the Adjustment Room, a watering hole frequented by those of questionable character.

D'Angelo's illegal empire thrived in part thanks to minions whose criminal proficiencies stretched far beyond the usual gambling, criminal usury, and extortion. After the passing of his elder brother, Carmine, Augie emerged as the sole ruler of the once-shared Lower East Side kingdom. Insulating himself through a series of fronts, Augie was the controlling partner in a number of prosperous enterprises—some of which were even legitimate.

Swing Blade had allocated part interest in the Adjustment Room to his son-in-law, Ernie Albertini. Albertini was responsible for the day-to-day operation of the business. But as far as the State Liquor Authority was concerned, the owner of record and head man was Walter Long—a mentally challenged local everyone knew as Wheezer. Augie had attended grammar school with his front man, who still lived with his ninety-year-old mother in the same tenement apartment he grew up in. Augie authorized Ernie to grease Wheezer five hundred dollars a month in return for his permitting the use of his name on the license.

Albertini, also known as "Ernie A," was receiving a disability pension from the City of New York Sanitation Department for a work-related injury that had left him with a slight limp. In addition to earnings from the Adjustment Room, his father-in-law also allowed Ernie to supplement his income with bookmaking and shylocking. The son-in-law, under Augie's protection, had a healthy amount of money in circulation on the street and was making a good living as Augie's partner in these ventures.

Augie insisted on his being a partner in everything he touched—it was his way. His value as a partner lay with the power connected to his name. Few people would fail to make nice once they understood they risked running afoul of Swing Blade and his crew. The D'Angelo name was known on the Lower East Side as a long-established organized crime power not to be taken lightly. Augie D'Angelo's notoriety was enhanced as someone to fear in no small degree by the looming presence of Red Harris.

Red was mentally prepared for the sit-down he intended to have with Augie. Looking to avenge his daughter, he was going into the gangster's courthouse to make a case. Red was seeking the authorization to kill Anthony Boy. His other intended executions, Joe Horse and Franny, needed the blessing of no one. Those two were freelancers without any organized muscle behind them. As independents, they were not on record with anyone, which meant they were without protection. Anthony Boy was with Augie...and *that* was a different story.

Red crossed the avenue and entered the social club. As Augie's assassin, he was a known entity who was afforded lots of respect by those frequenting the club. Once inside the social club, Harris scanned the room looking for Augie. Several tables were occupied by gamblers playing cards amicably, drinking espressos and Manhattan Specials. Any serious alcohol consumption inside the club was forbidden. That activity was reserved expressly for the Adjustment Room. Upon seeing the big man, several of the gamblers called out their greetings. "Hey, Joe"; "Hello, Red"; or "How is it going, Red?" were the most commonly heard expressions used to acknowledge the presence of Harris.

Red proceeded over to the bar area where Whiskey-Nose Ravetti was seated. To run the club, Augie enlisted the services of Ravetti, a longtime thief with a passion for burglary. His rap sheet, if laid on the floor, would extend out the door and onto the street. Red approached Ravetti, who greeted the big man with a wary nod.

"Swing around?"

"In the back, Red." Ravetti tossed his head in the direction of the office

Anthony Celano

behind the bar.

"Is he alone?"

"Yeah, I think so."

"Go in and see," Red ordered. "Let him know I'm here to talk to him."

"Sure thing, Red." Whiskey moved quickly to do what he was told. He knocked on the door before entering. After a few seconds, he emerged from the room to give Red the go-ahead to enter the office.

Augie D'Angelo, in his mid-sixties, was a stocky five-foot-seven, with a slight pouch visible around his waistline. His face was freshly shaved, his thick salt-and-pepper hair was neatly trimmed, and he was wearing an immaculate blue jogging suit. Around his bull-like neck, D'Angelo wore a thick gold rope chain with a golden horn. Augie was one of the few old-timers around who could be seen wearing a diamond horseshoe pinkie ring and not appear foolish. He'd picked up the name Swing Blade after he had sliced off the ear of a man who'd tried to listen in on a conversation he was having on a payphone.

"What do you say, Red?" Augie was usually casual when greeting his terminating machine.

Red responded somberly, "I got problems, Augie."

"What happened?" Augie sensed from Red's grimness that his visit was cause for concern.

Red followed protocol. "First off, I want to thank you for your support. I really appreciate it....It meant the world to me."

Augie waved him off. "We were all shocked over that, Red. I know what it is to have death come around. Look at my poor brother."

"Yeah, that was a shame too."

"So what's troubling you, my friend?" asked Augie.

Red got to the point right away. "I want my due, Augie. I want your blessing to do what I gotta do."

"What do you gotta do? I don't follow you."

Pointing his finger at Augie, the big man said two words. "Anthony Boy."

Augie responded immediately. "You talking about my Anthony Boy? What did that jerk-off do now? Tell me....If he got out of line, I'll crack his fucking head open myself."

"He had my daughter turning tricks, Augie. That don't go....You know that. It was to be just escorts...no tricks, no drugs. That was the arrangement."

"Ohhh, shit....You saying fucking Anthony was pimping her off? Giving her drugs?" Augie effectively exaggerated his bewilderment.

"He arranged it or he was letting it happen. Either way, he knew all along what was going on. I repeat...*he knew all along*! I hold that cocksucker responsible!"

"Are you certain about this, Red? I'm not disputing it...but I need to know how you know this for sure."

"I got it straight from the head bull."

"What head bull you talking about?" Augie was now concerned.

"The homicide sergeant—he told me direct...*to my face* when I had to go see him," explained Red. "I want this fucking Anthony's ass!" he demanded.

Augie looked at his torpedo suspiciously. "What exactly do you mean, you *had* to go see him?"

"Your fat boy fucking pimp called me to tell me *my* daughter may be dead *and* that I needed to check it out."

"He did?" asked the shocked D'Angelo. "What else did that asshole say?"

"He said that it was *you* who wanted me to go to the precinct and check it out." Red lied, trying to put Anthony Boy deeper in the trick box.

"*What*?! Are you fucking kidding me?"

"I don't kid around, Augie....You know that. I never ask for nothing. I don't ever question nothing. But now I'm asking my boss for permission....I want you to give me claim to Anthony's fat fucking ass!"

Red made it apparent there was little room for compromise. Augie looked to see if a nonviolent resolution could be worked out. "This fucking kid Anthony, even being the dumb bastard he is, knows how to earn for us. He is bringing in the green real good, Red. I'm talking about big money he's putting on the table for me here. How about we do this?...I give you a piece of his end in the business to make things right. Let's say half of what he takes in for himself now goes directly to you?"

"No soap, Augie. He's gotta be taken care of good. One way or the other, Anthony Boy is finished."

Augie was not used to such resistance. "Look, Red, back it up a minute over here...."

Red wasn't hearing of it. "I am more valuable to you than *ten* jerk-offs like Anthony Boy....He can't do what I do for you. People fear you with me on the team, Augie....You know that. They fear you!"

Augie could not argue the point being made. In one sense, the Death Maker was indeed more valuable to him than Anthony. With a guy like Red in his pocket, all of his rackets were protected against those apt to double-cross him. Plus, he could always collect from deadbeats with Red on board. The big man also made muscling in on businesses a lot easier. On the other hand, Anthony was a big earner, the one bringing in substantial coin. As one of Augie's top revenue streams, Anthony Boy had a long shelf life. He was still young and likely had many good earning years ahead of him. Losing Anthony would cost Augie money.

D'Angelo decided to offer Red one more alternative. "How about you take half his money, and I give you permission to administer to him a real good fucking beating to square the account and for using my name in lying to you? Would that sit right with you?"

"Square the account?" Red was astonished.

"Maybe you go and poke one of his eyes out, bust his back...you know, fuck him up good."

Red didn't even respond to the totally inadequate suggestion. The nonresponse told Augie everything he needed to know about the Death Maker's frame of mind. Augie's choice, with some regret, was to back Red's play. Not to do so would be a dumb move. Failure to get behind Red would result in his losing them both. He knew Red would kill Anthony Boy anyway, and then he would be compelled to clip Red for disregarding his order.

Augie shrugged. "Okay, Red, have it your way. Do what you like with Anthony; just do it quietly. I know I don't have to tell you that."

"I appreciate this, Augie. But what happens to the business with Anthony now out?"

"There will be some bumps...but I got it covered. I've been grooming that kid Jimmy over there anyway. He works with Anthony. Jimmy knows the routine, so he can carry on."

"Does the offer still go?"

Augie looked at Red as if confused. "What offer?" he asked.

"You know...a piece of the business for me?"

Red was pressing his luck. Augie looked at Red hard but ultimately conceded that it was in his interest to keep him happy. He would trim some off what had been Anthony's end for himself and Red, leaving less for Jimmy, which was no big deal. The new escort partner would be grateful for anything he received.

"You are on the wrong end of the team, pal of mine," Augie joked. "You should be the boss! Okay...let's say you and I split 25 percent of Jimmy's end from this point on. Happy now?"

"Thanks, Augie."

Red the Death Maker left satisfied; he'd walked out of the meeting better off than he could have anticipated. Now he had some work to do.

26

HEADQUARTERS HOEDOWN

"AL...I NEED YOU AT the puzzle palace tomorrow morning to represent the homicide squad at the meeting."

"Whatever you say, boss—no problem," replied Markie. The sergeant knew that his lieutenant hated to attend the accountability meetings at police headquarters.

"I have some work here to do...so I want you to go in my place. You can take Von Hess along if you like."

"No problem. We'll cover it."

"Are you up to speed on the homicides we are working on...just in case they call on you to weigh in about one of them?"

"No problem, boss....With Von Hess with me, we will be up to speed."

"Good man." The lieutenant felt confident he was covered.

The drama that unfolded during the grueling monthly meetings was nothing short of humiliating theater. The entertainment came at the expense of those commanding officers who entered the arena either unprepared or awkwardly nervous. Being part of a specialty unit such as the homicide squad limited any potential exposure to abuse. Such units existed to support the precincts, who held ultimate responsibility for the conditions and crimes occurring within their confines. Targeted for assessment were the precinct commanding officers along with their counterparts in the precinct detective squad. The two faced an interrogation concentrating on all ailments existing in their respective commands. The commanding officers, standing side by side in front of the ranking members in their borough, were forced to defend themselves against unfavorable crime statistics as highlighted by a team of three results-oriented executives. The spectacle of these meetings left those in attendance mesmerized as they witnessed their commanders being quizzed by the aggressive triad of superiors. The atmosphere was one of serial-like suspense, with each meeting representing another chapter. By the time the attendees headed out the door...they were excited, anxious to come back the following month to see what happened next to the latest head on the chopping block.

The follow-up would take the form of a lambasting if weaknesses went without rectification. Contributing to the anxiety was a wild-card factor: the chance that a fed-up commander would lose it under pressure. Creating a scene at one of these meetings could be career ending, but nevertheless, it was the reaction that people looked forward to most. A commander blowing up was always a showstopper.

The formula for the meeting was relatively simple. Those performing well were rewarded and their competency lavishly praised, while those falling short were publicly demeaned. The majority of flawed commanders fell in line to take their medicine like naughty children being reprimanded. Markie's favorite part of the meeting occurred when taskmasters with a reputation for being tough were under attack at the hands of a higher authority. Always a fan of the underdog, he relished seeing bosses who were considered pushovers surprise everyone by proving battle-ready when under assault.

Markie and Von Hess arrived early so that they could get good seats. The vast room was filled with everybody who was anybody in the targeted borough. One at the time, precinct by precinct, the commanders were called front and center before the tribunal.

"This is kind of like going to the fights," commented Von Hess. Markie laughed.

"Yeah...you got a point there."

"When they get down to specific cases, do you figure the two in the trunk will get much play this morning, boss?"

"I'd say so—I have not heard of too much else going on in that precinct to talk about."

"Do you figure Parlatto to hold up or choke under fire?"

"He's in trouble if they ask him anything other than his name," said Markie sarcastically. He then changed the subject. "Did you hear who died?"

"I heard it on the radio this morning....First Roy Rogers checks out, and now Gene Autry rides off into the sunset. There's nobody left."

"Autry was one of the richest guys in Hollywood," noted Markie.

Von Hess nodded. "He deserved it....I still remember Gene Autry's Cowboy Code of Honor."

"They should be teaching *that* in the schools," answered the sergeant. "But let's talk about that later. They are starting the meeting."

Sergeant Lance Parlatto's interrogation turned out to be the main event. When it was his turn to enter the ring, he did so with a slight strut, appearing full of confidence. The silver-haired precinct commander handled himself well. He was on top of his game, coming across graciously as the pinnacle of efficiency. But when the baton was passed to Parlatto, it was only a matter of time before things took a downward spiral.

The chief who chaired the meeting wore glasses with unusually thick lenses, making him something of an oddity in a department where excellent vision was required upon entry. They called him Bottle Caps behind his back.

"Lance, tell us about the double in the trunk," requested the chief.

Markie didn't miss the fact that Parlatto was known by the chief, who called him by his first name. "*Lance,*" he repeated with a cynical nod to Von Hess. "It's good to know the chief!"

"They respect ability, boss. You simply can't repress talent."

Parlatto's ability with computers was the halo effect incarnated: Bottle Caps presumed Parlatto would excel in his every undertaking since he had already proven to be proficient with technology. It didn't hurt that the squad commander made sure that he included a healthy embellishment of his own efforts during a commentary riddled with the word "I" as he detailed the case.

"He sounds like a professor up there," whispered Von Hess.

"Doesn't he, though?" agreed Markie. "What a pair of balls on this guy!"

Von Hess and Markie looked on as Parlatto unabashedly took liberties in doctoring the facts, inflating his participation in the storyline. Markie sat in his seat expressionless. But he was not surprised because he had previous experience with Parlatto's skill at revising history in his own favor. Markie recollected how the squad commander had shamelessly stolen his thunder by taking credit for closing over two hundred incidents of racially offensive white-paint graffiti being scribbled on commercial businesses—failing to mention that it was Markie who'd identified the vulgar culprit. He further neglected to mention that it was Markie who had notified all of the squad commanders in the borough, including Parlatto, and recommended they check complaint reports for past instances of offensive graffiti in which the markings were made with white paint. One particular accolade the chief used at the time still resonated with Markie: "Now this is a detective squad commander!" It was a public declaration that twisted Markie—one he would never forget.

But that was then. This was a new day, one that Markie hoped would prove to be not as amicable for Parlatto.

"What about the second perpetrator, Lance...the guy with the truck?" queried Bottle Caps.

It was a question that Parlatto should have anticipated but never saw coming. This was the payback Markie was waiting for.

Caught off guard, Parlatto was unable to offer any credible response. His hesitation in answering prompted another question.

"Well, do you have the second guy, the one with the truck, identified?" "Yes, Chief, we definitely do."

Markie noticed that Parlatto had shifted from using the word "I" to "we"—an effort to spread the misery.

"Okay, good....So now tell me, *sergeant*, what efforts have been made to apprehend him?" Bottle Caps had changed his tune. He was now suddenly condescending.

"Well...uh..." Parlatto's descent picked up speed.

"Well, did you at least check to see if there were warrants out on him, sergeant?"

Von Hess turned to his boss to enthusiastically whisper, "Yes!"

Markie just nodded his head in response.

"We are doing that now, Chief...." The squad commander was beginning to sink fast.

"You are doing that *now*? Did you check with the people from parole?" There was no immediate response to the question. The tone in the voice of Bottle Caps from this point on made his annoyance very clear.

"Yes, Chief, the one we arrested was on parole for drugs."

"Drugs?" The second man temporarily forgotten, Chief Bottle Caps fired questions at Parlatto in a barrage. "Did you look to see if the drug charges were associated with a violent crime? Did you compare notes with the borough narcotics division or the Drug Enforcement Task Force? Did the drug arrest stem from his role in a long-term drug investigation or part of a buy and bust? Did you see if the subject is currently part of an active narcotics investigation? Did you talk with his parole officer?"

Sergeant Parlatto wilted under the blistering cross-examination. It wasn't pretty, but it was a sight that Markie was glad to see. Parlatto deserved to go down in flames. Markie could have easily given the squad commander a heads-up had he wanted to—after all, he knew the questions that would be asked and had the right response to every question that Bottle Caps posed. The truth was, Parlatto knew very little about the case he'd been taking so much credit for. So Markie was glad to see the fame-hungry squad commander take it on the chin.

Markie and Von Hess returned to Brooklyn as happy campers. As they listened to a Gene Autry tribute on the radio, they spoke of how Parlatto absolutely had it coming. Markie considered his score with Parlatto now settled. Savoring his victory, he began singing along to "Back in the Saddle Again" during the ride over the bridge.

⊞ ⊞ ⊞

SIDNEY SCHIFF WAS CLEANING the crumbs off the top of his desk. As he was doing this, he glanced over at Fishnet's desk, where he observed his partner whispering into the telephone with his mouth covered. Curious, Schiff tried his best to overhear the conversation but was unable to. He waited for Fishnet to get off the phone to find out what was up even though he already had a good idea whom he was speaking to.

"Are you still screwing around with that wacko?"

The question took Fishnet by surprise. "What wacko?"

"You know who...Trudy, the woman with the necklace. What are you doing with that case anyway?"

"I just put a wanted card out for the Mask and notified the guys downstairs in the precinct. As long as it's not Halloween, he'll get picked up as soon as he shows that dopey face of his."

"Be careful, Fish. Don't forget...she still has a husband living with her," warned Schiff.

Fishnet, remaining in his chair, wheeled himself over to his partner's desk. Pulling up alongside Sidney, the detective lifted his wrist to show off his new watch.

"Talking about hubby, how do you like this baby?...It's an Omega! The band on this sucker is solid gold."

The watch did not appear to be brand-new to Schiff. "Nice. Where did you get it?"

"C'mon, you know. Trudy gave it to me....It was one of her husband's old watches." Sidney looked at Fishnet as if he were crazy. "You don't think he's gonna miss it?"

"Nah. She said he never wore it. He gave her the green light to donate it to some fucking charity for a silent auction or some horseshit like that."

"Just don't let him catch you wearing it," warned Sidney.

"You know *why* she gave it to me, Sid?"

"Tell me...why?"

"Because it took a man like *me*," said Fishnet, bursting with pride, "to get her hitting the high notes....You could have heard her in the street!"

Sergeant Parlatto, fresh from his meeting at headquarters, stomped into the squad room before Schiff could respond to Fishnet's statement. The two detectives watched their boss in silence as he entered his office in a huff. When the sergeant slammed his office door behind him without saying a word, the detectives knew something ugly must have gone down at the puzzle palace.

Fishnet was the first to speak. "Now, what the fuck do you think *his* problem is?"

Detective Schiff just shrugged his shoulders, knowing full well they would find out soon enough.

27

TWO MORE
NOTCHES

THE INDIGENT MAN STOPPED walking for a moment to lean into his shopping cart to tie off one of the large green garbage bags containing his belongings. Pausing to examine something he had just picked out of his hair, he took a second to look around. He spotted the Lincoln parked three cars off the avenue and decided to pay the man behind the wheel a visit. He flicked what was in his hand away and pushed his cart over to the car. The big man behind the wheel kept a distrustful eye on the beefy stranger as he approached. Red donned his black porkpie and placed a hand on his gun, anticipating the imminent interaction with the down-and-outer, who just might also be crazy.

"Excuse me, mister, I am a homeless Vietnam vet living on the street," the man said with a sad look. "I hate to ask you, but I'm desperate....I need something to eat. I don't like to bother you like this, but I'm desperate.... Could you spare a dollar, some change, or even some food?" The words flowed smoothly...perhaps too fluidly for Red's suspicious mind.

Red looked at the pathetic man without any sign of compassion. Seeing that he wasn't dressed too shabbily, another reason existed for Red's skepticism.

"I'm awful hungry," the beggar added in his "poor me" way.

Red didn't buy it. Harris was no new arrival to the big city—long faces and crocodile tears only worked with the hayseeds in his book. It would require the producing of dog tags to help convince him the man was legit...and even with that, Red would have still had his doubts.

"Take a fucking walk!" came the callous rasp from the car.

"Thank you, sir. Have a blessed day." The man slowly shuffled away from the car with his shopping cart.

"Yeah...you too, asshole," Red said as he watched the man walk off while scratching the stubble on his face.

Red Harris was a patient man when working, but he didn't welcome distractions. He had been laying for Anthony Boy, knowing that he was bound to show up one night. At the vantage point he had assumed, his view of the Star Light Social Club and the bar known as The Adjustment Room was unobstructed.

This was Red's third night on the street, observing people coming and going from the two locations. But this particular evening, Ernie A noticed Red hunkered down in his car. The sight of Red settled in anywhere on the street was sufficient cause for worry. Albertini's concern became magnified once it crossed his mind that Red was capable of doing something crazy inside the bar. Playing it safe, Ernie A decided to check in with his father-in-law to put his mind at ease.

"Is there a party tonight?" Ernie knew enough to speak cryptically when talking to Augie D'Angelo, a cautious man when it came to the telephone.

"What party? I know about no party." D'Angelo, wiretap wary, refused to make it appear that he knew what Ernie was talking about.

"I'm thinking that your friend, the *colored* guy, may be throwing a surprise party. He's got his party hat on."

The conversation was clear enough for Augie to understand that Ernie was talking about Red carrying his gun with the intention of killing someone.

Augie was abrupt in his response. "Forget it....Go leash and mind your business."

"Yeah...but the bar—"

"*Basta!*" came the shout from the phone. "That is it! Mind your own fucking business and be glad you weren't invited!"

Ernie knew not to question Swing's directive. When he said "enough," he meant it.

Augie's response confirmed his suspicion that someone had been put on the spot. He was relieved to know that he was "not invited" to whatever was about to go down. Ernie retreated to his small office in the cellar under the bar, leaving his bartender to handle things upstairs. He thought it would be a safe place to be in the event fireworks were forthcoming.

⊞ ⊞ ⊞

CONTRARY TO HIS UNIMPRESSIVE physical appearance, Anthony Boy was a disciplined hustler who got things done. A workaholic, he was dedicated to the pursuit of easy money. As long as violence was not involved, anything went as a means to accomplish this goal. Earning was injected into all aspects of his life regardless of where he was or what he was doing. In his role as a pimp, he would think nothing of peddling flesh at a funeral. If the demand was for some coke, he became the candy man. When wagering was desired...he was at the ready to take action.

Anthony viewed these ventures as giving people what they wanted. His ear was always available to listen to a proposal concerning a profitable scam. Part of Anthony Boy's professional routine was to identify talent he could exploit in his escort business.

Earning big served as an insurance policy that protected his health. He concluded that the best way to offset any potential beef with his criminal associations rested in his ability to enlarge the wallet of Augie D'Angelo. To Anthony Boy, it was a no-brainer to assume that ready cash solved all ills, and kicking upstairs was simply the cost of doing business. Insurance was important to a guy like Anthony Boy because he was, at heart, a risk-taker. With reckless abandon he kept a hand in narcotics trafficking. Anthony maintained a stash of cocaine as well as some heroin, which he procured through a couple of his more trustworthy escorts.

On a personal level, Anthony Boy was a recreational user of cocaine, a stimulant he found especially useful in getting close to women he was attempting to morally corrupt. Snorting a couple of lines with the girls always seemed to enhance his recruitment efforts with those who already had a fondness for the product. Those with a dependency often made the best escorts due to their being less inhibited and more willing to indulge the aberrations of clients. Those from the talent pool Anthony found attractive he sampled—it was a perk that came with the job.

Girls in his stable who were a cut below escort material were circulated in friendly locations such as The Adjustment Room, where they could generate a few bucks as long as Ernie A received his cut. Those with an ability to get on well with men in the bar were used as "party extras" whenever additional flesh was requested by Anthony's deep-pocketed clients.

The drug aspect of Anthony's business model was something he had to keep in the shade. In the Milano family, drugs were taboo—at least in theory. The antidrug edict had been established after family members and associates nabbed on drug charges began to roll over and become cooperating informants. The old-school bosses at the top of the ladder felt threatened by narcotics. They viewed the drug business as far too dangerous an enterprise—something with a reach that could potentially take them down.

As for Augie, he wasn't one to choke off a cash flow; as long as Anthony Boy was coming across with the green, Augie didn't ask questions. It would have been news to Augie that Anthony Boy's drug connection happened to be one of the best clients of the escort service...a Brooklyn dope dealer they called Joe Horse. Looking to kill two birds with one stone, Anthony used the women who serviced Joe Horse as his go-between in the drug transactions. Anthony felt insulated by having his girl pick up the product—this removed him from having any direct hand-to-hand transaction himself. The official position was that all the money coming in to Augie from Anthony was off the back of the escorts....The relationship remained uncomplicated that way.

⊞ ⊞ ⊞

SITTING QUIETLY IN HIS car, Red inserted a CD of Old Blue Eyes. Listening to Sinatra made his wait for Anthony Boy more pleasant. The singer had just finished his rendition of "Strangers in the Night" when the late-model white Jeep pulled up in front of the bar, blocking the fire hydrant.

"About time, you fat bastard...," said Red under his breath.

Red could see that there was a young, dark-haired female seated alongside Anthony Boy. The couple exited the Jeep and headed directly into the bar. Anthony was easy to spot from afar because he was attired all in white—a color that only emphasized his girth. As best as Red could make out, his companion had an exotic, Middle Eastern look to her. She was dressed in a black blouse and a pair of tight red-leather pants that showed off the contours of her figure. The pronounced clicking sound from her red heels echoed in the street every time one of her feet struck the pavement.

Red waited in the car. After about twenty minutes, Anthony Boy departed the bar alone. Returning to his Jeep, Anthony drove off, leaving the dark-haired vixen behind to fend for herself inside the saloon.

"Beautiful," said Red. "I got you all alone now, you motherless piece of garbage." Putting the car in drive. he proceeded to cautiously tail Anthony Boy at a safe distance. As he drove, he licked his lips in his unique fashion—he was looking forward to the dastardly surprise he planned to spring on Anthony Boy.

Red's rolling surveillance took him to a strip club on the west side, where Anthony appeared to be well known. His popularity became evident when the bouncer stationed at the door outside the club greeted him with outstretched arms, giving him a hug and a kiss on the cheek, signifying respect. It seemed to Red that Anthony might have passed something to the bouncer during the greeting. After the kiss, the two shook hands, embraced, and shook hands a second time.

"Look at this prick...making moves around town like he's somebody," muttered Red as he waited. "Just wait, fucko....Your big surprise is coming. Just you wait."

While Anthony spent about forty minutes inside the strip club, Red remained parked at a safe distance, smoking cigarette after cigarette. When Anthony finally returned to his vehicle, the waiting Red resumed his rolling tail.

Anthony took Red to the east side, where he picked up an attractive young woman on East Houston Street. She was an ash blond with a light complexion. The woman jumped into the passenger side of Anthony's Jeep without hesitation. Once she got in, Red was able to see her lean over to kiss Anthony Boy.

The Jeep proceeded further east and then headed south on the FDR Drive. Red followed at a safe distance, careful not to lose sight of the Jeep. The pursuit saw the Jeep exit the FDR and take to the streets. Anthony Boy turned into a dark, isolated street in Chinatown near the Manhattan Bridge and pulled over to the curb. Red was already into the turn before he realized the Jeep had parked on a dead end. Thinking quickly, Red pulled his vehicle over, stopping far to the Jeep's rear on the opposite side of the street. Donning his lucky black porkpie, the big man made no effort to be discreet when he opened the door of his vehicle. He exited quickly, spinning his torso around, careful to keep his back to the Jeep. Leaving the engine running and his headlights on, the Death Maker stooped, hoping to seem smaller as he began urinating. Once relieved, he got back in his car. Making a broken K-turn, he drove out of the dead end. As he pulled away, Red looked in his rearview mirror. He knew he was home free when the Jeep remained parked on the dead-end street.

The Death Maker drove two blocks away and then circled back, pulling his vehicle over just around the corner from where the Jeep had made the turn into the dead end. Red shut off his engine and headlights. With his lucky black hat still on his head, he walked along the building line to the corner of the dead end. He slowly poked his head around the corner, peering into the dead-end street. He was just in time to see the Jeep's interior sniper light go off. With the images of the two people in the car going black, Red waited a few seconds before entering the dead end. He crept slowly down the opposite side of the street from the Jeep, endeavoring to be out of the eye of Anthony's mirrors. As he neared the Jeep, the big man reached down for the gun he had jammed into his waistband. Once close enough to see inside the car, Red was able to make out the outline of only one person—Anthony Boy. With his seat back, he was reclining peacefully on the driver's side with the rear of his skull against the headrest.

Walking up to the driver's side window, Red made his move. In a matter of seconds, he was able to credit himself with two more notches. "So long, fucko," was all he said as he mercilessly emptied his handgun into the window of the car without hesitation. Anthony Boy took three bullets to the head with his eyes closed and a content look on his face. He never saw it coming. His companion, who was covered with shattered glass and blood, remained hunched over and frozen on Anthony's lap. Petrified, she never had the time to look up at Red as she received her allotment of lead...two slugs to the back of her head. The gun's attached silencer, a specially customized suppressor, served Red well in keeping things quiet, just the way Augie wanted.

After returning the gun to his waistband, Red lit a cigarette and briskly walked to his waiting car.

⊞ ⊞ ⊞

IT CAME OVER THE television in the squad room as a breaking story. "The bodies of a man and woman were found executed mob style in Lower Manhattan...," began the news report.

The story caught the ear of Detective Sidney Schiff. The detective had just turned on the television to listen to the news—he was looking to kill time as he waited for the clock to reach the end of his tour. Turning up the volume, he focused on the story of a double homicide: an execution-style shooting of a man and woman who'd been parked in a Jeep on a street in Chinatown. This being his turnaround tour, Sidney was impervious to the details of the bulletin once 1:00 a.m. came around. He had to be back in the office by 8:00 a.m., so any interest concerning a crime out of his command was understandably limited. His focus was on signing out, going home, and getting to bed. He shut off the television and met Fishnet at the logbook, where the two men ended their tour by signing off duty.

"Hey, Fish—looks like they caught a double over in Chinatown," Sidney told his partner. "It seems like it may be organized-crime related."

"Yeah? Did they say who bought it?"

"No names were released...just some guy and woman in a Jeep."

Fishnet thought a second. "A woman, huh? That's unusual....There must be a story connected to that one. Women don't usually get it like that."

"You want to take care of breakfast, or should I?"

"You'd better pick up bagels on the way in," replied Fishnet. "Make sure they're fresh....I'll be coming in with an appetite."

"Why's that?"

"Duty with Trudy tonight."

The two detectives shut the lights, locked the door to the squad and went their separate ways, planning to meet up again later in the morning for the day shift.

⊞ ⊞ ⊞

FISHNET WAS THE FIRST to return to the squad, arriving early at 7:30 a.m. Entering the precinct, he checked with the clerical office to see if any new cases had come in overnight. There were two new cases—a commercial burglary of a pharmacy and a criminal mischief to a school. Neither was considered an overly pressing matter. Fifteen minutes later, Detective Schiff reported for duty.

Schiff had picked up a half-dozen rolls on his way into work. He began the process of getting up a fresh pot of coffee for the pending arrival of Sergeant Parlatto. He took a minute to turn on the television set to listen to the news. The first story involved a city council member taking the witness stand in some corruption matter. The next concerned the suicide of a television personality. Then came the weather report. By the time the detectives and their boss were seated, comfortably eating rolls and drinking coffee, the big story of interest came on. When the names of the victims in the Chinatown double homicide were reported, Fishnet paid attention.

"Anthony Chiarello and Gloria Sloan!" Fishnet jumped to his feet. He then stood in front of the television to watch the remainder of the report.

"Hey, Fishnet," Sidney said, "wasn't that the name of the guy in your case?"

"Yeah...it was," commented Parlatto. "I'll bet it's the same guy—his escort service was in Manhattan."

"Maybe you should give them a call over at the Fifth?" Schiff suggested.

"Yeah," Fishnet agreed. "I'll bet this is our guy alright, but what about the girl...?" he said softly, addressing no one in particular. His mind was beginning to trail off.

"Gloria Sloan, they said. Did she figure in your case, Fish?" asked Sergeant Parlatto. But Fishnet was staring blankly at the TV and didn't answer. "Hey, Fishnet! I asked you something. Did Gloria Sloan come up anyplace in your case?"

His thoughts disrupted, Fishnet turned abruptly to his boss. "What was that you said?"

"For the third time...did Gloria Sloan come up in the case we had over here?"

"No, she never came up. They don't say if the squad has anything to go on?"

"You'd better get your ears checked," said the sergeant. "Call over to Manhattan to see what they have to say about this."

"Let me call our guys over in homicide first—they might have heard something. Alright?"

"Yeah...go ahead."

Fishnet picked up the phone to call Von Hess, who was assigned to work the same chart as Fishnet and Schiff.

"Hey...it's me, Fishnet. Did you guys see who got clipped in Chinatown?"

"Yeah," Von Hess replied. "I just got off the phone with Manhattan.... It's our boy."

"Do they have anything to go on?"

"They're looking to identify a boyfriend, husband, wife, or girlfriend.... They're checking for a possible love triangle."

"A fucking *love triangle*? Did you tell them about my case?"

"I did...but they're looking for an *amore* angle. They seem to have found the bodies in a compromising position. There was a small amount of drugs in the car as well."

"Blow?"

"Yeah, I think so," Von Hess confirmed. "The Manhattan crew said it looked like they did a couple of lines before getting amorous."

"You know what this looks like, Ollie...don't you?"

"I know, but let it play out. It's a Chinatown mystery, so we're out of it for right now. They'll be coming around with their hat in hand for sure if the love angle doesn't pan out."

"Right. Fuck it, it's a Manhattan problem." Fishnet hung up the phone. "What did they say?" Sergeant Parlatto asked.

"Manhattan thinks the killings are the result of a love triangle, so that's the direction they are pursuing. Von Hess already filled them in, so now we have to wait until they smarten up and get around to following up with us."

"Talk about following up! Listen...I already told you guys once, get going with that damn mover. You gotta put him in cuffs for me by the next meeting at headquarters."

"We will grab him, Sarge." Fishnet's tone suggested that Parlatto should not worry about it.

But Parlatto wasn't satisfied with the level of urgency in Fishnet's response. "I can't go back there and face Bottle Caps without delivering the second piece!"

"We have him identified, boss—we took care of that already," Schiff assured him. "We got his photo and everything."

"He's a two-bit fucking car booster," added Fishnet. "We're going out looking for him on this set of tours."

"He should be easy to find, boss....We have him living with his grandmother on Fort Hamilton Parkway," Schiff said confidently.

"Good....Then just fucking grab him already," ordered Parlatto. "Then I can finally put this mess to bed."

28

FRANNY
FISHING

FRANNY PARKED HIS TRUCK in front of the hydrant opposite Sal's Pizza Palace in Sunset Park. After crossing the avenue, he entered the pizzeria looking for Sal. A teenager worked behind the counter cooking up pies while waiting for his first customer of the day. Franny wondered if this young NI—his word for a non-Italian—was any good at making pizza. But he wasn't there to sample the food, so he would never know.

"Is Sal around?"

"Nah...he won't be back until later next week."

"Next week! Where did he go?"

The young man behind the counter raised up his arms, palms facing the ceiling. "He didn't tell me."

"Can you give him a call on his cell?"

"Nah...he don't like being bothered, man. I could get in trouble. He will be here next week."

"Then give me his number. I'll call him."

"You looking to get me fired from my job? I'd be taking a big chance, man...and for what?"

Smelling a shakedown, Franny frowned. "Thanks a lot, man....Forget it," he said, and he exited the store.

The man with the truck had no intention of slipping some snot-nosed

NI teenager a few bucks. He was desperate but not to the point of giving away his money. Spending his money was a behavior that went against Franny's grain. He was already upset about his cash flow being dented—his friend Joe Horse had been sent back up to finish a stretch, which meant a long-term impact on Franny's finances. With Joe in play, there was easy access to the heroin at a discounted rate—and his supply was virtually guaranteed. Without Joe stocking the shelves with product, Franny was compelled to go shopping on the street for another connection. He was routinely supplying a handful of users, who never caught on that he was stepping on the product he sold them in order to satisfy his own habit. In effect, he was supporting his own drug use off their dime.

Franny took a modest approach to his drug dealing—the fewer people he had to deal with, the greater his odds of staying out of jail. Having Joe Horse in his life had spoiled him. Now alone and left to his own devices, he was discovering that his former circle of contacts in the dope business were either dead or behind bars like Joe. With a horse stash running low, he was out beating the bushes to see who was still around that could supply him at a reasonable rate.

Franny set out to Coney Island to see if he could locate Little Louie Macho. Driving along Surf Avenue, he stopped his truck when he saw a familiar face opposite the Cyclone roller coaster. He pulled over to the curb and jumped out of his truck. With a smile, he approached a toothless Hispanic man stationed on the sidewalk in his wheelchair with an empty plastic cup in his hand.

"Hey, Zooko! How the hell are you?"

"Who you looking for, man?"

"What do you mean? Look at me....Don't you know me anymore?"

"Do I know you? Who are you, man?" Zooko asked warily.

"It's me...Franny!" But the man in the wheelchair still did not recognize him. "You know me, Zooko....I'm Fast Franny...the car guy who used to sell you and Junior the car radios! We took those two Staten Island girls to the boathouse in Prospect Park that time...remember? You remember.... We slipped them a couple of mushrooms...?"

The reference to getting the girls high did the trick. Zooko broke into a broad, open-mouthed smile that revealed nothing but his gums. "Ohhh, shit...Franny! How the fuck you been, man? I thought you was dead."

Franny was amused by that. "No...I'm still here. What happened? Where are all your choppers?"

"I got gum disease, man...lost all my stinking teeth! All I eat now is fucking mashed potatoes and soup! Take care of your teeth, man....Floss and do all that good shit."

"Too bad, man....And what the fuck you doing in a wheelchair?"

"I'm alright, man. This shit helps when I'm out here hustling for a few

260   *Anthony Celano*

bucks. Besides, the cops don't fuck with me when I'm in the chair."

"Listen, Zooko...I'm looking for Little Louie. Is he still around, man?"

Zooko turned somber. "Nah...Little Louie Macho passed away a couple of years back. He got AIDS or some shit."

Franny was sorry to hear the news. "Too bad. He was a good guy. I didn't hear about it. Any of that old crew around?"

But Zooko didn't hear the question; he was thinking of his deceased friend. "Yeah...leave it to Macho....He died with all his fucking teeth too! What you needing Little Louie Macho for, man?"

Franny leaned over to whisper into his old friend's ear. "I'm looking to do a little business, man...weight. You got anybody for me? I'll figure you in for something."

"Man...there ain't nothing around here no more. You need something? This ain't the place....There ain't nobody here you want to deal with."

Zooko then just came to realize that Franny had come out of the parked truck. "Hey...is that big-ass truck *your* wheels, man?"

Franny looked at his vehicle proudly. "Yeah...all mine. Like it?"

"Nice! You still got all your teeth, man?" inquired the man in the wheelchair.

"Yeah...except for one in the back. The dentist pulled that sucker."

Zooko was surprised to hear this. "The *dentist*! Man, you must be doing real good. I'm glad for you."

Expecting to be hit up for money if he prolonged the conversation any longer, Franny sought to make his retreat, taking a step back in the direction of his truck. He was too late.

"Hey, can I borrow a few bucks?...You know, man, things ain't been too good with me lately."

Franny pulled out two dollars to give to Zooko, but before the money even made it into Zooko's hand, the man in the wheelchair upped the ante. "Can't you make it a five- or ten-spot?"

Miffed, Franny returned the bills to his pocket. He headed back to his truck without ever turning around to acknowledge Zooko's ardent appeal to get the two dollars back.

Franny drove off, thinking he'd head over to the projects in Red Hook— maybe Sweet Apple was still in operation. But first he was going to grab a hot dog from Nathan's and enjoy it while he still had his teeth. It had been a long time since he'd had one of those babies.

⊞ ⊞ ⊞

FISHNET AND SCHIFF, who were now catching new cases that were coming into the squad, were devoting part of their tour looking for Franny Preto. Whenever they were able to take time away from the new work, they went on the hunt for the mover. But their efforts were proving to be fruitless. The truck was never parked by the grandmother's house when they went out to look for him, which meant Franny was either in the wind or out and about someplace. With the mounting pressure being placed on them by Parlatto, they knew they would have to step up their efforts on the next set of tours.

The two days Fishnet had off provided him with plenty of time to think long and hard about the things that interested him. Seated in a diner on Staten Island, the detective was having his breakfast alone while perusing a book on revenge that he'd recently picked up. As he was looking over the various ways to get even with people, it made more and more sense to him that Red Harris had murdered Anthony Boy out of revenge, with the pimp's gal pal having been in the wrong place at the wrong time.

Fishnet understood a man like Red because he and the killer shared the same innate vindictiveness. The demented detective accurately concluded that a thirst for vengeance existed and continued to linger in Red. Fishnet believed that Red would look to close the book by getting even with all those involved in the death of his daughter—just as he himself would were he in that situation. Consequently, the detective expected that Joe Horse and Franny Preto would soon be in the Death Maker's crosshairs too. As long as Joe Horse was living in a jail cell somewhere, he was pretty much untouchable. That left just one target for Red to pursue if he intended to satiate his craving for revenge: Franny Preto. And Fishnet was confident that it wouldn't take Red long to learn the identity of the man with the truck. On the strength of these thoughts, Fishnet took the express train to his mental dark side, a trip that came with illusions of gaining great notoriety at the expense of Red Harris.

With his mind far off, Fishnet took a slow drive into Brooklyn. Remarkably, his driving ability was pretty much unaffected during these mental excursions. His first stop was at the squad to remove the .25 automatic from the lining of his police coat. After leaving the precinct, he drove by the location where Franny Preto lived with his grandmother on Fort Hamilton Parkway. Of course, Preto was now small change— merely the bait that was going to draw out the big man with the bigger reputation. If Fishnet's fantasy was to be a reality, he was going to be shooting it out with Red Harris at the exact time Harris was closing in to snuff out the life of Franny.

Figuring Red would be concentrating on the truck—as he himself had done when laying for Franny—Fishnet stuck around the area of the grandmother's house for hours before calling it a wrap. With no sign of Red in the area, he finally headed home to Staten Island, where he would reenter the real world he actually lived in.

During the drive home, the detective remained undeterred in his commitment to play the long shot he had cooked up. He could not resist floating along in his fantasy land, fine-tuning his choreographed scenarios. The detective began thinking up ways to take down Red Harris while Red was in the act of whacking Franny Preto. One imaginative version saw the detective not just shooting Red but also engaging in a hand-to-hand death struggle for the murder weapon with Red's accomplice...an add-on who Fishnet would also send to his maker. The delusional sleuth then began leaning toward an alternative climax, one that saw Fishnet beating Red to a draw in an epic gun battle in the street, which included a thrilling foot pursuit, complete with shots exchanged every few steps. Whatever his decision, Fishnet was going to make Red's ending dramatic and self-serving. Fishnet was in the middle of reloading when the blast of a car horn interrupted his gun battle...snapping him out of his world.

"Hey....wake up over there!" yelled the woman from the Honda Civic behind him. "The light is green!" Fishnet drove through the intersection without giving her a thought. He was too occupied trying to recapture the daydream the motorist had so rudely interrupted.

When the detective returned to work for his first evening shift, he was still consumed with thoughts of Red Harris. He would be working with Sidney but had no intention of sharing his murder theory with his partner.

Sergeant Parlatto had been waiting for the two detectives to arrive at work. Upon learning that Franny Preto had still not been locked up, Parlatto came down on his team of detectives, adamantly insisting that Franny's arrest was an official priority. On the one hand, the sergeant's mandate fit perfectly into Fishnet's dream because it legitimately placed him exactly where he wanted to be in the event Red showed up. What was problematic was that he had Detective Schiff with him, which meant he would have to share some of the glory. Fishnet's ideal scheme had him working alone or off duty when the time came to take down Red.

"Remember, I want to hear some good news from you guys," said Parlatto just prior to leaving the office for the day.

"Right, boss. We're on it," answered Schiff. After the sergeant was gone, the detective turned his attention to Fishnet. He could see that his partner was in one of his...moods.

"Hey, Fishnet...come on," Sidney said impatiently. "We gotta get outta here. You heard the sergeant." Seeing that Fishnet was still staring blankly, he called to him again. "Yo, Fishnet! Wake up!...C'mon, it's time to saddle up."

Catching the words "saddle up," Fishnet voyaged back from dreamland long enough to respond. "I'm ready. Let's go."

"The sergeant said to put everything on the back burner and grab this guy...so let's go to the house and talk to the old lady. Maybe we can make something happen."

"Let me hit the head first," Fishnet told his partner.

"Okay," answered Sidney. "Try not to fall in."

⊞ ⊞ ⊞

ARRIVING AT THE GRANDMOTHER'S house, the detectives caught a break. They finally spotted the truck parked out front. It was around 6:00 p.m. when Fishnet and Sidney rang the bell at the small, two-story brick house on Fort Hamilton Parkway.

The elderly Italian woman who came to the door was about seventy-five years old, give or take a few years. She was an old-school woman from the other side, in all black—shoes, stockings, dress—and she even wore her gray hair in a bun. She'd been pretending to mourn for her husband, a man dead for the past twenty years. In life, he'd been a miserable old coot who hollered at children and harshly chased them away whenever they played in front of the house. His very voice made his wife jump every time he called her name.

"*Madelina...pera*," he'd say, and she would rush to get his fruit.

"*Madelina...bottone*," and his wife would make a dash for the needle and the thread.

The old woman could not have been more of a slave had she worked on the plantation of Simon Legree. But she was strangely out of hearing range the day she had "misplaced" the old man's dynamite pills. Her lapse in diligence resulted in his passage into the next world after his final heart attack. At the time of his death, he was sitting in a lounge chair in front of his house, listening to a ball game and snarling at any kids under ten who happened to be walking by. When his wife got around to checking in on him, she found him with a small transistor radio on his lap and an earplug screwed into his ear. Not being in any rush, she finished her housework prior to calling nine-one-one.

Once her husband was buried, all of her energy transferred to her grandson, Franco—her one purpose for living. Everyone called him Franny except his grandmother. The major difference between the old man and Franco was that the old man had to ask for what he wanted.

Franny had never met his parents. His father remained unidentified, and his unwed mother died of complications connected to the difficult delivery. This left Franny to be raised by his mother's parents, where he was subsequently spoiled rotten by his protective grandmother.

It had taken the old woman a few minutes to answer the door. When she got there, Schiff introduced himself and Fishnet. Her reaction to the authorities was lukewarm. She was   somewhat suspicious of the law at the best of times, and once the detectives asked to speak to her grandson, she was convinced that no good was in the air.

        Anthony Celano

"Who you wan-na?" she asked.

"We need to speak to Franny," answered Schiff.

"No Franny liv-a here."

"Where's your grandson, then?"

"Who you look-a-for, I say?"

"Your grandson!" snapped Fishnet.

"He move...long-a time ago. I dun-no where he go. I tink he maybe inna de army."

Fishnet could tell that getting any cooperation from her was a tall order. The detectives stood a better chance at getting nuked. "Come on, Sid, let's get the fuck out of here. This old crow is going to be no help."

"Hold on, will you?" Sidney said in a curt voice. He turned back to the old woman. "Your grandson...is he home? He's in no trouble. We just need to talk to him."

"Franco no here, I say!"

"But his truck is outside," Schiff pointed out.

"No his-a truck....You cra-zy!" She stubbornly maintained ignorance concerning her grandson or his owning any truck. The grandmother informed the law that she knew nothing about her grandson's whereabouts....She wasn't even in contact with him! It was the classic runaround.

Detective Schiff finally recognized the futility of the situation. Nevertheless, he thanked the woman and, with Fishnet in tow, departed her doorstep. The two detectives returned to their unmarked car. Fishnet ran the license plate on the parked truck. It had come back to Franco Preto at the grandmother's address.

"The little prick lives here. He's probably in the house someplace," Fishnet declared. "The old bag is full of crap."

"You tink-a so?" Schiff asked, trying to be funny.

"Tell you what, Sid....I'm going to keep coming back here until I grab the little shit...and when I do, the old bag will get a good look...as I put my foot up the ass of her little precious before I clamp the bracelets on him." Fishnet was putting on a show. He was perfectly happy with not finding Franny....He wanted to grab him alone and when Red was around.

"Let's notify the Six-Six Precinct that we're looking to pick up Preto. The anticrime guys over here, or even the sector, may spot him and grab him for us," suggested Schiff.

"Why? We'll get him," protested Fishnet.

"Let's just do it or else Parlatto will be up our ass, hounding us."

When fully inhabiting the real world, Fishnet resigned himself to the fact that the odds were greatly stacked against him. The notion that he could be present to interrupt Franny's assassination was a stretch. It seemed inevitable that Franny would be busted before Red Harris would have a chance to catch up with him. Still, Fishnet wanted to give it one last try.

"Okay...let's notify the Six-Six Precinct later, before we go end of tour," he told Sidney. "Meanwhile, let's you and me try to grab this guy ourselves."

⊞ ⊞ ⊞

RED HARRIS WAS OUT making the rounds in an effort to get a line on Franny Preto. He finally hit pay dirt when he went to see Squint Nolan, a seventy-eight-year-old fence who was known to have been doing business with all of the local petty thieves in Brooklyn for years. Nolan, who stored swag in the basement of his Coney Island house, would buy stolen property for a fraction of the actual value. Nolan's abode was packed with hubcaps, tires, paintings, jewelry, clothing, and almost anything else of value that could be carried out the back door of a store or residence or off the rear of a truck.

Squint greeted Harris with enthusiasm. "Red! How the hell are you? I thought you were in the joint doing time."

"No, I'm still here. You look good, Squinty," Red complimented the old-timer. "Some people never change. I bet you can even still pump oil...."

"Pump oil?" Squint scoffed at the idea. "Quit ya kidding, Red. Those days are long over for me. I'm closing in on eighty....I got no more interest in women."

"Ahh, fuck it. Who needs the headache anyway? You still look good, Squinty, like you can handle yourself."

"What can I tell you? I'm like a fucking old Studebaker...lucky to still be on the road. What brings you here?...You got something for me, or you looking for something? I got some nice rings."

Red turned serious. "I just need information, Squinty. I'm looking for a Brooklyn shithead they call Franny. His last name is Preto."

"Franny? The only Franny I know is a kid who used to boost cars. I'm going back now...."

"Tell me about him."

"Alright...yeah, sure....They called him Fast Franny because the kid could hot-wire a car, pop a trunk, or remove a radio in seconds. He was a real good technician in that department."

"This guy still around?"

"Yeah, I think so...at least as far as I know. Like I said, it's been awhile."

"What does this Franny look like?"

"When I last saw him, he was in regular clothes, dungarees...you know, nothing fancy. He told me he was in the moving business...had a truck and everything."

Anthony Celano

"That's good information, Squinty," commented Red. "You got the right guy...but describe him to me."

"Sure thing, Red....He's got no mustache or anything, about my height, on the thin side, and has all his hair...black. He gave me a business card the last time I saw him, but I threw it out. I guess I should have held onto it."

"Did the business card have a name on it?"

Squint answered enthusiastically. "Yeah! That I recall because it was an easy name to remember. It said, 'Fast Franny—Moving Specialist,' with a truck on the front of the card. Reminded me of Paladin...only the kid's card had a truck on the front of the card instead of a horse head. Remember Paladin?"

"Yeah, the *Have Gun–Will Travel* guy, he dressed in all black. I used to like that show. Any address on the card?"

"There was no address or anything, just a number...but like I said, I threw the card out."

"Tell me more about how he looked, Squinty...detailed, like."

"Well, there's really nothing special about him, Red. The only thing is... you know he used to be half a hophead, but I can't say for sure he's that way now. You can't miss him if you just look for that boxtruck."

"Okay, then....And one other thing, Squinty..." The Death Maker removed a hundred-dollar bill from a roll of cash, held together by a metal binder clip. He held the money up to Squint's face as he spoke. "If this Franny calls you asking about me, you just tell him you know me as Chester, and that you referred me to him for a move. Tell him Chester can pay plenty....That is all you tell him."

"Sure thing, Red, whatever you say." Squint took the money, sensing for the first time that this was a serious matter.

"Give him nothing else. You get what I'm saying here, Squinty?...No fucking around."

The message sent was not lost on Squint. "No problem, Red. Believe me, I know you good....I'll never ever speak a word other than I referred Chester for some kind of special move."

"Good. See you later, Squinty. I'll be back if I can't get a line on this guy. I may need you to ask around for me. Remember, keep it in the shade." Red left the house comfortable that Squint had gotten his message straight.

"I swear it, Red! Believe me...I never liked the little prick anyway," the old man yelled after Red as the big man walked off.

On his way to his car, Red lit up a Lucky Strike. The work he had performed concerning Anthony and now Franny was for pure self-satisfaction. These undertakings were something he felt compelled to do. While it bothered him a little that he was not making money from his labor, he managed to console himself with the thought that he was fulfilling a personal obligation. He was a believer that there were certain matters of honor that just transcended money.

Red took out his flip phone and called information, looking for a listing for Franny's business. After checking, the operator informed him that there was no such listing. Red was old school all the way. He wasn't computer literate, so researching on the internet was out—Red did not even own a computer. He considered all modern forms of communication other than his cell phone something out of Flash Gordon. After thinking it over a bit, the light bulb went on. A mover had to put the word out someplace that he was available for work. Where might a little shit like Franny advertise?

Red made the rounds of the local supermarkets to examine the community board postings. It wasn't long before he found exactly what he was looking for: a cheap paper posting that provided the number to Fast Franny–Moving Specialist.

The big man wasted no time calling the number. "Is this Fast Franny?"

"What can I do for you?" asked the male voice.

"I'm looking for Franny....You Franny?"

"I repeat myself....What do you need?" Franny knew he was talking to a street guy by the tone of Red's voice.

"I gotta move something. I was told Franny could help me. You Franny or what?"

"Who was it that told you to ask for Franny?"

"Squinty....You know Squinty?"

That did the trick. "Yeah, I'm Franny."

"When can I see you to work this out?"

"Tomorrow afternoon? I'm around."

"How about in a couple of hours? I got money, and I'm willing to pay. I'll come by your place....Where do I go?" Red was pushing.

"That's no good....Tomorrow works better for me." Franny wanted time to check in with Squint before entertaining someone he didn't know.

"When tomorrow?"

"In the afternoon is good."

Red disagreed. "Let's do it later at night....I got a late-afternoon appointment. Where am I going?"

"Call me tomorrow and I'll give you an address."

"Yeah...good. Figure on 9:00 p.m."

"This is to be private, right?" asked Franny. "Just you and me?"

"You got it right...just you and me."

"Okay. Tomorrow, 9:00 p.m. But now that I'm working at night, I have to tell you up front it's going to cost you extra." Franny intended to pluck the chicken for all he could get.

"No problem, pal."

"Hey, wait a minute....What is your name?"

Anthony Celano

"Chester."

Franny hung up the phone. This Chester sounded like a piece of work to him, but it made no difference to Franny as long as he had the money to back up his wants. Franny presumed this to be the kind of job he liked, one that came with a big payday. Between drug sales and legitimate moves, he had been making money—but it was this type of urgent request, the need for a "special" move for someone of less-than-stellar origin, that turned up the big coin for him.

Before he could commit himself, he needed to touch base with Squint and verify that this Chester was a known entity. Ever on the alert for a setup, Franny knew enough to be careful when it came to such sensitive matters. Squint had managed to conduct his shady business for a lot of years remaining under the radar of the authorities. For Fanny, this translated into proof of his guile, making the old man a wise sage whose assessments were to be trusted. The man with the truck would be guided by what he had to say. Once he received Squint's stamp of approval, Franny would go ahead with Chester's move.

There remained just one concern that extended beyond Franny's control. All he could do about it was hope that if things went sour, Chester would stand up and be half the man Joe Horse had been. So far Franny had no evidence to contradict his naïve belief that his friend Joe would do a stretch without squealing on him.

He was also clueless about the visit the detectives had paid his protective grandmother. Grammy was confident that she had taken care of the pesky local gendarme, so why would she bother to upset her Franco, who had been busy all day working? Why interrupt the private time he needed to get himself off?

29

LASTING
FAME

RED HARRIS WAS GETTING ready for work. He went under the shower—a cold one, one that would enliven him quickly. He was preparing for his date with Fast Franny. Murder had become so matter-of-fact for Red that on this occasion, he waited until the last minute before even considering how exactly he'd do it. Mulling it over, Red toyed with the idea of severing the mover's jugular with a bowie knife. This method would give him the pleasure of looking into his victim's shocked face as he sank into his own pool of drained blood. On the other hand, it had also been awhile since he had garroted anyone with a wire, so that was also briefly considered.

The downside to both methods was the unpredictability—such an engagement could involve a tussle. In the end, he remembered that he was no kid anymore. He chose not to put himself through the physical exertion of a potential struggle. As Red vigorously slapped himself about his naked body to neutralize the sting of the cold water splashing down on him, he decided to return to his most reliable tool for the eradication... the revolver with the specially made silencer.

⊞ ⊞ ⊞

IT WAS THE END OF Sergeant Parlatto's day tour. The last thing he did before signing off duty in the log was to again make it clear to Fishnet and Sidney that he wanted Franny Preto taken into custody at some point during the current set of tours...or else.

"Don't worry about it, boss. We're on it," Fishnet assured the sergeant. "We'll grab his ass."

"I've heard that song before," Parlatto said skeptically. "I need him in bracelets....Don't you understand that?"

Sidney saw that the tone of his boss was desperate. "If he's out there, sarge, we'll get this hump—we got everybody on the lookout for him. We're going out looking ourselves in a few minutes."

It took time to appease the sergeant, but the detectives managed to convince him that everything possible short of camping outside Franny's house twenty-four-seven would be done to apprehend the mover. Barring any pressing new cases, the two detectives intended to spend their evening tour conducting surveillance at the Fort Hamilton Parkway residence, waiting for Franny to show himself.

Parlatto was still not exactly happy, but he knew there was not much more that could be done. Had this been a straight-out homicide, he could have recruited the assistance of the career criminal apprehension unit to sit on the house around the clock and wait for Preto to show himself. But this was no homicide, and a misdemeanor did not warrant such attention. As a result, Parlatto's options were limited.

"Okay, keep trying...but I want you to document all of the efforts you have made in trying to apprehend him. If nothing else, at least I'll have that to talk about when they put me on the grill at the next meeting." The sergeant signed out, hoping that his detectives would come through for him; he could only hope that they would try their best. Parlatto went home to take another crack at beating the Oregon Trail.

⊞　⊞　⊞

RED LIVED IN A TRANQUIL little nest on the top floor of a four-story townhouse a couple of blocks from Pratt Institute, an educational facility renowned for its standing in the field of art. The owners of the brownstone were an older couple with a history of renting space in their house to people who would make the usual complaints tenants sometimes make. The couple held a tremendous appreciation for the tenant who never complained about insufficient heat, lack of hot water, or the neighbor's barking dog. Red had no pets, invited no guests, and paid his rent in cash—consistently and on time the first of the month. He was so ideal a tenant that he hadn't seen a rent increase in the three years he'd lived there. Around the holidays, Red would receive an open invitation to join the family downstairs for a drink and holiday dinner—a

Anthony Celano

consideration that he never took advantage of out of fear there would be questions relating to what he did for a living. As it stood, he presented himself to the landlord as a salesman for an electrical company.

While Red was not the invisible type, he was an accepted fit in the community once people got used to seeing him around. Among the denizens of this hamlet of creativity, he was known strictly as Mr. Harris. Every "Good morning, Mr. Harris," and "Hello, Mr. Harris" was received silently by an upward lift of his chin. No one around the campus vicinity ever dreamed that the man on the top floor was a prominent figure among those who comprised the underbelly of society.

⊞ ⊞ ⊞

SEEING THE TRUCK OUT front, Fishnet and Schiff positioned their unmarked car a full block away from the Fort Hamilton Parkway abode of Franny Preto. Sidney was behind the wheel. Seated alongside him, Fishnet kept an eyeball on the house through a pair of high-powered binoculars. From his location, he could see if Franny stepped outside or approached the house from the street. He would also be able to observe any activity around the truck. The detectives were set up perfectly to watch without worry of being spotted themselves.

"With the fucking truck still there, it's a cinch he's in the house," said Fishnet half-heartedly.

"Let's just hope he shows himself," replied Schiff.

"Yeah," Fishnet answered softly—any opportunity for his dream ending would evaporate the moment Franny emerged from the residence.

At 7:00 p.m. there still had been no activity at the house, and Detective Schiff was getting hungry. "What do you want to do about eating?"

"Anything you want is okay with me," responded Fishnet. "A hero is fine, pizza, or even Chinese is good."

"How about we do a couple of hero sandwiches? If we are going to be in the car eating, pizza or Chinese may get sloppy."

"Good....Italian, or how about we get Pete's Eats for a shrimp hero?" Fishnet suggested.

"We can't go all the way back to the command to eat. Let's do Gino's new joint....It is only a few blocks from here, and I haven't seen that guy in ages...since he opened this place over here."

"I forgot about him. You think Gino will be there?"

"I don't know. He could be in either joint."

"You want to walk over there and see? I'll stick here in case our boy comes out."

"So what do you want me to bring back?"

"Surprise me, Sid."

"C'mon, make a decision. What do you want?"

"What are you getting?"

"Me? I'm having gabagool and mozzarella with mayo."

"The Italian gabagool or the ham cappy? I'm not too crazy about the Italian gabagool," noted Fishnet.

"Who's eating the frigging thing, you or me?" asked an exasperated Sidney. "C'mon, willya?...What do you want?"

"Okay...okay...get me liverwurst and Swiss...with mayo."

Sidney just shook his head as he got out of the car. "Try to stay awake and not lose sight of the truck."

"Yeah, yeah, yeah....Go get the food."

Schiff had a history with Gino's place. Gino had run a small supermarket and deli in the precinct for years. In addition to food, he also sold other small items that included such things as razor blades, combs, lip balm, suntan lotion, and whatever else he could fit on a counter or hang off a wall. The owner got into a beef with a shoplifter who came into his store one afternoon to steal. The shoplifter had the misfortune of being spotted by Gino as he stuck half a dozen packages of nylon stockings, which were displayed on the counter, under his leather jacket. Gino overexpressed his displeasure by striking the bandit over the head with a wooden rolling pin he kept hidden behind the counter near the register. At the precinct, Schiff took the time to explain to Gino the best way to articulate the incident while still sticking to the truth. Inadvertently, this created a lasting gratitude that ended up with Schiff never having to worry about paying for eats at Gino's.

After picking up the sandwiches, Sidney returned to the car where Fishnet had been waiting patiently.

Fishnet took the bag of food from his partner. "Do I owe you anything?"

"It's covered....Gino was there. I got you a Coke with the sandwich and a quarter pound of potato salad. Okay?"

"Good. Gino's doing okay?"

"Seems alright. He asked for you," fibbed Sidney.

"He's a good guy, Gino." Fishnet took his food. After looking it over, he turned to his partner. "Is this *German* potato salad?"

"Let's just concentrate on the truck and stop busting my balls!" was the answer he received.

⊞ ⊞ ⊞

RED INTENTIONALLY ARRIVED to meet the mover a few minutes earlier than the specified time. Passing by the house, he spotted the box truck parked out front. The mere sight of the truck felt like the twist of a knife in Red's back—the thought of his daughter's sad ending only enhanced his desire for retribution. His mind worked cleverly as he fine-tuned the loose plan he'd formulated in the shower: if everything went according to his calculations, that truck would play a key role.

Red parked his car near the intersection, giving himself the choice of several ways to leave the area. Emerging from his vehicle, Red's hulking form slowly moved along Fort Hamilton Parkway toward Franny's address. Harris stood out as he walked along the sidewalk. He was simply too imposing a presence to go unnoticed. And Fishnet noticed.

Spotting Red outside Franny's place hit the detective like a thunderbolt—he could not believe his incredible luck. The two dimensions he lived in became one....His dream world had crossed paths with that of reality. Instinctively he reached into his jacket for the unauthorized Beretta he now carried when out hunting. Of course it was there, tucked nicely in his side pocket, just waiting to be put into service. Now the time was here. A hard, maniacal look of satisfaction came over Fishnet's face—a sinister smile straight out of a Chiller Theater flick.

Fishnet spoke in a low, calm voice that was eerily without emotion, as though he'd fallen into a zombielike trance. "All good things come to those who wait," he uttered. His eyes remained   fixed on Red as he continued to gaze though the binoculars. Fishnet was there...but yet somehow he wasn't.

"What's that you said?"

There was no answer from Fishnet.

"What do you see?" Schiff said louder after he received no response from Fishnet.

"He came," responded Fishnet blandly.

"Who came...Franny? You see Franny out there?" asked Schiff excitedly.

"No...the other one."

Schiff frowned at the vagueness of his partner. "What fucking other one? Who are you talking about?" Sidney was losing patience.

"The Death Maker!"

"What?" Schiff's eyes widened with excitement. "Are you fucking talking about Red Harris?"

"Red Harris," came Fishnet's robotic response.

"Are you sure it's him?" Schiff knew he was asking a dumb question. There weren't too many Red Death lookalikes out there.

Fishnet didn't reply to the question.

"So what the hell is *he* doing over here?" asked Schiff anxiously. "Give me the blow-by-blow, will you?!"

Fishnet obliged, dictating to his partner the details of every step taken by Harris as they unfolded before his eyes. Fishnet spoke, yet he was also elsewhere...far off someplace in his thoughts.

"He's walking in the direction of the house."

"He's on the same side of the street."

"He stopped in front of the house."

"He's looking over the front of the house."

"He stepped toward the parked truck."

"He's looking at the truck."

"Now he's going to the front door of the house."

"He's ringing the bell."

"The door opened...and..."

Suddenly, Fishnet stopped talking. He began to drift further into his darker side, caught up in his imagination. He was in that place where flying bullets and rooftop fights were rewarded with medals and glory.

The halt in the rundown caused Detective Schiff to abandon his normally calm demeanor. "And now what is he doing? WHAT?" he demanded at the top of his voice.

Schiff's yelling yanked Fishnet back to reality, at least temporarily. The detective resumed his description of events...only this time slightly less robotically. He knew where he was and what he was saying while his mind continued to walk a tightrope between two worlds. Fishnet was in a state of shock...listening to himself speak from an out-of-body vantage point.

"Franny's at the door."

"They're outside talking."

"What the hell kind of business could they have together?" Schiff wondered. "This can't be anything good...right?"

Fishnet offered no response.

"What do you make of this shit, Fish? Fish?"

The detective's state of mind had become conflicted. He was confusing his worlds. "He is going to take him out."

"Say what? What do you mean?" Sidney became excited. When there was no response, he became even more agitated. "You did say 'take him out,' didn't you? *Hey! I'm talking to you!*" Sidney stated loudly. The usually calm detective was evolving into a bundle of nerves.

"He's gonna clip him."

"*CLIP HIM*? How the fuck did you come up with that idea? "

Again there was no response coming from Fishnet, who was still intensely looking through the binoculars. He was well into his far-off trip...visualizing in his mind how the ensuing confrontation was going to go down.

"Fishnet! Wake the hell up, will you?...I'm asking you something!" Sidney was now really getting concerned over his partner's peculiar behavior.

Startled, Fishnet snapped out of it just long enough to answer his partner's question. "What did you say?"

"What did I fucking say? Where the hell are you today? Why did you say Red is going to clip him?"

"Oh, no...don't worry....All this may be nothing. It's just me guessing." Fishnet had returned. The detective was determined not to share what he alone had figured out....This was exclusively going to be his baby. There was no room for anyone else leading the safari's hunting expedition.

⊞ ⊞ ⊞

A MINUTE AFTER THE big man rang the doorbell, Franny came to the front door. The man with the truck straightened himself up at the mere sight of Red's imposing physical presence. Franny had met some hard cases while knocking around, but nobody he had ever met measured up to Red. He could tell immediately that Red played in the big leagues.

Red looked at Franny from a different perspective. He considered the man who answered the door to be a small-time junkie lowlife, hustling for chump change.

"You Franny?" The Death Maker spoke in his trademark rasp.

"You Chester?"

"Yeah."

"Then I'm Franny."

After taking a couple of seconds to measure each other, the conversation resumed.

"Your truck?" asked Red, pointing his thumb over his shoulder to the box truck parked in front of the house.

"Yeah, that's my truck. Look okay for what you need?"

"I think it can work. Let me take a look at the inside...hard for me to be sure from the outside."

"Sure." This was an odd request, but Franny wanted his client happy. "What do you need to move?" Franny was fishing for a little information.

"Let me first see what the inside of the truck looks like."

"Okay..." Franny said warily. "But I got to know what you need moved before I can give you a number....You know this is going to cost you a few bucks."

"No problem with that." Red flashed a wad of hundred-dollar bills that could choke a horse. "We can talk numbers once I see inside the truck."

Seeing the money caused Franny to pay attention big time as Red knew it would—they both operated in a world where greed always overtook better judgment. Red wanted to be seen by Franny as a sucker ready to be taken.

"Just one other thing...I get all the money up front once I'm on site for the pickup with the truck."

"If the truck is the right fit, you can name your ticket, pal."

This was music to Franny's ears—there would be no more questions.

Franny walked briskly to the rear of the truck with Red Harris following behind him. Franny lifted open the back so that Red could peer inside. The interior of the truck contained a large boxed flat-screen television, some rope, and a few quilts.

⊞ ⊞ ⊞

FISHNET CONTINUED TO WATCH the scene unfold at the truck through his binoculars. He was forced to keep Detective Schiff in the loop throughout.

"Red put something back in his pocket."

"They walked to the back of the truck."

"Franny opened the back of the truck."

"The two of them are looking inside the truck."

"Looks like the big guy might be having some need for the truck," injected Schiff.

"Franny just climbed inside the back of the truck."

⊞ ⊞ ⊞

FRANNY DID NOT WANT TO blow the deal, so he was as accommodating as possible. At the request of his potential client, he got aboard the rear of the truck to give his future murderer an idea as to the length and height of the vehicle interior.

"How does it look, Chester?" Franny asked as he stood in the center of the truck. "A lot bigger than you thought, right?"

Stepping toward the rear opening of the truck, Franny stooped down to talk to Red. "Well, what's the verdict? Are we good to go?"

"Looks okay....Move that television back so I can see things better. I'll come up and take a look for myself so I'll know for sure."

"Suit yourself....C'mon up. Let me move the television to the back."

"Does that TV work? Is it for sale?" Red was looking to throw off any possible suspicion.

Franny stopped a second to turn and look at him. "Sure, it works....It works good. It is brand new. Look, *if* we are doing business...for *you*, I'll let it go for three hundred and fifty bucks. How about it?"

"Wrap it up. It looks like we are good with the truck, so I'll give you a little something now with the balance coming once you show for the move. How does that sound to you, pal?"

Red was reeling the mover in....He was so close to popping him that he already could smell the gunpowder. As Franny bent over to pick up the flat-screen, Red looked quickly over his shoulder. Except for the occasional passing car, the street was quiet.

"That TV looks heavy. You might drop it. Let me give you a hand."

"I got it."

With Franny now at the back corner of the truck, Red withdrew his gun with the silencer already attached. He pointed the firearm and fired two slugs into the back of the mover's head. Franny dropped straight down as if his legs had been severed out from under him. Red quickly gathered a couple of the loose quilts and covered the dead mover. He peeked out of the truck opening, making sure the street was clear of pedestrians. Once it was good to go, he jumped down off the truck. Looking around, he saw no one who could cause him concern. He pulled down the back door of the truck and walked to his vehicle like a man taking a casual stroll in the park.

Everything had gone perfectly for Red.

⊞ ⊞ ⊞

"HARRIS HAS A SWIVEL NECK," said Fishnet. "He is looking around."

"Something is definitely up, then," commented Schiff.

"Red just climbed into the back of the truck!"

"Okay....Come on, let's start taking a slow roll down there for a closer look."

"Yeah, let's get in there," agreed Fishnet.

Detective Schiff pulled out and headed in the direction of the truck. As they got closer, the binoculars were no longer necessary.

"Fish...Harris just got out of the truck. What the...? He just closed up the truck with the mover inside. I'm really getting a bad feeling about this now. I think we may have made our move too late!" Sidney was genuinely anguished over his procrastination. "I'm heading in!" and began driving toward the truck.

The detective was upon the truck in a matter of seconds. He jumped out of the driver's side and opened up the back of the truck. He didn't have to remove any quilts to see what had happened. As he ran back to the unmarked car, he yelled to Fishnet, "He killed him!"

Schiff jumped behind the wheel of his car and sped off in pursuit of Red Harris, whose prominent figure Fishnet had never had lost sight of.

"There he goes, the son of a bitch....He never even looked back! He is walking without a care in the fucking world. He has to be going to a car," announced Schiff excitedly.

Detective Schiff was wasting his breath. He might as well have been talking to himself. Fishnet was ghoul-like as he stared ahead, intensely focused on the form of Red Harris.

Sidney spoke with trepidation. "Let's take him as he is getting inside the car. Watch yourself on this one, Fish."

Coming to sudden life, Fishnet bellowed, "GERONIMO!" in wild acknowledgment. This reaction caused Schiff to do a double take. Glancing over at his partner, he saw Fishnet braced tightly in the passenger seat as if taking a ride on a roller coaster. Fishnet had now gone off completely. Neither detective thought to call for a backup. The adrenalin rush was such that all they could focus on was the target before them.

Detective Schiff waited until the Death Maker opened the door to his Lincoln, and then he gunned the engine. Red never got fully inside the car—his attention was diverted to the vehicle coming directly at him.

Schiff pulled up to the Lincoln, stopping mere inches away from actually striking it. The mover's assassin was pinned, with his left leg still on the sidewalk. Fishnet was first to leap from the unmarked car, followed by Schiff a second or two later. Gun in hand, Fishnet ran directly at Red Harris. He opened fire as he rushed toward the big man, using bullets as his greeting, rather than the standard warning of, "Police!—Don't move!"

Sidney immediately took cover behind the open driver-side door of the unmarked vehicle, going into a crouch with his gun pointed at Red through the vehicle's open window. Fishnet fired off four rounds: two totally missed their mark, one took a piece of Red's ear, and the fourth caught Red in his right shoulder.

Red's reflexes did not fail him. He returned fire, shooting from beneath his left arm, which he held across his chest with his hand pressing into the shoulder wound. The big man's return fire saw his very first round hitting its mark—a lucky head shot that dropped Fishnet, with the bullet passing through the center of his brain. Lucky to survive, it was still a cruel trick that fate had played on the man of fantasy.

Detective Schiff came out best in the gun battle. He took one relatively minor hit that saw the bullet just graze his cheek. Sidney took a second to draw down on Red, firing off three rounds that went off in a cadence of bang, bang...pause...bang. The first of Schiff's bullets caught Red in the chest. It was the slug that took some of the fight out of the big man, possibly even rendering Red unable to continue his offense. The second of the detective's bullets was a complete miss, landing somewhere over Red's head. The final shot was a gold medal winner that spelled the end of the line for the Death Maker. For his last shot, Sidney put a bullet into Red's face. The slug whistled "Goodnight, Irene" as it caught the outlaw right in the center of his forehead. Sidney was playing for keeps—he was not about to take any chances. He left Red no opportunity to get off another round.

The Death Maker got the kind of send-off that gave Swing Blade and the boys another tale to tell about the bulls.

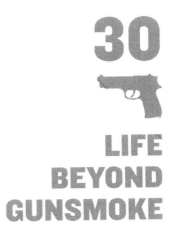

30

LIFE BEYOND GUNSMOKE

THE INVESTIGATORS RESPONDING to the gunfight were faced with the job of fleshing out what had happened. The task was not a terribly complex one.

The incident would go down in the annals of police-involved shootings as being a "good" one. The fireworks received massive media attention—a public-relations bonanza without the slightest inkling of a problem for the department. Based on the evidence, everyone was satisfied that the detectives had acted in accordance with department guidelines and were proper in the performance of their duty. Thanks to the amplification by the media of Red's criminal record and history of organized crime associations, the police department was widely lauded for taking down a leading underworld mobster known as Joe "The Death Maker" Harris. It all made such excellent copy that any alienation existing between the police and the press became invisible.

Old grudges were remedied, at least temporarily.

Statistically speaking, things also worked out well. Franny's homicide, like the shooting of Fishnet, were more or less open-and-shut cases. Red had killed Franny and shot Fishnet, while Sidney saved the taxpayers money by eliminating Red. The squad in Chinatown was able to clear the double homicide involving Anthony Boy and his lady friend. Ballistics evidence revealed   that the gun recovered from Red Harris matched the bullets removed from Fishnet, Franny, Anthony Boy Chiarello, and Chiarello's companion. The cases were all wrapped up in a nice, tight package...closed with positive results and filed in precinct basements, where they would remain forgotten until years later when it came time to burn the hard copies. Closure came complete with no additional overtime, burden to the courts, or further expectations.

As far as Red's departure from this earth was concerned, there were few people who cared. Augie D'Angelo wrote off the demise of his chief enforcer as one of those things...a cost of doing business. His compensation came in the form of a larger percentage in the escort business; he now assumed what he had previously allotted to Red. From an operational standpoint, Swing had to go out and find another tough guy to take Red's place. No one was going to miss the big man—other than perhaps his landlord, who would again have to worry about things like heat, hot water, and barking dogs.

Anthony Boy was waked at a Lower East Side funeral parlor, with what seemed like half the hookers in New York attending to pay their respects. Among those absent at the funeral parlor was his cousin, the FBI agent.

Fast Franny's grandmother kept her black dress on long enough to clean out his room. Being careful not to stick herself with any of the spikes she found, she wrapped up the hypodermic syringes in a newspaper. She then tied the paper with string saved from her last pastry purchase. Next she put the paper inside a triple plastic bag, which went into the center of a green commercial garbage bag filled with leaves the old woman had raked up from her rear yard. The final product was put out with the recycled trash, slated for pickup by the sanitation department.

After some brief contemplation, the old woman flushed her grandson's white powder stash down the toilet. She elected to hang onto the sixty-five grand that she found stuffed in a shoebox inside her grandson's closet. She also held onto the loaded Smith & Wesson 9mm automatic Franny kept in the top drawer of the nightstand next to his bed. Grammy relocated the gun to the top drawer of her own nightstand for protection now that she was living alone. It was later rumored that she was seen with her hair down, wearing a colorful flowered dress as she waited to board a bus loaded with senior citizens. She was said to be headed for Atlantic City in the company of an older man in a straw hat who was smoking a De Nobili cigar.

The sentence Joe Horse received saved his life, taking him on a path to regain his health. He had no trouble adapting to the incarceration experience because once among the general population, he put his brain to good use by reading law books. On the inside he became something of a minor celebrity as a jailhouse lawyer assisting many inmates in preparing their appeals.

Detective Von Hess was promoted to first-grade detective. The department had decided to throw a bone to the homicide squad. Not that Von Hess wasn't deserving—his promotion was long overdue—but it took a case such as this for him to get it. The detective never spoke about Fishnet or the case that had gotten him first grade.

Sergeant Parlatto, the squad commander, swaggered into his next meeting at the puzzle palace with his chest puffed and shoulders back, like General MacArthur returning to the Philippines. There was nothing for him to have to explain because performance expectations had not simply been met...but exceeded. He was called "Lance" once again by Bottle Caps, who was still running the show. Parlatto was restored as one of the fair-haired boys, skating by at least until the next caper.

Wires and Junior moved a step closer to acceptance by their peers in the homicide squad thanks in no small part to Sergeant Markie. Markie had seen some good in the two detectives. While he could never approve of how they had gotten into his unit, he nevertheless understood that the mistake made by Wires was purely one of judgment. What mattered most, he figured, was that the detective had seen the error of his ways. As far as Junior went, she was just a victim of circumstances. To Markie they represented the future of his squad—a worthwhile investment. Markie's blessing went a long way in the homicide squad, so Wires and Junior were eventually able to work within the unit without being ostracized. With the passing of time, even their nicknames became history, ceasing to be used behind their backs.

Detective Sidney Schiff's wound left a scar on his left cheek that he grew to be proud of. In the end, Sidney had proved himself to be a loyal partner, telling all who would listen how it was Fishnet alone who had the perceptiveness to decipher the demented mind of Red Harris. He would elevate his partner further by detailing how Fishnet had instinctively sensed before the shooting commenced that Red Harris was there to gun down Fast Franny. Sadly, few cared to listen to the details.

Sidney was awarded the Police Combat Cross, the second-highest medal awarded by the police department, in an all-hands-on-deck ceremony. He was promoted to detective first grade, the highest attainable level for an investigator. He walked on stage that day to accept his rewards quite proud of his accomplishments. He even flew in his elderly parents from Florida to be at headquarters and to sit alongside his wife and kids for the ceremony. His photo was in all the newspapers, and he was prominently advertised as the man who had outgunned Red Harris. The greatest of tributes was penned by Chick Aprile, who laid it on extra thick. He highlighted Sidney's years of service, professionalism, ethics, and morality. Aprile even made an open plea to the politicians, requesting they rename the site of the gun battle as Schiff-Milligan Square. Sidney was interviewed on television and radio. Police academy recruits listened attentively to Sidney's account of his heroics as the man who had saved his partner's life by outgunning one of the most dangerous men in the city...a serial-killing mobster called the Death Maker. Everyone from the American Legion to the Boy Scouts of America praised him. There was even some talk of Sidney being involved in a book deal and a movie. Detective Sidney Schiff became a blue living legend—he got everything Fishnet had ever wanted. After all, it was only right, as Sidney's mother liked to say....It was *her* Sidney who ultimately had taken out the Death Maker.

Once the doctors were through with him, Fishnet found himself unable to talk and restricted to a hospital bed. He was in a vegetative state...paralyzed with a fully conscious mind and just the ability to hear and think. His new routine relegated him to looking at and listening to the conversations of people entering his room to visit him. The information he gathered from listening was enough for him to create dramas that he could experience in his imaginary world.

Since he was limited to the confines of an uncooperative body, the only other thing he could do was blink once for yes and twice for no when asked a question.

Fishnet's spectacular exit from the department provided him with a promotion to second-grade detective, a tax-free disability pension, visitors to his bedside, and a prestigious department medal. It took receiving one to the head for Fishnet to finally reach a height that, to his great regret, he could no longer capitalize on.

The detective paid close attention when Sidney held photos in front of his face for his viewing. They were of the beautiful testimonial plaque that was hung over the precinct front desk as a tribute to the two detectives. Despite his unpleasant circumstances, Fishnet enjoyed the attention... however distanced he was. But when Sidney went on and on about movie offers, books, the multitude of people at the promotion ceremony... Fishnet became unglued. If only his eyes could communicate the four words he was thinking..."Go fuck yourself, Sidney!!!" Disheartened, Fishnet could do little else other than drop his eyelids and hope his next thoughts would come true..."Shut the fuck up, Sidney!"

Things got much worse for Fishnet when Sid spoke of the possibility of there being a Schiff- Milligan Square. Second billing was simply too much for Fishnet to endure. The internal agony at the very thought of Sid being the top banana enraged Fishnet. The words "son of a bitch" echoed loudly within in his head. The detective became so infuriated by the news that he miraculously was now able to move the pinkie on his right hand ever so slightly.

"Are you hearing me okay, Fish? Blink once if you are....," said Sidney.

Fishnet's thoughts were less than wholesome. "Me blink once for you, fucko...never!" Out of spite, Fishnet blinked rapidly five times...knowing Sidney wouldn't know what the hell he was talking about.

⊞ ⊞ ⊞

THERE WERE OTHER SMALL pieces of information that were to remain a secret. Markie and Von Hess had arrived at the scene of the shootout before the crime scene unit. Von Hess took charge of the weapons at the scene, including the .25 caliber Beretta whose outline he spotted in Fishnet's pocket. He was suspicious of the gun's origin because clearly it was not an authorized weapon to be carried on duty. Von Hess suspected the gun was a throwaway weapon. Von Hess brought the existence of the Beretta to Markie's attention. The sergeant moved to immediately send Von Hess to check to see if Fishnet had the weapon listed on his ten card, a document that recorded all of an officer's authorized guns. Von Hess later apprised the sergeant of his findings on his cell. Once Markie found out that the gun had no business being in Fishnet's pocket, he had a decision to make. After a few minutes of mental ping-pong, trying to figure out the smart thing to do, the sergeant made his choice: he took out his handkerchief and wiped the gun clean. He then placed the gun under the passenger-side front seat of Red's vehicle for someone else to find. Markie and Von Hess then went through Fishnet's locker, coop, and car for the purpose of disposing of any other questionable items...of which there were plenty. Not missing anything, before they were through they knew of the detective's lack of integrity...but remained in the dark as to his visits to his otherworld.

Markie didn't have trouble convincing himself that he had done the right thing. With everyone involved now gone and Fishnet out of circulation, why complicate matters? It was far more palatable for everyone to remember the participants in two distinct roles...bad guys and good guys. To Markie, putting it all to bed quietly seemed to be as happy an ending as any.

31

BILL AND COO TIME

ALLEY CAT SAT UP IN BED, evaluating her long red fingernails as she held them up to her face for a clearer look. They had been the same color for too long, she thought. She began wondering how her nails would look if she took them on a trip to the dark side. And the fact that black nails would seem bizarre to the regulars at an old-school joint like Fitzie's just made the idea seem more exciting.

She looked across the bed over to the new man in her life, wondering what he would think if she went gothic with the claws that he loved to have scratch his back. Being the impetuous sort, she could not wait for her new boyfriend to awaken naturally. Alley Cat needed to immediately find out his thoughts.

"Hey, cop!" she shouted as she gave Markie a hearty shove to stir him out of his deep sleep.

The sergeant's rousting startled him to the point of anger. "What the f—!" Markie was just awake enough to stop himself from actually cursing.

Unaccustomed to such rough treatment in the morning, he looked at her incredulously. "What's wrong with you?" He was clearly annoyed. "Are you going nuts?"

"Ohh...I'm so sorry!" she quickly said in good humor, realizing the effect her unintentionally alarming action had had on him.

"What the hell are you thinking? You looking to give me a lousy heart attack over here?"

The sergeant was emphatic in making it crystal clear that he didn't appreciate such an abrupt awakening. Alley Cat regretted her actions once she realized how upset he was.

In a low, guilty voice, she answered, "I'm sorry....I was just wondering something."

"Wondering what?" he shot back. "Wondering if you could kill me by shocking the shit out of me in my sleep?"

"You know what? Never mind, then....Forget about it," she answered, now annoyed herself. After his reaction, she chastised herself for caring what he thought about anything, least of all her nails.

Markie felt a little guilty after seeing that she was now pissed off. Going soft, he took the first step in trying to make nice with her. "No, c'mon...tell me. What's so important?"

Still pouting, she responded coldly, "I was wondering what you wanted to eat this morning. I can cook some eggs up with toast if you like."

Markie laughed. "Who you kidding?" he asked. "Since when do you cook anything?"

"Well, I just thought it would be nice....If you don't want eggs —"

"C'mon...out with it, will you please?...Come clean. I'm really interested. What did you want to say? Tell me."

This warmed her up again. "Say please."

"Please...okay?"

Now that she had won, things were again cordial. "Well, luv...it is silly." "Come on...spill it," he said, a little more gently.

"Okay, then...so how do you like my nails? Would you like to see them a new color?"

"Not really," Markie said honestly. "I like red nails."

"I've kept them red forever....How would you like to see them in black?" she asked with an intent look in her eye and a smirk on her face that suggested she was challenging him.

Markie's immediate response put a damper on any notion of black nails. He thought the idea absurd because black fingernails, like unpainted ones, seemed unglamorous to him while the color of bright red expressed a vibrancy.

"How can you even consider black? You are some piece of work! I like them red...hot frigging, flaming red, and no other color but red," came his declaration in a tone that seemed to be unwavering.

Her answer to the sergeant came in pantomime. Looking away from Markie, she curled her mouth downward, lowered her head, and closed her eyelids until they were almost completely shut. She had Markie's number good.

Anthony Celano

The sergeant again went soft, mentally chastising himself for the tone he had used with Alley Cat. He relented, as she knew he would, to her wishes. "Want me to paint them black for you?" he asked softly.

Alley Cat smiled. This was one of the things she loved about Markie.... She could win. Most times she never knew what he would do or say next, but he was predictable in this one way: when it came to her feelings, she had no doubt that he would cave in. However, she never expected his offer to perform the paint job. Alley Cat basked in her victory. Making her own concession, she was smiling when she passed him the red nail polish.

"Where is the black?" he asked.

"No, that is okay....I like them red too," she replied sweetly.

"Come on....Cut the crap....Out with the black."

Feeling better that she at least had made the offer; Alley Cat passed the black to him. "Toes first?" he asked.

"Yes...toes first, my dear," she answered with a coy smile.

She handed him her magnified reading glasses to make the task a little easier. Markie was brushing away carefully at the pinkie toe of her left foot when his cell phone rang. He put the brush back into its black bottle and answered his phone.

"This is Markie speaking."

"Markie...it's me, Lieutenant Wright."

"Hey, boss. Is everything alright?"

"Can you go to work?"

"What time is it?" Markie looked for his watch.

"It's 10:15 a.m....I need you to come in...okay?"

"Yeah, sure....What's up?"

"Headquarters called. They are forming a special task force in order to put the lid on a string of murders. They put the word out asking for a good boss from one of the homicide squads to work it. You were elected. I'm sending Von Hess with you as a consolation."

"No problem, boss...but any idea for how long?"

"Until you solve it, I suppose...and I hope you do it fast! Listen...it means lieutenant's money for sure if you do. I pushed for them to take Von Hess....My present to you."

"Where do they want us to turn out of?"

"Over at major case in police headquarters."

"Why all of a sudden did this become so important?"

"Some guy just took a slug in the eyeball this morning in Manhattan inside a commercial business in the West Village," Wright explained. "It seems like a woman managed to survive the attack, so they got something to work with over there. The powers-that-be figure you could be the right guy to take it home for them."

"When am I on the clock?"

"Starting right now. You and Von Hess are to report to Inspector McCoy's office over at major case at headquarters.

"I'll be there by noon, if not sooner."

Markie ended the call and turned to look at Alley Cat. As he was putting the reading glasses back on, he spoke to her.

"I have to go. Somebody got whacked, and they need me in."

"There is no one else working?" she asked.

It had been a long time since Markie had to answer to a woman who cared enough to ask such a question. "Hurry up and give me that foot if you want me to finish what I started."

Alley Cat shifted her position and lifted her foot to accommodate her Michelangelo. That was another thing about Markie. He was reliable—a man who did what he said he was going to do. She was confident that the person who had been shot and killed would be avenged. Alley Cat believed that there wasn't anything Markie couldn't figure out. She loved that he was a man who followed through....His willingness to finish her nails proved it. She touched the back of his head as she gave him her special "call of the wild" look. He reacted to the "on switch" by placing the paintbrush back in the bottle. She smiled, knowing that he had again proved her correct.

Markie figured out what was on her mind pretty quickly. Alley Cat's nails went unfinished that morning.

The End

57283055R00172

Made in the USA
Middletown, DE
29 July 2019